3/14

SIT

D0497126

WITHDRAWN

Books should be returned or renewed by the last date above. Renew by phone **08458 247 200** or online *www.kent.gov.uk/libs*

Jemma Forte grew up wanting to write for *Cosmopolitan* magazine, be a famous actress or work in a shoe shop (she loved the foot-measuring device in Clarks). Her parents didn't want her to go to stage school because, according to them, she was 'precocious enough already'. However, they actively encouraged her obsession with reading and writing and she wrote her first book, 'Mizzy the Germ', when she was eight. She sent it to a publisher (unwittingly backing up the whole precocious theory) and was dismayed when for some reason they didn't want it.

Years later, due to *The Kids from Fame* (and she blames them entirely), her desire to perform hadn't abated. Hundreds of letters, show-reels and auditions later she finally became a Disney Channel presenter in 1998. After Disney, Jemma went on to present shows for ITV, BBC1, BBC2 and C4 and, when not busy writing, can still be found talking rubbish on telly to this day. *If You're Not the One* is Jemma's third novel. She lives in London with her children, Lily and Freddie.

Also by

JEMMA FORTE

ME AND MISS M

FROM LONDON WITH LOVE

If You're Not the One

JEMMA FORTE

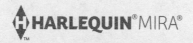

Harlequin MIRA is a registered trademark of Harlequin Enterprises Limited, used under licence.

Published in Great Britain 2014
by Harlequin MIRA, an imprint of Harlequin (UK) Limited,
Eton House, 18-24 Paradise Road,
Richmond, Surrey, TW9 1SR

© 2014 Jemma Forte

ISBN 978 1 848 45296 1

59-0214

Harlequin's policy is to use papers that are natural, renewable and recyclable products and made from wood grown in sustainable forests. The logging and manufacturing processes conform to the legal environmental regulations of the country of origin.

Printed and bound by
CPI Group (UK) Ltd, Croydon, CR0 4YY

For my nephew. Welcome to the world.

PROLOGUE

Friday May 18th

Jennifer Wright slammed the door and ran down the road as fast as her ill-fitting footwear would allow her to, tears blurring her vision. She didn't care who saw her. All she was conscious of was her need to get away from her husband and his ability to hurt her. Not that he was letting her get away that easily.

'Jen,' Max yelled down the road, clearly in no mood to consider what the neighbours might be thinking. 'What the hell do you think you're doing? Come back. For goodness sake, you've made your point.'

Jennifer ignored him. If anything, she picked up the pace, wishing it was dark so her flit could go unnoticed. She'd always loved living in the suburbs of South West London partly because everybody looked out for everybody else. Today however, it would have suited her far better if she'd lived in a place where people didn't give a damn about their neighbours. That way she could have wailed like a banshee and charged down the road without worrying she'd provided the man on the other side of the street (the dull husband of the quite nice woman at number forty-two) with a juicy bit of gossip.

She'd caught his look of alarm as he'd taken in her tear-stained face and heavy coat, which was far too warm for this unusually clement May evening. Not that there was any way she was taking it off, for what Jennifer knew, but the man from number forty-two didn't, was that all she had on underneath was a bra, a G-string, suspenders and stockings. The killer heels she'd originally teamed the whole ensemble with had been kicked off mid-argument, replaced by the footwear that happened to be nearest the front door, a revolting pair of lace-ups, usually reserved purely for gardening purposes. Without woolly socks, her stockinged feet were slopping about inside them.

Panting with exertion, Jennifer finally came to the end of the street. Briefly she turned round to see what Max was doing. She could just about still make him out, hanging out of their front door, obviously in two minds about what to do given that their children were sleeping inside.

Screw him.

Karen.

That's who she needed.

Fumbling in her pocket with shaky hands, Jennifer found her mobile which she'd had the sense to grab on her way out.

Half walking, half running now, she rounded the corner onto the busy main road and scrolled through her phone looking for her best friend's number. Wiping her face with the back of her hand she managed to rub away some tears but was surprised by how persistently they kept on coming. Briefly she acknowledged that there was a huge possibility she was having a nervous breakdown.

As she headed for the zebra crossing she listened to Karen's phone ringing and prayed she'd pick up. She did.

'Oh Karen,' Jennifer managed, speaking loudly against the traffic, choking on tears again.

'Oh my god, what is it? What's wrong?'

The concern in her voice almost floored Jennifer for a second. Thank god Karen's house was only ten minutes away. She couldn't get there soon enough. If only she'd chosen a less hot coat.

'Oh Karen, it's all gone wrong and I just don't think I can do this any more…' Jennifer broke off, half stumbling over an uneven bit of pavement. Wretched shoes. Then a bus whizzed past just as Karen was answering. It completely drowned out her response which forced Jennifer to say, 'Come again Karen, I couldn't hear you.'

'I said where are you? Do you want to come round?'

'Yes please,' Jennifer wailed, putting one foot out onto the road.

'Good,' said Karen 'Well just come straight away and I'll open a…'

But Jennifer never got to hear what her friend was going to open (though forced to guess she would have gone with a textbook bottle of dry white wine), because at this point her phone was flying high up into the air and she was staring at it aghast, wondering why everything had suddenly gone into slow motion. At the same time, although she didn't exactly feel it, she was also aware of the most enormous impact, of the most sickening crunching sound and of the metallic taste of fear, dread and regret coursing through her body which was now being flung skywards having been hit very hard by a car. For a brief moment, just as gravity was about to take command and begin Jennifer's terrifying and brutal descent towards the hard ground and the bonnet of a Ford Fiesta, she was filled with an illogical, yet undeniable sense of embarrassment. For the thought entering her brain at that precise moment was that there was a strong chance that whoever was driving and/or an ambulance team were about to discover what she had on under her coat.

And that was the last conscious thought she was to have for a very long time to come…

ONE WEEK EARLIER — FRIDAY

Jennifer Wright hadn't been entirely sure for a while now if she really liked her husband any more. As a result she'd been suffering from a sort of creeping, low-level anxiety for months. The thought of living out the remainder of her days in the suburbs with him terrified her, and she'd lost count of how many times she'd been struck by one solitary thought: *Is this it?*

To some degree, it was less a thought, more a feeling. She was only thirty-eight but felt like she was hurtling in slow motion towards middle age and decrepitude, while swept up in an unstoppable snowball of routine, malaise and domesticity. Lately, she could be in the middle of any number of mundane tasks, when from nowhere she'd be practically knocked over by a violent urge to run barefoot through long grass, dance till dawn (preferably on some form of narcotic), sleep in a yurt, or, failing that, to have the sort of passionate, filthy sex with a stranger that would leave her panting and covered in a film of sweat.

But Jennifer was a married mother of two, with a part-time job, and was fully aware, not only of how wildly inappropriate these yearnings were, but also how… impractical. There'd be consequences, ones she didn't have the heart to deal with, and besides, these days, if she danced till dawn it would take her at least a week to recover and quite frankly they couldn't afford the childcare.

'*Is this it?*' whispered her subconscious, again. The thought it might be freaked her out to say the least. However, at a loss to know what to do about any of it, she'd decided simply to wait things out, to try and remain positive, keep taking the Prozac and not to jump out of a window, for the time being.

Until one Friday evening in May that is, when Jennifer decided it was time to take matters into her own hands.

All relationships went through patches, she thought determinedly, clipping on her suspender belt and adjusting her newly bought black and red bra whilst manhandling her boobs into it. She owed it not just to herself but also to her children to try and make things better. Although she'd been hovering round the notion of what might happen were she and Max to split up, it was too terrifying a prospect to face head on as an actual possibility. And besides, after eleven years of togetherness she still *loved* Max. It was just a shame it was such a familiar, unexciting version of love, which occasionally had the tendency to veer off into violent hatred territory. The fact they hadn't had sex for over four months wasn't helping matters either.

Feeling surprisingly nervous Jennifer pulled open her wardrobe door so she could appraise herself in the full-length mirror that hung behind it.

Wow. She hadn't looked this tarty in a long time. The evening sunlight poured through her bedroom window, bathing the entire room in a golden glow, highlighting her cellulite and the fact they desperately needed a new carpet.

At first Jennifer felt incredibly self-conscious, standing there, trussed up in broad daylight. Eventually however, she grudgingly admitted that she kind of got away with it. She'd always had an hourglass figure and these days it was probably covered by less flesh than it had been even pre-children. In her twenties she'd taken her figure for granted. Post-partum however, not only had she been hit with the realisation that actually she wasn't immortal, she had also worked out that she was stood at a fairly major crossroads. One way led to elasticated waists, one-piece swimsuits and never being able to reveal her upper arms again, the other to still being able to look good in the odd bit from Top Shop, skinny jeans and the vaguely hateful yet better than frumpy 'yummy mummy' moniker. Terrified by the prospect of turning into her mother Jennifer had jogged determinedly in one direction, started doing boot camp at the park twice a week and stopped eating cake.

She peered at her face, wondering vaguely how old a complete stranger would guess she was. There was no denying she was in the midst of her fourth decade and yet it was hard to pinpoint exactly what it was that was different about her face now to how it had been in her twenties. Yet that difference was undeniable. She still had friendly, warm brown eyes but nowadays when she applied eye-shadow much of it disappeared into a crease she was pretty sure hadn't been there before. Due to her weight loss she had good cheekbones and her thighs looked good, yet she had to make sure she didn't lose *too* much weight or her face was in danger of starting to look gaunt. She had faint crow's feet round her eyes and a bit of a frown line which had deepened visibly around the time her babies had become toddlers at which point there had suddenly been more to frown about. But, she had a pretty face and, on a good day, could still scrub up well. She still had sex appeal, could turn a head and be whistled at by a builder and her wide smile, good, orthodontically-treated teeth (thank you, Mum) and long, thick head of brown (dyed) hair counted for a lot. Only for how much longer was anyone's guess.

Turning round so she could glance back over her shoulder and examine what her bottom looked like in her new very uncomfortable G-string, she decided that if she squinted she didn't look *that* far off the girl she'd been when she'd first met Max. Screw it, she thought, fired up by a growing sense of confidence. She was old and wise enough to know that any normal red-blooded man wouldn't care anyway. Rather than scrutinising her for

imperfections, surely he'd only see the naughty underwear, the effort she was making, the invitation.

She drew the curtains. Better. Direct sunlight and par-
tial nudity were best kept apart. Across the room her
phone was vibrating. She tottered over to it in her heels.
The display showed it was her best friend, Karen, phoning
to check up on her.

'I feel like a right old scrubber.'

'Good,' said Karen. 'You're supposed to. You're about
to seduce your husband.'

'Oh god,' groaned Jennifer, returning to the mirror to
examine herself from all angles again. 'I'm not sure I can
do this. I'm not sure I *want* to do it, truth be told. I've still
got this week's episode of *The Apprentice* to watch.'

'You have to,' Karen said frankly. 'Not see *The Apprentice*, though at some point do, it's hilarious, but have
sex first. If you don't do it soon he'll start looking elsewhere.'

Jennifer wasn't so sure. Karen had been flabbergasted
when she'd admitted how long their dry spell had been
and was clearly working on the proviso that no man could
live without sex, but then again, Karen was married to
a man who woke her up most mornings with something
hard jabbing into her back. Whereas these days, Max
seemed to have lost his sex drive completely.

'Still on for a drink next Tuesday?' Jennifer said,
changing the subject. It felt weird making small talk while
dressed as a sex worker.

'Definitely. I'll try and leave work a bit early and I think Lucy's coming but Esther still hasn't got a babysitter.'

Just then Jennifer heard the sound of Max's key in the lock. 'Ooh he's back. I'll call you tomorrow.'

'Good luck.'

Jennifer put her phone on silent then raced over to the bed and got herself into position. As she did, it suddenly occurred to her that instead of being consumed by lust, Max might find the sight of her trying to seduce him wildly funny. *Oh my god, what if he laughed at her?*

Quickly, she swerved her mind back round to the task ahead, acknowledging along the way that it was probably as much her fault as it was her husband's that they hadn't done it for so long. She was usually exhausted by the time he got home, busy trying to get the kids to bed and looking forward to nothing wilder than a glass of wine and some telly watching. Tonight however, with the girls at a rare sleepover at their grandparents, there was no excuse. They *would* have sex. Being physically close was what was required to lessen the emotional distance between them. She felt quite militant about it.

Downstairs she could hear Max taking his shoes off. She waited for him to call up the stairs, but instead it sounded like he was heading straight for the kitchen. Still, he'd come looking for her soon enough.

Minutes passed. There was no sign of him. Then she heard him leave the kitchen and go into the lounge. Damn.

This wasn't the plan. He was supposed to come upstairs and find her leaning back across the bed like a wanton sex goddess. Then, filled with raging desire caused by the fact she was wearing a bra that wasn't flesh coloured and pants that weren't large and from a Marks and Spencer pack of three, he was supposed to leap on her and ravish his way back into an intimate relationship.

Still nothing. Feeling irritated beyond belief, she now had no choice other than to heave herself back up and reach for the house phone, the suspender belt disappearing rather depressingly into the crevice of her belly. She rang his mobile.

'Hello?'

'What are you doing?' she asked, making a monumental effort to sound less irritated than she felt.

'Nothing. Got myself a beer and I'm watching a bit of sport. Why, what are you doing? What are we having for dinner?'

As Jennifer was treated to a crystal clear image in her head, of her husband in his usual position, lying on the sofa caressing his nuts, 'relaxing' with a bit of sport on, while waiting for dinner to magically appear in front of him, any vague urge she might have had to sleep with him evaporated. She was a woman on a mission though. The bra alone had cost forty pounds. She wasn't giving up that easily.

'Come upstairs.'

'Do I have to?'

'Please Max?' begged Jennifer, feeling the last vestiges of sex goddess slip away from her, like smoke.

'Can't you come here?'

'Just come for a second please. I'd really appreciate it.'

'Bloody hell Jen, I've had a long day and I've only just sat down. Ooof, great goal.'

Jennifer quietly put the phone down and stared into the middle distance for a while before slowly peeling off and unclipping her temptress outfit. Once she had, she shoved it all into the back of her drawer, and replaced the prohibitively expensive underwear with a pair of pyjamas before heading downstairs to cook lamb chops, baked potatoes and green beans, served on a bed of deep resentment.

Later, as she and Max sat masticating their overcooked chops in front of *The Apprentice*, Jennifer wondered if Max would ever desire or appreciate her body again, or whether that was it until she died.

Is this it?

'Good day?' she enquired feebly at some point.

'Er, would be if I could actually hear what was being said. Why would you speak right over the crucial bit?' He leaned over to get the Sky remote so that he could rewind.

Jennifer stared at her husband blankly, watching him ignore her.

In that moment it hit her that she couldn't bear for things to continue as they were. She was physically and mentally frustrated, unfulfilled by her job and sad, all of which she might have been able to accept. Only she'd also been reduced to one half of a couple who were sat next to one another on a sofa, bodies present but souls millions of miles away. And that she couldn't cope with.

Max continued to stare at the telly, oblivious to the maelstrom of potentially life changing thoughts which were swirling around his wife's head, unaware his other half was questioning how all the decisions she'd made in life had led to this bitterly disappointing moment in time.

Meanwhile Jennifer began plundering the reserves of her memory, something else she'd been doing a lot of lately, searching for feelings she longed to relive, for there was enormous comfort to be taken from the fact that, of course, things hadn't always been this way.

THE PAST — AIDAN

Summer 1994

The alarm beeped, penetrating the deepest of sleeps.

'Jen, wake up. It's already 9 o'clock. We've got to get ready and if you want a shower you need to hurry. I said I'd meet Mark at The Pink Flamingo.'

'Five minutes,' Jennifer answered drowsily, idly scratching a mosquito bite on her leg. The whirring of the ceiling fan was in danger of lulling her back to sleep again so she forced herself to open one eye, enjoying the gurgle of anticipation that was already building in her tummy, despite her groggy state.

They'd only arrived on the island of Kos five nights ago after a fortnight of taking it relatively easy on the quieter Greek island of Santorini. Before that they'd been to Mykonos and Rhodes. There had been the odd moment of tension, but generally speaking, she and her friends had managed five weeks of travelling with no major disagreements and were having the time of their lives. They'd originally planned on visiting a few more islands before heading home but Jennifer had a strong feeling that they'd probably spend the remainder of their trip here, until either their money ran out or their livers packed up. Whichever came first. Kos had simply proved too fun to leave, what with Bar Street (self-explanatory), the outdoor clubs that stayed open till the sun was starting to rise in the sky, the sandy beaches and the biggest appeal of all, tons of gorgeous men.

They'd all slept with someone, though if she were being totally honest, Jennifer rather regretted her liaison at the beach with a handsome Greek guy on their second night. She knew she'd lived up to the reputation English girls seemed to have, of being easy. By the same token, she'd decided not to lose any sleep over it. She wasn't proud of how little it had meant, but still didn't see why girls should feel any worse than guys did, about what amounted to nothing more than a consensual exchange of bodily fluids. The only thing that had been slightly awkward was bumping into him from time to time. Neither of them could be bothered to keep up the pretence of interest now the act had been done.

'Can I borrow your red dress, Jen?' asked Esther, emerging from the bathroom in a towel, strawberry blonde hair hanging in damp tendrils around her face.

Since arriving on Kos the four of them had eased into a routine which consisted of sleeping until midday, at which point they'd force themselves to get up, no matter how much their heads were splitting, for tanning purposes.

Then, after an afternoon of roasting themselves at the beach, they'd return to the apartment, shower, slather themselves in more after-sun than was probably necessary and have a sleep. Making sure first of course that they'd set the alarm so there was no danger of missing out on another night of partying.

Now, without waiting for a response Esther bent down to extract the dress, which was rolled in a ball and stuffed in Jennifer's rucksack. Only the minute she did, the red dress became exactly what Jennifer wanted to wear that night. Esther borrowing her clothes was starting to get on her nerves, partly because with her long freckled limbs, she looked totally amazing in all of them.

Esther was the rare sort of girl who actually looked better with no make-up on at all. She wasn't overtly sexy and yet was probably the most naturally pretty of the group. Back home in London, it was usually Jennifer's more obvious sex appeal or Karen's big boobs which guys noticed. However, whilst it might have taken their fellow students at College a few glances before they finally worked out just how attractive Esther really was, on holiday her tall physique and bare-faced beauty made her the instant star of the beach.

'Um, sorry babe I think I'm going to wear it,' Jennifer said sleepily.

Esther tutted. 'Shit, what am I going to wear then?'

'Don't know, but hurry up,' said Karen, drawing deeply on one of the two hundred Merit cigarettes she'd bought at Kos airport, before adjusting her dress straps in order to heave her considerable cleavage up as much as possible. 'I am so up for it tonight.'

'Makes a change,' teased Jennifer.

'Shut up,' said Karen, grinning, teeth white against her brown face.

Normally her deep tan would have really suited her but sadly on this trip, the browner she got the more alarming she looked. Not for the first time Jennifer visibly balked at the sight of Karen's hair. When they'd first arrived in Greece Karen had announced her intentions to go blonde with the help of a bottle of Sun-In. Typically, she'd ignored all her friends' protestations completely, despite the fact Sun-In was never designed to be used on dark hair.

As a result, instead of the sun-kissed highlights Karen had been imagining, her reward for being so pig headed was patches of dodgy orange hair which looked like straw and was brittle and coarse to the touch. It had looked horrendous when she'd first done it but at least then she'd been pale.

Luckily for Karen however, what she had in her favour was her attitude. She'd always had incredibly thick skin meaning that it would take more than orange hair to ruin her holiday. Whereas, had the same thing 'happened' to Jennifer, it would have been a complete game changer. And as for Lucy, who'd always been self-conscious about her looks, partly because she'd never had brilliant skin and suffered from a bit of acne, if she'd had to deal with the Sun-In disaster she probably wouldn't have left the apartment ever again, unless it was to go shopping for a burkha. But then Karen pretty much had a 'fuck it' approach to most things which would get her far in life, occasionally into trouble and lots of male attention.

Tonight she'd tried to mitigate the hair disaster by gelling it all back off her face. It looked seriously bizarre but, as ever, Karen preferred to concentrate on the positive so was reeking of confidence due to how good her boobs looked in her mini dress. Jennifer admired her for it.

As Jennifer looked at her friends, her best friends, getting ready for their night out, their biggest concern being what to wear, she was filled with the sense that this was a carefree time to be treasured. When they got home, A level results would be waiting for them and the next stage of education would begin. But for now they didn't have to worry about anything except getting a tan, a task the girls had applied themselves to with more zeal than they probably had to their recently taken exams. Only Lucy with her pale, almost translucent skin and mousy blonde hair was still roughly the same colour she'd started out, though not for want of trying.

'Do I look all right?' she asked now, having slipped on a halter-neck top and a pair of shorts.

'You look lovely,' said Jennifer sincerely, lazily stretching one brown leg out over the white sheet she was entwined in. She loved having brown feet. 'Those polka dot shorts are really cool.'

'Come on,' nagged Karen, who was dying to meet up with Mark. She'd met him four nights ago. He was twenty-four, from Wigan, and worked as a carpet fitter which had given rise to lots of predictable jokes about Karen getting laid.

'Right,' said Jennifer, finally heading for the shower.

*

Two hours, a quick pizza (they ate as cheaply as they could every night, preferring to save their money for drinks) and one bar later, they were in the best spot on the island. Club Kaluha. The club was huge, and outrageously expensive to get into unless you struck it lucky and got a pass from one of the PRs who scouted Bar Street looking for girls to entice in. Jennifer and her friends hadn't paid to get in once so far, but poor Mark and his mates had had to stump up every night, much to their chagrin.

There was an inside section of the club but the majority of it was outside and in the middle was a massive pirate ship surrounded by palm trees. Walking in, having greeted the bouncers who by now they were on first name terms with, they were met by a wall of house music and what felt like an electrical charge of energy in the air, palpable anticipation. Then again, everything was always going to feel magical when there was a warm breeze, everyone had a tan and people's biggest concern was who fancied them.

*

'You all right?' said Lucy to Jennifer, coming to join her on one of the outside seating areas where she had a good view of the ship and the main bar. She'd been sitting there for a while now, on her own, enjoying the music and watching the world go by.

'Yeah, well happy. You?'

'Good. Bit sad though. I don't want this to end.'

'I know,' said Jennifer. 'It's been amazing. Still, I reckon uni's going to be a right laugh.'

Lucy nodded. 'Wish we were all going to the same one. You and Karen are so lucky.'

'Look at Esther,' interrupted Jennifer, nudging Lucy hard and laughing.

The two girls chuckled as they watched Mark's mate, who for some inexplicable reason was called 'Bonehead', trying desperately to chat Esther up. Esther looked decidedly unimpressed as Bonehead advanced ever closer to her, shouting in her ear against the music. At the same time she was backing away, partly because he had a terrible lisp so was literally spraying her with his enthusiasm.

'Mark's a lovely guy but his mates are well annoying,' said Lucy.

'I know,' agreed Jennifer. 'I feel like we've slightly lost

Karen to Mark too which is a bit of a shame. She's bloody obsessed.'

And then, at exactly the same time, they saw him.

'Oh my god,' mouthed Lucy. 'Are you looking where I am?'

Jennifer certainly was. He was absolutely gorgeous. Without even realising she was doing it, she suddenly found herself sitting up and angling her entire body in his direction.

He was standing by the bar, to the left of the ship, and was nodding his head in time to the music, watching a group of girls who were dancing next to him. He completely stood out from the crowd. He was wearing a T-shirt and combat trousers but his body was that of a demi-god and to Jennifer he seemed to ooze testosterone, sex appeal and something more dangerous. His arms were muscular yet lean and brown and he put Mark and his mates in the shade. They were mere boys compared to this specimen of manhood.

Just then he turned and caught Jennifer's eye and as he did, a number of things happened. Firstly, Lucy realised in a nanosecond she was out of the running. Secondly, Jennifer suddenly sensed that the next few days were going to be very interesting, and thirdly he gave her such a confident grin she suspected he was thinking along the same kind of lines as she was. It was as if he liked what he saw but more thrillingly, clearly knew he could have it.

'He's coming over,' squealed Lucy all flustered.

'Oh my god,' panicked Jennifer, realising her friend was right. 'I shouldn't have had that slice with pepperoni on it. Quick Luce, smell my breath.'

'Fuck off, weirdo,' complained Lucy, shoving her away. 'And no, you're fine anyway.'

Quickly, Jennifer stopped breathing on Lucy, pulled her skirt down and rearranged her legs to look as slim as possible. Then, as he continued his approach, she flicked her long, brown hair over one shoulder, realising as she did how obvious she was being. She flicked it back again but then worried in case she looked like she was having some kind of attack.

'All right, girls,' he said, finally coming to a stop directly in front of Jennifer. His accent was broad and northern.

'All right,' said Jennifer looking him straight in the eye, acknowledging the instant flicker of attraction that she'd felt between them. This was going to be so much fun.

She frowned at Lucy who was making a silly face at her as if to say *I see you flirting, Missy.*

'Drink?'

Jennifer nodded, her eyes never leaving his. Nerves dissipating, she concentrated on letting him know she was more than a match for him and felt her stomach flip as he grinned again and looked her up and down in a way that could only be described as filthy. Every nerve ending fizzing, Jennifer watched as he returned to the bar where the queue for drinks was three people deep, while Lucy elbowed her excitedly in the ribs.

'Oh my god, oh my god, oh my god,' squealed Jennifer, eyes still glued to him.

Unsurprisingly, the barmaid noticed him at once and served him straight away. She obviously knew him and the easy way in which he bantered with her, made Jennifer briefly wonder what she was getting herself into.

A minute later he returned carrying three lethal-looking cocktails. Jennifer was pleased he'd got one for Lucy.

'Here you go. B52s'

'Thanks,' said Jennifer, tossing her hair again and shoving her breasts out as far as she could until, that is, she realised Lucy was laughing at her at which point she returned them to their normal vantage point.

'You're gorgeous,' he said, matter of factly.

'Not so bad yourself,' she shot back, thrilled by his flirting.

'Thanks for the drink,' said Lucy, giving her friend a large wink and slinking off to leave them to it and find some fun of her own.

*

Half an hour later, Jennifer had found out that his name was Aidan, that he'd been on Kos all summer and that he was the most exciting person she'd ever met. He didn't seem to conform to any rules. He'd left home, was travelling the world, his only real plan being to permanently escape his home town of Carlisle and to end up living in Australia. They'd already kissed and it was so charged with sexual excitement it had practically blown her head off. Now he was sliding his hand gently up and down her thigh, which tickled a bit, in a gloriously shivery kind of way.

'Do you want one?' he said suddenly, pulling a little bag of white pills out of his pocket. He took one out and offered it to her. It had a picture of a dove on it.

'Not sure,' said Jennifer truthfully.

'Your mates can have one too,' he said. 'I've got plenty and they're very clean.'

Jennifer shrugged, determined not to display how much her mind was racing while she worked out what to do. She'd not had ecstasy before but everyone she knew who had, like Karen, said it was amazing.

'If Karen's up for it I will,' she said, leaving Aidan behind to go and get her friend who was inside on the dance floor.

Once she knew she was out of his line of vision, Jennifer stopped trying to walk sexily and started practically galloping towards her friend, gesturing to Karen to meet her halfway. 'Aidan's got some e's,' she shouted into her friend's ear over the deafeningly loud music. 'Shall we have one?'

'Oh my god, so not only have you pulled the hottest person on the island, he's got pills as well?' she shouted back, out of breath from dancing, eyes shining. 'You are such a bitch. Why didn't you say earlier? Make sure he gives one to Mark too.'

Jennifer nodded and turned on her heel to find Aidan, hoping desperately he wouldn't have disappeared or met someone more interesting during the last forty seconds.

As she made her way back, she decided that with regard to the pill, she should probably just go with the flow. Her dad had always told her that in life it was better to regret something you'd done than something you hadn't which sounded like good advice to her, even if he probably hadn't had class A drugs in mind when he'd said it…

*

One hour later and Jennifer was standing in the middle of the club, with her hands in the air, feeling happier than she ever had in her entire life. 'Rhythm is a Dancer' by Snap was playing, a tune which they'd heard on average at least three times a day recently but at this precise moment it sounded more amazing than it ever had before.

Jennifer scraped her hands through her hair and exhaled noisily, letting the rushes she was experiencing travel up her body. Right now there was not one place on earth she'd rather be.

Suddenly she felt Aidan's hands on her shoulders, massaging her, kneading her. His touch was so firm and felt so good that she staggered a little bit, almost losing her balance. She turned round.

'All right,' he grinned, chewing gum, his eyes wide and pupils really black.

'Yeah,' was all Jennifer could manage to utter, but she grinned back at him and it didn't seem to matter in the slightest that she'd lost the power of speech. She literally couldn't care less. All that did matter was that she was with her best friends, and with Aidan, who happened to be the most beautiful man she'd ever seen in her life, listening to music that was literally transporting her to another dimension. She looked over at Karen who was dancing at a hundred miles per hour as if someone had told her all human life depended on it, Mark watching adoringly from the side, a daft grin on his face. Meanwhile, Esther and Lucy had kicked their shoes off and were having a chat on the cushions, stopping now and again only to give each other a big hug. God she loved them all.

'Good isn't it?' said Aidan.

But Jennifer was too fucked now to reply. Her jaw was trembling a bit and she could feel her eyes rolling slightly in the back of her head but she wasn't remotely bothered. Quite the opposite in fact. Instead she was relishing every minute of the warm, soupy sensations that had taken over her limbs and merely wanted to enjoy them flooding over her.

'Hey you, you OK? Come and sit down,' instructed Aidan.

Stumbling slightly but happy to do as she was told, Jennifer let herself be led to the cushions where her mates were sitting.

'Jen,' they said delightedly as if they hadn't seen her for a week, eyes huge and shining. 'Come here, babe. Love you.'

'Love you too,' she said softly before lying down on the cushions. She was overcome by a desire to writhe around on them but something told her it was probably best not to.

Maybe she'd run that thought past the girls.

'Don't you feel like rolling around on the cushions?'

'What?' said Esther, whose jaw was quivering slightly.

'I said,' repeated Jennifer, suddenly desperate for some water, 'don't you feel like rolling around on the cushions?'

Lucy nodded. 'I do, I feel like stuffing them up my top too and pretending I'm up the duff.'

This struck Jennifer as not only funny but wise.

'And I feel like sticking one down my pants so I've got a massive butt,' added Esther.

'And I feel like…' Jennifer tried to join in but was defeated once again by ever increasing sensations that were flooding her system. After a long pause, she uttered 'sticking one up my arse'. Only by then, the thread had been rather lost so it came out as a totally random statement. However, rather than feel embarrassed, she was amused by how ludicrous it all was. Besides, what anybody thought just didn't seem to be a problem.

'Stick what up your arse?' enquired Aidan, looking confused.

'Nothing,' muttered Jennifer, the notion of trying to explain her thought process far too daunting at this stage.

'You girls are funny,' said Aidan, head bouncing in time to the beat, and as they bathed in his compliment, it was like they'd known him for years.

'Where did you all meet?'

'School,' said Esther looking really out of it and clearly loving the next tune that had just come on: 'Everybody's Free' by Rozalla.

Karen came whooping over. 'Come on you lot. Fucking tune! Come and dance Jen, on your feet now.'

'Too wasted,' she managed.

'But happy?' checked Aidan.

'Oh yeah,' she said, flopping back onto the cushions.

Everybody's free to feel good.

She waved her hands around, playing air piano.

'Hey, you girls are great,' said Aidan, continuing on the same theme, chewing gum frenetically.

'We sure are,' concurred Lucy, trying to pull her friends in for a hug, but Jennifer was too wasted. She just wanted to sit in peace, in her own space, without being man-handled.

'Love you girls.'

'Love you too,' agreed Jennifer, hardly able to open her eyes, she was rushing so intensely.

'Even Bonehead's all right,' said Esther, looking over to where he was busy stacking boxes.

'I may have let Bonehead have a cheeky half, whereas this lunatic told me she definitely wasn't coming up so she's had a whole one,' Aidan said, gesturing to Jennifer.

'Have you?' said Esther and Lucy in unison, slack-jawed.

'Yup,' said Jennifer, collapsing into the cushions again. 'Oh my god this tune is amazing.'

'Nutter,' said Esther.

'Can I have another one?' asked Jennifer.

'No you cannot,' said Aidan, stroking her leg as her friends looked on, not knowing whether to be impressed or worried by how well Jennifer had taken to the drug. 'I can see I'm going to have my work cut out with you, you little minx.'

And that was it. From that sentence forward, continuing in the vein of giving everything little or no real deliberation, choosing instead to be steered only by instinct and desire, as you do when you're young, Jennifer and Aidan were an item.

PRESENT DAY

Everything was very, very quiet, apart from the dull, ominous thudding in her head. She was aware that there was stuff going on around her, commotion, chaos even, but she could only very vaguely decipher what any of it was. It all seemed so far away and she wasn't sure she had the inclination to tune in properly anyway, for instinct told her that if she were to, that suddenly everything would really hurt. So instead she let herself drift further towards a state of mental limbo, refusing to choose the path of either resistance or acceptance. Something terrible had happened. That was a certainty. Her entire body was like a piece of lead, and somehow didn't feel like her own.

A scream pierced the warm, dense fog she was in. It was a guttural, horrifying sound.

'Jen,' yelled the same voice, its tone desperate and distressed.

Karen.

It was Karen.

And then came another voice, one she didn't recognise, telling Karen to stay back. Not to touch.

She knew she should probably be feeling more than she was. Doing something perhaps, and yet doing anything was a complete and utter impossibility. She couldn't open her eyes and yet still managed to be dimly aware of flashing lights and at one point of someone manhandling her eyelids and asking her things. She wished they'd all go away and let the cloudy haziness which was shrouding her, envelope her completely. That would be easier.

SATURDAY

While Max went to collect the children from his parents, Jennifer raced round the house trying to get it into a vaguely fit state. Friends were coming for lunch and she was running behind. If she was honest she wasn't feeling a huge amount of joy about the fact they were coming. Lately they'd had a lot of people over and while it was nice to socialise, Saturdays were starting to feel as structured and routined as the rest of the week. What with the cooking, cleaning and never-ending washing up and putting away. Still, in reality, if it was Karen and Pete who were coming over, she'd be looking forward to it a whole lot more. Apart from anything else, Karen wouldn't care if the house was a tip, or if she served up a bit of old spaghetti for lunch.

Whereas with Judith and Henry Gallagher, she felt obliged to achieve that 'I've thrown this magnificent feast together effortlessly, à la Nigella, wearing an unstained silk dressing gown while simultaneously raising two angelic children in a house liberally festooned with fairy lights' look, that actually requires *tons* of effort, perspiration, lots of shouting at the children and some swearing. But then, when it came to Judith and Henry, 'friends' was probably rather a loose term and therein lay the problem.

Judith was a work colleague of Max's who was alright...ish, only she talked about work incessantly, in a way that tended to make Jennifer feel totally excluded from proceedings. With Judith always hogging Max, Jennifer was usually left feeling obliged to entertain Henry, who frankly was hard work. A quiet, uninspiring, humourless bloke, Henry was one of those people who liked to exist under an umbrella of shyness, as if by labelling himself thus, he was excused from having to make any effort on the conversation front. As far as Jennifer was concerned though, once past the age of twenty-one, no matter how bloody 'shy' anyone was, she felt they should at least pepper a chat with the odd question, thus making it a two-way thing. As it was, whenever Jennifer was doing her bit by talking to Henry she felt like she was interviewing him.

To add to the already non-enticing prospect of lunch with the Gallaghers, this was the third time in two years she and Max had invited them over for a meal and they'd never returned the invitation. Max insisted it was a good idea for him to 'keep in' with Judith, for work reasons. But Jennifer was starting to think it was probably Judith's turn to spend hundreds of pounds in the supermarket on feeding *their* faces, and that furthermore, perhaps she didn't give a shit if they 'kept in' with her or not.

Having finally finished tidying downstairs, even going so far as to squirt a bit of polish on the coffee table so at least the room *smelled* clean, she started on the children's bedrooms. By the time she'd got to her and Max's room though she'd lost the will, and was suddenly overwhelmed by the prospect of still having to produce a meal for four adults, three children and a baby. So, after she'd stuffed everything that was on the floor into the laundry basket, she stopped for a second and sunk onto the bed, taking advantage of the unusual silence. For a few minutes she reflected on how easily she'd given up on her mission to seduce Max. As she did, the disappointment from the previous evening washed over her once more, and she found herself wondering idly when and indeed *if* she should try donning her new underwear again. After all, Max wasn't psychic, so to be fair to him how could he have known what she'd had in mind? If she'd been really serious about having her wicked way with him she probably should have gone downstairs and shown him what she was wearing because if he'd had the visual stimulation she suspected he definitely would have gone for it. So why hadn't she done that?

She sighed. Marriage. It was such bloody hard work sometimes. Make an effort was all anybody said and it *was* an effort. That was the problem. She missed the days when being with each other wasn't any effort at all. The days when *not* being together were the ones which felt like the effort.

Jennifer willed herself to get up and continue her attack on the house but it wasn't happening, mainly because her thoughts had turned to a subject which had been occupying her mind a lot lately. Sex. Or rather, her lack of it. As soon as she allowed the thought in, she felt a lurch of possibility in her nether regions.

The next thing she knew, despite the fact the potatoes desperately needed peeling if lunch had any hope at all of being served for one o'clock, her hand had slid into her knickers. Right, she needed to be quick so who should she think about? Aware that time wasn't on her side she turned to an old favourite, if you like, a golden oldie, though part of her detested the fact she was still dining out on sex she'd had nearly twenty years ago. However, when it came to fantasy, Aidan was still guaranteed to get her going. And fast.

Once again Jennifer returned to a hot, airless room, which had a bed with a squeaky mattress and a ceiling fan, and replayed the best sex she'd ever had in her entire life. Images of brown limbs entwined and his strong hard body pressing into hers, manoeuvring her into positions she hadn't even known existed, swam into her head. An enjoyable three minutes later, and her very old flame was just on the brink of giving her an almighty orgasm when she became dimly aware of the key turning in the door downstairs. She couldn't believe it…

'We're back,' called Max up the stairs.

'Muuuuummy,' two little voices yelled in unison, feet charging up the stairs.

'Shit,' gasped Jennifer, withdrawing her hand, and springing into an upright position, feeling utterly frustrated. Thirty seconds more and she'd definitely have been there. 'Hello-ooo,' she called back, slightly screechily. 'Have you had a lovely lovely time, kids?'

As she leapt up from the bed she experienced a bit of a head rush. Quickly she patted her hair down and did her jeans up, legs feeling slightly wobbly.

The children barrelled in. 'Mummy.'

'Hello my little loves, how are you?' she warbled 'I've missed you. Were you good for Grandma?'

'Yes,' said Eadie.

'What about you, Pol?'

'Yes,' her youngest agreed, though she seemed more interested in trying to get her T-shirt off.

'What are you doing?'

'I need a wee.'

'OK, well you don't need to take your top off to have a wee do you? Come here.'

Just then Max called up the stairs. 'Jen, what the hell have you been doing? You haven't peeled the bloody potatoes. They're going to be here soon and nothing's ready. You haven't even laid the table.'

Jennifer rolled her eyes so vigorously they actually hurt a little bit. 'Well...feel free to go for it.'

'All right, there's no need to be sarcastic about it, it's just you said you'd get things under control while I got the girls and nothing's done.'

'All right,' said Jennifer testily, stomping onto the landing and into the bathroom so she could plonk Polly on the toilet before heading downstairs.

She found Max in the kitchen, peeling potatoes angrily. Whole chunks were coming out.

'I'll do that,' she said, trying to grab the peeler off him.

'No, it's fine, I'm doing it.'

'What are you so grumpy about anyway? Is it that much of a big deal that little wifey hasn't done everything by the time you've got back?'

'Little wifey hasn't done anything, let alone everything,' muttered Max.

'Oh rubbish,' disagreed Jennifer. 'The house was a complete state if you must know, and besides, I'm getting a bit sick of having people over every single weekend when we don't even enjoy it.'

'Yes we do,' said Max, shooting her a look of real disdain.

'No we don't,' she replied petulantly, simultaneously acknowledging that now they were sounding like their children.

'We do,' said Max, oblivious.

'Oh yeah, we're having a great time preparing for the arrival of smug-arse, "high powered" Judith and dullard

Henry. And it goes without saying I can't wait to spend the rest of the day washing up after them while you bum lick her,' huffed Jennifer.

Max wrinkled up his nose at her choice of words, which actually made Jennifer giggle for a second and broke the tension a little.

'Muuuuuuuuuuuum,' yelled Polly from upstairs. 'I've got wee wee on my sock.'

'Yours,' said Max.

Jennifer tutted before turning on her heel, faintly wondering if she'd get away with quickly locking herself in the spare room, so she could finish what she'd started earlier. Hmm…probably not.

Half an hour later the doorbell rang meaning the people she couldn't be bothered to see, let alone entertain, had arrived.

Taking a deep breath and summoning up a smile she opened the door.

'Hello everybody, come in, come in,' said Jennifer, ushering them all into the house and down the hallway. 'It's so lovely to see you all. Oh my look at James, hasn't he grown and doesn't he look *so* like you, Henry?'

'He's a chip off the old block all right,' agreed Judith, immaculate as ever in tasteful navy, which she'd offset with funky 'weekend' jewellery and ballet pumps. 'No questioning who his dad is.'

Jennifer agreed totally, because actually James really did look exactly like Henry, only given that he was only

ten years old, looking like a gone-to-seed, middle-aged
man wasn't necessarily a good thing. 'So how was your
journey?' Jennifer enquired brightly, snapping out of her
reverie before anyone noticed her staring.

'Fine,' said Judith, kissing her on both cheeks and
handing her a bottle of wine. 'Sorry we're a bit late.
Work's been sooooo manic this week I simply had to have
a bit of a chill out this morning. I bet Max did too, we've
literally been working like Trojans this week.'

'I can imagine,' said Jennifer, quite wanting to punch
her.

*

An hour and a half later than planned, lunch was finally
on the verge of being served up.

The children were all starving despite having been fed
various 'just to keep you going' snacks and were getting fractious. Judith and Henry had polished off two
entire bags of Kettle Chips and had already had an
argument about who was driving home. Oscar, their
eighteen-month-old baby, was having a sleep upstairs and
they were well into a third bottle of wine. Meanwhile,
Max was sucking up to Judith so much it was making
Jennifer's skin crawl. She herself was worryingly pissed
given that she still had to get lunch on the table.

As Judith roared with laughter at yet another dull
work anecdote of Max's, Jennifer flinched. The way Max
was giving her his undivided attention was grounds for

jealousy quite frankly, only she couldn't be bothered to make a fuss. Instead she just felt saddened that every time she tried to join in with a vaguely witty remark he barely looked in her direction. Perhaps she should get her tits out she thought wryly. Run round the kitchen with them jiggling about.

With little enthusiasm Jennifer replenished the crisp bowl (this time with Frazzles and Pom Bears instead of posh Kettle Chips—it was all she had left). As she did so she smiled weakly at dull Henry who was sat on a stool by the island like a fat useless turd. She was just about to ask him yet another question about how his work was going when she realised she didn't care and couldn't be bothered. So instead she turned her back on him, and bent down to open the oven to investigate what might be happening in there. As boiling hot air blasted her in the face, she realised she was one hundred percent, definitely, without a shadow of a doubt, drunk.

She was also glad, and a little bit smug, that for once she'd cut corners by picking up (on Karen's recommendation) some small stuffed chickens from the local deli. Not having to cook a meat dish of some description meant all she'd had to do in theory was make the roast potatoes and cobble together a salad. So why did it all feel as stressful as though she'd been preparing a banquet for eighty under the same conditions as the *Masterchef* final?

Seconds later she emerged from the oven once more, red in the face, sweating, and clutching the ludicrously heavy tray in an oven glove only to realise that the island needed clearing before she could put it down.

'Max,' she called over, to where he was deep in conversation with Judith about something tedious.

'Max!'

'Hey, there's no need to yell. What is it?' he said, trying to sound like he wasn't snapping when in fact that was exactly what he was doing.

'Sorry,' she said, not sorry at all. Her hands were practically on fire. 'I was just wondering if you could clear a space for this. It's very heavy,' she grimaced.

'Oh right,' he said, finally realising her plight.

Once dumped on the side, one by one, Jennifer lifted the little chickens out of the roasting tray and onto the chopping board. They were less chickens really, more parcels of poussin, tied up with string and stuffed with pork and herbs. Jennifer immediately decided that she wouldn't bother fobbing the meaty creations off as her own. After all, she'd never boned a piece of meat (fnar fnar) in her life and had certainly never been arsed to tie up anything you could eat with string.

'Ooh, those look wonderful, Jennifer,' said Judith, gliding over to have a look at what she was about to stuff her self-satisfied face with. 'Aren't you lucky, Max? That's what comes of having a wife at home who's got time to actually create things like this. Poor Henry is lucky if I remember to buy him a ready meal aren't you?'

'I do work,' said Jennifer, probably a bit defensively.

'Do you?' said Judith, looking first surprised and then apologetic, as if she'd just realised her error. 'Oh god of course you do, and it goes without saying that looking after children is probably the hardest job of all. I certainly wouldn't have had another if I'd had to stay at home and look after them,' she honked, loudly enough for her offspring to hear and therefore quite possibly need therapy in the future.

'No, I mean, I do work. I have a job,' explained Jennifer '*And* I look after the kids. I work at an estate agent's on the high street three days a week.'

'Oh god brilliant,' said Judith lamely, 'that must be really fun.'

Jennifer picked up the carvers and tried not to look menacing. She really needed to eat.

'Those look good,' said Henry, ambling over.

'Right, well, why don't you all sit down?' ordered Jennifer with meaning, wanting them all just to get out of her face while she plated up. 'Judith, get the kids sat down. We'll do their plates first.'

'Oh right,' she said, looking startled at having been asked to do anything.

Jennifer didn't care though. She was too busy trying to figure out if the chickens were definitely cooked through. To her alarm they looked a bit pinky inside and a bit…well… unappetising really.

'So, what's that then?' Max asked, also looking mildly alarmed by the colour of the meat.

'Oh, that's just the pork they're stuffed with. Don't worry, it's supposed to look like that,' Jennifer assured him, secretly wondering if a night on the toilet lay ahead for them all.

'They don't carve very well do they?' Max added, in a muted whisper.

Jennifer gazed hopelessly at the chickens which had sort of collapsed in on themselves and were looking less and less appealing by the second. Sort of like grey and pink mush.

'Just get it on the plates,' she muttered, feeling deeply stressed now and too pissed and hot to handle the situation. She was pretty certain it was just the pork stuffing that was lending them that strange hue so they were just going to have to go with it. Frankly she was past caring, though she did add as an aside, 'But make sure you give the kids the bits from around the outside.'

Once the children had all been given their plates of food (which they unanimously declared they didn't like before having even tried it) and their drinks (one beaker of juice being knocked over immediately as tradition required), the adults got on with helping themselves to lots of salad and potatoes.

'You didn't make these yourself did you?' Judith asked Jennifer, looking slightly worried as she surveyed her plate of unidentifiable meat.

And here it was, crunch time, time for Jennifer to

explain that no, of course she hadn't made them and that yes, they did look a bit weird didn't they? And this answer was on the tip of her tongue, and yet for some reason known only to the inner machinations of her befuddled brain, that isn't what came out.

Instead, what she experienced in that moment might well be what happens to mass murderers when they hear voices in their heads telling them to do things. Or, to put it another way, the normal Jen, the one who was usually pretty down to earth about stuff, and who ordinarily felt strongly that not making other women feel less able was hugely important, was punched in the head, literally knocked out flat by the other part of her. That is to say, the part that felt belittled by Judith and who had been battling for hours with the desire to yell very loudly and directly into her smug face that actually she'd got a 2:1 in her degree and that giving up her career in order to play an active part in her children's upbringing had been a choice (albeit one she struggled with sometimes) so shouldn't be sneered at. The part of her who was exhausted by the daily grind, that was strung out, in need of a long holiday and some rampant sex, and who was also suffering from a monumental mid-life crisis and had been prescribed anti-depressants only a few weeks earlier. That Jennifer took over and said, after an unnaturally long pause 'Yes I did...I did make them.'

At the other end of the table Max looked baffled and just stared at his plate.

'Wow,' said Judith tentatively. 'They look really…
complicated. How did you go about it?'

'Well…' Jennifer said gingerly, feeling suddenly
drowned by her own lie. 'I…er… bought them, boned
them…and then stuffed them with pork and herbs
before…kind of, tying them up.'

'Right,' said Judith and in that moment Jennifer knew
that Judith knew that she was talking absolute bollocks.

'Mum,' piped up Eadie, looking miserable.

'Yes, darling,' said Jennifer, teeth gritted. 'What is
it?'

'I don't like my beef. It tastes like cat poo. Can I have
some toast?'

'It's chicken not beef and it's *please may I have* some
toast?' replied Jennifer.

'Please may I have some toast?'

'Yes,' sighed Jennifer faintly. 'Anyone else?'

For a second Max looked sorely tempted but soon
readjusted his expression when Jennifer glowered at him
on her way to the toaster.

The rest of the meal was pretty torturous. Only Henry
seemed blissfully unaware that he was eating something
which resembled road-kill. Everyone else performed a
sort of cutlery ballet-dance around their plate, consuming
lots of potatoes and salad, and expertly leaving a pile of
pinky grey mush to one side, with either their knife and
fork, or a napkin, placed cunningly over the top.

After the meal Jennifer cleared away, scraping tons of

discarded meat into the food recycling bin. As she did so, she wondered at what point she'd become so sad and pathetic that she couldn't have admitted that she hadn't made the disgusting food herself and that probably none of them should have touched it, in case they all got the chronic shits. When had she become the sort of person who cared what people like Judith and Henry thought anyway? When had she transformed into such a middle-class stereotype, desperately trying to impress? When had she turned into Max's mother?

Much later that night as she climbed gratefully between the sheets, head thumping with a same-day hangover, she said to Max who was already half asleep, 'The chicken was a bit weird wasn't it?'

'It was all right,' he said, his eyes shut and his body turned away from her. 'It just looked a bit like cat food. Why did you say you'd made it?'

'Don't know,' she replied truthfully, staring at the ceiling, hot with embarrassment just thinking about it.

'You did yourself a disservice anyway,' he added. 'Your cooking's far nicer and I think Judith doesn't cook much so it's not like you needed to compete. She works too hard to ever get round to doing any domestic stuff.'

'Oh, so now you're having a go at me for not making something are you?' she retorted defensively, because in truth she was feeling gradually more and more embarrassed that she'd passed off the stupid, dodgy looking ruddy chickens as her own creations. Her tone wasn't helped by the fact that the mere mention of Judith's name was starting to send shivers up her spine.

'No,' he sighed, now clearly wishing she'd shut up and go to sleep. 'I'm giving you a compliment on your cooking really but I'm also saying I think they knew you hadn't made it anyway.'

'Really?' she said, despite the fact she'd figured this out on her own, having it confirmed was mortifying, to the point where *another* bad night's sleep was probably on the cards. 'Why?'

'Because you went weird and replied really slowly, so it was obvious.'

'Oh god I'm so strange,' she whimpered. 'The thing is I'm very tired you know.'

'I know,' he said, and with that he fell fast asleep, as he had an annoying habit of doing when he was tired, leaving his wife to ponder in the darkness the fact that lying hadn't really achieved anything. In fact, it was clear to her that the only thing she'd stuffed by doing so (and it certainly wasn't the chickens) was herself.

Perhaps the whole debacle was a sign that she needed to be more honest about a whole load of things.

Two hours later, bored of her insomnia, head whirring, Jennifer slipped out of bed and crept into the spare room. Able to spread out she tried to relax, and then decided to finish what she'd started much earlier in the day in the hope that a good healthy orgasm might help her get to sleep. And so it was that she returned to that hot summer back in 1994 when, unlike now, food was of little or no consequence to her or her friends because they'd had far more interesting things to worry about.

THE PAST — AIDAN

Summer 1994

'Come with me,' said Aidan, the green eyes she'd got so used to, boring into her, pleading with her. 'I know we've only known each other five minutes but what we've got doesn't come along every day. I'm telling you.'

'How can I come with you?' repeated Jennifer, who inside was in complete turmoil. Something was pulling her, like a magnet, telling her to throw caution to the wind, to follow her heart, or possibly more accurately, her loins. They'd barely come up for air since they'd met and Jennifer had never known anything remotely like it. She knew she was relatively inexperienced on the sex front, having only slept with three people in total (actually four, she kept forgetting Greek bloke on beach), but Aidan had made her feel things she hadn't dreamed were possible. In bed they made total sense and as far as she could tell he was also an exciting person, someone who was creating his own path in life to tread, one which wasn't constrained by parental pressure or some traditional idea of how things should be played out. And that was the problem in a way. Jennifer had always *liked* knowing how things should map out. It had never occurred to her to stray even remotely from the plan which she and her parents were in agreement was the right one for her. The right one for most people.

School, college, travelling. Next on the list was university, followed by career, marriage, babies. That was life. Wasn't it?

And yet here was someone asking her to go completely off piste. And she was actually tempted. Sorely tempted. She was pretty sure she loved him, or was definitely on her way to falling in love with him and knew if she let him go she might regret it forever. The thought of never sleeping with him again and therefore not experiencing that unbelievably exquisite pleasure was unbearable too. She licked her lips and stared down at her green flipflops. Her feet were pleasingly brown. It was so hot.

'Look,' said Aidan, 'I'm not going to beg. That's not my style. And if you say no I guess I'll understand, though I think you'd be making a massive mistake. Like I said, what we've got is special. I know it is, and besides, what's the worst that could happen? I'm asking you to come away with me, but I wouldn't be kidnapping you. If it didn't work out you could just get on a plane home.'

'But my university place…?' questioned Jennifer, wondering if she could really deny herself the opportunity to be with him when he'd turned her entire world upside down in a matter of days. University was something she'd always wanted to experience but he was right. She could always change her mind, so maybe she needed to be more adventurous? But as this thought trailed away it was replaced by the feeling of absolute certainty that her parents would be beyond livid with her for being so irresponsible and for not consulting them. Then again, it was her life. She was so torn.

'Look, the boat leaves in half an hour. I'm going to be on it,' said Aidan. 'If you're coming with me, you need to say goodbye to the girls and get your stuff. What's it to be?'

'Oh god,' said Jennifer. 'I don't know.'

And for precisely ten more minutes she still didn't.

And then she had a chat with Karen who looked at her with such horror that she was even contemplating the idea of going off with someone she'd known for a total of seventeen days that something took over. Something irritatingly sensible.

And so it was that the boat sailed off with a hurt and more devastated than he'd imagined he might have been Aidan, taking him off for adventure and ultimately Australia.

She may have made what she thought was the 'right' decision but that didn't prevent Jennifer from feeling utterly desolate and distraught. She wailed as that boat sailed off into the distance and at one point even contemplated throwing herself off the jetty and swimming after it. Anything to have just one more feel of those arms around her. What had she done and would she regret this for the rest of her life?

PRESENT DAY

'Stay with us Jennifer, come on love, you can do this. Hang in there.'

Why was everyone yelling? She was so tired. All she wanted to do was sleep. She was so close to being able to just slip away yet simply wasn't being *allowed* to. She felt very muddled and had the vague sense of being bullied.

'Patient's suffering agonal respirations and has a CO2 of eleven. Probably in anaphylactic shock so let's commence CPR.'

'Jen, please hang in there, I'm so so sorry. I love you.'

'Sorry, Mr Wright. Can you stay out of the way? It's very important.'

What was Max doing here, she wondered. For a second she was tempted to open her eyes to have a look but she wasn't able to because suddenly a burning sensation swept through her so violently she would have done anything to make it stop. It was pain on a level she wouldn't ever have thought possible. Every cell in her body was on fire, doused in hot, white agony. Then, as quickly as it showed itself it subsided, and once again she reverted to her numb state of nothingness.

Then, someone was applying pressure to her which hurt in a different way. She didn't really want to be awake any more. She craved peace and sensed a way she could achieve it. There was definitely a direction she could go in that would remove all the pain, plus any further possibility of it.

She reflected for a second, feeling as though she were suspended in time and space, floating almost. In all honesty she wasn't totally sure she wanted to go that way either. She wasn't ready, which meant there was only one option left available to her. So once more she submitted to the grey fog of nothing. And as she sank back into it, more cries of panic sounded around her.

Meanwhile, as the paramedics went about their frenzied business of trying to save her life, the strangest things were happening in Jennifer's bruised brain.

None of us can really comprehend what the human brain is capable of doing, in the same way that Jennifer had no clue as to the true capabilities of her laptop. All she tended to use her PC for was to write emails, do a bit of shopping or social networking, meaning its dual core processor was never fully taken advantage of. She was always stunned when Max, who was far more tech savvy than her, did some simple task on her computer, in a way that made her realise she was only ever utilising around ten percent of what it could probably do, if only she knew how to operate it properly.

It's the same with the human brain, only on a far grander and more mysterious scale, its true power being so tricky to tap. Most of its work and activity happens at a deeply subconscious level and yet even beyond that, there are areas of it which we never unearth even when dreaming.

Psychics do better than most. Whether you believe in them or not, they at least have more awareness of the various possibilities which we *could* perhaps utilise if only we tried.

Right at that second, within Jennifer's skull, a series of lightning-fast connections were being made, ones which she never usually would have been privy to if her head hadn't made contact with the hard ground quite as brutally as it had, thus flinging her software into disarray. Something extraordinary was happening.

As her synapses furiously connected and fused, three tunnels of white light suddenly showed themselves to her. There was one to the left, one straight ahead and one to the right. Was this what death looked like? Instinct told her it was something different though and suddenly she knew, without needing to be told, that rather than leading her to the afterlife, instead these tunnels represented different lives she could so easily have led. Parallel universes, ones which were usually buried and hidden, deep in the core of the brain.

What she was being given here was a gift. The gift of being able to see what life would have been like had she chosen *another* route, or made a different decision, at three separate points during her life. And so it was that Jennifer allowed herself to fall into a deep and very informative coma. As her own private miracle started, she began to glide towards the first tunnel, the one to the left which was swirling with clouds of light at its entrance. This was the one marked Aidan

TUNNEL NUMBER ONE

What Could Have Been—Aidan

Jennifer slipped out of bed and padded across the room to pull the curtain back. Sunlight immediately poured in and though it was still only early, she could feel the heat of the day penetrating the glass. She gazed out at the view, loving the way the sea glinted and twinkled through the gaps in the rooftops. Their little one bedroom apartment in the bay-side suburbs of Brisbane was very basic, very compact, but it was also only a twenty-minute walk from the beach.

She opened the window a fraction and breathed in deeply. Then she tipped her face back and let the already strong rays bathe her skin with their warmth.

It was strange getting up every day knowing it was going to be hot and that the sky would almost definitely be blue. She'd always considered herself a total sun worshipper but having been away for so long now, the sense of urgency to get out there and work on her tan had started to fade a bit. Sometimes, if she were being totally honest, she even found the constancy of the temperature a little relentless, a tad monotonous, to the point where recently she'd found herself secretly craving a bit of grey sky. This was ironic given that she was always the first to moan about the abysmal climate in England and yet what she missed about the British weather was that subtle change of seasons. Nothing beat a glorious, breezy, spring day, or that first sniff in the air which told you that autumn had arrived, when the light became more golden and the leaves were falling from the trees, crunchy and brown.

'Hey sexy.'

'Oh, you're awake,' she said, turning round to see Aidan grinning at her from the bed. He was brown, toned and fit from all the hours of running on the beach he was doing most days. She still felt a lurch of desire every time she clapped eyes on him.

'Yeah funny that, given that you've pulled the curtains wide open. Now, seeing as you've woken me up, get your sexy bum over here,' he said, eyeing her greedily.

She was only wearing a small vest top and a pair of knickers.

'I know what you're after,' she grinned back at him, knowing full well he'd have a raging hard on. He woke up with one every morning. In that way he was a bit like the Queensland weather, predictable.

'Just shut up and come here,' he said, flinging back the sheets to reveal that her guess was indeed correct.

Not needing to be persuaded, Jennifer approached the

bed and succumbed to half an hour of intense passion. Before Aidan, she hadn't been aware of ever having such a voracious sexual appetite but he'd definitely woken something up inside of her that she supposed must have been lying dormant before.

After what was, as ever, mind-blowing, energetic sex, they both lay flat on their backs panting, sated, sweating.

'You're amazing,' said Aidan, idly tweaking her left nipple.

'So are you,' she replied. 'Seriously amazing.'

'Love you,' he said, hugging her tight. As he did so Jennifer marvelled at how safe he made her feel. The chemistry between them was something she doubted could ever be replicated with anyone else, to the point that sometimes they were almost savagely passionate with one another. She didn't think there was anything she wouldn't be prepared to do with him physically and, as a result, she had never felt so confident in her own body or so empowered in terms of the effect she knew she was capable of having upon him.

'Are we going to the beach then?' said Aidan.

'Not the building site?'

'Nah, that can wait. It's too much of a scorcher. Maybe tomorrow?'

'OK,' she agreed, flopping over to her side so she could get up and start getting the beach bag ready.

Just then the phone rang.

'Yours,' said Jennifer lazily, though a second later she regretted this when she remembered it would probably be the scheduled phone call she'd arranged with her parents before they retired to bed on the other side of the world.

'Yup, here she is,' Aidan was saying, in a fed up, vaguely unfriendly tone which simply confirmed it was them.

Jennifer sat up and reached over for her vest top which she pulled back over her head before taking the phone from him. It was such a small apartment that there wasn't anywhere for her to go where she could talk without Aidan listening in, so rather than standing up in the tiny kitchen, where he'd be able to hear every word anyway, she just stayed where she was. Never having any privacy did get to her sometimes.

'Hi Mum, how are you?'

'Oh all right,' said the so familiar voice, made tinny from the sheer distance it was travelling.

Jennifer pictured her parents, sitting by the phone together, probably ready for bed in their dressing gowns, in the lounge with the radiators blasting.

'What have you been up to this week, Jen?'

'Oh, this and that,' she replied 'Working, bit of beach action. You know? The usual really.'

'I thought you were going to that Surfers Paradise place.'

'Oh yeah, we were, but we didn't in the end,' said

Jennifer, turning around so she had her back to Aidan. He was looking grumpy like he always did when she chatted to her parents. It was getting on her nerves.

*

Three months ago, at exactly the time her mum and dad had been expecting her to be landing at Gatwick, back from her holiday with the girls, Jennifer had rung them from Athens to break the news that she'd essentially decided to throw caution to the wind and take an unplanned gap year. In Australia...

To say they'd been furious had been an understatement. Her dad had shouted, her mum had wept though, as it transpired, it was less the fact she wasn't coming home which enraged them so much, but more the fact she wasn't coming back because of a man they hadn't met.

Their reaction had been *so* bad that Jennifer had seriously considered giving up on her adventure altogether. Had even thought it might be best just to admit defeat and head home straight away, tail between her legs. In fact she'd just been about to tell them that she was sorry and that she would do exactly that, when her mother had interjected with, 'One whiff of male attention and you go and lose your head, Jennifer. It's pathetic when you think about it.'

And that one comment changed everything. For at that point, Jennifer's mood had switched from apologetic and shamefaced to resolute and determined. She'd been utterly insulted by her mother's accusation and had said as much to Aidan when she'd got off the phone a few minutes later in order to have a think, on the proviso that she'd call them back with a decision.

She'd left him drinking a beer and smoking a cigarette in a dusty roadside cafe in a busy square and as she'd approached, it was obvious to her that despite trying to appear nonchalant he was in fact really nervous.

'What happened?' he'd asked, as soon as she was in earshot.

'They went bloody mad,' she replied, still a bit shell-shocked from the whole experience. She jumped as a moped whizzed past, almost knocking her off her feet.

Gathering her wits and checking left and right she finally reached his table, mind whirling as she tried to comprehend what had just happened.

She'd always hated confrontation and miraculously had managed to avoid too many bust-ups with her fairly conservative parents up until this point, which was partly why she was so livid with them now. How dare her mother have talked to her like that? Like she was some stupid, dozy tart who was so needy of male attention she'd do anything to get it. She'd never given them any cause for worry or upset in the past and yet now she was deviating off the path just a little bit, they didn't have the patience to at least try and understand her reasons. Yes, Aidan had been a massive part of the decision not to go home, but that was life. You met people and things happened and given that they hadn't even met him it seemed ridiculous for them to have formed an opinion of him already. It was so unfair. They gave her no credit whatsoever.

'So what's the score then?'

'I said I'd call back in ten minutes so we could all cool off,' she'd replied, avoiding both the question and his stare.

'And?'

'Oh I don't know,' she'd replied truthfully, feeling unbelievably torn 'They're really mad at me, Aidan, and it was awful hearing them so pissed off. Plus, Mum's desperately worried that if I defer I might lose my place altogether.'

'Well she would say that wouldn't she,' suggested Aidan.

Jennifer shrugged, doubtful her mum was that manipulative. 'I'm so thirsty I almost feel faint, have you got enough money for me to get a beer?'

'Yeah, go for it,' said Aidan pulling some ancient Drachma notes out of his pocket and signalling to the waiter.

A few minutes later, once Jennifer had had the chance to glug back some of her cold lager, he enquired again. 'So what's it to be then, babe? Sunshine, the land of opportunity and some hot romance with me? Or back to mummy and daddy and the rain?'

'I don't know,' Jennifer had replied honestly. She felt really conflicted and a bit stupid. She'd probably been deeply deluded thinking her parents would just accept her reasoning for ducking out. Plus, deep down she really didn't want to throw away her chance to go to university, even if it meant admitting she'd been rash. Their fury had knocked her though and treating her like a child made it harder for her to decide what to do. She was so cross with them.

Realising she needed time to think Aidan dropped the subject so they sat in slightly tense silence, watching the world go by, until Jennifer got up. 'Right, there's no point sitting here putting it off. I'd better go and ring them back.'

As she marched back across the busy road to the centre of the square where the phone booth was, her head was spinning. What should she do? She still had no idea, so decided it would probably be best just to see how the conversation panned out.

Her dad had picked up the phone. 'Right, now I hope you're phoning to tell us you've seen sense.'

This wasn't a good start in terms of making her feel like returning to the bosom of her family.

'I've phoned to discuss things like an adult,' she shot back.

'Well, that's a start,' he said. 'So in that case, surely you can see that running off with some good for nothing beach bum, while ruining your life in the process, is entirely the wrong thing to do?'

It was a shame he'd taken that approach. It was a shame

he hadn't simply asked her how she was and how she was feeling because he might have got a very different response to the one he received and the conversation may have played out another way.

As it was, three days later Jennifer and Aidan boarded a plane to Australia and, although she was experiencing an underlying sense of panic as to whether or not it was definitely what she really wanted, the fact she was proving a point to her parents had become enough to prevent her from changing her mind.

If relations had been bad at that point they'd taken an even worse turn once she'd phoned them again from Sydney, where they'd stayed for the first few weeks before heading to Queensland, at which point her furious dad had demanded to speak to her boyfriend. At first Aidan had refused, which had made Jennifer feel very uneasy. Eventually however, sensing that if he didn't Jennifer was going to freak out, he'd eventually acquiesced, albeit reluctantly, at which point her dad had given him very short shrift, venting all his frustrations and feelings of helplessness at the person he held responsible for his daughter's unfamiliar behaviour.

Aidan hadn't appreciated being shouted at though. Rather than taking the reprimanding on the chin, he'd retaliated with a few barbed insults of his own which hadn't helped matters in any way. Now, a few months on, things had calmed down a bit but no matter how much Jennifer tried to explain that Aidan had only been sticking up for her, her parents wouldn't budge on their opinion of him. Meanwhile, Aidan refused to understand that perhaps they were only feeling protective and worried about their daughter.

So here she was having yet another awkward conversation with them while Aidan glowered and sulked next to her.

'So why didn't you go to Surfers Paradise then?' her mum asked now, in a way that sounded to Jennifer somehow accusatory.

'Because we decided to go another time,' she lied. In reality they couldn't afford to hire a car or go at all but she certainly wasn't going to tell them that.

'Hmm, well it seems a shame since you are there not to be doing anything, or seeing anything other than Brisbane,' remarked her mother pointedly.

Jennifer swallowed, determined not to have another row.

'How's dad?'

'He's right here, do you want a word?'

'Please.'

'Hello, love,' said her dad and Jennifer blinked back a tear. She didn't half miss them.

'You'll never guess what happened to Martin at work the other day.'

It was true, she never would, so Jennifer let her dad witter away, filling her in on the day-to-day minutiae of his life in a way that made her feel closer to home.

Afterwards her mother came back on the phone. 'I saw Karen's mum the other day.'

'Oh yeah,' said Jennifer, rolling her eyes and wishing Aidan would stop staring and listening, while simultaneously preparing herself for the next dig.

'Yes. Karen's loving university apparently. She's got loads of new friends and is really enjoying the course.'

'Good for Karen,' huffed Jennifer.

'Oh don't be like that Jen, I'm just saying. There's no need to be so defensive.'

'You're not just saying though are you? You're having another go at me for coming here, only I don't know how many times I have to tell you that I can go next year.'

'*If* they agree to you deferring your place. We've still not heard yet have we?'

'No, not yet,' she agreed.

Minutes later as she finally put down the phone she swallowed hard.

'Hey you, you OK?' said Aidan. 'Don't let them make you feel like shit.'

But Jennifer's previous good mood had dissolved entirely. Every time she spoke to them it was the same. It stirred up so many mixed emotions, doubt, fear and anger at both their handling of the situation and her own.

'Listen, fuck 'em. Just forget about them, babe. Now let's get up and head to the beach.'

'I don't know,' she said flatly, wishing it were that

simple. 'Perhaps we shouldn't be going today you know. Perhaps it would be more sensible to head down to that building site to see if we can get you some work.'

Aidan rolled his eyes. 'You're such a killjoy you are. Don't let your parents ruin our day. Just because they want to be miserable buggers doesn't mean we have to be. I mean, look how gorgeous it is out there and you want to sweat into town because some idiot from the cafe says there *might* be some work going. That's hardly making the best of the day is it?'

Jennifer despaired. 'I don't know to be honest. I mean, yeah, it is a beautiful day, just like it was yesterday and the day before and the day before that. But it would also be good to be able to tell Mum and Dad that between the pair of us we had a bit more money coming in. Besides, we're not in England now you know? We don't have to drop everything just because the sun's out. I suspect it will be a beautiful day tomorrow too, only by then, if there is any work going it will have gone.'

Feeling decidedly grumpy now, in that second Jennifer wished heartily that it would start chucking it down with rain. A bit of damp and drizzle might force Aidan into doing something useful and they could have a day off from feeling required to be on the beach. She only had a couple of shifts in a cafe every week and he was working as a bouncer every Friday but that was the sum of their income at the moment. They were totally skint and their lack of a 'plan' bothered her greatly, though every time she raised the subject Aidan didn't seem to understand what her problem was. As far as he was concerned, they were living in hot sunshine, near a beach and having a lot of sex so there wasn't anything else to worry about. His needs were pretty simple.

'Look, I'll go tomorrow when you're at work. There's no point wasting a day when we could be together, hanging out,' he said.

'All right,' she said, suddenly too hot and lethargic to protest. Besides, by now she was also keen to get out of the stifling apartment. She decided to make an effort to snap out of the mood which she knew deep down had been caused by speaking to her parents. She just wished they would be a bit more supportive. Aidan, who could see she was feeling tense and sad, came over and started to stroke her back in a way that instantly made her shiver with physical pleasure.

'Hey baby, it's OK,' he soothed.

'I know,' she said unconvincingly.

His hands carried on lightly travelling up her back and then around to her front where he gently rubbed her breasts. His touch was incredible and never failed to arouse her.

'Is that nice?'

'Mm,' she sighed, giving in to the sensations and reaching around to feel if he too was getting excited. He was.

'Wow. We only had sex five minutes ago.'

'That's what you do to me, little baby,' he whispered in

her ear before pulling her around and kissing her passionately and deeply.

They fell into bed and gradually her troubles faded away. There was no point stressing about anything too much, she supposed. She was in Australia so had to just make the best of it and to enjoy being with this amazing man who had the ability to frustrate and delight her in equal measure. Had she done the right thing? Who knew? Ultimately, she guessed, only time would tell but for now she was lost in the moment, and the moment felt unbelievably good.

PRESENT DAY

Jennifer didn't exactly emerge from the tunnel. The sensation felt more like an expulsion, one which was sudden, brutal, and delivered with precisely no warning whatsoever. She was left feeling confused and utterly depleted. Her brain desperately needed time to rest and recover from what she'd just experienced, which was frustrating because there was so much she wanted to absorb, mull over and digest. But for now she was nowhere near capable. She needed to sleep. Before she surrendered to the grey ether however, she quickly glanced around and noted that the three tunnels all still existed, though the first was definitely shining ever so slightly less brightly.

She knew then that she would have another opportunity to visit each of them and was swamped with relief. She wanted to find out more about how things would have gone with Aidan. This was the most fascinating, terrifying, yet privileged gift she could ever have been afforded. For now though it was time to regain some strength and with that final thought she allowed herself to slip away.

SUNDAY

'Polly and Eadie need to get out and burn off a bit of energy,' announced Jennifer.

'Take them to the park then,' said Max, finishing the last bit of his toasted bacon sandwich, and only narrowly saving himself from being swatted with a copy of *The Sunday Times* by winking, to make sure his wife knew he was joking. 'Come on then, let's take them to the swings now, and then perhaps we should go out for lunch, so you don't have to cook?'

Jennifer acknowledged that this was a kind thought but couldn't help but wonder what was preventing him from rustling anything up.

'Or should I say, so you don't have to buy in any revolting stuffed chickens that don't actually look or taste anything like chickens.' Another wink.

'Ha bloody ha,' said Jennifer, laughing despite herself. 'OK, that sounds good. And there's a pie in the fridge which we can all have for early dinner but not much more than that so hopefully it'll be quiet at work tomorrow, so I can do a shop in my lunch break. Otherwise I'll have to go later.'

'Good,' said Max, who didn't really care. Food was his wife's department as far as he was concerned. 'Right, Po-lly, Ea-die, come and get your shoes on, we're going to the park,' he yelled in the general direction of the kitchen door, getting up to put his plate in the sink.

'Let's aim to wear them out as much as possible,' said Jennifer.

'Definitely,' Max agreed. 'Then we can plonk them in front of a DVD this afternoon totally guilt-free.'

'Sounds good to me,' said Jennifer, wondering hopefully if that meant that he was thinking they might be able to sneak back to bed for some canoodling.

'Because I hope you don't mind,' added Max, looking sheepish, 'but there's a footy match on that I really want to watch this afternoon and I told Ted he could come round and watch it here. He still doesn't have Sky Sports at his.'

'Oh…right,' she said feeling crestfallen and bored already.

'You don't mind do you?'

'No,' she lied.

*

Later that afternoon, despite having been run out in the park all morning, like dogs, Polly and Eadie were still full of energy. They usually got on pretty well but today were directing it all towards fighting with one another, forcing Jennifer to act as both bouncer and mediator. When she wasn't stopping them from killing each other over, of all things, a broken Barbie, she was putting on washing, taking it out or shoving it in the mountainous ironing pile. All in all not the most riveting of afternoons and, as she took out load after load, she thought wistfully of pre-children days when Sundays meant lying in bed with a hangover, which would eventually be cured by a Bloody Mary and a roast dinner at the pub, followed perhaps by a movie and some lovely sex. God, she was becoming obsessed. This must be how people felt when they came out of prison, or the army.

'Come on, you two,' she said now, or rather yelled, because by this point both her daughters' whining had developed into full-blown wailing. 'Eadie, bash your sister again and I'll bash you.'

Of course she would never bash her kids in a million years so the threat was rather empty which Eadie could tell.

Eadie eyeballed her mum through the wonky brown fringe Jennifer had gifted her with only the week before, as if weighing up how much trouble she'd be in if she ignored her. Then, obviously having concluded she could handle whatever was flung at her, proceeded to whack Polly again.

'Right,' growled Jennifer, who had now officially had enough. 'That's it, up to your room.'

As Eadie burst into noisy sobs, Jennifer sighed heavily, sick to the back teeth of all the squabbling but partly blaming herself for it. No doubt her children had picked up on her generally unenthusiastic mood? Perhaps if she'd been perkier today and more inventive in finding ways to entertain them, they'd be behaving fine but frankly she just wanted to be able to leave them to their own devices for more than five minutes. She was tired and would like nothing more than to get into her pyjamas and zone out to a bit of crappy afternoon telly.

Max scampered into the kitchen.

'All all right in here?' he said, charging to the fridge to get a couple more beers. 'Did I hear wailing?'

'Yes you did,' snapped Jennifer. 'They're behaving like a couple of deranged chimps. I've sent Eadie to her room for bashing Polly.'

'Yeah Daddy, she hit me really hard,' said Polly, rubbing her arm to demonstrate how much it hurt.

'Er, it was the other arm, Pol,' said Jennifer wryly.

'How could you miss that, you bloody idiot?' Ted yelled from the front room at which point Max literally ran back out of the kitchen, bottles of lager in both hands and one under his arm, skidding on the wooden floor of the hall in his socks. As he disappeared he yelled over his shoulder, 'Be good for your mother.'

'Come on you, let's get some colouring stuff out,' said Jennifer to her youngest, 'but hurry up because I need to go and make sure Eadie's OK. And don't think I'm massively happy with you either, Madame,' she added, noting Polly's smug expression as she gloated over how much trouble her sister was in.

Later, after thirty minutes spent with Eadie in her bedroom, who by now had worked herself up into such a state she'd needed soothing and stroking, despite the fact it had been her who had been in the wrong, Jennifer decided to join the boys in the lounge. That way if the children wanted anything their father might be forced to do something.

'Hello,' Max said, looking distracted and surprised to see her standing in her own front room.

Max was on one sofa and Ted was on the other. Both were sitting wide-legged on the edge, beers in hand.

'You all right? Second half's just started. Why don't you see if there's a nice movie on upstairs? There might be a rom com or something.'

'Because Eadie's watching *Tangled* on our bed and as much as I actually quite enjoyed it the first time round I can probably live without seeing it again,' she replied, flopping onto the sofa that Ted was sitting on. He shuffled up, slightly reluctantly, to make a bit of room, his eyes never leaving the TV.

'All right, Ted?' she asked.

'Yeah, great thanks,' he said, reminding her of when Eadie's friends came round to play and answered her questions about school politely, with enough clues in their tone to suggest they'd rather not be talking to her at all.

'How's Annabelle? Is she well?' she continued, not really caring if Ted didn't want to talk. She did. She was bored.

'Not bad thanks. Bit stressed. Callum's been off school with tonsillitis but other than that OK.'

'Good,' she said, flicking through *Style* magazine.

'Hey, have you seen your ex's latest chart position in this year's Rich List?' said Max, throwing the supplement in her direction.

'Oh god.' Jennifer rolled her eyes. 'Go on then, let's feel sick for a second.'

'reUNIon floated this year,' Max informed Ted, almost proudly. 'He's worth a billion now.'

'You are having a laugh,' said Jennifer, though soon she knew it to be true for there it was in black and white, accompanied by a picture of him. Tim Purcell. The ex-boyfriend she'd put up with for two and a half years, now worth a billion quid. She scrutinised the picture of him. His blond hair was slightly silvery around the edges, but only slightly. He was a little more jowly but on the whole looked remarkably similar to how he had done fifteen years ago. He was good looking in a Nordic sort of way and had always had incredibly good skin, though his blue eyes were flinty and rather too deep set and his nose was a little too sharp. His face couldn't have been more different to the one she'd eventually married. Max's mop of brown hair and friendly face may not have been anywhere near as chiselled but it was one that overall she far preferred staring at.

She wondered what it would be like to see Tim now, after all these years. Would they get on? They'd had a strange relationship really. She'd always felt as if more than anything she'd *amused* him. She'd known he'd found her funny and sweet but she'd never got the impression that he massively fancied her. Then again, for her, it hadn't necessarily been a relationship based on physical attraction either. She'd just been so terribly impressed by him, by his flair, and had liked being associated with someone who everyone on campus was aware of. If she did ever meet up with him again she'd love to ask him what he'd seen in her. She doubted they ever would though. They were hardly likely to bump into one another. They mixed in totally different circles. Plus they'd never kept in touch due to the fact that they'd broken up on such desperately bad terms, which ironically was the one time he'd demonstrated that actually she had got under his skin. Or had it just been his ego making him so angry and upset when she'd told him she wanted to split up?

'What I'd do with a billion quid,' mused Ted.

Buy yourself a Sky Sports subscription hopefully, Jennifer thought to herself, smiling blankly at him.

'Perhaps I should get in contact with Tim and ask him if I can have a thousand pounds that I could use to get the tumble dryer fixed, pay some bills and have a splurge in Whistles eh? It would be pocket money to him,' she joked.

'Bet you wish you'd stuck with him, eh Jen? Instead of hooking up with this here loser,' said Ted.

Jennifer smiled and shook her head. 'Not at all, Ted. He may be rich but he was a bit of a cold shit really.'

'Bloody clever though,' said Max, 'I mean, who hasn't been on reUNIon at some point or another? Apart from my parents, who are literally the only people I can think of.'

It always struck Jennifer as slightly strange when Max went on about how clever Tim was. It was almost as if he was proud of the fact she'd gone out with him yet she'd have preferred it if he was a little bit jealous. As it was she suspected he'd probably love to meet him, have dinner with him, be able to discuss his career with him. In fact, given the choice, these days it wouldn't surprise her if he were to choose going to dinner with him over dinner with her.

Jennifer's phone beeped. It was a text from Esther, saying she was round the corner at the park with Sophie and could she pop in for a cuppa.

Jennifer phoned straight away. 'Please come round. Max and Ted are here watching footy and I would love to see you. Also, Sophie can sort my two out and give them something more interesting to do than killing each other.'

Bored rigid of the swings, Esther was round in minutes.

'I am so glad to see you,' said Jennifer flinging her arms round her friend as soon as she'd opened the door. 'Hi Sophie, how are you sweetie?' she asked her goddaughter.

'Good,' said Sophie.

'Go on then, Eadie's upstairs and ah…here's Pol. Have you finished colouring?'

'Yes,' said Polly, looking delighted to have a playmate that wasn't Eadie.

As the girls scampered upstairs Jennifer ushered Esther into the kitchen.

'Am I glad to see you? What a dull weekend I've had, bloody hell.'

Esther giggled. 'Why? What have you been up to?'

'Ugh,' groaned Jennifer. 'Well, we didn't have the kids Friday night but we managed to totally waste that window of opportunity to have some fun by doing jack shit. Then on Saturday we had Judith and boring Henry round for lunch.'

'Oh god,' said Esther, who had heard enough about them to imagine what that would have entailed.

'Quite, although I did nearly give them food poisoning which added a very small frisson of excitement. Then today I thought we were going to have a nice family day but it's ended up being a day of sport watching and beer drinking with good old Ted.' This last bit she said in a hushed tone.

'All sounds joyous,' laughed Esther, slipping off her jacket. She looked great as ever, but today she also looked tired. Under all those freckles she was pale, though as ever her naturally strawberry blonde hair was shiny and brushed and no matter how tired she'd always look attractive. She'd aged really well and always dressed in a way which made other women want to know where her clothes were from. She always bothered to add accessories and put outfits together in a way that told you she hadn't just picked up whatever was on the floor and thrown it on.

Today her printed scarf and Alex Monroe gold bumblebee necklace were the items Jennifer was coveting.

'Sounds like you need a good night out with the girls.'

'I do,' agreed Jennifer. 'You know we're going out on Tuesday don't you? Only to the Hare and Hounds but perhaps then we can get our diaries out and arrange something proper. Something which involves cocktails and dancing. Love that scarf by the way.'

'Thanks, it's River Island and yeah, I do know about Tuesday, although I'm not a hundred percent sure I can come yet,' said Esther. 'I still need to get a sitter sorted out.'

Jennifer suspected at that point she definitely wouldn't be coming then. Such a shame and it grated ever so slightly that she wasn't making it a priority.

'Tea?'

'Yeah please.'

'Anyway, enough of my boring weekend, how's yours been?'

'Not bad actually,' said Esther, a sly grin lighting up her face.

'Go on,' said Jennifer getting mugs out of the cupboard, happy that her friend was round. Her proper friend. It had restored her equilibrium.

'Well, Jason and I are pretty skint at the moment and we've been in loads, but on Friday my mum babysat so we went out and got hammered. I'm talking properly pissed and when we got home and Mum had gone, we ended up…' Esther grinned and started shaking her head '…doing it in the hall. And then we actually did it…' again she had to stop while she snorted with laughter at the memory '…in the downstairs loo.'

'You are kidding me,' said Jennifer, full of mixed emotions. She was deeply impressed, terribly envious and strangely proud to hear that people were still having wild sex with their husbands, even if she wasn't.

'I'm not,' said Esther, giggling. 'It was hilarious. You know the type of sex you have where afterwards you're almost a bit embarrassed.'

'Wish I could remember,' said Jennifer drily, grabbing the milk out the fridge. 'By the way, they are brilliantly quiet up there aren't they? Thank you so much for coming round and saving our day.'

'Pleasure,' said Esther. 'Thanks for saving *me* from hours more of pushing Sophie on the swings.'

'No worries,' said Jennifer dolefully, her mind still on Esther's exploits. 'Do you know the last time I can remember feeling faintly embarrassed after sex was probably with Tim.'

'Really? Why? What did you do?'

Jennifer grimaced. 'You don't want to know.'

'Er, well that's where you're completely wrong.'

Jennifer wrinkled up her nose, embarrassed 'Let's just say he was quite kinky and leave it there shall we?'

'No way!' protested Esther. 'I'm sorry but you have to spill the beans now, Missy. If you don't I'll end up imagining all sorts of things that are probably far worse than the reality.'

Jennifer sighed, knowing she was beaten. 'OK, but tell anyone this and you're a dead woman.'

Esther pretended to pull a zip across her mouth.

'OK, so basically, towards the end of our relationship Tim was only really up for it if I was…um, pretending to be someone else.'

Esther's eyes widened. 'You mean he liked role play?'

Jennifer nodded, went red and chewed on a fingernail. Liked was an understatement.

Esther laughed heartily. 'Oh god. I think I can vaguely remember you saying something about that at the time.'

'Hmm,' Jennifer said, wrinkling up her nose 'Anyway, maybe I should have just put up with his weird ways. Let me show you something.' She hurried into the front room and returned with the Rich List.

'Bloody hell,' said Esther, wide-eyed once she'd been shown the relevant bit. 'That is a sick amount of money. God, I can't tell you how much we could do with just a little bit of that. Things are really tight at the moment to the point where we're struggling some months to make the mortgage payments. I certainly shouldn't have treated myself to this scarf I can tell you. I feel guilty every time I put it on. Can't you phone Tim and ask if we can have some?'

'I wish,' said Jennifer.

'That could have been you,' said Esther.

'Well, I don't know about that.'

'It could. Don't you remember how gutted he was when you broke it off? You could be that rich.'

'Ooh listen to you, last of the feminists. I'd prefer not to be sponging off Tim Purcell thank you very much. Though, having said that, I'm not totally sure what the difference would be to how my life is now. I hate being so bloody dependent on Max these days. In fact I've been thinking recently about retraining in something in an attempt to improve my pathetic earning potential.'

'Like what?'

'Dunno, haven't got that far yet,' admitted Jennifer flatly. 'Any ideas are very welcome.'

Esther giggled suddenly. 'So, hypothetically, if you had stayed with Tim, do you think you'd still be friends with us lot now?'

'Course I would,' said Jennifer, insulted. 'What do you take me for? Although I'm not sure Karen would have been popping round the mansion that often. She hated him didn't she?'

'She did,' confirmed Esther. 'I always thought he was OK though. He was so clever wasn't he? Had an answer for everything. Oh and I'll never forget that party he threw in your house that time. The one where Karen shagged Pete for the first time. It was awesome. Maybe even the best party I've ever been to.'

'God that party was fun wasn't it?' agreed Jennifer. 'Or are we looking back through rose-tinted glasses?'

As her mind returned to Tim, for once she allowed herself to be transported back to how life had been then, all those years ago. She always pretended she couldn't care less, but in truth, being permanently reminded by the business section of the papers that one of your exes was doing amazingly well in life was a little galling.

And deep down she knew it probably *could* have been her enjoying the fruits of his labours, if she'd stuck with him. If she hadn't let her concerns that he didn't love her as maybe he should overwhelm her. Or, more to the point, if she hadn't decided that despite his protestations, he cared more about work than any living human being, and that that in itself was a problem she'd never be able to overcome.

Still, that was all firmly in the past and besides, she suspected that no amount of riches would ever have made up for the fact she'd spent much of their time together dressed as a police woman.

THE PAST — TIM

April 1997

Jennifer was just about to pour her powdered Cup–a-Soup into a mug when she made the mistake (or not as the case may be) of glancing inside the empty vessel, at which point she retched violently.

'Oh my god that is so disgusting,' she exclaimed, stomach heaving.

'What?' said Karen, coming to join her in the small kitchen, opening the fridge and peering hopefully into it.

'That mug's got mould growing in it. I think I'm going to puke.'

'Gross,' said Karen, closing the door again. Neither a stick of limp celery, a jar of Pond's Cold Cream or a Fray Bentos were really what she fancied.

'Shall we just get some chips before we get there?'

'OK,' agreed Jennifer, unable to bear the surrounding debris a moment longer.

As a student you expected to live in a certain amount of squalor but the house they'd moved into for their

third and final year of university, veered dangerously into
unsanitary territory. From the outside it was amazing:
a huge, grade-one listed, Regency terrace, located smack
bang in the middle of a square just off the Brighton sea
front. The paint may have been peeling (not helped by
the saltiness of the atmosphere), but when you stood at
the other side of the square, with your back to the sea, it
looked exceedingly grand and still possessed the majesty
of its era. Inside, however, it was a different story. The
house had been adapted so it could be rented out with the
student market in mind. On the ground floor there were
three bedrooms and a bathroom, on the middle floor there
was a vast communal lounge along with a further two bedrooms and a tiny kitchen. The third and final floor comprised three more bedrooms and another bathroom. Curi-
ously there was no dining table anywhere in the house,
something which all the parents who had visited at one
time or another found baffling and commented on, but
which none of the students cared about one iota. Meals
tended to be consumed standing up or lying down.

Of course eight bedrooms meant eight housemates.
Eight studenty human beings, whose priorities didn't
remotely involve anything like rubber gloves, cleaning
fluid or tidying. As a result the mess was unprecedented.
The house permanently looked like it had just been bur-
gled and the kitchen existed under a coating of grease.
Washing up was done on a need to eat basis and everything generally felt a bit…sticky to the touch.

The only part of the house which wasn't completely grim to be in was Tim's room. His was on the top floor and was by far the largest in the house, a privilege for which he paid £20 rent a week more than the others. Not only was his room the best in terms of size and view, but in startling contrast to the rest of the house it was also kept clean and tidy. Not that Tim was getting busy with the Marigolds. Instead he paid fellow student, Amber, a Chinese girl, £6 an hour for three hours every week, to come and clean his room and also to take away, wash and iron his clothes. This completely set him apart from his peers but then Tim was a rare breed of student altogether. The most glaringly obvious thing that separated him from the rest of the student community was the fact that he always had a bit of cash. Not just the odd tenner either, but wedges of the stuff which he kept folded in a money clip. He'd gone to a very expensive public school so undoubtedly had financial support from his family, but he also always had money-making schemes on the go, ones which tended to actually be successful, and this was reflected in his standard of living. Tim had his own fridge which was always well stocked with lagers and nice food, ready meals like lasagne and curries from Sainsbury's and sometimes even M&S. He had his own desktop computer complete with Windows 95 and a two-seater sofa positioned against the window, meaning that when you lay on it you could fully appreciate the sea view. He also had his own hi fi and a kettle, making the room more like a self-contained studio apartment. Jennifer loved spending time in it. It certainly beat her tiny box room on the ground floor at the back of the house, with its own rather desultory view of a back yard which belonged to an unsavoury Mexican restaurant.

For Jennifer, climbing into fresh clean sheets once a week also felt like a huge perk of going out with Tim. Unless, of course, the night after Amber had been and cleaned it coincided with one of Tim's 'work' nights or, as Karen referred to them, his 'I want to be alone' nights. Jennifer was used to Tim's ways though, and in all honesty Karen constantly going on about how weird they were was sometimes more annoying than her boyfriend dictating when she could and couldn't stay in his room.

Now, as Karen and Jennifer gave up the futile task of looking for anything that might be worth eating, they retreated to the lounge where Pete and Jim were playing Fifa on the PlayStation and listening to music. Empty McDonald's bags littered the table and, with the curtains drawn, the only real light source other than a small side lamp came from the tropical fish tank which belonged to another of their housemates. Jim was only wearing his pants, which wasn't a pleasant sight but one which the girls were used to enough that it didn't warrant a comment.

'Tim's not coming out tonight is he?' asked Karen, collapsing onto the sofa, her short skirt riding up her firm but chunky legs. Her question sounded more like a hopeful statement and told Jennifer everything she needed to know.

'Don't know,' she replied, immediately on edge. She wished Karen would get over her dislike of Tim once and for all. 'Why?'

'No nothing,' said Karen, 'I don't mind either way, I just assumed it wouldn't be his bag. That is to say fun. Joking!'

'You going to that karaoke thing?' enquired Pete, his eyes not leaving the screen.

'Yeah,' said Karen.

'Do you want some draw?'

'Why not?' said Karen.

'OK, you sort that out and I'll go and find out if Tim's coming or not,' said Jennifer, pointedly ignoring her friend's dig.

She thundered up the stairs to the third floor, taking them two at a time in her platform trainers which she was wearing with a crop top which showed off her flat belly and an A line short skirt.

'Are you coming out tonight or what?' she panted, having banged on Tim's door and received a 'Come in.'

'I'm not, my precious,' replied Tim, not looking up from his desk. 'Sean's coming over to show me the code he's written. We're having a meeting.'

'Ooh,' she moaned. 'Please come?'

Tim turned and gave her an approving look followed by a lopsided grin so endearing it made her want to run over and kiss him. Not that she did. Tim's demeanour was generally one which encouraged people to keep their distance. But while they didn't tend to go in much for spontaneous affection, what they both did relish was sparring with one another verbally.

'Hmm, let me think about it. My options are A: stay here and see all my ambitions and dreams come to fruition. Or B: go out in the rain to watch you and Karen murder what were perfectly decent songs to start off with in a shitty karaoke gay bar on the sea front. You're all right thanks.'

'Vicky's coming,' joked Jennifer, grabbing the life-size cardboard cut-out of Posh Spice which Tim had pinched from Blockbuster Video the previous week when he was pissed.

Ms Adams was wearing the white mini-skirt and bra top she'd worn for the Brits. Ginger Spice was downstairs in the lounge too, in her iconic union jack dress, casually leaning against the wall, only with an extra black moustache and glasses which someone had thoughtfully drawn on.

'Well, that's a different story then,' said Tim. 'If old lovely legs is going.'

But he didn't mean it. His attentions were firmly back on his computer.

Jennifer tried not to feel put out. She'd been going out with him long enough to know he wouldn't change his mind and that there was no point grumbling given that his drive, ambition and clever brain were the things that had attracted her to him in the first place.

Admittedly half the time she didn't entirely follow what he was on about when it came to his plans to cash in on what he felt was going to be a huge surge in terms of internet usage but his passion for the subject was infectious. His latest idea was to create some kind of platform on the world wide web for people to find old university, college or school friends, that then allowed you to find out how they'd done in terms of what jobs they'd gone on to, whether they were married or not, and if they'd had children. It would be called 'reUNIon' and was less a social networking experiment than a way for people to be utterly nosey. It would allow you to link up with people and then, once they'd given their permission, you'd be able to see their page which would be formatted almost like a CV. However, before you could see it, the site would ask you to predict what you thought those people were doing. In other words, if you'd signed up to it you might receive an email from an old classmate asking if you wanted to see what they had predicted about you. Tim was convinced that people's natural desire to know what others thought of them would be the key to its success.

'So what's Sean bringing round?'

'You wouldn't understand,' said Tim bluntly.

'Try me.'

'He's been developing some programs. I *told* you. He's written some code.'

'For reUNIon?'

'Yes,' Tim said, sounding exasperated, which in turn made Jennifer feel sad.

Just then, Pete yelled up the stairs.

'Tim, someone here for you.'

'Great,' said Tim, bounding into action, brushing past her in his eagerness to get to Sean, practically flattening her as he did so.

Jennifer gave up and sighed. She'd lost him so she might as well get on with her evening. Karen would be pleased anyway, she thought, as she picked her way across the landing which had piles of dirty laundry strewn all over it.

*

Later that night, or rather, in the early hours of the next day, Jennifer and Karen staggered home. After five minutes of taking it in turns to stab the front door with their keys they finally made it into the house. Giggling like schoolgirls, cross-legged and clutching one another in an attempt not to piss themselves laughing, it took them an age to get up the stairs. Once they had they both raced to the loo and then reconvened in the lounge,they peeled their coats off and Karen got out all her skinning up para-phernalia.

'I'm going to see if Tim's still up,' said Jennifer, who couldn't be bothered with pretending she wasn't dying to see him.

'Fine,' said Karen, only slightly huffily. 'No doubt he will be because he hasn't taken over the world yet.'

As Jennifer bounded up the stairs she decided it was probably time to have it out with Karen once and for all. Her constant jibes were getting on her nerves. It wasn't her fault Karen was single at the moment.

'Tim,' she said, banging on his door, having seen light coming from beneath it. There was no reply but there was music playing, Oasis by the sound of it. She barged in.

Tim and Sean barely looked up, so engrossed were they, huddled over the wretched computer.

'Er...yoohoo, hello, Earth calling my saddo geek boyfriend.'

'Oh hello you,' said Tim looking up. Despite looking exhausted and having the pallor of someone who hadn't had any fresh air all day, his eyes were shining and he looked excited and thrilled. As he leaned back his shirt rode up exposing a glimpse of his lean hairless stomach.

'How's it going?' said Jennifer, suddenly feeling slightly queasy. Running up the stairs probably hadn't been the wisest of moves given that she had litres of various spirits swooshing around in her belly. She swayed across the room and sank thankfully down onto the bed. She reached down to pull off her trainers and once she'd manhandled them off, chucked them across the room. They made a huge thudding sound as they made contact with the wall.

'Amazing,' said Tim. 'We're doing fucking amazing, thanks to Sean.'

Jennifer smiled weakly in Sean's direction. Sean had the social skills of a jellyfish as far as she was concerned and, if she were being completely honest, she was a bit jealous of him. Tim never looked this happy and satisfied after a night in with her, that was for sure.

'Come downstairs and have a drink with me and Karen?' she said, trying not to sound petulant but not sure if she was succeeding due to being so drunk. Ugh, now that she wasn't breathing in lungfuls of sea air, the alcohol was making its effect well and truly known.

'Um…'

Jennifer got up, rolling her eyes heavenward, bracing herself for the inevitable no.

'…yes, why not, my little drunkard? I'd love to. And then you can tell me all about your evening.'

Jennifer smiled. 'I'll re-enact it if you like.'

'Even better,' said Tim pulling a face. 'Come on Sean, we should have a break.'

'Cool,' muttered Sean, not moving.

Tim rubbed his face with both hands, then came over to where Jennifer was and regarded her with interest as she bent down to retrieve her clumpy shoes.

'I can see right up your skirt,' he said, in a way that gave Jennifer an immediate thrill.

He lightly stroked her belly, in a way that was a mixture of quite nice yet also irritating.

'You are wrecked aren't you,' he stated, suddenly noticing how much she was frowning. Her brows were knitted together partly due to how much concentration was required simply to stand up straight.

'I'm fine,' she said defensively.

'Good,' he said, running his hands up her back.

It was the affection she'd been craving for days, only right this second being touched was making her feel vaguely nauseous. She needed to eat. She needed toast.

'Can I have some of your bread?' she said, pulling away and gesturing to his fridge. She lumbered over to it before he'd had the chance to answer.

'But of course,' said Tim. 'Eat an entire loaf if you like, my sweet. And if reUNIon takes off like I think it's going to, I shall buy you your very own bakers.'

Jennifer wasn't really listening. She was too intent on getting at the sliced white which she had confidence would restore her sugar levels and hopefully make her feel less pissed. She had planned on toasting it but in the end was so desperate for some starchy carbohydrate, she just ripped a slice in two and shoved one of the halves into her mouth plain.

As she chewed, it stuck to the roof of her mouth.

'Don't ever let anyone tell you you're not completely classy,' joked Tim. 'Third class that is.'

'Come on, let's go and have a drink then,' she said, mouth full.

'Yes,' said Tim. 'Because you look like you definitely need one.'

Jennifer tried hard to think of a witty riposte but it was too much effort so she gave up and staggered towards the door instead.

Tim followed her but seemingly Sean couldn't be torn away from his computer for neither love, money nor vodka.

In the lounge Karen was reclining on the main sofa which was so threadbare and ancient it had pretty much collapsed in on itself a long time ago. Lying on it felt a lot like you were lying on the floor. She was doing some impressive recreational multi-tasking by building a spliff, keeping one eye on the telly and listening to music. 'Don't Speak' by No Doubt was blasting.

'Evening, Karen,' said Tim, in a tone that suggested he was up for a bit of a wind-up session.

Jennifer sighed inwardly as she realised she'd now be in charge of keeping the peace.

'Right…booze,' she said. 'Shall I make us all a vodka?'

'Yeah,' said Karen. 'Where's the bag, we didn't leave it did we?'

'No, it's here by your feet,' said Jennifer, extracting the plastic bag which had a half bottle of vodka and some orange juice in it from where it was wedged down the back of the sofa.

Of course it went without saying that there were no clean glasses or mugs to be found in the kitchen so she went downstairs to her room to fetch some paper cups which she'd purchased only the other week precisely for times like this.

Due to being so utterly rat-arsed, the effort of now having charged downstairs at high speed left her swaying in the middle of the room for a few seconds while trying to remember what she'd come down for. Her mind had gone completely blank and she could hardly keep her eyes open. Finally it came back to her. Cups. Paper cups. Now she felt smug. Well done her. She was conscious of getting back to the lounge quickly though, so as soon as she'd retrieved them she raced back, leaving her door wide open in her haste. It wouldn't do to leave Tim and Karen alone for too long. They'd only end up sniping at each other.

It was too late though. As she approached the lounge her heart sank.

'But wanting to know what people "do" is just blatant snobbery isn't it?' Karen was arguing, albeit from a lying down position which put Tim, who was sitting upright, at an immediate advantage.

'Oh fuck off Karen, you should hear yourself. What's snobby about being curious? About being interested?'

'Because you're suggesting that what we "do" defines us, like some middle-aged fart at a drinks party saying "And what do you do?" she said, in a voice like Maggie Thatcher.

'Here are your drinks,' said Jennifer brusquely, splashing liquid into the paper cups until they were pretty much two parts vodka one part juice.

Tim took his and slugged it back. As he did he winced. 'Oof that's strong?'

'Poof,' said Karen unnecessarily, downing hers in one and instantly looking like she deeply regretted it.

'Anyhow,' said Tim, 'the point is, Karen, that if you think reUNIon is such a shit idea you won't go on it, that is entirely your prerogative. And yet I'd bet good money that in five years' time, if you got an email telling you that Ed Fisher wanted to find out what you were up to, and not only that, that he'd predicted what he thought you were up to, you'd be intrigued. Don't try and tell me you wouldn't have a look at that point.'

This was a bit below the belt. Ed Fisher had been, up until five weeks ago, Karen's boyfriend. Then he'd dumped her, cruelly, by text, telling her it was because he didn't really fancy her and saw her more as a friend. She'd cried pretty much for a week.

'If that arsehole got in touch with me in five years' time I'd be fucking livid,' she yelled.

Jennifer slugged back her drink nervously. 'You two,' she interjected. 'Can we talk about something else for once?'

'Like what?' said Tim sarcastically. 'What do you want to enlighten us with, my angel?'

Jennifer gulped and as she did so she became aware of a horrid metallic taste in her mouth. This was swiftly followed by an ominous lurching sensation in her stomach. Horrified, she brought her hand up to her mouth.

'You OK?' said Karen.

'Gonna puke,' Jennifer just about managed, racing from the room as the cocktails she'd drunk earlier made an unscheduled reappearance.

'I am one hell of a lucky guy,' said Tim.

'Yes you are actually,' replied Karen loftily, though the sound of Jennifer puking violently into the kitchen sink wasn't really helping her case.

PRESENT DAY

'What's happening, Doctor?' asked Max, the scraping sound of the plastic chair against the floor indicating he'd leapt to his feet the second the doctor had appeared through the door.

'Well, we're encouraged that she's made it through surgery. At one point we were extremely concerned about the build-up of blood around the skull but it appears to have eased off. Having said that, she's not completely out of the woods yet, although her vital signs have stabilised.'

A pause.

'Perhaps we should continue speaking in the corridor, Mr Wright.'

*

Good, thought Jennifer. She needed quiet and wanted to be left alone. In sterile silence. Once more she felt herself slipping a little further back towards oblivion, only as she did so she was suddenly hooked violently back to reality again for the second time that day. As though a giant fist had gripped her purposefully, purely so she could address a thought which had been loitering on the periphery of her consciousness, tapping her brain, desperate for her attention.

Polly and Eadie. As maternal instinct took over and penetrated everything, her daughters were flung into sharp reality. Her babies, her girls. The stab of emotion she encountered in that moment as she thought of them was gut wrenching, panic inducing. She didn't know if they were OK and during this rare moment of lucidity she fully understood that she was powerless to find out. She couldn't be like this. They needed her. What was happening? She felt like a prisoner in her own body, helpless, petrified. If Max was here, wherever 'here' was, then who was looking after them? Her mum? Karen? But as quickly as panic and fear welled up, it subsided again as confusion swamped her once more.

She battled in vain to stay attached to the awareness of her daughters, but it proved too difficult. As quickly as their images had formed, they slipped away again, until within seconds she couldn't remember anything. Instead, all that remained was the overriding sense that she was detached from whatever was happening, and that she was being encouraged to drift further and further from it. Perhaps she should? At first she'd been pleased to emerge from the fog but it was enticing her back again. And so she succumbed once more to the new murky world she now existed in. Furthermore, as Jennifer drifted away she let the falling sensation overwhelm her again, this time confident of what to expect. There they were, the tunnels of light, and for the second time she was carried towards the still open portal on the left.

TUNNEL NUMBER ONE

What Could Have Been—Aidan

Gasping, Jennifer jabbed Aidan in the ribs, signalling for him to roll off so she could lie back and enjoy that brief period of utter contentment which follows an epic orgasm.

'Wow.'

'Hmm,' agreed Aidan, reaching over for his rolling tobacco. She surveyed his back. Since he'd hurt his ankle he'd not been able to go swimming or running and he'd piled on the pounds.

He still had a lovely broad body though; even if it was remarkably pasty and carrying a lot more fat than it had done. Still, his physique would always err on the side of good for his frame was masculine, tall and well proportioned. She surveyed the tattoo which spanned the width of his lower back. It was bizarre to think he'd had it done sixteen years ago, six months after they'd arrived in Australia. Sun-drenched, heady, exciting days when it had still seemed like anything was possible. It was a Celtic pattern with a large sun in the middle and recently Jennifer had started to hate the very sight of it. It represented the elusive sunshine which Aidan had spent ever since hankering after, chasing, but which somehow always remained just out of their reach. Just then, the strong, very wet Carlisle rain started hammering against the window panes as if to illustrate her point.

'Typical,' muttered Aidan.

'Why, what are you up to? Are you going to fetch that paint for Nathan's room?' asked Jennifer hopefully.

'No, I'm supposed to be signing on at three and I'm probably not going to have time to do that and get the paint am I?'

'Guess not,' said Jennifer flatly, hoping he wasn't trying to wriggle out of it. The feeling of peace she'd had from their physical exertions was short-lived as ever. She'd finished work very late last night, was exhausted and, frankly, picking up the paint was the least he could do. She had absolutely no idea why he couldn't get round to it. It was as if he was deliberately not doing it to spite her. She was almost tempted to get the bus and collect it herself. That way they could make a start on Nathan's room like they'd been promising him they would since his birthday. Only, Aidan collecting the paint had become a point of principle.

She inhaled deeply through her nose, as she'd been taught to in yoga class, desperate to remain in a good frame of mind a while longer.

Aidan sucked deeply on his skinny cigarette.

'Did Olly say if he had any more decorating work?' she said, knowing he'd hate her asking but unable to help herself.

'He didn't,' he replied tersely.

'All right, I'm only asking,' said Jennifer, getting up abruptly, knowing her mission to remain Zen was futile, so infused with intense frustration was she. She grabbed her old, tatty dressing gown from the hook on the back of the door and wrapped it around her thin body. Between working in the restaurant, Aidan's insatiable sexual appetite and the stress of never having enough money, keeping the pounds off wasn't something she'd ever had to worry about.

'Well don't. You know I'll tell you when he's got something. Why would I not?'

Jennifer didn't reply. There was no point. There'd only be a row and she could do without one on her only day off. Instead she left the bedroom and went into the tiny kitchen to make a cup of tea.

'Do you want a brew?' she called, biting her lip in an attempt to quell the angry tears which were suddenly threatening to spill down her cheeks.

'Go on then,' called Aidan. 'Seeing as I've got to go out in this rain I may as well.'

As Jennifer waited for the kettle to boil, she wished Aidan would go. Apart from anything else her new book on reflexology had arrived and she wanted to start reading it in peace. She was seriously considering applying to do a course. Emma, a friend of hers from yoga, who was already a qualified practitioner, had told her a lot about it. The subject completely fascinated her. Becoming a certified reflexologist would not only provide a way to earn some more money but she suspected would also be something she'd actually enjoy.

If only Aidan would find something to get enthused about. It would make life a lot easier. She was unable to prevent one solitary tear from rolling down her cheek and onto the laminate worktop which due to how old it was never looked totally clean no matter how much she scrubbed it. She wiped the tear away impatiently, bored of feeling down. Bored of feeling bored.

She glanced at the cork notice-board which was covered in bills, all of which needed paying, takeaway menus, letters from Nath's school and, in the middle, a photograph. A tatty, dog-eared photo of her mum and dad, whom she hadn't seen for eighteen long years now. For what felt like the thousandth time her hand went to her dressing gown pocket to feel the letter she'd received from her mother only a week ago. It had come to her work address and she knew it pretty much off by heart.

Her mum wanted to see her. Her dad still hadn't come round but her mum had decided it was finally time to let bygones be bygones. The only decision that needed to be made was where and when. Possibly the most surprising thing of all to Jennifer was that, rather than questioning the decision to contact her mother in order to hold out an olive branch, all she found herself debating was why she'd left it this long.

As she was stirring the teas Aidan appeared behind her and wrapped his arms around her.

'All right, gorgeous?'

'Yeah,' she said miserably, feeling anything but.

'You just rest up while I go out. Put your feet up,' he said, as if he was bestowing some massive favour upon her.

Too right she'd be putting her feet up. She had a double shift tomorrow, and one the day after that and besides, 'putting his feet up' was all Aidan seemed capable of doing these days, so why shouldn't she?

'Even go back to bed. I know you've been dying to start reading that book. Then maybe me, you and Nath can have something from the chippy tonight?'

'All right,' she agreed, slightly mollified. 'Sounds good.'

'Eh, what's up?' he said, spinning her round to face him. 'If you're still worried about my mobile bill don't be. Worst comes to the worse I'll get my old "pay as you go" out but knowing you you'll rake the tips in tomorrow. I know my girl and not only are you my sexy little minx, you're a bloody good little waitress too.'

In that instant Jennifer figured she should just tell him. After all, given everything she'd given up for him over the years, friends, family, an education, prospects, surely he wouldn't begrudge her the chance to rekindle relationships which had been put on hold for long enough now? There wasn't so much water under the bridge as opposed to an entire river.

'Mum wrote to me,' she said calmly, deciding to omit the fact that she'd been the one to get in contact first.

Aidan's face froze.

'She wants to see me and I think I'm going to go.'

'Why?' he said, looking totally flummoxed.

'Honestly? You need to ask why?'

'Of course I need to ask why,' he exclaimed, looking thunderous. 'After all these years of them being sanctimonious, judgemental arseholes, I hardly think I'm weird for thinking you should give them a wide berth. They treated you like shit.'

Jennifer shook her head. 'No. That's the thing. I don't think they did. Not really,' she said. 'In fact, the older I get the more I think I treated *them* like shit. I'm the one who disappeared off to the other side of the world. I'm the one who gave up going to university so I could disappear to Australia with a bloke they'd never even met. And I'm also the one who then had to break it to them that that particular pipe dream had been ruined due to you getting caught with drugs. I happen to think *most* parents would take a pretty dim view of that.'

'This again,' cried Aidan, outraged. 'Are you ever going to get over it? It's not like I was dealing heroin or anything. A bit of pot it was. Where's the harm in that? I was bloody unlucky to get caught but I was hardly ruining lives.'

'Except you were,' Jennifer muttered, feeling on the brink of a very dangerous conversation.

'What's that supposed to mean?' he said, his face stony.

'Nothing,' she said rolling her eyes in frustration 'It's just that…well, you have to remember that the whole point of me not going home was because we decided we wanted to live in the sunshine, to build a life in Oz, in the sunshine. Only it didn't quite work out like that did it?'

'No, it didn't Jen, but then you forgetting to take your pill was hardly the plan either was it?'

Jennifer shrugged. The memory of finding out that on top of everything else she was pregnant at the age of twenty-two was still more bitter than sweet.

'But I stood by you,' retorted Aidan, indignant and hurt. 'I stood by you when thousands of blokes might have left you to it, or forced you to have an abortion. I was a free spirit remember? Having a wife and kid wasn't exactly part of my master plan either but I'm glad we did it. I wouldn't be without Nath, would you?'

'Of course not,' said Jennifer sincerely. 'Of course I wouldn't be, but I'm not so sure I should have had to go without having my mum and dad in my life for all this time either. And…perhaps if I'd been less chippy with them, maybe even a bit apologetic about how things had turned out I wouldn't have had to be.'

Finally she met his gaze. He looked defensive and

huffy, knowing full well that her words were an accusation aimed firmly at him for he'd always encouraged her to be on the offensive with her parents.

'Look at us,' she said, gesturing around the small kitchen and flat. 'I'm thirty bloody eight, Aidan. Thirty-eight and living in a shithole. I work every hour god sends in a stinking restaurant which I'm starting to hate and for what? I've got no real friends here apart from Emma and she's flaky at the best of times, no family, except you and Nath of course, and I spend most of the time feeling…'

'Feeling what?' he said stonily.

'Feeling…a bit…embarrassed about how things have turned out,' she admitted quietly, knowing that although it was a terrible thing to say it was also unutterably true.

'Well, screw you,' Aidan said and, as he did, the lurch in Jennifer's stomach told her she may have said too much. There were some things you couldn't take back and as much as she resented him he was still her man and for all their problems he still held her tight, each and every night, which did much to soothe her troubled head. They were still intimate all the time and although things had hardly turned out like they did in the movies, their physical bond, the child they shared and the years they'd been together, were a pretty efficient type of glue.

'I'm sorry,' she called after him.

'Whatever Jennifer, I don't want to hear it,' he said, going into the hall and pulling on his Doc Marten boots before storming out, presumably (hopefully) to go and sign on.

Jennifer flinched as the door slammed. She stood still for a while, soaking up the silence and wondering what to do. Eventually she decided upon nothing. He'd be back later and they could talk then. In the meantime she'd got a few things off her chest which might be healthy and she was still determined to meet with her mother. No matter what he said. So nothing had changed.

TUNNEL NUMBER ONE

What Could Have Been—Aidan

'Someone here to see you love,' said Lindsay, the manageress of Red Peppers, the brasserie where Jennifer worked. The conspiratorial wink which accompanied this piece of information told Jennifer it was definitely Aidan. She confided in Lindsay a lot. The older lady was kind, always had time to listen and usually appreciated having a bit of gossip to think about other than what was happening at the restaurant. So last night, when things had quietened down at around ten o'clock, Jennifer had told Lindsay how Aidan was sulking with her and had been ever since she'd announced her intention to see her mum. Lindsay's advice had been concise and to the point: 'Tell him to bog off and to stop being such a baby.'

'Go on, you can have a quick ten minutes,' Lindsay said now, grabbing an apron 'I'll cover for you. Have table nine had their wine?'

Jennifer went to the front of the restaurant where Aidan was indeed stood waiting for her, incongruous in his huge woolly cardigan and combat trousers. For a while now his hair had been slightly dreaded and not for the first time Jennifer wished he'd smarten up his act a bit. If he stopped dressing like some kind of crusty perhaps there'd be a sliver of a chance he could get himself some work? Funnily enough there wasn't a massive demand for middle-aged, pot-smoking surf dudes in Carlisle.

'Is Nath at home?' she asked, exhausted to her very bones now that she'd stopped for a second.

'He's next door, getting a drink from the newsagents.'

On cue, Nathan appeared, clutching a can of Fanta.

'All right, babe?' said Jennifer, pleased to see him. He was still in his uniform. 'Has your dad given you some tea?'

Nathan nodded.

'What did you have?'

'We had egg didn't we?' answered Aidan on his behalf.

'Shall I ask Lindsay if there's any spare banoffee?' said Jennifer, knowing it was his favourite and wishing she had more time to cook for her son. He was looking so tall. His body, which at one point had been quite scrawny, all arms and legs, was starting to fill out. He was sixteen and growing before her very eyes it seemed. Her beautiful boy was on the verge of becoming a man.

'Banoffee would be ace if there is any,' Nathan said,

still boyish enough to get excited about his favourite dessert.

Jennifer gestured to Aidan to head out to the back of the restaurant while she got Nathan settled at one of the only spare tables with a huge slab of creamy pie.

'There you go love, get that down you. Right, I'd better go and see what your dad wants.'

'OK…oh, hang on a minute Mum, I've got something for you.'

Jennifer watched as her son stood up briefly again so he could get into the pockets of his trousers. He fished out a crumpled ten pound note and five pound coins and placed them on the table.

'What's that for?' she asked, bemused.

'It's for you,' Nathan said, sitting down again and making a start on his dessert, eyes practically rolling to the back of his head as he enjoyed his first hit of thick cream and toffee.

'What's the money for, Nath?' repeated Jennifer.

'I earned it the other night, didn't I? When I babysat. I want you to have it.'

'Don't be silly,' she said immediately.

'I'm not. You're always working in here and I know Dad hasn't done much lately. I just want to help out a bit.'

Jennifer swallowed, touched by her son's gesture; yet despairing that her boy was learning to be a man, not by example but as a result of his father's glaring uselessness. She was also deeply saddened that he'd picked up on how much they were struggling. She went to give him a hug across the table.

'Mum,' he protested, embarrassed by her public display of affection.

'Sorry,' she said, grinning. 'It's just I don't half love you, my precious, generous boy. And I don't want you worrying about money. We're fine.'

'Pack it in,' said Nathan, smiling.

'Right, I'd better go and see what Dad wants,' she said, wishing it was the end of the night so she could go home with them. It had been a busy lunchtime shift and the evening was shaping up to be the same, which was great in terms of tips but not so good for her aching feet.

*

Round the back of the restaurant, in the small courtyard, Jennifer breathed deeply. The fresh May evening air was good for the soul. Occasionally, when she could afford it, she liked to go to a yoga class in the church hall round the corner from the flat. The teacher, Kerry, was amazing. She was fifty years old with a figure most thirty-year-olds would be proud of, which she attributed entirely to daily yoga. Kerry had once told Jennifer that everyone had a finite amount of breaths to take during their lives, hence, if you could slow down your breathing and therefore your stress levels, you would live longer.

Whenever Jennifer remembered this and made the effort to become 'aware of her breath' she was dismayed to discover how sharp and quick her intake was. It was always a depressing reminder of the pace she was going at. She often worried that if she didn't slow down and her teacher's theory was correct, she might keel over any minute.

'You all right?' asked Aidan, looking sheepish as she approached and flicking away the ends of a roll-up which he stamped out with his boot.

'Yeah, what did you want to talk about? Has this got anything to do with Nath? I'm worried about him you know. He's not stupid. He can tell when things aren't right between us.'

'Nath's fine. Come here, you,' he said, drawing her tense body in for a hug.

Ordinarily she would have enjoyed the comforting sensation of being encircled in his arms only right now she was too in need of a shower to relax into it properly. Red Peppers was a lovely restaurant but she'd be quite happy never to see a piece of deep fried camembert again as long as she lived. It was their most popular starter and the stench of fried cheese seemed to be ingrained into the fibres of every top she owned.

'So anyway, I came to say that if you really want to see your mum, it's fine by me.'

'That's good of you,' she said sarcastically.

'Look, you have to remember that up until a week ago I thought we were on the same page as far as your parents were concerned, you know? I mean, you're the one who used to get so fed up with their attitude and with how judgemental they were.'

Jennifer shrugged. She couldn't agree or disagree because if she were being totally honest, she couldn't really remember how things had managed to get as bad as they had. She also wasn't sure she really cared any more either. All she did know was that she had a family, and that many moons ago she also used to have good, good friends, better ones than she'd ever made since. Only the other day she'd looked up Karen on reUNIon. It hadn't taken long to find her at which point she'd written her prediction of what she'd thought she'd be up to now. She'd written that she thought she'd be happy, married, possibly with a couple of kids and no doubt in some high-powered impressive job, living the high life. She was still waiting to hear back though, and if her old friend did ever make the effort to respond, she wasn't sure she'd be brave enough to read what Karen had predicted for her.

After all this time she still missed her. She missed all her old friends, in fact, but not as much as she missed the feeling of belonging. Furthermore, these days she was starting to think she might need, or maybe just want, more in her life than she had at the moment. Hence the reflexology course. She'd given up a lot to be with Aidan and knew she was in danger of growing bitter if she didn't take charge of her own destiny a bit more because if she was being honest to the point of being brutal, she wasn't totally one hundred percent sure he'd been worth it.

It hadn't mattered how many times she'd tried to stick up for him, or had tried to explain that actually, dabbling with a bit of marijuana hardly made him an evil drug baron, it had been a pointless task. Her parents were the kind of people who considered all drugs to be inherently dangerous and wrong. Full stop. Worse still, what they really couldn't get their heads around was why he would have taken such a risk when he was responsible for their only daughter.

At the time Jennifer had refused to even consider that they may have had a point for if she had, she would have also been admitting to herself and everybody else that she'd made a mistake. A huge, life-changing mistake.

She regarded Aidan now. Her man. He was so bloody useless and yet there was something about him which still, after all these years, she was drawn to, and whatever it was, it was a force to be reckoned with. She stepped towards him and held his face in her hands, looking up at him as she had a thousand times before.

'It's fine, let's forget about it. I'm just pleased you're cool about me seeing her.'

They hugged and as they did Jennifer buried her face deep into Aidan's side. As ever she drew comfort from the physical sensation of being held and used it as a balm to soothe her sad, troubled soul. This felt normal to her, but what she didn't realise was that she'd forgotten what it was to feel truly happy.

THE PAST — MAX

June 2004

'I'm knackered,' declared Jennifer, flopping backwards onto the huge bed and instantly disappearing in a cloud of tulle, satin and net. The net at the bottom of the dress was no longer white but grey from where it had trailed along the ground all day.

'Tiring business getting married,' agreed Max from the other side of the room, 'but did we have the best wedding or what?'

'By miles,' said Jennifer contentedly, stretching her arms above her head and then swiping them up and down, enjoying the feel of the luxurious damask she was lying on.

'You look like a snow angel,' said Max, swaying by the mini bar as he tried to fix them both a drink.

'You look like a handsome movie star,' said Jennifer, feeling totally drained yet exquisitely happy that after a long year of planning it was all over, it had gone well and they were finally alone. The two of them. Mr and Mrs Wright.

'You're my wife,' Max stated.

'You're pissed. You're my pissed husband.'

'You're sexy, give us a flash of your knickers.'

Jennifer acquiesced.

'Ooh that is sexy.'

'Stop making drinks and come here, you big lug.'

Max seemed more than happy enough to go along with that. Getting the tops off various bottles was proving too much effort anyway. He weaved his way across the room and flopped down beside her on the bed, turning onto his side so he could stare into her eyes. 'Is this the bit where I'm supposed to make mad, passionate love to you?'

Jennifer wrinkled up her nose, not wanting to be unromantic but at the same time not in the mood to pretend. 'To be honest I'm quite happy just lying here for a bit. This corset's bloody killing me and actually...'

'Go on...'

'I am absolutely starving. Do you think they're still doing room service?'

'Er, didn't we just pay for a three course dinner and evening buffet?' said Max, twiddling a lock of her hair idly between two fingers.

'Yeah and I hardly ate any of it,' admitted Jennifer.

'Well, in that case, my beautiful bride must have some chips.'

Max heaved himself into an upright position and reached for the phone.

'Yes,' said Jennifer punching the air. 'Chuck a burger in while you're at it. Cheeseburger please.'

'And they say romance is dead,' he quipped, shaking his head as he proceeded to place their order. Cheeseburger and chips for two.

When he'd finished, the two of them lay on the bed, both in their own world, quietly reliving parts of the day until Jennifer said, 'I loved the part in your speech when you said you'd never met anyone who loved celebrating birthdays as much as me, and that you'd see to it forevermore that mine would always be celebrated properly.'

'I meant it. I've never forgotten that little speech you gave about birthdays when we met. It was sweet. Slightly weird, but mainly sweet. What other part was your favourite?'

'This is my favourite part,' she laughed, reaching across to grab a certain bit of his anatomy.

Max grinned 'That's another reason why I love you. You're terrible. Ooh, hang on a minute, I've just remembered I've got something for you.'

'Oh no! You haven't have you?' Jennifer sat up, looking worried. They'd made a pact not to buy each other presents, having gone way over budget on the wedding as it was. She for one had adhered to it so now felt dreadful.

'Don't panic, it's only something silly,' said Max, who had got up and was now scrabbling around in his suitcase.

Eventually he found what he was looking for, a beautifully wrapped, rectangular shaped present.

'Oh my god, thank you so much,' said Jennifer.

'Open it then.'

Jennifer pulled off the velvet ribbon which was tied around it and pulled away the paper to reveal a smart blue box. She took off the lid. Inside was a photo frame, face down so she could only see the back. 'Oh baby, how lovely. A frame! We can put a wedding photo in it.'

Max shook his head 'There's already a photo in it. Turn it over.'

Jennifer prised the frame out of the box and turned it round. When she saw what picture he'd chosen, she felt instantly sentimental but also a bit confused. 'It's me.'

'Certainly is.'

'In my pink dress.'

'Yup,' said Max.

'On the night we met.'

Max nodded.

'In a photo which was taken by my ex?'

This was the bit Jennifer didn't really get.

'It is indeed.'

She studied the photo for a while. She looked so carefree and even she had to admit, quite sexy. Her younger self was gazing straight down the lens, her hair an unruly mane tumbling around her shoulders, her eyes full of promise and mischief. It was just slightly disconcerting knowing that the person she was staring at in such an uninhibited way wasn't Max, but ex-boyfriend Steve.

'So, why this one? It's so dog-eared. Shouldn't we keep one of us together in it?'

'No.'

'But…'

'No buts,' said Max, sitting down next to her on the bed again. 'I chose that one for a reason. I love that photo. Always have. Apart from anything else, it's a reminder that I should never take you for granted because no matter how long we're together, how married we are, or how old we get, you will always be that incredible girl in the picture. That girl who I spied at the party, wearing that sexy pink dress, who made my stomach flip. And yes, someone else did take the picture, someone else who loved you because you're bloody easy to fall in love with, which is yet another reason for me to always look after and treat you as you deserve. Look at you. You're so beautiful. Sometimes I still can't believe you're with me. I never want to stop feeling as lucky as I did back then and as lucky as I do today that you're mine.'

Jennifer had to look up to quell the tears that by now were threatening to glide down her cheeks. She thought her heart might burst with love and she leaned forward and kissed him tenderly on the mouth. 'That's so lovely. Thank you so much, baby. I love you so bloody much.'

'I love you too.'

'And I promise we'll have sex tomorrow.'

'Come here, silly,' said Max, signalling to her to lie down and tuck in at which point he wrapped his arms around her and held her tight. Minutes later his hold on her slackened and Jennifer realised he'd fallen asleep. Right on cue there was a knock at the door. Oh well, she thought. Two burgers for her then.

*

Half an hour later Jennifer was stuffed to the brim and Max was still passed out, fully clothed and snoring like a walrus. From time to time she glanced back at the picture of herself which she'd placed on the bedside table. She marvelled at how happy she was and how loved she felt and, as Max continued to snore noisily away beside her, her heart expanded with emotion. He was right of course, she had chosen him and she was glad, for nobody who'd come before had ever suited her quite like he did and no one ever would. How amazing it was to feel so utterly sure.

THE PAST — TIM

August 1997

Things hadn't been particularly great between Jennifer and Tim for a while now. Throughout their final year at Sussex, his obsession with reUNIon had overridden everything, including his studies, meaning that instead of achieving the first he'd been predicted he'd ended up with a 2:1. Jennifer probably only truly realised the extent of his passion for reUNIon when he didn't seem bothered. She may have given up trying to compete ages ago but that didn't mean she didn't feel jealous of the object of his obsession sometimes. If reUNIon were a woman she'd merrily scratch her eyes out.

As for Jennifer, degree-wise she also came away with a 2:1 which for her was a massive achievement. But now, with university over, she was finding it hard to adjust and was worried that their student days may have been the glue holding her and Tim together.

Her mood was mainly despondent but then she was in a huge amount of debt, was living back at home and could only find a part-time job in Miss Selfridge; whereas Tim had (typically) managed to rent a flat which was ridiculously luxurious for someone of his age, companies were beginning to take an interest in his software designs, plus he had lots of meetings lined up and a potential job at Apple. Being around him was enough to make Jennifer feel like one massive loser.

The pressure was on. This summer was the last bit of time she could get away with being directionless before people (her parents) started to lose patience. It was already the last day of August, summer was officially drawing to a close and she was half expecting a claxon to go off, along with a Tannoy announcement saying, 'Jennifer, your time's up. You are now officially expected to get your shit together and be a responsible adult.' It was terrifying and yet the hardest thing was having to constantly pretend that inside she wasn't panicking and on the verge of a full-on meltdown.

Last night she and Tim had been out for drinks at a bar and had come back to his after (always preferable to hiding up in her small room at home, her mum banging on the door every five minutes asking if they wanted a cup of tea when in fact what she was really checking was whether or not they were having sex).

'Shall we go out for breakfast?' asked Tim now, still bashing away at his computer. He'd been up for a while, had showered, got dressed and probably changed the world while Jennifer had been dozing and trying to figure out whether she wanted tea or coffee.

'I don't know,' she said unhelpfully, staring into the middle distance.

Tim lived in Notting Hill in the most beautiful flat Jennifer had ever been in. It had one spacious, light bedroom and a luxurious bathroom complete with power shower. The living room, which was where they were sitting now, had wooden floors, was big enough to include two large grey sofas and led onto a small kitchen diner which had been painted a startling but gorgeous shade of bright sky blue, the perfect contrast to the pale wood units and stainless steel appliances. The living room walls were taupe and had two sets of floor to almost ceiling-height glass doors, framed by wrought iron Juliet balconies. The doors were open now and the morning breeze was blowing the calico curtains into the room.

'It's like a soft rock video in here,' she joked absent-mindedly but Tim didn't reply. Instead he finally shut down his computer and almost without taking a pause between activities, leapt over to where she was sitting and made what can only be described as a lunge for her. With a look of intent and a mischievous, somewhat off-putting schoolboy grin on his face, he grabbed her, stuck his hand up her jumper and started massaging her left breast. He wasn't particularly tender about it though. If anything it was slightly painful. However, mistaking her gasp for one of passion he upped the ante, and before she knew it he was really going for it, tuning in her nipple like he was trying to get an FM frequency.

Still, it seemed to be working for him for his breath grew short and as he huffed and puffed in her ear Jennifer decided she ought really to try and get into it. She was still in her pyjamas so he had pretty easy access to everything. However, when he suddenly stopped and looked at her with a pleading expression she'd come to know only too well, her heart sunk.

'Estate agent?'

'Really?'

'Yes. You should go out into the corridor and pretend you've arrived to do an evaluation.'

At this Jennifer felt full of irritation and decided she couldn't pretend any more. 'Why can't I just be naked for once?'

'What?'

'Plain old me is never enough is it? You always want me to be someone else these days. But to be honest I don't really feel like putting on a suit right now and acting like I'm terribly excited by your flat's potential.' Her frustration was a long time coming. 'Just for once it would be nice if you wanted to have sex with me, Jennifer. Not Trixie the masseuse, Suzy the police officer, Laura the teacher or now Jane the frigging estate agent.'

At this Tim pulled away, practically throwing her onto the other side of the sofa 'Oh well that's charming. Talk about know how to get rid of someone's erection for Christ's sake.'

'Well, I'm sorry,' said Jennifer primly. 'But perhaps you need to take into consideration what I want for a change, which is not necessarily always having to remember my lines and be in fancy dress every time I want to have sex with my boyfriend.'

'No, all you want is to whinge at me,' he said, though Jennifer noticed that at least he'd had the decency to blush a pale pink.

'That's out of order,' she snapped. 'As if I whinge?'

'It's true. Nag, nag, nag, that's all you do,' he said.

'That's rubbish,' she said, hurriedly pulling up her pyjama bottoms. 'What on earth could you say I nag you about?'

'Ooh, well, let me see now…my work, er…seeing you, what I'm up to on a day to day basis, Sean, whether or not I'm coming out to whatever night of torture you and Karen have arranged.' He paused, letting his mean words sink in. He looked very defensive and Jennifer sensed he was only lashing out so much because he was still embarrassed about his ridiculous addiction to role play.

'Frankly, what you should be focused on,' he continued now, unable to look her in the eye, 'is what you're doing with yourself and with your life.'

'Oh well, it's all coming out now,' said Jennifer, who by now was so angry she'd started contemplating what to throw out of the window. On a braver day she'd have plumped for the computer but knew it would result in death and not just hers if it landed on a passer-by's head.

'I'm just saying that if you spent a little more energy deciding what it is you want to do, rather than worrying about how much time I spend with Sean, or how little time I spend with Pete and bloody Karen you might be better off.'

'Oh will you get over yourself,' shouted Jennifer. 'Honestly, if I hear you mention Karen in an argument one more time I'll lose it. What have you got against her? I mean, I know she can be prickly sometimes but now she's with Pete she's calmed right down and she's been so much more tolerant. Why can't you be the same?'

'Tolerant?' spat Tim. 'If two people have to be tolerant of one another then I would suggest they shouldn't bother going to the effort full stop. Life's too short. And yes, the fact she's had a complete personality transplant since getting together with Pete hasn't escaped me but why I should be a slave to her ridiculously volatile state, which seems solely dependent on if she's getting any sex, is anyone's guess.'

'Well at least she's not permanently trying to remember which accent she's supposed to be putting on,' stormed Jennifer, livid beyond belief, springing up from the sofa and heading for the bedroom. Arguing while wearing pyjamas was making her feel weird. She needed jeans and a jumper for this.

She had been so happy when Karen had got together

with Pete at the end of university. Her friend was at last
happy, and although nobody could have predicted that
after a whole two years of living under the same roof,
barely noticing one another, she and Pete would have
finally found each other (underneath a pile of coats in
Jim's room to be precise), it had taken the pressure off
Jennifer enormously. 'At least Karen's got a personality unlike the almost mute freak that is Sean,' she yelled
from the bedroom where she had already yanked on some
knickers and jeans and was in the process of doing up her
bra.

'And at least he's got a brain and knows what he wants
out of life,' retorted Tim.

And in that instant Jennifer stopped feeling angry and
went cold. And a fraction of a second later she decided
that she might be finished. Because actually, deep, deep
down, she knew that what he'd said earlier was probably right. With Tim she *did* turn into a harridan, a nag,
a banshee. His success made her feel inadequate and yet
didn't inspire her to do anything about her own situation.
Instead it merely fed her permanent sense of insecurity.
Did she love him? She didn't really know, so perhaps that
answered that one. Did she like him? Sometimes. She
loved the way he challenged and stimulated her intellectually. Did she admire him? Hugely. There was something
about Tim that screamed 'I AM GOING PLACES'. But
did she want to go with him? She was no longer entirely
sure she had the energy or the desire to. If she really

thought about it she might possibly love his flat more than him. It was a tricky one though, a dilemma. There would be plenty of girls lining up to take her place if it came up for grabs. And no doubt they'd happily dress up like bloody Minnie Mouse if it made him happy. Was this something she'd regret further down the line? Would she ever meet anyone else as eligible? Was the fear of ending up alone enough reason to stick with a relationship that didn't really make her happy?

Pulling a sweater over her head she decided what to do and as her decision was made she was flooded with an eerie sense of calm.

'Tim,' she said, wandering back into the sitting room.

'What?'

'I can't do this any more. We don't really make one another happy so why are we bothering? I think we should call it a day.'

'What?' he repeated, completely thrown. He sunk down onto the nearest sofa, pulling his trousers at the thigh in order to achieve a bit of give, an action which reminded her of something her dad would do.

'I just think we should admit defeat,' she added more gently. 'You see, you're right, I do spend far too much time having a go at you, mainly because I get jealous of how much attention you pay your work all the time.'

There, she'd said it.

Tim sighed. 'And I only get frustrated because I know how much potential you have and it irritates me to see you procrastinating all the time and never actually…actioning anything.'

'Which just goes to show how different we are as people and that we'd probably be better off without one another,' she said flatly, knowing she was right and just wishing she'd had the balls to say it about two years earlier.

Tim got up and paced the room. 'You're wrong,' he said.

'Am I?' said Jennifer.

'Totally wrong,' he said firmly. 'You're right for me, Drew. Opposites attract and I don't really mind your inertia. It's only you I worry about because I know not having any direction gets to *you*. Personally I wouldn't care if you never did anything because I'm more than happy to take care of you. You know I am. You know I'm an old-fashioned bloke at heart and I have no problem with men taking care of the finances and women looking after the home.'

'We're not living in the dark ages,' she spluttered. 'I don't want looking after thank you and I don't necessarily want to be a ruddy housewife either.' Jennifer was surprised by her own use of the word 'necessarily'. It was as though she was hedging her bets and disappointingly meant Tim was probably right. She really didn't know what she wanted out of life.

'Oh well that really is a load of crap if you don't mind me saying,' said Tim. 'Of course you do. I've been looking out for you ever since we met, but I'm saying that I don't mind. I like it.'

Now Jennifer was completely on the back foot. Was that really how he'd seen it all these years? As though she'd been some pathetic freeloading sap he'd had to look out for. And anyway, what exactly had he done for her? Though even as this last thought was formulated she was already thinking back to university and of all the times Tim had bailed her out. Of all the times he'd 'taken care of' a phone bill she couldn't afford. Of how much food she used to squirrel out of his fridge, secretly acknowledging that she was saving herself a few quid each time. She hardly ever paid when they went out and when she did, she used to make a thing of it, making sure he got the message. Ultimately however, if she had occasionally taken advantage of his deep pockets it had only been because she knew he could more than afford it and because he never minded. She felt ashamed. It was time to get a backbone.

'Well, I do mind you saying,' she said. 'I don't want to be taken care of and I wasn't really aware that I had been or that you'd noticed. I mean, you've always been very generous but I wasn't aware I was riding on some Tim Purcell gravy train.'

'Oh come on, Drew,' he said, 'don't give me that bullshit. And don't make some big issue out of it. I like that you're a bit scatty, that you're quirky. I need that. It's a good foil for me. You're funny, you're sweet. I like your little eccentricities.'

Jennifer gulped and felt really, really sad that in two and a half years this was the first time he'd been able to articulate what it was he liked about her. She'd always wondered.

'You make me sound a bit…simple.'

'Well, I have to say Drew, at times I do wonder.'

Tim's attempt at a joke wasn't appreciated though.

'My name's Jennifer,' she said firmly, annoyed at his constant use of her surname as a term of endearment. 'Not Drew. Just Jennifer. I am not a public school boy.'

Tim's face was grim, his eyes flinty and confused. She could practically see his mind racing, so desperate was he to regain control of the situation. For a split second she felt really angry with him because actually he was quite controlling in a passive aggressive kind of way and perhaps if he hadn't put her down as much as he had she might have a bit more confidence in herself.

'So what are you saying? Do you want a break?'

'No,' she said quietly, 'I think we should split up. I'm saying that while we've had some great times, we've forgotten how to have fun and that we're only young so that's not on. I'm saying that we don't necessarily bring out the best in each other and that I don't want to compete with reUNIon any more. I'm really sorry.'

Tim gazed at her in shock from across the room and if she'd had any small lingering doubts as to whether or not she was doing the right thing they now all disappeared, because there wasn't just a physical distance between them but a whole aching chasm of wrongness. If she ended up lonely and depressed for the rest of her life so be it. It was surely better to be single than in a vaguely dysfunctional relationship.

She waited patiently, expecting Tim to digest what she had said, to think logically about it, before analysing the facts and then to interpret and manage them dispassionately. To her surprise though, instead he did something very out of character and that she never would have expected. He cried.

'Don't do this, Jen,' he pleaded, his blue eyes suddenly brimming with surprised desperation and tears.

For a while she didn't reply. She was simply too surprised by his...surprise.

'I just don't think we bring out the best in each other,' she repeated, now feeling a definite and very welcome sense of relief about having formed her decision. It was then that she realised just how many doubts she must have been having for some time now. 'I'm sorry.'

'I can't believe you're being such a bitch,' said Tim.

'Don't get nasty,' she warned.

'I have done nothing but love you,' he ranted. 'And this is how you repay me. How could you?'

She sighed and not wanting to continue the scene went to get her stuff from the bedroom. Though she'd probably leave the police woman outfit where it was.

'Just think about it for a few days, Drew...um...Jen. Just don't do this on a whim, you'll regret it.'

'I'm sorry,' she repeated. 'I've made up my mind.'

She gathered all her stuff into her holdall and switched on her phone. How odd. She had eight new text messages and the voicemail symbol was flashing. The first message she read simply said 'have you seen the news?'.

'Weird,' said Jennifer.

'What?' said Tim, looking fairly pitiful. His tears were terribly disconcerting. So out of character. They didn't suit him.

'Switch on the telly a moment,' she instructed, and when he ignored her she went back into the lounge and did it herself.

Within seconds the reason she had so many messages, five of which were from her devastated mother, became clear. Princess Diana had died.

For the next three hours what had just passed between them became irrelevant, unimportant and completely secondary to the story which was unfolding on the news. Tim and Jennifer sat gazing at the footage in shock, feeling desperately sad. Jennifer was in floods and Tim was pretty choked, which was unexpected given that he was completely anti-royalist. A long while was spent wondering how it was that things could change so irrevocably on the turn of a sixpence before Jennifer finally felt able to wrench herself away from the telly to make her journey back to her mum and dad's. As she said goodbye she suspected it was the last time she would see Tim. Deep down she doubted they'd remain friends.

She was partially right. It was the last time Jennifer would see Tim in the flesh and yet a mere twelve months later there was no escaping his face and she saw him practically every day. For when reUNIon finally, possibly inevitably, took off, it was everywhere, and so therefore was Tim, including, on one occasion, on the ten o'clock news.

THE PAST — MAX

2006

'Off out somewhere?' Jennifer's boss Janine half yelled after her departing back.

'Er, family dinner, but I'll be in early tomorrow.'

'No problem,' replied Janine, wafting her hand in an airy manner, obviously designed to suggest that she was totally cool either way, when clearly she wasn't. Clearly she was actually flabbergasted that, shock horror, Jennifer was doing the unthinkable and committing a huge office offence by, wait for it…*leaving on time*.

It annoyed Jennifer. Strictly speaking her hours were nine thirty till six but her colleagues were miserably competitive. Staying at their desks later than was really required had practically become a professional sport, meaning anyone wishing to attempt some sort of a life during the week appeared to be slacking.

Still, she wasn't going to fret about that now. She had bigger things to think about.

*

Half an hour later, she emerged from Clapham North tube and as she headed purposefully in the direction of home, she ended up breaking into a trot, unable to prevent a wide grin from spreading across her face. She had the distinct feeling that passers-by must be able to tell that she was a spectacularly clever and useful creature just by looking at her.

Happily, Max had obeyed orders and arrived home as promptly as she had.

As soon as she walked in the door, he looked up and raised an eyebrow, not wanting to pre-empt what she was about to say but unable to hide his anticipation.

By way of reply she simply nodded, eyes shining, and to fully prove it, pulled out the stick she'd urinated on eight long hours ago now. She loved what that stick had told her so much, she'd allowed it to remain alongside the luxury lining of her beloved Miu Miu handbag, despite the fact it had wee on it.

'I knew it,' said Max, punching the air and leaping up to come and hug her. 'Oh Jen, you clever, clever thing. That's amazing. When did you find out?'

'This morning,' she said, so relieved to finally be able to talk about it. 'I just had a feeling. My boobs were really aching and I had this odd crampy feeling so I thought, right, come on, no point putting it off.'

Max hugged her tightly.

'But we're not allowed to get excited yet,' instructed

Jennifer pointlessly, 'and I don't want to tell anyone until we've had the scan. Except my mum. Obviously.'

'Agreed,' said Max solemnly. 'Oh my god Jen, I can't believe it.'

*

Later, as they ate dinner in front of the telly, grinning like idiots at one another, it was impossible to ignore the fact that all being well, in around thirty-four weeks' time, their lives would change forever.

In the end it was Jennifer who gave in. 'I guess we'll definitely need to move then.'

'Guess so,' agreed Max. 'God, suburbs here I come. Shall I just buy some Hush Puppies now and be done with it? I'm going to need a shed obviously and to start getting excited about stuff like mowing the lawn.'

'Janine's going to be gutted you know,' replied Jennifer distractedly. 'She won't want anyone else handling the Lancing project. Perhaps she'll make Ed and Sue share my workload till I get back, rather than get a freelancer in?'

There was so much to consider it was quite overwhelming.

'What do you mean?' replied Max immediately. 'I thought you said you don't want to be one of those women whose nanny knows more about their child than they do.'

Jennifer finished her mouthful before replying.

'I don't. And I'm not sure if I will be going back yet,

but I might, and either way it's going to affect things massively for all my colleagues. And besides, what I said didn't necessarily mean I don't want to work.'

'Oh right.'

Jennifer twirled her spaghetti. She wanted to leave the subject but it proved impossible. Perhaps it was her heightened hormones but his question had made her feel uneasy, like they weren't quite on the same page.

'But seeing as you've brought it up, the last time we spoke about it, I *told* you I wasn't decided either way. Don't you remember me saying I might go part time? You seemed completely cool about it.'

'I am cool about it,' Max said. 'Whatever you decide to do I'll be right behind you.'

'OK. Good.'

'Course I will be. Though what I will say is that knowing Janine, if you go part time she'll want her pound of flesh, only for less money than you're on now, which frankly might be more stress than it would be worth.'

Jennifer had to concede he may have a point. Janine could be a taskmaster.

'So if you work, great, the money will be handy and I'm sure we'll make it work somehow, but just be prepared to hand the majority of your wages over to a nanny.'

Jennifer had assumed they'd both pay for a nanny if they both worked. She wasn't sure what to say.

'And if you don't, then that's great too and you'll be doing the most important job in the world.'

Jennifer wished he'd stop addressing the television and look at her.

'But whatever you do is great by me and we shouldn't be having this discussion now anyway,' he added, reaching over to give her foot a squeeze. 'Tonight we should be just enjoying the fact that after all these months I no longer have to shag you on command or be constantly aware of what your eggs are up to at any given moment.'

Jennifer smiled and concentrated on feeling reassured, determined not to let anything ruin the evening. This was what they'd both wanted for a long time. So why did what Max wanted seem so apparent? *The most important job in the world.*

Later, Jennifer phoned her mum. She'd been dying to make this exact call for so long. Her mum was predictably thrilled so it was a very special moment, marred only by the cogs which persisted on whirring in her brain, to the point where she ended up broaching the subject again, keen to get another point of view.

'What do *you* think, Mum?'

'I think it's a bit early to be worrying about all of this but I agree with Max. It's up to you, love. Though, for what it's worth, I would think very carefully before giving up your financial independence.'

Jennifer was surprised. Her mum had been a housewife all her life so she'd have bet heavily on her having the opposite view.

'Why?'

'Oh I don't know; I just think times have changed. You young women have so much more choice than my generation did and that freedom has been fought for, so you should be careful with it.'

'OK,' said Jennifer. 'I will be, and I haven't decided either way yet anyway. I like my job but I want to be the best mum in the world too and I'm not sure if I'll be able to pull both things off at once.'

'True,' chuckled her mum. 'Well, whatever you decide we're very proud of you. Proudest day of my life was the day you graduated from university and I'm sure the next one will be when I see you being a wonderful mother. But just don't forget you've got a clever brain in there. Working isn't just about money; it's about your identity as well. And you're very lucky to have the choice.'

'I know,' said Jennifer ruefully. 'Although sometimes I think having no choice is almost easier because then you just have to get on with it, whereas having choice means I have to make a decision which could turn out to be the wrong one.'

'Well that's life isn't it? A series of decisions, some bigger than others of course, and some which we don't even realise will affect our lives but do. Should I turn left or right? Get the bus or the train? Stay in or go out? But enough of this gloomy talk, we've got a lot to be thankful for and I've got booties to knit so let's speak tomorrow shall we?'

'Thanks, Mum,' said Jennifer sincerely, grateful that

her mum didn't seem to have any agenda and was happy to be objective in order to let her come to her own conclusion. Unlike somebody else.

*

Later that night Max snuggled in for a hug. 'You asleep?'

'Nearly,' murmured Jennifer. 'Why?'

'Nothing, it can wait, night night.'

'No, go on, you've got to say it now,' she said, irritated. This whole hormone thing wasn't boding well so far.

'I was just going to say that I really don't want you worrying about work during this pregnancy. I know you love your job but you're growing our baby now and I will always look after and provide for you both.'

'I know,' said Jennifer, wondering if her husband was going to go the full hog and put her in an actual cave and perhaps start venturing out to hunt for their food. 'Now go to sleep, I'm knackered.'

MONDAY

For three days a week Jennifer worked in Hayes and Ludlow, one of the many estate agents on the High Street. She was permanently amazed by how any of them managed to stay in business. So many shop fronts had changed in recent years, hit by the recession, but it seemed that in this enclave of South West London, if you were a hairdresser's, an Indian restaurant or an estate agents you could weather any financial shit storm.

Sometimes, when she thought wistfully of her old job, it felt more like an old life. A life where she'd worn a suit, and used to go for after work drinks with colleagues. A life where once a year they'd all travel by coach to Swindon and have an uproarious few days which made all the long hours, tricky clients and ever decreasing budgets they endured the rest of the time, seem thoroughly worthwhile. Still, after having children it really hadn't made much financial sense for her to continue working. Plus nothing could have prepared her for the demands of motherhood or how intensely she'd love her baby. Ultimately, with Max growing more and more resistant to the idea of her going back, it didn't seem worth the battle anyway. Going back would have compromised everybody's set up and would only really have benefited her, in terms of retaining her sense of who she was and continuing to utilise her brain. And life wasn't all about her any more. So the suits she could no longer fit into properly had been put away, as had any shoes with a vague heel. Gradually she'd come to terms with the fact that the hours between six and eight were no longer nice ones to drink during, unless you counted a quick swig of wine gulped directly from the bottle in order to get through bath time, and on the whole she'd been happy with this arrangement. When considering leaving her offspring in a nursery or with a child-minder when she didn't really have to, she'd experienced so much emotional guilt she hadn't known whether she'd have coped with the separation anyway. So it was fortunate that Max's wage was enough for them to survive on. Just about. Although their monthly expenditure certainly became something that had to be planned down to the last penny.

However, as soon as their youngest, Polly, had started school in September, working had become a sensible option again. The money couldn't be anything but extremely useful and it certainly beat feeling obliged to clean the bathroom on a day to day basis. Of course, having been out of the rat race for so long and with jobs so scarce, Jennifer had known she was unlikely to get anything even vaguely resembling her old career. She did take

Janine out for a hopeful coffee at one point but swiftly realised that as far as her old boss was concerned, she was already from a different era in terms of how much the business and their practices had changed in just a few years. So, although being an estate agent hadn't exactly been her burning ambition in life, when she was offered the job, she'd decided it was far, far better than nothing. She got to poke around people's houses, it got her out of her own house and into other people's, and there was the added bonus that she got to chat to Lee all day.

Lee was lovely. He was young and really quiet, or at least he was until you got to know him. He had a kind face and a shaved head, usually two things that don't go hand in hand and yet possibly should, for as it turns out they're a remarkably good combination, and as he grew more comfortable around Jennifer, that is to say once he'd got the measure of her, his true personality unfurled, revealing charm, wit and a pretty sexy glint in his eye. A glint that Jennifer knew she was too old to reciprocate and yet couldn't pretend she hadn't noticed. Due to the fact she wasn't dead and that her womb was still intact and in good working order.

Every day, Lee travelled miles into work from his flat in Wood Green which was pretty much at the end of the Piccadilly line, meaning his commute consisted not only of a very long tube journey but also a bus ride from Hammersmith. How far he was prepared to travel to work amazed Jennifer, but then she had enough self-awareness to know she'd probably adopted her fellow neighbours' rather parochial attitude that unless something was happening within spitting distance of your front door it was all a mammoth effort. Take going out for instance. Many of the mums at school would speak of 'going into town' as if it were akin to trekking in the Himalayas in terms of adventure. Popping into nearby Richmond or to the Kew retail centre was considered pretty adventurous so hopping on a bus and then a tube to get anywhere was positively outlandish. Jennifer liked hearing about Lee's exploits, partly because they were varied, but mainly because they didn't involve anywhere local.

Right now he was filling her in on what he'd been up to at the weekend.

'So then where did you go?'

'So after that we ended up going on to this amazing club in Shoreditch. Have you heard of East Village?' he asked, at which point Jennifer decided she might quite passionately love him for assuming there might be even a vague possibility she'd know where the hell he was talking about.

'Um,' she turned her head to one side, in what she hoped was an attractive fashion, 'I've definitely heard of it,' she lied. 'But I don't think I've been there.'

'Oh right, well you should. It's brilliant. There was this one DJ who I'd definitely go and see again. He was amaz-

ing. He played, like, really, really good Dubstep mixed up
with more commercial tunes. Like remixes of pop tunes,
Adele and that.'

'Cool,' said Jennifer, wondering what Dubstep was and
deciding to Google it and find out the minute she could.
God she'd love a night out clubbing. She hadn't had a
proper dance since…well, probably New Year's Eve and
that was in someone's kitchen surrounded by balding
men who were wearing cords or chinos. When she was
at university she'd loved raving, had discovered it with
a vengeance and for the first two years had spent a lot
of time getting wasted. Thinking about it, she'd spent a
lot of the third year getting wasted as well, only with a
bit of studying thrown in for good measure. Then, after
university, once she'd got a job and had started working,
she'd continued to go clubbing regularly at weekends, liking nothing more than getting sweaty in a room full of
strangers who only had the music and the atmosphere in
common, rendering small talk impossible. Instead it had
been enough simply to grin at one another like loons, and
dance. All pretty tribal and primitive if you really thought
about it, and yet perhaps more natural than endlessly dis-
cussing secondary education over Jamie Oliver recipes
and never-ending bottles of wine. Better for the waistline
too.

She smiled ruefully now as it occurred to her that in
those days she could have told Lee where all the best
nights in London were, who played at them, plus could

have sorted out the guest list to boot. Not any more
though.

'What did you get up to?' asked Lee.

'Oh…er, well the kids had a sleepover on Friday so
we just had a night in,' she said, blushing as she did so,
hating how that mere sentence sounded so full of innuendo. Wasted innuendo. 'Then, on Saturday, we had some
mates round for lunch which was really fun,' she fib-
bed.

'Oh cool, that sounds nice,' he said politely.

'How old are you, Lee?' she asked suddenly, changing
the subject.

'Me?' said Lee, looking surprised.

'Well there's no one else in here right now.'

'Twenty-one.'

'Ooh lucky bastard,' she replied flatly.

He shrugged, conveying that of course there was nothing lucky about it at all. Twenty-one years was simply the
amount of time he'd been on the planet.

'I'll be twenty-two in October,' he offered, almost
apologetically. 'Why? How old are you then? You're not
that old.'

'How old do you think I am?' she said, noting the word
'that' and not liking it. She knew full well asking him to
guess was a horrible thing to do to him, but didn't care
sufficiently to stop herself.

'Um…'

She could see Lee concentrating, desperate not to mess

his answer up thus offending her. She knew then that whatever age he thought she was he would undoubtedly shave a few years off, just to be polite.

'Thirty, thirty-one?'

'Thirty-eight,' she said, surmising that in that case he must think she was about thirty-four, which wasn't bad at all. She'd take that.

To her immense pleasure Lee looked genuinely surprised. 'Oh right, well you definitely look younger than that. You're a proper...'

'What?' laughed Jennifer.

'Nothing,' blushed Lee, looking mortified. 'I was about to say something really out of order. Something which would have put you well within your rights to think I was an utter twat.'

'Oh go on, you've got to say now,' urged Jennifer. This was more fun than she'd had in ages, only just then Patrick Ludlow, one of the partners, came in, putting paid to any more inappropriate, non-work based, flirtatious chat with a minor.

Reluctantly Jennifer picked up a set of keys on her desk and went to meet her two-thirty viewing, the last one she'd do before picking up the children from school.

In that moment she hated herself slightly because deep down she'd been hoping that Lee had been about to call her a 'Milf'. A word which was tasteless at best, offensively sexist at worst and which would ordinarily have her feminist hackles up. Yet had Lee thought she was one, if she was being entirely honest, she would have felt rather chuffed. Oh god, she was definitely going through some kind of rather worrying 'phase'. There was no doubt about it.

As she showed a couple around a rather pokey, over-priced, two bedroom flat, all she could think about was how, despite his youth, Lee afforded her the respect of speaking to her on his level. He didn't treat her, or make her feel like, a middle-aged housewife but instead spoke to her as a friend and as a woman, reminding her along the way how good that felt. She liked having a younger friend and briefly wondered whether she should suggest joining him and his mates on a night out at some stage. Or would he balk at the idea of being seen out with someone who occasionally bought clothes from Marks and Spencer, albeit only from The Limited Collection (never from Autograph and *certainly* never from Per Una)?

She was pretty sure Max wouldn't mind if she said she was going clubbing with Lee. He'd probably take the piss out of her a bit but to be fair was usually pretty cool about things like that, allowing her freedom, because he trusted her implicitly. Maybe she should stop being wet and just do it?

Still, twenty-one. That had been a fairly devastating moment. She'd had him down as at least twenty-five. What had she been up to at twenty-one she wondered once she'd said goodbye to the by now disillusioned and thoroughly depressed couple who'd just realised they probably couldn't ever afford to get on the housing ladder unless they bought a skip and lived in that.

At twenty-one she'd been in her last year at university and was going out with Tim of course. Tim who was busy planning the empire he was going to build, rule and dominate. God, it all felt like a million years ago in some ways.

*

That night Jennifer cooked an especially nice dinner for herself and Max, insisting that they ate it at the table over a bottle of wine.

'So, how was your day?' asked Jennifer.

'Good thanks, Judith and I had to give a presentation this morning which went really well. She certainly knows how to communicate that one. I'll give her that for nothing.'

'Did she ever "communicate" anything about last weekend by the way? Like, for instance, did she have chronic diarrhoea on Sunday night or was she OK?'

Max grinned. 'I think she was fine, although I had to come clean about the chickens.'

'What do you mean?' said Jennifer, frozen in horror.

'It's not a big deal, I just told her they were from a deli and that we'd been a bit worried that we might have poisoned everyone.'

'Oh god,' cringed Jennifer, wishing he hadn't and feeling inexplicably furious that he was always being so fucking chummy with Judith.

'She was fine,' added Max. 'We laughed over it. We also laughed about the fact that Henry just shovelled it all in without even a second look, while we sat there, not saying anything but all privately worrying for our guts.'

'So you were laughing at me basically,' mumbled Jennifer.

Max tutted. 'No, we weren't. Funnily enough Judith and I don't spend our time being mean about you.'

'Oh, well what do you and Judith spend "your time" doing then?' spluttered Jennifer, shaking parmesan unnecessarily vigorously over her spaghetti bolognese.

Max sighed but said nothing.

'What?' snapped Jennifer.

'Nothing.'

'No seriously what? Don't just sigh like that. I'm not stupid. I can tell you've got something to say.'

'I'm just a bit fed up with you being so…angry all the time. I don't know what's got into you lately. You're so aggressive about everything.'

Jennifer put the cheese down and regarded her husband before exhaling hard. He had a point. Yet what she wanted to articulate but for some reason couldn't, was that she was only acting aggressively because lately the way he was being made her feel so defensive. 'I know…you're right. I don't know what's got into me lately either.'

'Not me, that's for sure,' Max quipped, which did at least raise a smile, albeit a sad one.

'I just…'

'What is it?' he said and for the first time in a long time Jennifer felt like he really wanted to know.

'I don't know,' she said truthfully. 'It's just lately I've been questioning everything, you know?'

'Like what?'

'Like what the hell I'm doing with my life. I mean, I'm thirty-eight, I work three days a week in an estate agent, which is perfectly fine, only I earn pretty much less money than our weekly food bills, which is ironic because if I'd stuck at my old job I wouldn't be paying for much childcare now the girls are at school.'

This was a familiar, well-trodden theme which she glossed over slightly, not wanting to annoy Max so much that she lost his attention.

'You and I seem to be in a bit of a rut. Plus I seem to irritate you more than I used to, and I know we've got everything and that I should be bloody grateful for that…but I just feel so sad at the moment. And…frustrated…And, if I'm being totally honest, I'm getting a bit fed up with hearing about flipping Judith every five seconds.'

Max looked at her for a while then shovelled some more spaghetti in his mouth, seemingly unmoved by her outburst.

'You,' he said, pointing at her with his fork, 'are having an MLC.'

'A what?' said Jennifer, irritated that he had already come up with some crap acronym for what she personally felt was a pretty life-changing and difficult phase. Was that the best he could come up with?

'An MLC,' he repeated. 'Mid. Life. Crisis. You've always been a bit impatient so instead of waiting to get to forty you're bringing it forward to thirty-eight.'

'I'm not sure it's as simple as that,' said Jennifer, feeling flustered. 'I mean, admittedly I'm sure there is a bit of that in the mix. I hate being our age sometimes. I hate the fact we never go out dancing and that a lot of people my age wear boot-cut jeans but it's more than that, Max. I don't think they just hand out anti-depressants to anyone.'

'I know,' he said, not looking totally convinced. 'And I know you've been really down but you've got to remember that you're doing great. You're busy with the kids and you've got a job, which helps bring in a bit of spending money.'

'Patronising.'

'Sorry.'

'How about a holiday?' suggested Jennifer, suddenly desperate not to be anxious and confused all the time. 'I know we said we weren't going to have one this year but you know what? I think it might be just what we need, as a family and more to the point as a couple.'

'No,' said Max. 'You were the one who wanted to paint the front of the house last year, plus we don't know what's happening with my work so let's just stick to the plan. We can go to my parents in the holidays for a while.'

'Oh well that'll be a stress buster,' said Jennifer deeply sarcastically, before taking a deep breath and trying again. 'OK, look, I know money's a bit tight but how about if I take on some extra days at the agency? Then I can pay for us to go away.'

'Er…where?' laughed Max, in a way that made her want to grab the grater and use it on his face.

'I don't know. Perhaps we could get a good deal somewhere last minute in Spain, or wherever. I just think I've been feeling so down lately that a change of scene might sort me out. Give me something to look forward to. I don't care if it's somewhere cheap and cheery.'

'I think it's a bad idea,' said Max. 'I would rather not go anywhere than go somewhere shit and depressing just because it's the only thing we can afford. If my contract gets extended we'll go on holiday next year, but this year we're in the middle of a massive recession in case you hadn't noticed so we have to go without and that's that.'

'Again. Patronising,' said Jennifer.

Later, as they sat in silence watching telly, Jennifer thought despairingly of their earlier exchange. She wasn't naive or stupid. She knew there was a bloody recession on but sometimes wished Max would be a little less cautious. Yes, they would have to scrimp a bit to go away but wouldn't it be worth it? Wasn't getting things back on track between them worth splurging on? After all, a divorce would be far more damaging to their finances than a holiday, she thought bitterly, deciding against voicing this out loud.

For some reason her ex Tim popped into her head. There was no chance he'd be going without a holiday this year, she thought wryly. His wife was probably permanently on one long holiday, like a leathered lizard bedecked in jewels. In fact they probably owned a frigging island somewhere. Like Richard Branson.

'Do you want to watch another episode?' yawned Max.

'No, you're all right,' she said. 'I think I might go and have a bath.'

Ten minutes later as she slid into water hot enough to cause serious problems with her veins, Max suddenly gave her a terrible shock by poking his head round the bathroom door on his way to bed.

'By the way,' he said, 'if you start wearing miniskirts with knee-high boots we can definitely confirm the MLC.'

Jennifer summoned up her most sarcastic face possible and casually flicked him the bird before sliding into the water, thinking as she did so, 'And I can confirm that you are well and truly getting on my tits.'

TUESDAY

'How did it go?' mouthed Karen, as Jennifer barrelled towards her friends in the pub, looking flustered.

'Fine,' she said dismissively, not wanting to discuss the disaster that had been last Friday night and her failure to lure her own husband into bed.

'You all right? You look stressed.'

'Oh it's just Max,' she said. 'He knew I wanted to get out tonight and promised he'd get back early but of course ended up *having* to stay later at work. He's being really weird at the moment.'

'Well it's not his fault if he has to work late I guess,' said Karen mildly, holding her handbag on her lap, like the queen. Having come straight from work herself she was wearing a rather staid black skirt suit and not for the first time Jennifer thought it a shame her friend refused to ever do any exercise. She was still carrying an awful lot of the extra weight which she'd put on when pregnant with Suzy. It didn't really matter of course and yet being a bit tubby and having such a huge bust made her look rather matronly which in turn aged her considerably. She didn't

really resemble the feisty, big-boobed sex bomb she'd
been in her youth.

In stark contrast, these days Lucy was looking better
than ever. Having been the ugly duckling of the group
when they were younger, nowadays she'd taken firm control of her appearance. She was gym and yoga honed,
spent a considerable part of her wages on good hair-
cuts and highlights and had finally worked out that what
suited her most were slim-fitting clothes in shades which
complemented rather than battled with her English complexion.

'Anyway, enough of all that,' said Jennifer now, not
wanting to sound like an old harridan yet still not able to
quash the uneasy niggle she'd had for ages that all was not
right with her husband. 'How are you both and where's
Esther?'

'Couldn't get a sitter,' said Lucy. 'Or…wouldn't get a
sitter, not sure which. I think money's a bit tight for them
at the moment.'

'Ah, fair enough then,' said Jennifer, thinking what a
shame it was and also in a sense how pathetic it was that
these days it was seemingly impossible for their foursome
to be precisely that. It always proved so difficult to find a
time when they could simultaneously abandon the respon-
sibilities of work or childcare simply for a few paltry
hours. 'I'm going to the bar. Are you both on wine? If so
I'll get a bottle.'

Karen and Lucy nodded, though as soon as she was

out of earshot, Karen, pulled a face. 'She's not happy is she?'

'She's all right I think, not her usual bubbly self admittedly but she seems OK,' said Lucy.

When Jennifer returned from the bar though, Karen was determined to get to the bottom of things. 'Come on Jen, you're obviously fed up. Why don't you tell us what's really wrong? It can't just be Max getting home late. Surely that's not such a big deal?'

'Oh I don't know,' replied Jennifer, smiling wryly at how well Karen knew her. 'It's no biggie really. I'm just generally feeling a bit down. Bit depressed about being so unemployable and unsure how to fix it. Plus, things aren't that brilliant between me and Max at the moment, which he keeps blaming squarely on the fact that I'm having some sort of mid-life crisis, which to be fair I probably am.'

'Aren't we all,' laughed Lucy.

'Probably,' agreed Jennifer. 'It's a weird stage of life I think. I keep reminding myself that I've "got it all", two lovely children, a husband and a nice roof over my head etc etc. Yet, if you'd told me when I was twenty-one that by the time I was thirty-eight I'd be permanently exhausted, work part time in an estate agents and that my marriage would be a bit stale, I'd have been horrified. Still, I'm probably not the only one feeling like this am I?'

'Course not,' agreed Karen vehemently. 'Take last

week for instance. I got told by my bitch boss that I can't have a pay rise *yet again*, then five minutes later found out my male equivalent is earning ten grand more a year than me, so believe me when I say I know that "how did it come to this" feeling.'

'Well there you go then,' said Jennifer. 'Only due to the fact I don't have any hope of resurrecting a decent career for myself, I probably focus more on how drab things are between me and Max.'

'Oh, you and Max are solid as a rock,' protested Lucy, which Jennifer thought was a bit weird. It was her relationship after all. She was the only one of them actually in it so surely the only one with the right to make big sweeping statements about the state of it.

'Christ, if you two are in trouble what hope is there for the rest of us?'

Jennifer shrugged, not wanting her and Max to be held up as an example of the perfect couple all the time, a symptom of having married someone who got on well with all her friends. 'Well,' she answered eventually, thinking it was probably time to inject some positivity into the conversation before they all got the urge to smash their wine glasses in unison and communally slash their wrists. 'I think there probably is hope actually, and it comes in the form of Esther and Jim because although they've been together since the dawn of time, I don't think *they* have any problems in terms of staleness. I know they've got their problems financially but the other day she told me that after a recent night out they ended up doing it in their downstairs loo! I couldn't believe it.'

'You're kidding me,' gasped Lucy. 'They're like rabbits those two. How do they manage to keep things so fresh? I'd genuinely love to know.'

'Why? Aren't you and Dave getting on?' asked Jennifer, curious to hear, especially if it meant finding out that someone else felt even remotely like she did.

'Oh we're all right,' Lucy said flatly. 'You know, we're fine, although recently I've wanted to murder him on a pretty much daily basis, not helped by the fact I've got a terrible crush on someone. There's this guy who works in the deli round the corner from my work and I've developed a complete fantasy about him. I know it's because my sex life is so non-existent at home but I've been going there fully made-up most days. We've never had so many olives in the fridge. The kids actually know what a pimento is.'

'I had no idea you and Dave didn't have a great sex life,' said Jennifer, genuinely shocked.

'It's not really the sort of thing you broadcast is it?' shrugged Lucy. 'And it goes without saying I would appreciate it if you kept it firmly under your hat please.'

'Of course,' said Karen, who was dying for a cigarette. Usually she'd have already gone outside to have one by now but she didn't want to miss any of the conversation. It was all coming out tonight.

'Oh Luce, I know how you feel,' said Jennifer, full of

empathy. 'I know Max loves me, but sometimes I feel like he hasn't looked at me properly for years. It sucks doesn't it?'

'It's awful,' agreed Lucy, leaning in suddenly and lowering her voice to ensure only her friends could hear what she was going to say next. 'I mean, you know you've hit rock bottom when you go to the clinic for a vaginal probe, to check you haven't got fibroids…and you actually enjoy it.'

Karen recoiled, her face a shocked picture, turning this way and that to check no one anywhere near them had heard. 'That's one of the funniest and yet also most disgusting things I've ever heard in my life.'

'I know,' said Lucy. 'Or the most depressing, I'm still not sure which. I even told Dave about it, to demonstrate how truly desperate I am for him to get his mojo back but he just grunted and called me a weirdo. Now come on Jen, Max can't be that bad.'

'Mm…you say that, but I can't remember the last time he told me he loved me. Every time I try to reach out to him he's either too tired, or can't be bothered. He's so….casual about me, so complacent that sometimes I just really wish…' Jennifer stared down at her glass and for a worrying moment her friends thought she might be about to cry '…sometimes wish I could have that feeling again, you know the one you get when you first meet someone and everything's amazing and they're madly in love with you and can't keep their hands off you.' She stopped, needing to express herself fully but slightly embarrassed by the next bit. 'I suppose I want to be…grabbed. I want to be…desired, loved.'

'But Max does love you,' insisted Lucy, seemingly determined not to hear what she was saying. Possibly Jennifer's woes held a mirror up to her own marriage, only not one she wanted to look in. 'Any fool can see that.'

'Oh I don't doubt he loves me, like he loves his slippers or his iPad, but I don't think he *fancies* me any more. He never wants to throw me on the bed, or stroke my face or stare into my eyes.'

'Oh for god's sake,' giggled Karen despite herself. 'You've got two children, of course he doesn't. That sort of passion never lasts, but it doesn't mean he doesn't find you attractive any more.'

'Then how come we haven't had sex in months?'

'How many months is months?' asked Lucy.

'Four…no, actually five now.'

Already privy to this information Karen simply looked on, though her face demonstrated exactly how dire she thought this was.

'I'm not kidding,' said Jennifer in case anyone thought she was.

'Well I don't think that's that bad,' admitted Lucy, looking miserable.

That shut them up.

'You are joking?' said Karen. 'Why? How many have you gone without for?'

'Six ish?' she half whispered.

'That's awful, Lucy,' stated Karen.

Jennifer agreed. She was dumbfounded really and wondered if there was an actual complacency virus going about.

'Well, it's probably not *that* out of the ordinary,' said Lucy, suddenly defensive. 'I mean we have got two children who never sleep. Honestly, it's like I've literally given birth to vampires, and Dave's been so stressed since losing his job he's lost all his confidence. Sex is the last thing on his mind right now.'

'Fair enough,' agreed Jennifer. It was true. Dave's sense of self-worth had diminished before their very eyes after he was made redundant. 'And I suppose with me and Max, we were never the sort of people who liked doing it in the evening. We always used to like doing it at the weekends, you know, when you could be leisurely about it in the mornings, so when you have children there's just never really an opportunity.'

'Blimey,' said Karen, still looking like her friends were talking another language. 'I think Pete would prefer doing it in *front* of the children, no matter how scarred it would leave them, rather than go without.'

Jennifer sighed. 'It's not really sex I miss. It's excitement. Sometimes I find myself worrying that I could be on my death bed thinking, "Why didn't you get your kicks when you could, you silly woman? Before you were too old and ugly to do anything about it." I found myself remembering the time we went to Kos the other day.'

Her friend's faces immediately lit up at the memory.

'Oh my god, what were we like?' grinned Karen. 'Do you remember that awful carpet fitter I was seeing?'

'Mark,' said Lucy.

'Yeah, Mark. Did I tell you he sent me a Facebook friend request?'

'No way,' said Lucy. 'He remembered your name after all these years?'

'Yup,' said Karen proudly. 'He sent me a prediction via reUNIon too. Sorry, Jen.'

'Do you remember sexy Aidan?' asked Jennifer, ignoring the reference to reUNIon. She was used to it.

'God yes,' said Lucy. 'I was so jealous of you. He was beautiful.'

'I know. I'd love to know what he was up to now.'

'Drug dealing in Australia?' suggested Karen drily.

'No,' tutted Jennifer. 'He probably is in Oz but I don't think he'd be doing that. Don't you remember he wanted to start up a scuba diving school? He's probably living the life of Riley, on the beach, brown as a berry, healthy and happy.'

'Do you remember how close you came to going off with him?' asked Karen. 'I still get palpitations thinking about that now. I remember standing on that jetty thinking, oh my god I'm going to have to explain to her mum when she comes to pick us up at the airport. "Ah hello

Mrs Drew, no, Jennifer isn't with us. She's decided to stay with a sex god called Aidan and his nice big bag of white doves, which are the other thing she's taken quite a fancy to.'"

They all laughed.

'I seriously considered going with him you know,' said Jennifer.

'I know you did,' said Karen indignantly. 'Don't you remember me crying about it?'

Jennifer nodded vaguely. She could remember only too clearly the details of that scorching hot afternoon. Only she'd hate her friends to know quite how often she'd found herself recalling them lately.

'You were always lucky on the man front. Do you remember Steve?' added Karen.

'Ah lovely Steve,' cooed Lucy, looking positively drippy. 'He was such a poppet wasn't he? I always had a bit of a soft spot for him, and in terms of someone adoring you, my god Jen, you literally couldn't have asked for anything more. He used to look at you like a puppy dog. Now there's an example of a man who would have walked on hot coals for you and was permanently complimenting you but, if you remember, it used to drive you mad,' she said, practically wagging her finger. 'To the point where it was the precise fact that Max was a bit cooler with you that made you feel like you'd met your match. You loved the fact he wouldn't let you get away with stuff like Steve did.'

'True,' said Jennifer. 'I did love Steve though and I did always appreciate how lovely he was to me. Finishing with him wasn't an easy decision by any stretch of the imagination. I got rid of a good man there and we all know they don't grow on trees don't we.'

'We do,' said Karen 'which is why you're so bloody lucky to have bagged another one. Babe, I reckon you need to stop thinking there's something better for you out there. Stick with what you've got. It works, you've got a lovely house, two happy secure children and if you upended all of that who knows how difficult life would be?'

'Who said anything about upending anything?' said Jennifer, unnerved by Karen's ability to not only hit the nail on the head but then also to smash it hard with a mallet in order to really illustrate her point. She'd never been one to mince her words but Jennifer didn't like how close to the bone she'd got this time.

PRESENT DAY

'How is she today? Any change? Sorry we're late, we would have been here earlier but I thought it important we check on the girls first.'

'Thank you,' said Max, bursting into tears which surprised him more than it did anyone else. He had thought he was bearing up well but the sight of Jennifer's parents looking so flooded with anxiety for their daughter was too much and brought home the severity of the situation once again. The guilt was practically eating him alive.

'Oh you poor man,' said Lesley, his mother-in-law, drawing him in for a hug. It was the first time such a physical exchange had occurred between them during all the time they'd known each other but he went with it and was surprised by how comforting it was to be drawn into her ample, rather matronly bust.

'How are the kids?' managed Max eventually, coming up for air. 'They don't know anything yet do they?'

'They're fine, don't you worry about them. They've still no idea, which personally I think is for the best at this stage. Till we've got a better idea of what's going on. Anyway, we left them with Karen, happy as pie, making fairy cakes. She's been a star.'

'When's the doctor coming round?' asked Jen's dad, Nigel.

'I didn't know he was unconscious,' joked Max weakly.

Lesley and Nigel looked baffled.

'Sorry. That wasn't even funny was it? In fact it's the sort of feeble joke Jen would usually crack at a time like this,' Max babbled. 'Out of nerves. Completely inappropriate. I haven't slept much lately. I think I might be going a bit doolally.'

'It's all right, love,' said Lesley, eyeing him with such a mixture of concern and pity it was obvious she concurred with the analysis of his mental state. 'Do you remember when Uncle Ken died and Jennifer got the giggles at the funeral because the vicar's toupee was blowing around in the wind then half slipped off his head at the graveside?'

'Oh gosh yes,' said Max, smiling sadly at the memory, grateful to Lesley for bearing with him.

'Thinking about it now, it probably was quite a comical sight, but at the time I was furious with Jen for not having more decorum,' she added wistfully.

They all fell silent for a second, lost in memories. Max hated it. The atmosphere they were creating was too similar to how people reflected about the deceased, yet his wife was still alive, sort of.

'Anyway, thinking about it, the doctor should actually be here by now,' he said eventually, determined to change the mood despite the fact he was still pretty choked up and having to use every ounce of bravery in order to stay composed. 'The thing is, you don't like to make too much of a fuss because the staff have all been amazing so far, but at the same time, they never come when they say they're going to.'

'Oh but you're right, you mustn't make a fuss,' agreed Lesley, horrified at the mere thought.

*

Inside Jennifer's bruised head, what her mum had just said was one of the few things to penetrate her consciousness.

It was a typical comment for her mum to make. She was the type of woman who'd rather eat a dish she hadn't actually ordered in a restaurant, even if she hated it, rather than 'make a fuss'. The familiarity of this personality trait was in itself a comfort. It was also a comfort to be aware of people's presence, ones she knew cared about her, only she was still very confused about why she required comfort. Something terrible had happened. But what?

Hearing her mum's voice had made her desperate to find out whether or not she would have rekindled her relationship with her had she stayed with Aidan. She hoped they would have done. It wouldn't say much for them if they couldn't have found it within themselves to have salvaged something of it.

The next thing she knew she was tumbling through space once more, a sensation she was starting to become accustomed to. Hovering outside the portal she was reluctant to go down, *scared* to go down. It would be beyond devastating to discover that their relationship hadn't been able to survive one lousy decision. One mistake. She waited, floating, like a fish suspended in a bowl, wondering what was going to happen. There were, after all, two other portals to go down. She did want to discover what would have happened between her and her parents eventually, but perhaps that wasn't supposed to happen right now after all, for she suddenly found herself being pulled in another direction. It was time to explore the second portal. The one marked Tim.

TUNNEL NUMBER TWO

What Could Have Been—Tim

'So you can't come?'

'I'm so sorry Karen, I would have loved to but I'm meeting Tim. He's taking me to some do. In fact, I'm in a bit of a mad rush to be honest. I couldn't get out of work as early as I wanted to and I've still got to get ready.'

Jennifer could practically hear Karen's irritation crackling down the phone but there was no way she was going to cancel her plans just to placate her. She wasn't going to apologise either. She hadn't done anything wrong and was getting fed up of always being made to feel like she had.

'What's it tonight then?' asked Karen reluctantly and Jennifer could picture only too well how she'd be rolling her eyes with disdain.

'Tim's got tickets to the Serpentine party in Hyde Park. It's supposed to be pretty amazing. There'll be lots of people from the art world there but also loads of celebs and cocktails and canapés and all of that malarkey. Tickets are a few hundred quid a pop.'

Jennifer winced. Had that sounded like she was showing off? She hadn't meant it to. She was simply trying to
demonstrate to Karen that her plans weren't all that easy
to break.

'Oh well, having a curry with me and Pete can't compete with that,' said Karen.

Jennifer despaired and not for the first time wished
she'd never told Karen about the argument she'd had with
Tim the day Princess Diana had died. It was nearly a year
ago now but ever since she'd confided in her that for
an insecure moment, she'd briefly considered finishing it
with him, Karen had acted like she had carte blanche to be
as scathing as she liked about their relationship.

Now Jennifer felt a constant need to justify her decision
to stay with him. Yet it didn't seem to matter how many
times she explained that ultimately she'd decided not to
dump him because he had so much to offer, in many different ways, her friend refused to listen.

She was sick of it. It was her life and it wound her up
that Karen acted as though by comparison her and Pete's
relationship was so perfect, to the point where the more
she thought about it, the more she was starting to think
that perhaps she might just be a tiny bit jealous. After all,
Karen and Pete struggled to make ends meet most months
whereas she'd finally got herself a nice job in marketing
and Tim had made it. He'd done what he had always set
out to do. He'd invented something and it was all coming to fruition. He was rich. reUNIon was taking off and

that was entirely down to his hard work, vision, drive and dedication to making it happen. She was *proud* to be with him. He was so clever. A genius to some extent and yes, he may appear distracted much of the time but then of course he was. He had a growing company to manage. He had the attention of many major captains of industry, from politicians, the media and not just in Britain but globally.

'Well have a great time,' Karen said flatly.

'I will,' said Jennifer, sad that once again Karen had rained on her parade. She sighed but, keen to keep the peace, attempted to make sure their conversation ended on good terms. 'Can I come round next week instead?'

'Course,' said Karen, who at her end was determinedly pulling herself together. She had enough self-awareness to know she was giving Jennifer a hard time but couldn't help herself. Tim made her skin crawl. Always had done. Physically he reminded her of Beavis from *Beavis and Butt-Head* which was how she and Pete referred to him in private. She found him repellent and arrogant and was convinced her friend could do better. She could only think that Jennifer was still with him purely for the money and lifestyle that being Tim Purcell's girlfriend provided.

'Why don't you come round next Tuesday or Wednesday?'

'It's a date,' said Jennifer. 'Though Tuesday probably works better for me and it's nearer so stick it in the diary.'

After they'd got off the phone Jennifer allowed herself

five minutes just to sit on the bed and gaze dolefully at the wall, until she realised that unless she got a move on she'd be horribly late.

*

Forty minutes later, Jennifer was dressed and ready to go. Tim had bought her a beautiful Diane Von Furstenberg wrap dress from a very expensive shop in Notting Hill. It was silk and beautifully made and the colours were vibrant, fiery oranges and reds. The style was slightly too conservative for Jennifer's taste but she appreciated how lucky she was to have it and wanted to please Tim by wearing it, even if she did think it would be better on a woman in her forties. He'd suggested she go to the hairdressers and have a blow-dry but being totally honest she preferred her hair more natural. All the moneyed women round Notting Hill looked like clones of one another as far as she was concerned with their coiffeured, crash helmet, invariably blonde highlighted hairstyles.

*

Just as she was applying a final slick of lip gloss the doorbell rang, so she picked up her clutch bag and clacked to the door in her high heels.

Tim's driver was standing on the front step.

'Oh hi Ray, is Tim not with you?'

'He got held up Jen, but said to say he'll meet you there.'

Jennifer's smile slipped off her face slightly but there was no point saying anything to Ray. In fact there was no point saying anything to anyone. Her boyfriend would be there when he could be and if she had to sit outside the Serpentine in the car for a while that's what she'd do. There was no way she was going into that party on her own.

Twenty minutes later Jennifer was idly daydreaming out of the window about nothing in particular when the car glided up to the pavement.

'Hang on a minute, we're not here yet are we?' asked Jennifer. Why were they stopping in Knightsbridge?

Ray turned round from the front seat. 'Mr Purcell requested we make a quick pit stop here, if you don't mind.'

'Oh right…er…shall I wait in the car then?'

'No Miss, if you would be so kind, there's someone waiting for you inside so you should come with me.'

Thoroughly confused, Jennifer looked out of the window again. They were outside The Mandarin Oriental hotel and by now Ray had already come round her side of the car to open her door. Wondering what on earth was going on Jennifer got out, hoping this wasn't going to take too long. She'd be annoyed if Tim was still doing business. She hadn't seen him properly all week and he'd promised her that tonight he'd finish at a decent time so that they could enjoy the party. As she followed Ray up the steps of the hotel, she got the strangest sense that the hotel doormen were half expecting her. She was probably being paranoid though.

'What's going on, Ray? Where are we meeting Tim?'

'Don't you worry,' he said mysteriously and she knew then that she wasn't going to get any more information out of him.

'I'd best leave you to it, Jen. I can't leave the car here I'm afraid, I'll get a ticket.'

'Oh…really…' she began but he'd already turned and gone, and was hurrying back to his waiting car.

Feeling rather self-conscious and a tad irritated she resigned herself to the fact that she now had no other choice but to go into the hotel and find out what was going on. So she let the incredibly enthusiastic doorman usher her through to the main reception where the first thing she noticed within the opulent surroundings was a uniformed member of the hotel staff standing clutching an enormous bouquet of white flowers. There were lilies, roses and huge white delphiniums so large they pretty much covered the woman's entire face. They were absolutely beautiful and Jennifer wondered who they were for. Just as she was thinking this the legs beneath the flowers started walking towards her.

'These are for you, Miss Drew,' said the woman, once she was only a few feet away, almost teetering underneath the weight of the blooms and handing them over to Jennifer.

'Oh my gosh,' she gasped, overwhelmed and enjoying

the incredible perfume that was coming from them. 'They're amazing, thank you so much. Are you sure they're for me? Are they from Tim?'

'Indeed they are, Miss. Now, I'd like you to follow me, only perhaps let's leave the flowers with reception to look after and we can collect them again later. They're a bit too big to carry around aren't they?' she said smiling.

At this point all the irritation and confusion Jennifer had been experiencing dissolved completely and instead she started to get seriously excited. There had been so many times over the years when she'd had to put up with broken arrangements, or had to wait around for Tim for hours on end while he finished up his business but never had any of these times involved being handed a massive bouquet. She felt like Pretty Woman. Not because she felt like a prostitute but because she was being spoiled by a millionaire in a fairy-tale type of way. It was pretty intoxicating and was also obvious by now that Tim must have planned something. Dinner before the party maybe? She was really touched. It had been a long time since he'd done anything romantic for her. For a brief second she wondered if he was going to propose but as quickly as the notion came to her she dismissed it again. No, he wouldn't. Not yet.

Once they'd disposed of the flowers she followed the woman through the hotel towards the lifts. Jennifer watched as she pressed a button for one of the very top floors. As the lift made its ascent through the building the two of them stood in vaguely awkward silence, grinning inanely at one another. What on earth was going on? It was so exciting.

Coming out of the lift Jennifer found herself in a spacious corridor, decorated in decadent red.

'This way please,' the woman said with a polite smile.

Jennifer followed, full of nerves. They walked right to the end of the plush, thickly carpeted corridor at which point the woman took a key card out of her pocket.

As she inserted it, she stood aside to push the door open so that the room was revealed.

Jennifer gasped. The room, which must have been the hotel's most luxurious suite, was full to the brim with candles, carpeted with them if you like, save for a path through the middle which led to a terrified looking Tim.

'What's this?' squawked Jennifer. 'What are you doing?' Not the most romantic or profound thing to say but she was terribly nervous by now.

'Well come in then,' said Tim, encouraging her to stop standing gormlessly in the doorway.

Doing as she was told, Jennifer made her way towards him, picking out a path between the flickering candles. Once she'd reached him she watched incredulously and for a second it was as if life had gone into slow motion as Tim slowly got down onto one knee, simultaneously producing a duck-egg blue box from his pocket and saying, 'Jennifer Drew, I know I'm not perfect but I hope I'm perfect for you. Please will you marry me?'

Tears filled her eyes. She couldn't believe it. Couldn't believe she was being asked for starters but also couldn't believe how much effort Tim had gone to and that he had it in him to be so romantic. By now he'd opened the box and for a second the sight of the ring completely distracted her. It was amazing. Not the kind of ring she ever would have imagined a girl like her to wear. It was from Tiffany's for a start and was a ring for a rich person, a statement ring. The kind of ring that would need insuring and to be locked in a safe when on holiday. The sort of ring you couldn't in all seriousness contemplate wearing if you planned on doing any washing up, gardening or swimming. The diamond was enormous, a proper rock, which glinted and twinkled in the candlelight, and was set off by a traditional platinum band.

Eventually she tore her gaze away in order to look at Tim. He looked nervous. Tim was never nervous. Why was he nervous? Oh yes, he'd just proposed. Her mind was swirling this way and that. Did she want to be his wife? Did she want to spend the rest of her life with him?

She gulped. She'd always known this moment could be a possibility and she wouldn't have stayed with him all this time if it wasn't ultimately what she'd always wanted. Would she?

'Well?' said Tim, looking positively pained by now.

She laughed. Poor man. He was waiting. He was on one knee. She did love him. Of course she did. It had to be a yes.

'Yes.'

'Thank goodness for that,' exclaimed Tim. 'And thank goodness I can get back up, my knee's killing me.'

Getting to his feet he shook out his cramped leg then came towards her. They both smiled at one another, digesting what had just happened.

'So Mrs Purcell, are you happy?'

'Ycs,' said Jennifer, eyes shining, wondering who to call first. Probably not Karen. She batted that decidedly depressing thought out of her head, determined not to give any headspace to anything as gloomy as her friend's disapproval at this special time.

'I suppose I should probably kiss you then,' said Tim.

'Yes, you probably should,' agreed Jennifer, laughing at how deeply unspontaneous he was. God forbid he ever just grabbed her and kissed her because he was overwhelmed by the desire to do so.

Tim came towards her and, bending forward slightly, met her mouth with his. It wasn't the best kiss in the world but it was a happy one that firmly sealed the deal and she hugged him with real affection.

So that was that then. She was going to marry Tim, her boyfriend of four years. She would be Mrs Tim Purcell, wife of the founder of reUNIon. She could hardly believe it. Her mum would be ecstatic. Karen, not so much…

PRESENT DAY

Max tore through the hospital searching for a doctor, frantic in his pursuit. Finally, after much helter-skeltering up and down slippery corridors, he spotted a nurse he recognised.

'Hello,' he panted, relieved beyond belief. It was so frustrating when you desperately needed but couldn't find someone medical. It made him feel so helpless. 'I need you to come to Jennifer Wright's room right away please.'

'Everything OK, Mr Wright?' she enquired calmly.

'Yes, I think so. Well I'm not sure really, but unless I'm hallucinating, and I'm afraid there's a chance I could be because I can't remember the last time I had a proper night's sleep, I think my wife just smiled.'

'OK…' said the nurse looking grave but not as excited as Max thought she should be.

'Seriously, her face definitely changed, which is amazing, because surely that must mean she's thinking about something, or dreaming, or hearing, which in turn must mean her brain is functioning on some level?'

'I'll see if I can find Mrs Wright's consultant and if

he's here I'll ask him to come and see you in your wife's room. But please try to stay calm. I'm afraid that sometimes, when a patient is in a coma, their body can make involuntary reflex movements. It can be very distressing for relatives because of course this can give what usually turns out to be false hope.'

Max stared blankly at her. He knew his wife better than anyone and would stake his life on the fact that she had just smiled. Voluntarily. He was convinced of it.

'Hmm, well thank you, and if you could find someone that would be great please,' he said, on the verge of tears. Not just any old tears either but violent sobbing which he was determined to hold back until he was alone. He headed away from the nurse and traipsed back to Jennifer's room. When he got there he closed the door behind him and allowed the inevitable tears of frustration to pour down his face. Collapsing into the chair he'd spent an unreasonable amount of time sitting in lately, he wept noisily until some of his grief and helplessness had worked its way out of his stressed-out system.

When he'd finished he felt calmer. He also felt exhausted, drained and very sad. He stared at his wife. His silent, slightly waxy-looking, shell of a wife. Was she still in there? Could she hear him? Would there be a day when they'd be cuddled up in bed, feet entwined, talking about how lucky they were to have got through this nightmare and to still be together? If she did wake up would she ever forgive him? He'd give anything for the opportunity to tell her how much he loved and missed her, how much he'd taken her for granted and that he was sorry. He reached over for her hand. It was warm but disconcertingly limp. Was he being punished? It felt like it. He was a pathetic cliché. When Judith had showed him some attention it had flattered his ego so much. It had been fun to be flirted with and thrilling to think that someone found him sexually attractive. Plus, if he were being totally honest, the prospect of touching someone who wasn't his wife had been a huge aphrodisiac. They hadn't slept with each other but god he'd wanted to and the few kisses they'd shared had been unbelievably erotic. Only the minute Jennifer had found out, any 'feelings' he may have had for Judith had vanished without a trace, completely annihilated by the horror and realisation of the upset he'd caused. He remembered now being age fifteen and his mum walking in on him and Sarah Fisher in his bedroom. He'd had his hand in her knickers at the time and had been about as excited as only a straight fifteen-year-old boy could be in the same position. Yet the minute his mum had appeared his ardour had been instantly extinguished by embarrassment and shame. This situation felt similar somehow which only made him feel more foolish. Lust. Not love. That's what he'd been experiencing. He didn't give a shit about Judith really. He'd wanted to fuck her. And because of that, this had happened. Why?

Not wanting to go down that particular path which only led to more frustration he thought back instead to what had just happened. The smile which had brought with it such an incredibly soothing rush of hope it had almost bowled him over.

He'd been half dozing at the time and although the memory was a bit hazy now he was pretty sure it had been the slight rustling sound of a sheet which had made him look up. Rustling was probably too strong a word, for it had been a minute sound, barely discernible but there none the less.

As he'd glanced up, instantly alert, yet still groggy from sleep, it had seemed like Jennifer's hand might have been in ever such a slightly different position to the one it had been in before. And then, without question her face flickered. Her mouth definitely seemed to curl in an upward motion and it looked to Max like his wife was smiling.

*

Later, as the weary consultant and even wearier Max discussed what he'd seen (or as the consultant preferred to put it 'what he *may* have seen') deep inside Jennifer's psyche a different type of debate was going on.

*

She'd re-emerged from the portal marked Tim and was still mulling over the fact that if she'd stayed with him they would have ended up engaged. Who'd have thought it? She wondered what she should do now. Usually after a trip to one of her alternate universes she was so depleted her body took time out in the grey ether to recover and recharge. However, now she felt fine. She was just totally intrigued, fascinated in fact to find out more. It seemed her brain agreed for she found herself floating towards the tunnel again where no doubt she would discover how things would have gone. Would she have been blissfully content, living out many people's version of a fairy-tale? This certainly seemed like a possibility.

TUNNEL NUMBER TWO

What Could Have Been—Tim

'You look nice, Mummy.'

'Thank you Hattie, come here darling,' said Jennifer, beckoning to her youngest daughter to come for a hug.

Hattie padded across the room to where her mother was sat at her dressing table, in her vast dressing room, putting the finishing touches to her make-up and spritzing her neck, wrists and hair with perfume. Eau d'Hadrien by Annick Goutal, the one she always wore. Years ago Tim had told her it was really attractive for a woman to have a signature scent, so she'd stuck with the one she'd had at the time and it had indeed become the smell her children would always associate with her.

She drew Hattie towards her. The little girl was already in her White Company gingham pyjamas and had obviously had her hair washed as it was still damp and drying into natural ringlets.

'Are you OK, sweetheart? Where's Deck?'

Hattie shrugged, looking fed up. 'Putting Jasper to bed, but I want *you* to read my story today.'

'I can't tonight. You know Daddy's got all his work people coming and Mummy's got to be there.'

'But you haven't read stories for ages.'

'Yes I have,' said Jennifer, refusing to be put on a guilt trip, something Hattie was very good at. 'Who read *The Selfish Crocodile* to you yesterday?'

Hattie tried to continue looking hard done by but ruined the effect by allowing a small grin to escape. 'But before that you haven't.'

Jennifer paused. Her daughter's cut-glass accent took her by surprise sometimes. She was starting to sound more and more like the Queen, or perhaps an Enid Blyton character, a result of the very expensive school she'd started at last September. Jennifer wasn't entirely sure it sat all that well with her. She worried that later on in life if her daughter sounded too posh she might be bullied. She wondered what she could do to combat the problem. Force her to watch box sets of *Towie* or *EastEnders* perhaps? Get her a job in a garage? Get Aunty Karen to give her anti elocution lessons maybe?

'Look, I know it's been a busy time sweetie, but Daddy goes to Hong Kong next week and then I won't have so much on in the evenings. So I promise I'll make up for it on the stories front then. But right now I've got to get downstairs or otherwise the first guest will arrive and I won't be there, so go back to your floor and find Deck will you?'

Hattie turned round and padded out of the room, an

air of weary resignation about her, which made her look even more adorable. It was her little shoulders which got to Jennifer somehow. She sighed, wishing she didn't have to go downstairs and play the corporate wife. Deep down she was only too aware that recently she seemed to be permanently telling all four of her offspring that she didn't have time for anything that mattered to them. Still, Tim had never been so busy, so she didn't have much choice.

If only she could convey to Hattie that given the chance she'd do anything rather than have to entertain the bunch of stiffs that were on their way right now. Gouge her eyeballs out with a spoon. Anything.

*

Forty minutes later and the evening was well underway. Nearly all of the twenty guests had arrived and were being plied with drinks and canapés. As ever Jennifer had done her homework so knew not only what everyone was called, but also what they 'did', what their other halves were called and how important to Tim they were in terms of business on a scale of one to ten. She would allocate time devoted to making sure they were being 'looked after' accordingly.

*

'Darling, will you make sure there's some more claret for Jeremy?' said Tim now, as an aside. He didn't even look her in the eye, just gave her elbow a discreet nudge before turning his attentions back to the man who had a redder nose than Rudolph. However, it appeared Jeremy's attention had been stolen away by a woman with an impressive cleavage which he was now practically dribbling into.

'And try to look a bit happier,' added Tim, seeing as he wasn't being listened to any more. 'You look like you're here under duress.'

Jennifer gave him a withering look. 'Ten out of ten for accuracy,' she shot back.

'Don't fuck this up for me, Jen,' he said resolutely, a fake smile plastered across his face. 'I need all of these people on side if there's going to be a merger. And if it's so much of a chore for you to be here, try thinking of it as your job.'

'All right,' she agreed between gritted teeth, nodding politely at someone who'd just arrived. 'But stop lecturing me will you?'

Tim looked at her with enormous disdain, only she couldn't take him seriously because she'd just spotted a tiny piece of lettuce on his nose.

'You've got canapé on your nose. It looks ridiculous.'

Tim looked immediately chastened and patted his suit jacket, searching for a hanky. 'You could have told me earlier,' he snapped.

'Terribly sorry, I didn't realise I was supposed to be monitoring your face,' added Jennifer primly, her own face a mask of composure. 'Though if I had I would have told you that you've also got what looks like a piece of duck stuck between your teeth. I'll get that claret.'

Over the years Jennifer and Tim had got saying one thing while looking like they were saying another, down to a fine art. Anyone observing would probably have thought the couple had just shared an affectionate private joke as opposed to a couple of scathing put-downs. But then, as the wife of someone as powerful as Tim, over the years Jennifer had learnt how to play the game and how to cope with tedious evenings spent entertaining his dull clients and associates. Not that it was exactly hard. All she had to do was look groomed, make polite conversation and give instructions.

Come to think of it that was pretty much what she did in a nutshell these days. She gave instructions to the chef about what everyone would eat and then, when it was served, everyone complimented her on how amazing the food had been, which always felt weird when she hadn't even shopped for it, let alone prepared it. She gave instructions to the agencies she hired staff from when they needed extra help, on top of the help they already had. On this occasion she'd 'instructed' that they needed an experienced cocktail maker to work behind the bar, plus three waiting staff who could pour drinks and serve dinner. This afternoon she'd instructed her hairdresser and her personal trainer on when she wanted her next lot of appointments to be and on Monday she would give instructions to their housekeeper who worked five days a week, the gardener and of course their two Filipino nannies who between them worked every day, meaning that Jennifer never had to 'do' anything.

A few weeks ago, on a rare night out with the girls she'd said as much but hadn't received much sympathy from Karen. 'Oh my heart bleeds,' she'd said. 'Well how about instructing them all to fuck off for the day and doing your own cooking and cleaning for a change? Or maybe, and call me crazy for suggesting it, try looking after your own kids for a whole twenty-four hours? You never know, you might enjoy it. Give Ant and Dec the day off.'

Jennifer's Filipino nannies happened to be called Deck and Annie, a source of great amusement to Karen, Esther and Lucy.

Karen had been particularly brutal because she was drunk but Jennifer was glad she hadn't sugar-coated what she really thought. It was just so difficult to explain to her friends that 'doing' everything herself actually sounded unbelievably appealing; liberating even, yet at the same time the mere idea of it frightened her half to death. Having so much help all the time had gradually made her feel superfluous to anyone's needs, especially when it came to the kids.

*

Tim had paid for maternity nurses to be there from day one. When their eldest, Edward, had been born she'd never forgotten the feeling of elation she'd had. She'd produced a human being, a breathing little person and furthermore, despite having him at The Portland, had managed to buck the trend and have a natural delivery. It had been painful, brutal, bloody. She was a total hero! It was the first time in a long time she'd felt worthwhile, clever almost. And then the maternity nurse had arrived and taken her little bundle away. Never had anything felt so utterly wrong.

Despite her protestations Tim had insisted. She never need have an uninterrupted sleep he'd said. She could remain in the marital bed at night and by day concentrate on getting her figure back.

This 'luxury' was the saddest thing she'd ever experienced. To this day she was certain it had contributed towards her postnatal depression. Only the worse the depression got, the more it was deemed a good idea for her to have more 'help'.

Sometimes she couldn't believe that she and Tim had gone on to have a further three children. Or more accurately she couldn't really understand why they'd bothered. Edward was thirteen now and on his way to becoming a moody teenager, Tilly was ten, Hattie was six and Jasper was four. They were four children with enormously different personalities, interests and needs. She loved all of them, of course, yet there was no getting away from the fact that neither she nor Tim had played much of a role in actually raising them. In fact sometimes she felt that as far he was concerned they'd been churned out like status symbols. The only thing that made her feel better about her mothering skills was that no matter how dubious they were, they were hundreds of times better than Tim's fathering ones. At least she'd changed the odd nappy herself, when she'd been allowed. At least she'd tried. Plus, much of her time was spent torturing herself with maternal guilt whereas she was pretty sure that for Tim, the way he was as a parent wasn't something that ever pricked his conscience. He paid for everything, so in a very old-fashioned sense he felt that was all that was required.

Now she slipped away from the drawing room leaving her guests (not one of whom she considered to be a friend) to mingle, drink champagne and eat their canapés.

Frankly she was grateful for an excuse to leave for a minute. Prior to Tim's request/order she'd been struggling to make small talk with the wife of his financial advisor. At one point things had got so desperate they'd discussed whether or not children should be allowed to give up the piano or not for *twenty-five minutes*.

Jennifer made her way through the corridors and into the spacious hallway, stopping only to check her appearance in a huge gilt-edged mirror which hung on one wall.

She looked immaculate. Her hair had been blow-dried that afternoon into the look which tended to be preferred by the ladies of Notting Hill and Chelsea. It was big, slightly stiff but with a wave at the bottom. Very Kate Middleton. She was wearing a new silk shift by

Stella McCartney which probably wasn't quite conservative enough for Tim's tastes but which she loved, with some gorgeous Marc Jacobs heels. Her skin was looking far younger than her thirty-eight years due mainly to some expertly injected Botox and aided by monthly facials. She looked rested, slim, toned and totally dead behind the eyes.

Her phone vibrated in her pocket. It was a text, one which improved her mood beyond measure. It was the fix she needed and she responded quickly before continuing her way to the staircase which led down to her vast kitchen. So vast in fact, it actually took up the basement floor of the entire house and was larger than most people's flats.

*

Downstairs, their chef, Joe, and two of the waiting staff were milling around, engaged in one activity or another.

'Hello Jennifer, everything all right?' asked Joe, treating her to a big friendly grin. He'd been with the family for four and a half years now.

'Fabulous thanks. The quail eggs are disappearing at a rate of knots as are those homemade cheese straws.'

'Oh good, that's what I like to hear.'

'I'm here to ask if you'd mind awfully going to the cellar and grabbing another bottle of the Montrachet for Jeremy? You know Jeremy, the one who's got a face like a side of beef.'

'I do indeed,' laughed Joe.

'I can get it if you want,' offered one of the young waiters.

'No, don't you worry,' insisted Joe. 'The starter's all plated up so I'm fine to go. Besides, it's best to make sure we open the right one eh? Some of those bottles are worth more than you'll earn in a year, young man.'

'Thanks Joe,' said Jennifer, leaving them all to it and clip-clopping out of the kitchen and back upstairs.

Back in the hallway she hesitated for a fraction of a second, checking to make sure no one was around. Then, certain she was alone, instead of making her way back to the party she turned left, heading with purpose towards the rear of the house and ultimately the largest of their three sitting rooms. She closed the door quietly behind her and picked her way across the room stealthily to the French doors which led out onto the garden, one of the largest in London. The striped, immaculate lawns almost went on for as far as the eye could see and the rest of the garden had been designed as if it belonged to a stately home with lots of topiary and neat beds which were completely colour co-ordinated. Despite having four children there wasn't a plastic slide in sight.

Jennifer ventured out onto the flagstones and tiptoed along the side of the house until she came to another door which was slightly ajar. As soon as she reached it a hand appeared and yanked her inside.

She immediately giggled and felt a lurch of happiness and desire as those same hands drew her in and then started to explore every inch of her body.

'Oh my god you feel so good in this dress.'

'Do I?'

'Yeah, you look amazing in it too. Absolutely gorgeous.'

'Oh, I do love you,' she gasped, her heart full to the brim with love and lust. How was it even possible to feel this turned on so quickly?

'I love you too, gorgeous girl,' said Joe, his hands everywhere, his mouth in her hair, kissing her face, her neck. 'What's the situation later?'

'I don't know,' she said doubtfully. 'You know how he gets at these things, he'll probably be up till five am, talking utter shit, but if I can come and see you I will. I'll have to play it by ear.'

'Please try,' groaned Joe, pulling her into him 'I've missed you so much it's ridiculous. It's been far too long since I've had my lovely girl lying next to me.'

'I know, you don't need to tell me,' said Jennifer, wide-eyed. 'I've been pining for you the whole time.'

'But if you can't get away, no worries my love, I don't want it to be a stress.'

'OK, speaking of which, how long have I been?'

'Don't know,' said Joe, pulling away, but stroking her face so tenderly she experienced the most enormous pang for him. His expression was pained, par for the course these days. Their affair was getting harder and harder the deeper they fell.

'I love you,' she said for the second time, meaning it passionately.

'I love you too, little squidger,' said Joe, his Yorkshire accent such a contrast from Tim's clipped public school tones. Then again everything about him was.

'Don't forget the wine,' she whispered, tearing herself reluctantly away and back outside.

'I won't,' he said, disappearing back towards the cellar.

*

'Where've you been?' asked Tim five minutes later, having spotted her as soon as she'd reappeared in the drawing room. 'I asked you to get more wine, not drive to France and stamp on the grapes yourself.'

'Sorry,' she replied. 'I was just making sure everything's under control for dinner. I think we should start thinking about getting everyone into the dining room. Otherwise we won't be eating till ten.'

'Right you are.'

*

As the evening progressed, Jennifer's mood took a serious nosedive.

She did her best to be engaging, to be the perfect host, but her heart wasn't in it. It wasn't even in the same room. It was languishing downstairs in the kitchens where Joe was of course. She played with her food. Joe had cooked the most incredible rib of beef which he'd served with creamy artichoke mash, perfectly cooked vegetables and a fricassee of mushrooms that was out of this world. But she had no appetite. The latest anti-depressant she'd been prescribed made her feel permanently a bit wired and not for the first time she wondered if they were a waste of time. Was she actually clinically depressed? She was starting to doubt it gravely because she never felt even remotely miserable when she was alone with Joe. Quite the opposite. And yet for years doctors had told her she had depression when in fact there was a distinct possibility she'd just been fed up, bored or in a bad mood.

*

For what felt like the thousandth time that hour her thoughts returned to the man who had been her best friend for two years now and her lover for seven months; seven amazing, painful, confusing, sad, yet unbelievably golden months. Since having Joe in her life she'd reassessed everything. She was permanently saturated in intense stress and guilt, not surprising given that she was committing adultery, and yet also felt more *herself* than she had in a long while.

Joe, it seemed, was her soul-mate, her rightful other half, but while that bit was clear, the situation was so complicated. For both of them.

Joe was a good man, for whom sleeping with someone

else's wife had never been the plan. He'd fallen hard and was never going to be satisfied simply with being Jennifer's bit on the side. The two of them were smitten, utterly and hopelessly in love to the point of obsession. Every meeting was tinged with tragedy, with worry about the future and with deep frustration. Whenever they had sex, the strength of her feeling meant she always ended up in tears at the end because she was in a terribly painful quandary. If she were to leave Tim she'd be breaking up her family, turning her back on a man who may be flawed but had always stuck by her. She'd be doing the 'wrong' thing no matter how right it felt and would be losing everything familiar to her. If she stayed however, she'd ultimately lose Joe and that was too unbearable even to contemplate.

The situation was starting to make her feel ill. Having to decide whether or not to leave the father of your children was excruciatingly hard. She'd also been with Tim since university and to this day people constantly told her how ridiculously lucky she was to have landed him. As if she was almost a booby prize by comparison. Then, of course, there was the lifestyle she enjoyed, the money. Tim had made her sign a prenup and being the romantic idiot she was she'd agreed happily, wanting to prove the point that she wasn't with him for his cash.

Now, as much as Joe told her there were more important things in life than money she had her children to think of and was unable to comprehend how she would cope, having been dependent on Tim for so long. Was she mad for even considering leaving him? Look what she'd be giving up? She glanced around the opulent dining room, the work of an over-enthusiastic interior designer desperate to justify his grotesque fee and the bunch of corpses who were sat around the Louis XVII table. On second thoughts…

'So tell me Jennifer, what are your plans for the summer?' asked Maurice Fellowes, one of the largest shareholders of reUNIon who Tim had cruelly placed her next to.

Maurice was quite literally the short straw from what was already an unbearably tedious crowd. In fairness, not all the entertaining they did was quite this bad. Sometimes they had uproarious dinner parties with clever, creative people. People who had helped make reUNIon what it was or others whom they simply knew for social reasons. However, these days reUNIon was only a fraction of the business which Tim was involved with and it seemed to Jennifer the more money you accrued, the more you were obliged to socialise with people you wouldn't ordinarily give the time of day to if you were skint and didn't need to.

'Well, we're going to our place in the South of France as soon as the children break up and then, at the end of August, Tim and I leave them there and we go to the Earl of Bradwick's boat. You know Bradwick I'm sure?'

'Oh yes, frightfully nice chap.'

Jennifer smiled pleasantly, wishing she could think of

a reason to go and see Joe in the kitchen. The thought of being separated from him for a whole summer was unbearable. She was already determined to concoct some story so she could return to the UK for at least a week. He'd asked her to come to Yorkshire with him and there was nothing on earth she would rather do than spend time hidden away in a little cottage with him. It would be heaven. By contrast, the prospect of spending weeks in luxury with Tim was one that filled her with nothing but a sense of dread and foreboding.

She sighed heavily.

'So what are you and Margaret doing for the summer, Maurice?' she asked politely, despite the fact she couldn't give even the smallest of shits.

'We're braving Cornwall, and just praying it doesn't rain like it did last year.'

How brave, thought Jennifer wryly, fully aware that the house they owned there was more like a castle and was fully staffed. She was pretty sure they'd survive.

'And then we'll be going on to Tuscany where we shall stay until the end of September, which is always the nicest month there I find. This is excellent meat by the way. Wonderful food, you're a marvellous host Jennifer.'

'Thank you,' she said. As it occurred to her then that he'd just complimented Joe's meat it made her laugh inside. She wondered briefly if that made her a very sordid individual.

Urgh, what she wouldn't give for a normal night out. With normal people. Thank god she still had Karen, Lucy and Esther in her life, although even with her old friends, having so much money still sometimes created problems, no matter how hard they all tried to pretend it didn't. Not for her. She couldn't care less about it and would gladly have given them all as much as they wanted. Writing cheques meant nothing to her and if paying meant they all got to do things together she was more than happy to facilitate that. But her friends had their pride, and how much generosity it was appropriate to accept was one of the things Karen found particularly tricky to handle. As a result it was often them, as opposed to her, who were guilty of making an issue out of her wealth. Sometimes they didn't include her in stuff because they assumed she'd turn her nose up at it, when actually she would have loved to have been invited. At other times, when she invited *them* to events or to come abroad with her and Tim, they couldn't necessarily afford the flights or the spending money that was required but didn't know how to tell her without it sounding like they wanted her to cover it. The one saving grace was that every April, without fail, they allowed her to pay for the four of them to go on a girls' skiing trip. It was always the best week of her entire year.

Her phone vibrated in her pocket. Expertly she managed to slip it out and onto her lap, her gaze never leaving Maurice's rheumy eyes as he blathered on about restaurants in Tuscany and how much he loved peasant food.

As soon as she thought she could get away with it, for a

mere second, her eyes flickered onto her lap. The text read 'Hello sexy. Hope you're not bored rigid. Have put something special in Tim's dessert. Hopefully see you later xxx'

WEDNESDAY

'Why does everything in life have to arrive ruddy flat packed?' swore Max, who was struggling to make sense of the instructions he was holding. Not surprising given he was staring at the section which was written in Swedish.

'It can't be that hard,' said Jennifer.

'Eurgh,' said Max, which didn't mean much but was simply an expression of how hung-over he was feeling. Last night Ted had come round to keep him company (to watch Sky Sports) while Jennifer was out with the girls, and between them they'd managed to get through more beer and red wine than was probably necessary. Apart from a bit of a furry mouth he hadn't felt too bad at work, but the hangover had finally caught up and now he was severely regretting his ill-advised decision to embark on a major bit of DIY. The fact that Jennifer had predicted that precisely this would happen only made matters worse.

Meanwhile, Polly and Eadie were watching agog, thrilled because they knew full well that whilst bedtime might be imminent it would also be impossible due to the chaos in Polly's room. There were bits of wardrobe every-where, plus the contents of Max's tool box all over the floor.

'Yeah, come on Daddy,' joined in Polly now. 'It can't be that hard.'

'When I need your opinion…' he said, frowning at her. 'Christ Jennifer, in future perhaps we should pay a bit more for furniture so that it doesn't need making entirely from scratch.'

Jennifer was livid. 'Er, hang on a minute, the reason I went out of my way to drive all the way to flipping Brent Cross to get this was because you moaned so much when the last credit card bill came in. I thought you wanted us to cut back!'

'If I moaned it was only because you spent fifty pounds on your mother's birthday present,' Max muttered, refus-ing to catch her eye. He knew how inflammatory this com-ment would be.

'You're out of order,' seethed Jennifer.

Max just shrugged.

'Why shouldn't I treat my mum on her birthday? And why should I be made to feel guilty every single time I buy something from our joint account?'

'And why haven't I got any furniture for my room?' piped up Eadie, looking miffed.

'Because you don't need it,' said Jennifer, taking a monumentally huge deep breath to bring her temper down. 'You've got a whacking great wardrobe in your room and poor old Pol has had to make do with no hanging space at all until now.'

'Hold that a minute, Jen,' said Max, still looking flummoxed. 'I think this screw needs to go in there.'

'Are you sure?'

'No, but at this point I can't stare at these stupid indecipherable things any more and you never know it just might be worth a go, so humour me.'

Jennifer rolled her eyes.

'What?' snapped Max.

'OK,' said Jennifer, growing tired of the grumpy tone of voice he was using with her. 'Firstly I'm wondering why you have to do this now when the girls need to get to bed, when it could easily wait until the weekend, and secondly I'm still furious that you're making me feel bad for spending fifty quid on my mum when she's helped us out so much lately. And thirdly I was just thinking how quickly Steve would have had these up.'

This last comment was a reference to her ex which she was confident her husband would find amusing. She'd made her point so now hoped to cajole him out of his mood with a private joke.

She couldn't have been more wrong. At first he just gave her a look and a faint smile but seconds later, once he'd had the chance to fully digest what she'd said, he retaliated in a way which seemed really uncalled for.

'As it happens I'd rather get this out of the way, as opposed to spending my day off on Saturday doing it, and

with regard to Steve, we can't all be good at everything,'
he said, looking decidedly pissed off. 'Just as you aren't
a breadwinner like Judith for example, I'm not good at
sodding DIY. Though if you would rather be with someone who is, perhaps you should look Steve up and tell him
you're on the market. I'm sure he'd leap at the chance to
meet up.'

'All right,' said Jennifer, stung by his hurtful words.
'There's no need to jump down my throat. I was only joking. Usually you're always up for a laugh about Steve.
And there's no need to bring up frigging Judith's name or
to pit me against that silly witch. Or to point out I'm not
a "breadwinner". That's just nasty. And if that's what *you*
want then perhaps you shouldn't have made me feel so
guilty about wanting to have a career.'

'Oh get over yourself,' said Max.

Now Jennifer really was fuming.

'Stop arguing,' barked Eadie fiercely. Both children
had gone very quiet up until this point.

'Sorry love,' said Max immediately, 'we're not arguing, just having a debate.'

*

That was rich thought Jennifer, who was itching to say as
much only didn't for the girls' sakes. They didn't need to
hear them squabbling any more. Not for the first time she
despaired over Max's recent attitude towards her. Why
was he speaking to her so dismissively? And how dare

he put her down for not being an equal breadwinner. That part was unforgiveable, especially given the fact that as well as everything else she had a job which paid for all sorts of bits and pieces. He was an arsehole. The thing she used to treasure most about their relationship was the fact that he was her best friend and that, together, they usually saw the funny side in everything. She missed it and realised then that their relationship was in decline and heading for a slow and painful death unless they did something about it and fast. The saddest thing of all was that it wouldn't take much to get things back on track. They just needed to be nice to each other, to treat one another like friends. Something they'd managed to do even when the children were babies and life was much harder than it was now. Familiarity breeds contempt, it was the biggest cliché of them all.

THE PAST — MAX

Max and Jennifer were on a mission. A mission to leave the house, something Jennifer hadn't done for ten whole days now, ever since she'd arrived home from hospital with her second baby girl.

Of course, when you're recovering from a caesarean section there's really no point attempting much. She had, after all, been opened up like a tin of peaches in order to produce her own fruit. The hours leading up to major surgery hadn't exactly been restful either. She'd endured an intense thirty-six hours of ultimately pointless contracting due to the fact Polly's noggin was in totally the wrong position to ever allow a natural delivery. Still, as Max had kept reminding her, it could be worse. If she were a Tudor or medieval woman, she'd be dead. Not that this had come as a massive comfort at the time.

Physically she'd been through an awful lot, but now, thirteen days after the birth, she was getting better in small increments. She was capable of mild shuffling and of get-

ting in and out of oversize tracksuits and Ugg boots all
by herself. Bending down to put tights on still couldn't
be contemplated and other small tasks had become huge
mountains to climb. Post-op and with a new-born and tod-
dler to cope with, simply finding the time to have a shower
for example was a huge deal and her first post-op poo
was worthy of a phone call to her mother. So, the whole
family attempting to leave the house en masse, dressed,
and with everything they needed in order to go shopping,
was always going to be a drama of epic proportions.

As she and Max packed bags, cajoled Eadie into getting dressed, changed nappies and generally tried to make
it all happen, Jennifer couldn't help wondering what the
hell she was going to do when her husband had to return
to work the week after. How would she ever cope?

'I'll never manage,' she whimpered now.

'Nonsense,' said Max, trying in vain to collapse the
new, so far unused double buggy so he could get it into the
boot of the car.

'You can't leave me. Ever. You'll have to resign and go
on the dole.'

'You'll be fine,' he reassured her, albeit absent-
mindedly. 'How on earth does this frigging thing work?
Eadie darling, get out of the way please, Daddy's trying
not to lose the plot here.'

Eadie looked militant. She had done ever since Polly
had arrived, clearly not at all sure how she felt about this
young upstart, this pretender to her throne, pitching up and

taking her mum's attention away. Polly was a sucky baby and pretty much never off the breast so it was hard for Jennifer to give her eldest the attention she required.

Jennifer winced as Polly sucked away. The idea was to stuff her to the brim in order to give them all more shopping time. Her nipples were on fire though and the fact she was so exhausted wasn't exactly helping her pain threshold. She'd probably averaged around four hours sleep a night for over a fortnight now. Not that Max was faring much better. Polly was sleeping, or not as the case may be, in their room and Jennifer was insisting he helped out with the odd bottle during the night. Although in reality, whenever she missed a feed her boobs would swell to such gigantic milky proportions she'd end up positively itching to ram them back into the baby's mouth again just to relieve the pain.

Still, they were muddling through, helped by enormous amounts of hormones and the wondrous feeling that they'd pulled off some sort of miracle by producing an actual real-life person. And love. The fact they loved one another and their offspring helped enormously.

Now though, as Max struggled to collapse the monstrous double buggy she suspected their 'love' was about to be sorely tested.

'Look, just try and cast your mind back to how they did it,' said Max, looking despairingly at his wife. 'You must have some idea surely?'

'Don't call me Shirley,' she retorted, easing Polly off

her boob. Gingerly she stood up and placed the baby casually over her shoulder in order to rub her back and wind her. 'I told you. I think you pull that lever thing and then sort of bend it backwards.'

Max sighed. 'I'm not being funny but surely you must have thought it worth finding out how to use it when you bought the bloody thing.'

'Obviously,' said Jennifer, feeling defensive. She collapsed back onto a kitchen chair. She had been shown numerous times how to do it but for the life of her couldn't remember. 'I was eight months pregnant,' she said huffily. 'So it's not like I had a proper working brain. Besides, you need a degree in physics to work it out. Why can't they just make these things simple?'

Almost by way of reply Polly suddenly did the most enormous belch and puked down her mother's back.

'Oh god,' sighed Jennifer, defeated.

'OK,' said Max, literally throwing the double buggy to the ground in disgust. 'Unless we can collapse it we can't get it into the car, so we're going to have to think again. What if we take the sling and Eadie walks?'

'Can you get me a tissue or something? I'm covered in sick.'

Max raced to the sink and chucked a damp cloth at Jennifer which she caught skilfully with her free hand.

'It's not going to work,' she said, sponging herself down with one hand, trying not to drop the baby with the other. 'Eadie will go a few yards and start whinging and if it's going to take ages we can't go anyway. We need to leave now so that we've got enough time to get there and back before Polly needs another feed. Especially seeing as her tummy's basically empty again and I'm not whacking these udders out in any old place. I'm also not going out only to end up sitting in the car feeding.'

'Right,' said Max. 'Well I don't know why you got rid of the old buggy.'

'Not helpful.'

'No it wasn't.'

'I meant your comment wasn't helpful. I got rid of the bloody thing because there wasn't room in the hall for two massive wheeled contraptions.'

'OK. Look, I'll just put Eadie on my shoulders then, or carry her. Let's just go though, otherwise we'll never get out.'

'OK,' whimpered Jennifer. 'Except next week when I've got to get her to nursery on my own what am I going to do? I've got stitches. I won't be able to carry her then. I need a buggy, Max.'

To Max's horror, Jennifer suddenly succumbed to a huge rush of hormones, and started to weep.

'Right, you stay here with the baby,' Max said, realising how much he needed to take charge of the situation, '…and I'll take Eadie with me. Where's the video camera?'

'What are you on about?' said Jennifer, who wasn't even entirely sure what she was crying about, though being covered in sick might have something to do with it. Still, by the sounds of it at least she didn't have to go out any more and for that she was pathetically grateful. She wasn't really fit for public consumption and there was nothing she wanted to buy anyway, unless you could buy sleep.

*

An hour and a half later and Max was back having filmed a slightly bemused and self-conscious sales assistant at John Lewis demonstrating slowly and methodically exactly how the new buggy folded and collapsed.

'You're brilliant,' said Jennifer, as she watched the footage over and over again. She hadn't been as impressed by anything for ages. 'A proper evil genius.'

'No, you're brilliant,' said Max, handling the buggy like an expert, unfolding and folding it repeatedly. 'There's no way on earth I would have remembered how to do it either. Stupid machine.'

Later that night, Jennifer was sat in the kitchen feeding Polly (for a change), Eadie was fast asleep and Max was washing and sterilising bottles and tidying up.

Jennifer was so exhausted her eyes were practically rolling to the back of her head. Still, as she looked down at her little bundle with her soft, downy cheeks and tiny wrinkled foot which was poking out the end of the blanket she was wrapped in, she felt a huge pang of love.

God her back ached though, the after effect of the

epidural. And she still felt very strange in her under-carriage. Her stitches were particularly sore tonight too. She was due a painkiller and had probably overdone the shuffling today. As for her boobs, they were literally burning.

'Ow,' said Max, throwing down his tea towel in disgust.

'What?' asked Jennifer, squinting at him through tired, grainy eyes.

'My hands are so sore. So dry! Must be from all the washing up. They really hurt.'

Jennifer couldn't believe what she was hearing.

'I'll have to get some hand cream, they're actually incredibly painful...'

As Max looked up and caught his wife's eye he trailed off.

'Oh,' he said, not taking long to cotton on as he took in the pathetic state his wife was in.

'Oh god,' he chuckled. 'How much of a prat am I? I'm so sorry. Shall I shut up about my slightly chafed fingers?'

'If you know what's good for you, you big lightweight,' said Jennifer, suddenly finding the whole thing very amusing. She started to laugh. 'Oh shit, actually don't make me laugh because it hurts my stitches, you know, where I've been *sliced open*?'

'Ha ha, Oh my god don't,' wailed Max, laughing really hard now. 'Oh poor me, my fingers are terribly dry. I can't bear it. My wife doesn't understand, she's so unsympathetic sitting there with her non-chafed fingers.'

Still laughing, he discarded his tea towel and came to sit next to his wife. 'Oh Jen, I'm so in awe of you. You've been so brave and so bloody amazing.'

'Have I?' she said, feeling choked.

'Oh my god yes, I mean look. Look what you've done,' he said, gesturing to Polly who had fallen asleep on her mum's boob. He bent down to take his daughter, still handling her like she was the most fragile thing in the world and kissed the top of her head. Then he kissed his wife tenderly on the cheek. 'And you did it with no fuss.'

'Apart from when I called you the "c" word and threatened to kill you.'

'Apart from when you called me the "c" word and threatened to kill me,' he agreed, regarding her with real affection. 'I think you're amazing Jen, you're my hero. I love you so bloody much. And I know sometimes you find it hard being stuck at home and get frustrated but I want you to know that you are doing the most incredible job.'

'But will you ever fancy me again?' she asked. 'Look at me, I'm a big fat lactating cow and I look so pale and tired and ugly.'

'Oh shut up you silly moo. I love you to bits and to me you're the most beautiful woman in the world. I don't care what you're wearing or how tired you are; to me you'll always be my girl in the pink dress.'

'Really?' squeaked Jennifer.

'Really,' said Max. 'You're still the love of my life.

Admittedly I've seen you look better than you do this precise second and you might want to wash your hair at some point, though I've got nothing against dreadlocks per se...'

Jennifer laughed and then gasped as her stitches twinged again.

'Painkiller?'

'Please.

'And then shall we go to bed? Not that there's much point of course,' yawned Max, who had quite impressive black rings under his eyes, 'given that this little one will be up in a few hours. But we could give sleep a go I guess. And we can also have a cuddle.'

'That would be nice. But no hanky panky.'

'What do you take me for?' Max winked. 'Besides, that tracksuit's good birth control for now. It stinks of sick.'

WEDNESDAY CONTINUED

'Right, come on then you two,' said Jennifer firmly. 'It's time for bed and your father clearly isn't going to be finished for hours so Polly will have to go in our bed and I'll move you later.'

'O-oh,' whined Eadie. 'That's not fair.'

'Tough,' said Jennifer.

Once the girls were finally asleep, Jennifer got the chance to tell her husband exactly what she thought of how he'd behaved earlier.

'Every chance you get you compare me to that bloody woman. Why do you do it?'

'I don't,' said Max.

'You do,' said Jennifer, despairing. 'You bring her name up all the time to the point where at one stage I even thought you might be having an affair with her. Though in reality I think you'd be more discreet about it if you were. As it is you're permanently going on about her or comparing me to her. It's not bloody on.'

'You're being paranoid,' said Max, just a tad too defensively.

Jennifer leapt on her instinct.

'What? What is it, Max? What aren't you telling me? Do you have feelings for her or something?'

'No,' he said, outraged.

'Promise,' she said faintly, suddenly terrified in case she was about to discover something she didn't really want to confront as a result of her digging.

'Will you stop going on,' said Max, looking monumentally pissed off.

'It's just you're being so snappy with me at the moment, Max.'

'Not this again,' he shouted. 'Will you stop going on and on about how I've changed. It's driving me mad.'

Jennifer blinked and wondered whether to press the issue further. After all he'd kind of just illustrated her point. Plus she still wasn't wholly convinced there wasn't something to get to the bottom of, and yet if there was, did she even want to know?

Max let out a huge sigh. 'Look Jen, I'm sorry. I'm tired and grumpy and bored of having the same conversation over and over again.'

Jennifer's eyes filled with tears and she sniffed hard in an attempt to keep them at bay.

'Look come here, look how keyed up you are. Relax these shoulders,' said Max, coming over and kneading her shoulders with his hands. They were so rigid it hurt but in a pleasurable kind of way.

'Hmm,' muttered Jennifer, still not wholly placated.

She closed her eyes. 'That's nice,' she mumbled, giving in to the sensation.

'Good,' said Max. 'Maybe that should be your birthday present. A nice massage somewhere.'

'OK.' A solitary tear escaped and ran down her cheek. She quickly wiped it away.

'Or perhaps ring Steve and ask him to do it seeing as he was so brilliant with his hands.'

Jennifer pulled away, ready to retaliate but to her relief she could see immediately that Max was only joking.

'Idiot,' she said softly, playfully hitting him on the chest.

'Aah Steve,' mused Max, a smug grin on his face. 'Do you remember the party?'

'Course I do,' said Jennifer.

How could she forget? It was the day she'd met her future husband and the day poor old Steve had suddenly realised he had major competition. She still felt mildly guilty even now after all these years. Steve had been nothing but lovely to her and if Max hadn't turned up she'd probably still be with him. But Max *had* turned up and ultimately she'd gone for it because she'd recognised a twinkle of something in his eye that she'd suspected Steve would never quite be able to muster up.

She looked at him now, hating how detached she felt from him almost as much as she hated the fact she'd had these suspicions and doubts about him. She'd always trusted her husband but lately it was almost as if she didn't trust herself. It wasn't that she'd ever do anything but she definitely felt at a bit of a crossroads in general. Recently she'd found herself thinking about the past all the time, about how things had turned out and how things might have been. So perhaps she was projecting her own rubbish onto Max? In which case she needed to stop, because it simply wasn't fair. She sighed. When was she going to shake this miserable feeling of malcontent?

THE PAST — STEVE

January 2000

At long last the most anticipated New Year's Eve in history was finally out of the way and Jennifer couldn't have been happier. It was enormously comforting to know she'd never be required to suffer the question 'what are you doing for the millennium' ever again. Well, not unless she planned on living for another thousand years. And in the unlikely event she did, at least by that point she'd be perfectly within her rights to answer, 'Nothing. I'm not doing anything. I don't get out much these days because by rights I should be *dead*.'

The pressure to do something 'amaaazing' had bored the pants off her. At work, what everyone was going to 'do' for the big night had been all anyone could talk about for months. Inevitably of course there had been a handful of smug people with bigger pay packets than her who had been able to say things like 'We're off to the Pyrenees', or 'I'm going dolphin watching in San Diego' and even 'we're just going to a small bash for five thousand, in

Paris, with fireworks'. It goes without saying that these people didn't just earn more than her but also must have been stupidly organised. She and Karen hadn't been able to find even a local restaurant for them and their friends to go to, that wasn't either fully booked or extortionate, so as far as they could work out this lot must have booked these 'experiences of a lifetime' events when they were toddlers.

In the end, Pete and Karen had hosted the night at theirs. Dinner for twelve with lots of music and, if that had been that, it might have been a pretty enjoyable evening. As it was however, some bright spark had thought it would be a good idea to splash out on a couple of grams of cocaine, given the hugeness of the occasion. Only it was cut with laxative, so all taking it really achieved was to make everybody in desperate need for the toilet. Unsurprisingly it wasn't long before the evening had taken a slightly grim turn for the worse. The bathroom had been permanently occupied, either because people were inside talking incoherent babble while preparing to shove some more powder up their noses or, because they were about to soil themselves. At times there'd even been a queue. Those who finally made it into the bathroom, after a buttock clenching wait, ventured out again looking sheepish and despite it being minus five outside, the window was required to remain open for the entirety of the evening. Not massively pleasant.

Karen had invited Pete's cousin David to the dinner,

purely so she could try and match-make him with Jennifer. David was relatively good looking but had been excruciatingly dull even before he'd got a line of crap cocaine up his nose. Mainly due to the drugs, his mouth had gone incredibly dry (unlike his sense of humour), to the extent that his tongue kept getting stuck to the roof of his mouth as he talked. Only to Jennifer's horrified fascination, instead of deciding that talking therefore probably wasn't worth the effort, he'd battled on regardless, waffling away and only trying to combat his startlingly bad dry mouth by glugging back litres of red wine. This did nothing to solve the problem but everything to ensure that over time his teeth were stained red and his breath became properly vile. Jennifer would honestly rather have slept with a member of her immediate family than have sex with David.

The final nail in that possible date coffin was delivered once and for all, hard and severely, when he proceeded to talk at length about how reUNIon was such a great invention and how his sister had reunited with her now fiancée on it...

By this stage Jennifer was seriously considering getting a cab home despite the fact it wasn't even midnight yet.

*

The next morning she woke up to the first day of the new millennium feeling not only hung-over and rancid, but also horribly anxious. Dumping Tim may have been a huge mistake. For a start she hadn't met anybody else even remotely worth seeing since they'd split up and to make matters far worse, he was now a bloody millionaire, a fact that seemed to be rammed down her throat wherever she went.

Deep down she knew she'd done the 'right' thing because she didn't really miss him. However, what she worried about was that if no one else came along she might always regret leaving him. Ending up with a clever, multi-millionaire would have been far better than nothing.

*

On the upside, the millennium New Year was over and for that she was both grateful and relieved.

So frankly the greyness and general frugality of January was very welcome, until Wednesday 7th January when her boiler broke down. And then it was just shit.

*

'Coming,' called Jennifer, rushing to answer the door, wishing she had slippers on as the floor tiles were so cold underfoot, even with tights on. Her tiny one bedroom flat in Tooting, which was hers and hers alone, and therefore a space she usually adored, was completely freezing. Last night she'd slept in a tracksuit and a coat but when she'd woken up, her nose, the only thing that hadn't been submerged under the covers, had been cold like a dog's. Unable to have a hot shower, her hair resembled a bird's nest and was far greasier than she'd normally ever allow it to be. Getting ready for work this morning she'd tried to solve this dilemma by scraping it all back into a pony-tail and had compensated with extra make-up, which on her pale, winter-worn face, made her look a bit like a drag queen. She was cold to the bone and simply couldn't warm up.

'Hi,' said the affable looking plumber, who was standing on her doorstep and who was hopefully going to be the answer to her prayers.

'Oh my gosh, thank you so much for coming. I'm literally desperate,' she said, pulling her coat even further around her. Underneath she was wearing a suit, ready for the day ahead. 'I don't suppose there's any chance you could have it fixed sooner rather than later, it's just I've actually got a massive day at work and should really be there right now but didn't think I could cope returning to this ice block again.'

'Er, well, give us a chance to at least have a look at what's happening and I'll let you know. But if I can, I shall get it sorted for you asap.'

He had an Essex accent.

'Oh gosh, I'm so sorry, you must think I'm insane. I think the cold may have actually frozen my brain.' said Jennifer, standing back to let him in, a good start in terms of him being able to fix anything. 'Then again I may have just got confused because I think it might actually be warmer outside than it is in here.'

'No worries,' said the plumber politely.

'Sorry, I'm Jennifer,' she said, starting again.

'Pleased to meet you, I'm Steve.'

*

Forty-five minutes later and the boiler had clunked into action, hot water was swooshing round the pipes and Jennifer was free to escape to work, unwashed, but confident that when she returned she wouldn't have to sleep in a coat.

'Thank you so much,' she gushed.

'No worries,' said Steve. 'Glad I could get it sorted and thanks for the tea.'

She was struck by what a nice face he had. During all the time they'd been chatting away, he'd been on his knees half inside the cupboard where the boiler lived so all she'd really been able to examine so far had been his backside. It was a nice backside but it was rather heart-warming to discover that he had a face to match. It was an open face which wasn't dazzlingly good looking but was really pleasant. He had a good even smile and blue eyes. He smiled back at her. 'So, you off to work now then, you said you're in marketing but what does that actually involve?'

'Er, well, basically it's all about identifying who your customer is, then creating value for them and making sure you keep them,' said Jennifer. She really did have to get going, so went to get her bag so she could write Steve a cheque and leave.

'Yeah I know that,' he said, rolling his eyes. 'What do you take me for? What I mean is who do you do marketing for? Or, if you like, who's your market?'

'Oh right,' she said, surprised. She grinned at him, though as she did, her teeth almost chattered together she was still so cold. She honestly felt like she might never be warm again.

'Big questions,' she said, deflecting them, mainly because she was in a rush and her mind at this point was now fully focused on the meeting she desperately needed to get to.

'Sorry. You've got to go haven't you?' he said, taking the hint.

'I do I'm afraid,' she replied, rooting around in her bag until she finally came across a biro at the bottom. 'How much is that then?'

'Eighty,' said Steve.

'O-K,' said Jennifer, trying to mask her disappointment as she scribbled down the amount. There was no way she'd be getting the shoes she'd been lusting after this month. She should have been a plumber. She ripped the cheque out and handed it over.

'Thanks a lot. So anyway, sorry, because I know you're in a rush but I don't suppose, and I promise I never usually do this, but do you fancy going for a drink one night?' asked Steve suddenly. As Jennifer looked up to check she'd heard right his cheeks flamed red. 'And I promise, no more dull questions about work.'

'Er…I don't know,' replied Jennifer honestly.

'OK, no worries, I shouldn't have put you on the spot,' said Steve, turning away and bending back down to rummage in his tool bag as if he suddenly needed to find something when really he was obviously just masking his embarrassment.

Jennifer regarded him. He seemed like a perfectly decent bloke and he had just fixed her boiler. Plus, who else did she think she had lined up exactly? Pete's cousin David? Her last meaningful relationship had been with Tim and that had ended over two years ago. She'd had a couple of terrible dates, thanks to being forced by Karen to give online dating a go, and a one-night stand she could hardly bear to think about it had been so unbearably clunky.

So why would she now turn down a date with a man who had all his own teeth, four limbs, was seemingly nice and who had just saved her, definitely from hypothermia, if not death by frostbite? Was she insane?

'Actually…I'd love to go for a drink,' she said shyly.

'Really?' He looked pleasingly delighted and flashed her a wide grin.

'Yeah,' she grinned back. His smile was infectious. He had lovely teeth.

'Great, that's really good then,' he said. 'OK, well I've got your number, I'll give you a call and perhaps we could go for dinner after or something?'

'That would be very nice,' she said. They both stood

there, still grinning but now also feeling mildly awkward.

'So...anyway...' she said, reaching for the front door at the exact same time he did.

'Oh sorry,' he said.

'No, no, after you,' she said as he went to grab his tool-bag, realising they were now going to have to cope with leaving the flat at the same time and therefore continuing the conversation even though really it was clearly time for it to end.

Feeling gauche they shuffled out of the door together.

'OK, well I'll see you soon then,' said Steve once they were both outside and Jennifer had locked the door behind her. 'I'm just going this way, to the van.'

'Oh...er right,' said Jennifer, now wondering whether to pretend she was headed the other way but knowing it would only make her even more late 'Um...I'm going that way too actually, towards the tube.'

'Oh cool,' he said, his face colouring a little.

They ended up strolling down the road, together but not, both smiling manfully despite the awkwardness of the situation. Eventually Jennifer decided to do them both a favour by saying something. 'So where do you live then, Steve?' she said at the precise moment he decided to say, 'Well, this is me, my van's parked here.'

Their sentences collided awkwardly.

'Oh right...well...not to worry then,' said Jennifer, cringing and feeling unbelievably self-conscious by this point yet also really hoping he would definitely ring her. There was something about him that appealed to her more and more by the second.

'At the moment I'm staying with a mate in Mitcham though…'

'Oh great, not too far then I suppose,' she said. 'O-K …well…see you. Give me a ring.'

'Will do,' he said watching her go up the street. And although he knew it hadn't been the smoothest of meetings and that he wasn't going to win any points for his chatting up technique, Steve drove away feeling chuffed and had a little spring in his step for the rest of the day. You see, underneath all that make-up and that huge coat he could tell that Jennifer Drew was cute. More than cute. She was gorgeous. His cup of tea. Strong and sweet.

PRESENT DAY

'Jen, I don't know if you can hear me, but it's me, Max…'

Jennifer waited for him to continue but when silence followed she assumed she'd imagined what she thought she'd just heard. But then he spoke again.

'….anyway, the doctor's think it's worth a go. Talking to you that is, so I'm going to sit and chat anyway, just in case.'

It was strange. She kind of understood what he was saying on the surface and yet at the same time it was as if he were speaking a foreign language. She strongly suspected her brain couldn't really cope with the task of listening and understanding at the same time. Instead the words were just noise really.

'We're all really missing you. It's very quiet at home without you. The girls are fine. They know Mummy's having a long sleep and they say a little prayer for you every night. I'm keeping close tabs on them and the school have been brilliant actually, especially Miss Kelly who's really been keeping an eye on Pol. So that's all OK.

Think they might be getting a bit fed up with my cooking though…'

Max's voice cracked and he stopped talking for a moment, though Jennifer had no clue that the pause was necessary so he could regain his composure. She was still numb to reality. He cleared his throat.

'For that matter I am too. Anyway, I've brought a paper with me so I thought I might just read some of it out to you.'

*

But Jennifer had tuned out again; had slipped back to where she'd come from, with intent, for the last time she'd emerged from a portal she'd noticed that the one to the left, the one marked Aidan was growing faint. She'd had a strong inkling at the time that if she wanted to find out anything else from that parallel universe that she'd have to do it quickly, while it still existed. She'd even considered what might happen if it closed while she was inside. Would she be trapped? Would she remain Jennifer from that life forever? She hoped that wasn't a possibility. There was nothing about that life that made her feel proud or happy particularly. Had she gone with Aidan it seemed she'd have had a forlorn existence compared to the one she enjoyed with Max. In her real life she'd got her education, stayed in touch with her friends and family and ultimately gone on to create a safe, secure and largely happy family unit of her own. In the world of Aidan she felt sorry for Nathan. Sorry for her own son. The son she might have had...

As the drop began she was suddenly desperate to know that there was some form of resolution, if not for her then for the boy. He needed his extended family she decided. Not just a worn-out mum and a lazy, workshy dad.

She arrived. The portal was weaker than ever and as she glided towards it she felt more nervous than she had about anything in the whole of her thirty-eight years.

TUNNEL NUMBER ONE

What Could Have Been—Aidan

Jennifer sat in the cafe drumming the fingers of one hand on the formica table while decimating yet another packet of sugar with the other. She wished she hadn't ordered coffee. She felt jittery enough as it was and the caffeine she'd consumed wasn't making life any easier.

Where was she? Why wasn't she here yet?

For the hundredth time she glanced at the black and white clock on the wall. Three thirty-two. Her mum was now officially two minutes late for their meeting. Still, it wasn't like she was coming from round the corner she supposed. She had a horribly long train journey from the suburbs of London right up to the very North of England and then a cab ride to contend with. The wait was unbearable though and now she needed the loo again. Blooming coffee.

Jennifer stood up and for the second time since she'd arrived, headed for the tiny toilet at the back of the cafe.

Once she'd finished she checked her reflection in the cracked mirror above the small basin.

She didn't usually wear a great deal of make-up but today she'd taken extra care with her appearance. In the days leading up to this she'd agonised about what to wear for hours. She didn't want to appear dowdy or plain in her standard jeans and same old tops that she wore day in day out. But she only had them or a couple of dresses she reserved for special occasions. She'd decided that what she needed was a happy medium, because as much as she wanted to look nice she also wanted to avoid looking like she'd tried too hard. In the end she'd splashed out on a new top from Oasis. It had been so long since she'd treated herself to anything, she'd decided the occasion merited it. Besides, it had been on the sale rail so had only cost her £28.00 as opposed to £42.00. It made her feel a million dollars. Well, maybe a thousand...

Anyway, the point was it was *new* which was thrilling.

She sighed at her reflection. No matter how many layers of blusher she added, deep down she knew her mum would undoubtedly detect the tired aura that permanently existed around her. Would it also be noticeable that she dyed her own hair and that she looked a few years older than the thirty-eight she'd lived?

Suddenly it occurred to her that if her mum had arrived by now, she might think she hadn't turned up so, with a start, she hurried back out of the loo only to immediately spot her mother sitting at a table, looking as nervous and anxious as she felt.

She was so much older.

Of course this was obviously going to be the case and yet no matter how much common sense told you to expect someone you hadn't seen for decades to have aged, it didn't stop it from being a shock. Her mum looked far more like a grandmother these days. It was the strangest thing.

Tears immediately pricked her eyes. It was so ridiculously good to see her but perhaps it wasn't until this very second that she realised not only just how much she'd missed her but also how much she'd missed out *on*.

Unsure how to behave, she was a bag of nerves as she approached the table.

'Mum,' she said, completely choked.

'Oh Jennifer,' said her mother, leaping to her feet, nerves clearly frayed by the stress of the situation. 'You're here. I can't believe it.'

'Neither can I,' said Jennifer and the two women stared at one another, both too moved to speak.

'Oh come here,' her mum said eventually, gesturing to her daughter to give her a hug.

As they embraced Jennifer couldn't help it, she sobbed noisily into her mum's shoulder. Eighteen years was a long time to go without seeing your mum.

'I'm sorry,' she repeated, that being all she could manage for now.

'Me too,' said Lesley with meaning. Finally she broke their embrace and motioned to Jennifer to sit down opposite her.

'Now,' she said briskly, determined not to let the emotion of the moment overwhelm proceedings. 'Come on, we'd better pull ourselves together or they'll be sending in the men in white coats for us. Shall we order some tea and cake?'

Jennifer nodded as she sat down, before grabbing a white paper napkin out of the stainless steel holder to blow her nose on. 'Oh gosh, I'm so sorry about weeping. I really didn't want to be like this.'

She looked up to see that her mum was staring at her and for a few seconds she stared back.

'Do I look awful?' asked Jennifer feebly.

'No, love,' said her mother, her whole face suddenly crumpling, 'you look absolutely wonderful, a sight for sore eyes.' And with that, despite all her best efforts not to, she burst into tears herself.

'Oh Mum,' said Jennifer, feeling stricken and standing up to reach across the table. 'Come here.'

Her mum gladly accepted a second hug and they stood like that for some time, in a very awkward position, one that neither of them wished to change. Suddenly what anyone else in the cafe might be thinking was totally unimportant.

Finally they let go again and as they both sat down Jennifer absorbed every detail of her mum's face. She was so lined, so grey. She'd put on weight and looked quite tubby around her middle. She also looked like home.

'So, have you been happy?' asked Lesley, getting straight to the heart of things.

Of all the questions her mum could have started with, Jennifer wished it hadn't been that.

'Um…yes,' she replied hesitantly after a lengthy pause, which kind of said it all.

'And Aidan, has he been good to you?'

'Yeah Mum, Aidan's fine. I know you have this idea that he's some kind of monster but he honestly isn't.'

'And Nathan?'

'He's amazing. It's just so sad you've never been able to find that out for yourself.'

'There's still time,' said Lesley, pulling a hanky from her handbag and gripping it so tightly that the blood drained from her knuckles. 'If he'd see me I'd love to take him out perhaps? I don't know, I mean what do you think?'

Jennifer's heart ached as she took in her mum's pained expression. How much time had they wasted?

'I'm sure he'd love that,' said Jennifer at once. 'He's a real sweetie. Tries to pretend he's all cool in front of his mates but it's all a front. Underneath he's soft as butter.'

'You've got a Northern accent you know.'

'No,' said Jennifer. 'Have I?'

'Ooh definitely,' replied her mother.

'So what do you want to do now then? Shall I get you

this tea and cake?' asked Jennifer after a time, not particularly relishing the idea of showing her the drab flat where she lived. Ideally she'd postpone that a while longer.

'Do you know what? I think I might have changed my mind. I'm not sure I could eat cake after all. Not like me…Shall we have a little walk instead?' suggested Lesley. 'That train journey was a long time sitting down. It would be nice to stretch my legs.'

'Good idea,' agreed Jennifer, motioning to the waitress that she'd like to pay for her coffee.

Then they gathered their bags and left the warmth of the steamy cafe for the cooler streets of Carlisle.

'It's so good to see you, Mum,' she said.

By way of reply her mother extended a hand out of the sleeve of her coat and reached for Jennifer's in order to give it a little squeeze.

And in that small moment it appeared that things were perhaps going to be OK.

THURSDAY

Jennifer left work at six o'clock on the dot after what had been a relatively successful day. That afternoon she'd managed to secure a deal on a three bedroom house which had been lingering on their books unsold for far too long. The manager had been so happy to finally get shot of it that he'd been particularly complimentary to Jennifer about her selling skills. Although deep down, Jennifer wondered if anything she ever said when showing people round properties actually made the blindest bit of difference to whether or not they ended up deciding to buy them. When guiding people round she sometimes caught herself solemnly saying things like, 'And this is the bathroom', as if she were enlightening them with knowledge they'd otherwise not have been able to figure out themselves. Still, she wasn't about to let her boss know that she'd been pretty much superfluous to the buyer's decision making process and allowed him to believe instead that without her the agency would still be lumbered with a three bed that most people in their right minds would never purchase due to the fact the ground floor was so dark it felt like a dungeon.

Feeling chirpier than she had in a while, having for once been surprised by a bit of job satisfaction, as she wandered home she contemplated the upcoming weekend. Tomorrow was Friday and once the children were in bed she planned on reprising her original plan of putting on some tarty underwear and seducing her husband. And this time it *would* work and they *would* have sex and they would reconnect on lots of levels and all would be well. After all, there was a huge possibility that a lot of this angst she'd been experiencing lately was down to the fact she simply needed a good shag.

Then, on Saturday, the girls both had parties to go to and she and Max were out in the evening for dinner with friends she actually liked.

Yes, she'd definitely been worrying far too much lately about stuff that in the grand scheme of things was probably all fairly manageable and not too disastrous. No one was dying. Everyone had their health. She was a lucky girl and needed to keep reminding herself of this fact.

Nearly at the bottom of her road she realised her phone was vibrating away in her handbag.

Scrabbling around for it, she caught it just before it went to answer phone.

It was their nanny, Ivana.

'Hello,' she said, wondering what she wanted and betting they'd run out of something.

'Jennifer…'

Oh god thought Jennifer at once for Ivana sounded very distraught. Her heart skipped a beat and hundreds of thoughts flashed through her mind in a nanosecond before Ivana finally managed to utter 'I'm so sorry, I think Eadie's broken her arm.'

Oh. My. God.

Later, around the time Jennifer had originally been hoping to be sliding into a nice relaxing bath, she and Max were sitting at Kingston hospital, feeling traumatised and looking almost as white in the face as the cast that was now wrapped around their eldest daughter's arm.

Jennifer felt a shadow of her former self having experienced the most stressful few hours of her life. The image of Eadie's arm sticking out at such a bizarre angle seemed to be burned into her retinas and would undoubtedly never leave her.

Upon racing into the house she'd found her daughter in a state of shock, lying on the couch in a daze, white as a sheet with her arm at said disgusting angle which Jennifer had struggled with even being able to look at. She'd stroked her daughter's brow and told her everything would be all right, grateful that Eadie was so still and calm because being totally honest the arm thing made her feel very nauseous. Ivana had already called the ambulance but she was wracked with guilt and worry and was literally wringing her hands, pleading with Jennifer for forgiveness. Not that by the sound of it she could have done anything to have prevented the accident. Eadie had simply been bouncing on the trampoline in the garden just as she did most days after school. She'd slipped, had landed awkwardly and that had been that. Jennifer knew this was the case and despite maternal instinct wanting desperately to have someone or something to blame she knew this wouldn't be fair so kept her counsel.

The minute the ambulance arrived though, Jennifer burst into tears, simply at the relief of someone medically trained finally being in their presence.

'Is she going to be all right?' she wailed.

'She'll be fine, but let's get her to the hospital as soon as we can.'

By now the shock was starting to wear off, meaning Eadie was suddenly far more aware of the pain she was in. At this point she started really crying and repeatedly yelling 'Ow, ow, ow' until she'd wound herself up into a terrible state. She didn't want the ambulance men or anyone else for that matter to move her so getting her into the ambulance was a bit of an ordeal to say the least.

Jennifer hated seeing her daughter so distressed but knew she had to remain strong at least till Max could join them. Thankfully she'd got through to him on his mobile straight away and between them they'd decided that the best plan would be to meet at the hospital while Ivana stayed at the house to look after Polly, the only one in the family who seemed perfectly oblivious to the drama going on around her.

*

Eventually, in the ambulance, the medics were able to administer some heavy duty pain relief to Eadie which they assured Jennifer would slightly sedate her and calm her down. Jennifer spent the rest of the journey wondering if it would shed her in a bad light if she were to ask if she could have some too.

Once they'd finally arrived, the hospital was really busy so they had to wait for ages in A and E before anyone could attend to them properly. When Eadie was eventually wheeled into a room to have her arm x-rayed and set in a cast, Jennifer was still without her husband so had to continue being stoic while ignoring the desire to retch every time her gaze fell upon her little girl's bent arm. When Max eventually arrived at the hospital, having jogged all the way from the train station, he was a sweaty stressed mess and Jennifer realised she had never been so happy to see anyone in her life. He was waiting for them as they emerged from the treatment room. Eadie was on a trolley, pale and whimpering, and he immediately gave his daughter an enormous, reassuring hug.

'Are you OK, Eadie Beady?' he soothed, stroking his daughter's hair and kissing her puffy face so tenderly it nearly set Jennifer off.

'It still hurts,' Eadie moaned, holding her rigid

plaster-casted arm out. Remembering what lay beneath and the process which had occurred in order to get it back into a normal position Jennifer's stomach turned yet again. She'd have made a truly lousy nurse. Doctors and nurses were saints as far as she was concerned.

'You are so brave,' Max said to his daughter. 'And you know what brave people get?'

'Presents?' Eadie tried hopefully, her puffy, tear-stained face looking something other than pained and distressed for the first time in hours.

'Too blooming right they do,' said Max. 'Sackfuls of them, maybe even a Wii?'

'Yeah,' squealed Eadie, her face a picture of disbelief. Her parents had always said she couldn't have a Wii for another two years. Maybe it had been worth breaking her arm after all?

Seeing her little girl look vaguely comforted meant Jennifer didn't even get annoyed by Max's slightly dubious parental approach. Sod it, if Eadie wanted a Wii, at this stage frankly she could have one. She was just grateful that Max was here. For the first time in a long while she recalled how much she loved him, why she'd married him and the security and comfort that doing so had brought into her life.

It's amazing how things can turn on a sixpence.

As soon as they'd got Eadie to the ward, off the trolley and settled into her bed Max suddenly turned to his wife and said 'Can I have a word?' which struck Jennifer as a bit odd. He was her husband. He could say what he liked. He hardly needed to make an appointment.

'Course you can. Eadie darling, you try and close your eyes now and have a little rest.'

Eadie must have been completely exhausted because she didn't put up any resistance to her mother's suggestion at all and merely closed her eyes at which point Jennifer and Max pulled the curtain shut around her bed and tip-toed out into the corridor.

'Who was keeping an eye on her when it happened?' Max demanded to know as soon as they were out of ear-shot. His voice was full of rage.

'What do you mean?' said Jennifer who by now was so tired she could only think about getting home and to bed. 'You know who was—Ivana.'

'Well, how could she allow this to happen? I know the kids like her but after this I think we have to ask ourselves if we can really entrust the care of our children to her.'

'Oh for goodness sakes, Max. It could so easily have been one of us. It was an accident. It's not like Ivana went up to her and snapped her arm in two.'

'But that's the thing,' retaliated Max. 'It wasn't one of us. It was Ivana, who's a very nice girl but is she respon-sible enough to be in charge of our kids? Given that we're standing in a hospital I'd suggest the answer might be no.'

'Why are you sounding annoyed with me?' seethed Jennifer. 'What the hell have I done? Our daughter's bro-ken her arm and you're standing here yelling at me.'

'I'm not yelling,' yelled Max, 'but to be honest I do resent the way you've always made me feel like a bastard for preferring my kids to be looked after by one of us rather than a stranger. And then this happens.'

'Well then why don't you bloody well resign then and look after them yourself?' said Jennifer, who had probably never been more angry in her entire life. 'Because what you're basically intimating is that I'm a terrible mother and that somehow this is all my fault because I had the audacity to be at work today. Well fuck you, Max.'

Max flinched but his expression remained stony. 'Don't make a scene, people are watching.'

'I couldn't give a shit,' she said, lowering her tone slightly. 'And don't you dare make Ivana feel bad when we get back either, because if you do I will be absolutely livid. No one feels worse about what's happened than her right now. She loves the girls to pieces and all my friends comment on how wonderful she is when they see her out and about with them. Now, before I lose it completely, we need to find out when we can get out of here. Eadie's exhausted.'

'She's not the only one,' said Max, looking shifty and Jennifer could tell then that deep down he knew he'd been out of order.

Suddenly she didn't feel cross any more, just tired to the marrow of her bones.

'I'm sorry,' mumbled Max.

'Whatever,' said Jennifer, past caring.

'I'm sorry,' he repeated. 'It's just stressful that's all. On the way here I kept thinking how I was in and out of A and E as a kid but you still can't help panicking.'

'I know,' said Jennifer. 'And I was here and had to deal with it. But we have to keep it in perspective. It's a broken arm and it'll mend. What we should probably be more worried about is the fact that our youngest might be a psychopath. I've literally never seen anyone so unbothered by witnessing someone in horrific pain as she was.'

'Right, I'll go and see if we can get out of here,' said Max, looking sheepish. 'I know they said we should wait to have the cast checked again but I'm tempted to say that we'll bring her back in the morning and get it looked at then.'

'OK,' agreed Jennifer, equally keen to get home. As Max went off in search of a doctor, Jennifer returned to Eadie who by now was fast asleep, worn out by her stressful experience.

When Max arrived back ten minutes later he gave her a thumbs up. 'We can go, we just need to sign a form on the way out.'

'Great,' said Jennifer. 'Though it almost seems a shame we'll have to wake her up now.'

'Well when our cab's here I'll carry her, that way, with a bit of luck she might stay asleep. Then, when we get back, I might eBay that bloody trampoline you know.'

'Do it,' said Jennifer vehemently.

'And perhaps I'll take the day off work tomorrow,' he

suggested. 'That way we can bring Eadie back here to get checked together?'

'If you want,' said Jennifer who could tell he was trying to make amends.

'Plus we're both knackered so it would give us a chance to have a bit of a chill out.'

'I suppose….oh shit.'

'What?'

'I'm supposed to be seeing my therapist tomorrow. My appointment's at eleven. I'll have to cancel if Eadie's not at school.'

'You didn't tell me,' said Max regarding his wife quizzically.

'It's no big deal,' said Jennifer.

'Well, you shouldn't cancel. Doesn't she charge for missed appointments?'

'Yeah.'

'Well, you go then and I'll bring Eadie on my own,' said Max still trying to make up for what he'd said earlier.

'Fine.'

'Great.'

Inside Jennifer still felt murderous towards him but teetering on the verge of wanting a divorce was so ter- rifying it galvanised her into making more of an effort than she normally would. 'And then tomorrow night,' she found herself saying, 'we should perhaps, you know, have a bit of a romantic night in. If you know what I mean?'

'Sounds good to me,' said Max hesitantly, wondering

what to do with this slight curveball. 'And impressive that despite the strip lighting, smell of antiseptic and our bandaged child being only feet away you've still got sex on your brain whereas here I am thinking how I might finish that wardrobe off properly.'

'Yes, well it would be nice not to have it lying on the floor any more,' Jennifer replied, faintly embarrassed and fed up beyond belief.

'I'll get you lying on the floor,' said Max, assuming he'd been forgiven and pinching her bum.

'Maybe,' said Jennifer primly.

'And after your Steve "jokes" the other day I'd better pull my finger out and show you that actually I can be quite useful to have around. Otherwise you might run off with the plumber.'

'I doubt it,' said Jennifer. 'You saw the last plumber we had round. Mick with no front teeth.'

'True,' said Max. 'He hardly lived up to "sweet" Steve's standards did he?'

Jennifer didn't reply. Steve had been sweet. Really sweet and there was no harm in that. He'd been her 'one before the one' who could have been 'the one' if fate hadn't stepped in and brought Max to her. Perhaps she should have stayed with him after all? He would never have spoken to her like Max had before.

'Anyway, you sit down and I'll go and sign this form and then come back for you both.'

'OK,' agreed Jennifer.

She sank into the plastic chair next to Eadie's bed and wondered how it would feel to deal with incidents like this as a single parent? Horrible no doubt. Terrifying in fact. Still Max had offered to take the day off tomorrow. It was a start and with a bit of luck she wouldn't have to set foot in a hospital again until the cast needed taking off, which suited her fine.

THE PAST — STEVE

January 2000

Jennifer had been looking forward to her date with Steve all day, which was a good sign. First dates were usually horribly nerve-racking events but she wasn't dreading this one at all. They'd had a couple of fairly long chats on the phone already which helped. Both times the conversation had flowed easily and had given her an indication that the date would be enjoyable as opposed to a terrible ordeal.

She'd taken all the first date precautions of course. She'd washed her hair the night before, and when she'd got home from work to shower and change, she'd also shaved her armpits, sorted out her bikini line and legs and put on a sexy, matching bra and knickers. She certainly wasn't planning on sleeping with him tonight but would be prepared nevertheless. Just in case.

They'd agreed to meet at Pizza Express. Not very imaginative but at least she knew the food would be nice and that she could dress pretty casually. She was wearing boot-cut jeans with a top from Whistles and high-heeled ankle boots. Despite feeling relatively confident she still had butterflies as she approached the restaurant at seven minutes past eight.

As soon as she walked in she spotted him. Good. She would have hated to have arrived first. She was quite taken aback by how good he looked. She'd remembered him as having a really nice face but actually on second sighting she realised he was far better looking than she remembered and had the sort of face most women would probably notice in a crowd. His eyes were really blue and you could tell that although he wore his hair short it wasn't because he was going bald but because he had a lovely shaped head, good bone structure and it simply suited him that way.

He waved at her as soon as he spotted her and got up from his seat which she thought was chivalrous. He'd obviously made an effort. He was wearing a shirt and looked clean and smelled of some nice herby aftershave.

'Hi, you look nice,' he said, leaning in to give her a kiss on the cheek.

'Thanks,' she said shyly, sitting down in the chair he'd just pulled out for her. His manners were impeccable.

'Did you come straight from work?' he asked.

'No,' replied Jennifer. 'I popped home actually as I tend to have to wear suits and stuff to work. You know, really "officey" clothes.'

She decided it probably wasn't necessary to add '*I also needed to sort my pubic sideburns out.*'

'Cool,' he said. 'Do you want a drink?'

'Yeah definitely, I'll have a glass of white wine please.'

The waitress who had just come over scribbled this down. 'And I'll have a coke please?' said Steve which Jennifer slightly cringed at. Fizzy drink for dinner? Really?

'Are you not a big drinker then?' she asked, wondering what kind of a person it made her that she'd rather he was than wasn't. At university being able to drink huge amounts had almost been a badge of honour.

'Not really. I quite like lager,' said Steve 'But I'm not massively into wine if I'm honest.'

'Fair enough,' said Jennifer.

'So, tell me about yourself,' Steve started manfully. 'How come a gorgeous girl like you is single?'

Pretty smooth, thought Jennifer. She grinned, flattered 'Well, I was in quite a long-term relationship at university. Two and a half years to be precise.'

'OK, so what happened, if you don't mind me asking that is?'

'No, not at all. Um…well, I'm not sure really. I guess it wasn't so much a case of anything specific happening to end it but more realising we just weren't compatible. He was a really clever guy and interesting to hang out with but to be honest he was a bit of a cold fish at times. He was incapable of expressing his feelings so I spent the whole time wondering if he actually did fancy me or whether he was just with me for the sake of it.'

'Really?' said Steve. 'If I was your boyfriend I wouldn't be able to stop telling you how pretty you are.'

Jennifer didn't know how to react. What a lovely thing to say. He sounded so sincere too. Not creepy or disingenuous at all.

'Thanks,' she managed in the end, once she'd got over the shock of being complimented. 'Um, anyway, I guess it just didn't feel like he loved me in the right way which probably sounds a bit weird but by the end, as far as I was concerned, it felt more like we were friends than boyfriend and girlfriend. I don't know.'

'Fizzled out?'

'Yeah,' said Jennifer a bit doubtfully. By now she was revealing slightly more than she had originally intended to but was unsure how to stop the snowball of information that was rolling out of her mouth. 'Though to be fair it wasn't ever massively sizzling even at the beginning so there wasn't a great deal of sizzle to fizzle. Besides, he had a wife of sorts.'

'What do you mean?'

'He was literally married to his work,' said Jennifer, teetering on the verge of telling him about Tim, only half wondering if she should so early on. Still, she'd gone this far. Perhaps she'd just get it out of the way. 'Have you heard of reUNIon?'

'Course, yeah.'

'OK, well he kind of invented it.'

'You're kidding? He isn't that Purcell bloke is he?'

Jennifer nodded.

'Wow,' said Steve, trying to recover from having been emasculated within the first few minutes of the date. 'OK, so very clever bloke then, although if you don't mind me saying?'

'Go on,' encouraged Jennifer. 'Say what you like.'

'I always think he comes across as a bit arrogant in interviews.'

'I agree.'

'And he can't be *that* intelligent if he let you slip through his fingers,' he added, going red as he did so.

Jennifer grinned. He'd already paid her more compliments than Tim had in the first year of being together. It was nice.

'Well that's very kind of you to say. And what about you? How long have you been single for? Not long I bet.'

Jennifer cringed. She'd been trying to match his kindness by saying something nice herself but in the process had managed to make herself sound like a cheesy old lothario.

'Oh blimey, let's see now, about six months.'

'OK and who was your last girlfriend?'

'Lauren,' replied Steve and as he said her name Jennifer could tell that Lauren had meant a great deal to him. 'We went out for about three years.'

'Right, so a long time then,' she said, slightly unsure as to why, or how they'd got onto the subject of their exes quite so swiftly. Surely this was more of a third or fourth date kind of chat? Oh well they were doing it now. 'So was it a difficult break-up?'

'Yeah I guess.'

'So...what happened then?'

For the second time Steve's face coloured and he seemed distinctly unsure about replying.

'What?' said Jennifer, his reluctance to answer making her far keener to find out more details.

'Well, it'll probably sound a bit heavy and I don't want to scare you off. We haven't even ordered yet,' he joked, looking more than a little uncomfortable.

'I know,' grinned Jennifer. 'I was thinking the same thing myself when I told you about Tim but you've *got* to tell me now and I promise I won't get scared,' she said, despite the fact she wasn't one hundred percent sure she meant it. If Lauren had found out he was a crossdresser or that he had a penchant for sleeping with goats she couldn't be totally sure she wouldn't be leaving before her Fiorentina pizza had even gone in the oven.

'Thanks,' she said to the waitress who had just arrived back with their drinks.

Steve seemed grateful for the distraction and said that they'd like to order their food. So they did, though Jennifer wasn't letting him off the hook that easily.

'So,' she prompted as soon as the waitress had left, 'what happened?'

'OK, well before I say, just bear in mind that we were together for a pretty long time. So I guess you consider lots of things that don't even enter your brain when you first start going out with someone.'

'Good disclaimer. Now tell me,' she insisted.

'Right,' said Steve, who'd accepted that he wasn't going to be able to wriggle out of an explanation. 'Basically, what happened was, I realised we weren't on the same page as far as what we both wanted out of life was concerned.'

'In what way?'

'She didn't want to have children. Ever.'

'Ah,' said Jennifer, feeling mildly relieved. That was a fair enough answer, one that didn't have her running for the hills. 'OK, well fair enough then. I would say that's a pretty sensible reason to have ended things if you know you do definitely want them.'

'I do,' said Steve with feeling. 'I love kids. Ideally I'd like three I reckon. Not that I said that to Lauren. I mean, if she'd agreed to trying just for one at some point I probably would have stayed with her but she point blank refused even to consider it.'

'Was she a real career girl then?'

'Er, no not massively,' said Steve, shaking his head. 'She's a beautician. She just doesn't like being around kids. It's weird. Her sister's got a couple you see and she kept saying that her sister had lost her life. That she was always tired, that she was fat and never had any money. Only whenever I went round there I always thought her sister looked fulfilled and like she wouldn't change her life for anything. Besides, I think not wanting to lose your figure is a pretty lame reason for not wanting to have a child.'

'Was the sister fat?'

'Hardly the point.'

Jennifer blushed. Only the other day she'd heard a story on the news about a man who had murdered his wife after cooking dinner for her and all she'd been able to wonder, apart from how awful it was, was what he'd cooked her. It was just the way her brain worked. The details seemed important.

'I know it's not the point,' she agreed now. 'And I know I'm awful, but I still have to know now, was she?'

'Um, yeah, a bit,' said Steve, rolling his eyes in mock disapproval but clearly amused.

Jennifer nodded, while considering everything he'd just said in the last few minutes. It was endearing hearing a man speak in the way in which he had. In her experience it was usually women who dreamed and talked of motherhood in the future, and on the whole men who just appeared to go along with it when the time was right. She tried to think if she and Tim had ever discussed if they'd want to have children one day but she couldn't remember. She didn't think he'd be against it but she certainly couldn't remember him ever definitely stating that he wanted to as a fact. Besides, being a dad would take some of his attention away from reUNIon and that would never do.

'Have you seen *Chitty Chitty Bang Bang*?' she asked. Steve nodded.

'Did she share the Child Catcher's views on kids?'

'She did, though fortunately she was slightly better looking,' said Steve amiably. 'Not such a big pointy nose.'

'And she didn't wear black tailcoats and carry a massive net around with her.'

'Only on a Tuesday.'

There followed a bit of an awkward silence, only because given what had just been said, Jennifer now felt vaguely obliged to announce her own views on procreation. After all, if she didn't want to have children one day there was almost no point her being there. No point in him treating her to a casual pizza. Steve was right of course. Only insane people would think about such things when they'd only just met someone and yet the stark reality was that once you ploughed deeper into your twenties you only really embarked on a relationship if you thought it might end up leading somewhere. Otherwise what was the point?

'Well, for what it's worth then,' she said in a voice that she hoped sounded light-hearted but actually sounded vaguely like Alan Partridge, 'I'd like at least a couple of sprogs one day.'

'OK,' said Steve, raising his glass of coke to her. 'Well good for you and don't worry, I'm not planning on impregnating anyone in the near future.'

He smiled cheekily, acknowledging that he fully

comprehended how crazy this conversation was, given that they hadn't even slept together. Just at the thought of that her stomach flipped in a very good way. Suddenly coy she looked around the restaurant at nothing in particular.

'Anyway,' he continued, 'that was a bit awkward wasn't it? Sorry about that. I honestly didn't mean to extract your personal views on whether or not you'd like to be a parent or not within the first ten minutes of the date.'

'It's OK,' laughed Jennifer, who actually thought he'd managed to break the ice quite successfully. At least he could take the piss out of himself. It was sweet.

'Right, so what shall we talk about now?' he said.

'Ooh why don't we just go straight for another contentious and deeply personal subject,' said Jennifer. 'Maybe, who we'd vote for in the next election? Or, how much we earn? Something nice and delicate like that.'

'Good idea, or perhaps you could just tell me how your day's been. Might be less controversial?'

'OK,' agreed Jennifer and from that point onward the evening veered into more standard first date territory only with the edge of nerves having been extinguished completely.

*

Later, after they'd had their meal, they left the restaurant and stood out on the pavement, both reluctant for the date to end but unsure as to whether the other person felt the same. In the end Steve broached the subject.

'Well, I've had a lovely time but if I'm honest I'd like the evening to continue a bit longer. It's only nine-thirty after all. But if you're tired…'

'No,' said Jennifer, 'I'm fine, why? What were you thinking?'

'We could go for a drink in a pub?' he suggested. 'Or, and I hope you don't think this sounds forward, perhaps we could go back to yours for a cup of tea and just chill out for a bit or something?'

'Could do,' said Jennifer who quite fancied doing that. She really wanted to snog him. 'Or we could go to yours? Mitcham isn't far.'

'Ah,' said Steve. 'Actually, I'm not based in Mitcham any more.'

'Oh right,' said Jennifer wondering why he suddenly looked so sheepish. 'Where are you then?'

'I've, er, moved back home, just for the short term,' he said, and Jennifer realised at this point that he blushed incredibly easily.

'You mean with your parents?'

'Just with my mum actually. My dad died a few years ago so Mum's on her own. Well, strictly speaking that's not true. She's got a boyfriend called Derek only they don't live together.'

'So where's your mum's place then?'

'Leytonstone.'

'Leytonstone?' she exclaimed. 'That's miles away isn't it?'

'It's not close,' he agreed. 'But it's not that bad. When I'm working I drive a motorbike to get down to these parts and just leave the van parked somewhere overnight. I biked here tonight as it goes.'

'Right,' said Jennifer, trying not to feel so downcast about the fact he lived so far away. With his mother! He was twenty-eight years old for Christ's sakes. Her expression must have given her away because Steve suddenly piped up with, 'Like I said, it's only temporary. It's just I was spending so much on rent that it was getting really difficult to save. Living at home for a few months means I can save for a deposit for my own place. And besides, living with Mum isn't so bad. We get on really well. Plus, I get a great dinner every night. She even does my washing and ironing.'

'Ah, that's nice,' said Jennifer, though if she were being totally honest she would have been more impressed if he'd said he looked after his own washing. If he wasn't paying rent surely it was the least he could do? There was nothing sexy about imagining his mum washing his underpants for him.

'So, can we go to yours, or would you prefer the pub?'

'Let's go to mine,' said Jennifer, her mind racing as she tried to remember what sort of state she'd left the flat in. She prayed she'd put away the hair removal cream. Otherwise that disgusting fishy odour would be lingering in the air. She'd have to get him in the lounge so she could have a quick whizz round.

*

One hour later and Jennifer was on the verge of her first ever kiss with Steve. They'd had cliché cups of coffee and had sat on the sofa together chatting away about this and that, both keen to get to the point where they could go in for a snog, wondering who was going to instigate it. Finally, just as he had all evening, Steve took the lead and reached over gently and turned her cheek so she was facing him fully. Then, staring at her with real tenderness he pulled her towards him and kissed her gently on the lips in a way that made her feel like the most beautiful girl in the world. Then he slowly opened his mouth a bit until she could feel his tongue and kissed her more expertly than anyone had since Aidan all those years ago. It was absolutely amazing and when his hand started stroking her leg she almost melted with pleasure. It wasn't long before their breathing got heavier as they became more aroused and the kissing became more urgent and deeper. God she'd forgotten how much she loved snogging and it appeared he did too because instead of immediately try-ing to move things on he kissed her for ages, really taking his time over it and seemingly enjoying it as much as she was. It was incredible. So sexy and so sensual. By the time he did start touching her elsewhere she was desperate for him to and was hinting at him to do so by pushing herself against him. He knew exactly what he was doing though and seemed only too aware that in itself the wait was one of the horniest things about the whole experience. Jennifer was so taken aback by how good Steve was she was practically grinning as they kissed.

It was worth the wait too, because when it came his touch was incredible. Every time his hand made contact with any part of her it felt insanely good so when his hand slid to the top of her jeans she couldn't resist letting him undo the fly. He touched her through her knickers in the most sensual way imaginable. He stroked her gently yet firmly in a way that left her panting for more. However, remembering this was a first date, eventually she pulled away, breathless, knowing that despite the fact he lived with his mum and drank fizzy drinks with his dinner she definitely wanted to see him again.

'Are you OK?' he whispered into her ear, his voice thick with desire.

'Yeah,' she said. 'You're an amazing kisser.'

'So are you,' he said. 'I am so turned on.'

Her gaze went to his trousers where she could see for herself exactly how turned on he was. She clearly wasn't going to be disappointed in that department either.

'I think perhaps we should stop though,' she said. 'I mean I don't want to, but it's probably for the best don't you reckon? It being our first date and everything.'

'Whatever you say, beautiful.'

It was the 'beautiful' that did it. It almost made her cry.

She had longed for Tim to say nice things to her for years. Had yearned for a bit of attention to the point where at times she'd been reduced almost to begging for compliments sometimes, like a dog sniffing around a table for crumbs. Now here was Steve, who she hardly knew but who had been so lovely all evening, telling her she was beautiful and it was so unbelievably lovely to hear. It was like pouring water on a dried up old plant.

'Perhaps let's just do some more kissing,' she suggested.

Steve was more than happy to go along with that plan, although predictably, it didn't quite end there. Half an hour later, unable to resist, Jennifer ended up having sex with him. On her sofa. And it was bloody great.

PRESENT DAY

What Jennifer couldn't have possibly known was that by now she had been in a coma for three weeks. Three long weeks during which her friends and family had had to come to terms with the fact that she may not return to them. No matter how many times they asked the consultant for his opinion he could only offer them vague replies. The fact was no one knew what was going to happen to Jennifer, whether she'd live, die, or remain in no man's land until someone else made the heart-rending decision for her.

Of course this was far harder for them than it was for Jennifer for she was oblivious, cocooned in her own little world. A grey, foggy world which she drifted around in, sometimes aware of her anchorless state, occasionally surfacing to hear snippets from the real world before descending back to the place she was far more able to handle.

Meanwhile, her body was doing its very best to recover from the shock it had endured and her brain was scrambling to repair itself, to reboot if you like. Currently she wasn't wired correctly which was why she was able to experience things which normally one couldn't ever be privy to.

Right now her consciousness was buzzing, yearning to make another journey, desperate to find out more about how life could have been.

She started her descent.

It took a while but when she reached the tunnels, as she'd suspected it would have, the first portal had disappeared completely. Instead of a grey swirling, cloudy mist, there was now a black seal in its place. Tunnel number one was most definitely shut for good so she would just have to accept that and be thankful for what she had learned from it. However, the second portal, the one marked Tim, was still very much available, though it was a few shades weaker than it had been before. The third, which she had yet to explore at all, was still as bright as anything.

Tim or Steve?

So far she'd learned that by staying with Tim she would have turned into the kind of woman she'd probably detest if she were to meet her at a party. Groomed, pampered and not really serving much purpose other than to be a wife. She also appeared to be miserable, unconfident and too hung up on her 'lifestyle' to do much about it.

There didn't seem any point checking out life with Steve yet. He could wait. She could visualise it so well anyway. Whereas she couldn't even begin to guess what would happen to her in the second portal. Would she leave Tim? Would she break Joe's and indeed her own heart for the sake of her children, or out of fear?

TUNNEL NUMBER TWO

What Could Have Been—Tim

'But what I don't understand is why you can't just fly Karen out here?' repeated Tim, regarding Jennifer in a way that told her to tread extremely carefully.

He was perched on the edge of their enormous seven-foot bed which was still rumpled from where he'd had his post-lunchtime nap. Their housekeeper, Jacqueline, ensured that more often than not lunches were the sort that needed to be slept off. She lived locally in Antibes and brought all their meals to the villa every morning, on huge earthenware platters, or in brightly painted dishes that were synonymous with the region, along with fresh baguettes and croissants for breakfast and copious bottles of wine. Life in France tended to be one long blissful blur of eating, drinking, swimming, fending off cheese and rosé top-ups and playing with the children. This year however, as far as Jennifer was concerned, there was nothing blissful about it. She was in her own private hell, missing Joe while feeling painfully stressed and confused about the decision she needed to make.

'Why on earth do you want to leave here when you could just as easily invite her to come and stay with us?'

After his nap Tim had showered and changed into olive green linen trousers, a white shirt and Hermes dark-brown suede loafers with no socks. His helicopter was due to meet him at the helipad but he seemed reluctant to get going, preferring instead to watch his wife pack whilst trying to get to the bottom of what her last-minute trip to the UK was really all about.

Jennifer wished with every fibre of her being that he'd just leave so she could have some space, stop being questioned and concentrate on what she wanted to take. She was feverishly excited by the prospect of her escape and nervous that something would happen to prevent her from going. She also felt guilty as hell and was aware that no matter what, it was vital she appeared nonchalant and normal. She was being scrutinised. She could sense it. It was all so exhausting.

The large terracotta floor tiles were cool under her bare feet. She was wearing a bikini with a flimsy Melissa Odabash kaftan over the top yet still felt hot and flustered. It was thirty-six degrees outside and although they had a very sophisticated air conditioning system installed throughout the villa, in the daytime she preferred the windows to be open. Firstly so that she could fully appreciate the breath-taking view. Their house was situated high up in the mountains of Antibes, in between Nice and Cannes, and the view of the twinkling Med was phenomenal. She also liked the windows open so that she could hear her children's squeals from the infinity pool down below where they played for hours every day under the supervision of Annie and Deck and a life guard. The grounds were so vast there was enough distance to render their boisterous screams of excitement and all the splashing into an extremely soothing sound.

'Do I look all right?' asked Tim, bored of waiting for his wife to give him a straight answer.

'Yes,' she replied, not giving him so much as a glance to at least pretend she was interested. If she had, she would have thought he looked smart, Sloaney, older than his years and conspicuously wealthy. Joe would never wear such a stuffy outfit.

Joe.

Would there ever be a minute, a whole sixty seconds when he didn't pop into her brain? He consumed her thoughts. She was so in love and for the first time in her life finally understood why people spoke of being 'crazily' or 'madly' in love for what she was experiencing felt like madness.

*

Distracted, what Jennifer didn't pick up on was that had she given Tim just a second or two of attention it would have appeased him greatly and made her getaway far easier. As it was, it was totally obvious his wife's mind was elsewhere. Tim's eyes narrowed and briefly he wondered if he should cancel his trip to Monaco.

'When's your flight again?' he asked.

'First thing in the morning. Early.'

'So what are you doing this evening?'

'This evening?' she repeated, going to the closet to find socks, which were almost an alien concept when you'd been barefoot for weeks.

'Yes, this evening. What are you doing? Are you eating here? Do you have dinner plans with anyone?'

'No,' she said, irritated. 'Course not. I'm just going to be here. I want to spend time with the children before I leave. And besides, I've had enough dinners out recently to last me a lifetime.'

'Right,' said Tim. 'I didn't realise it had all been such a chore for you.'

Jennifer rolled her eyes.

'It's just I thought you might have arranged to see Gail and James or something.'

'God no! Why would I want to do that?' she replied, a little too vehemently. Gail and James were two of their oldest friends but this holiday Jennifer had had her fill of Gail who had become increasingly materialistic and superficial as the years had rolled by. These days she wouldn't contemplate eating at a restaurant unless she thought it was one worth being seen in, which frankly made the holiday not feel like a holiday at all. Gail had also really overdone it on the fillers and cosmetic surgery front so now looked permanently like she was trapped in a wind tunnel.

'What about you? Are you going out this evening?' she asked, realising too late how shirty her tone had been and changing the subject in order to avoid a row which would only delay his departure further. Tim loved Gail and James.

'Not sure,' said Tim. 'Pierre's having something on his boat tonight so I may go to that. It depends on these viewings and how long they go on for.'

'You don't really want to live there do you?' asked Jennifer wearily.

'I wouldn't be looking if I didn't want to,' said Tim, sounding irritated. 'Why would I waste my time?'

'Well, it just might have been nice to have had a discussion about it,' she replied, wondering idly which jeans suited her best from the pile she'd selected.

A fortnight ago Tim had suddenly announced that he was going to look into making Monaco their primary country of residence.

'Well, when *you're* earning billions of pounds and the government want to fleece you for half of it, despite the fact you've done more for their economy than the majority of the population put together, plus contributed to endless charities, then you can have your say can't you?'

Jennifer clenched her fists so tightly, her nails made indentations on her palms.

She stayed silent though, despite the fact that if Tim had bothered to ask whether she wanted to uproot the children in order to live in Monaco or not, she would have told him she had no desire to live there whatsoever. She would also have added that her socialist roots found the whole idea repugnant. They had so much wealth they could easily give far more than fifty percent away and still never have to work another day in their lives.

'Anyway, Monaco aside, which we can discuss when you're back, I have to say, I still don't get why you're going to Karen. Or why you're avoiding giving me an answer. I mean, if she's prepared to take days off work just to hang out with you then surely she'd rather do that here in the sunshine than there in the pissing rain?'

Jennifer glanced at the clock on her dressing table. His helicopter was due at four. It was five to. By this point she was so tense she would have done anything to make those five minutes pass more quickly. Only once Tim had gone would she relax and then their paths wouldn't need to cross again until she returned from her trip.

She sighed heavily, hoping that would be enough to shut Tim up. Apart from anything else she wasn't getting very far with her packing. This was another perfect example of where less would be more. She had such a stupid amount of clothes to choose from that trying to condense what she'd laid out on the bed as possibilities was more of a stress than it would have been if she only owned a few pairs of jeans in the first place. Next month she was going to have a huge clear-out and give loads away to charity.

Right, she needed to stop faffing about. Joe wouldn't care what she was wearing, as long as her knickers were nice of course, and she should be ruthless because ideally she'd just take hand luggage, a luxury she could never enjoy when travelling with four children plus staff.

She glanced up. Tim was still staring at her and not in a soppy way. He was watching her like a hawk. The clock said two minutes to and they could both very clearly hear the chopper arriving. She suddenly felt horribly uneasy.

'So, Karen calls and you just go running. Again, it just seems a bit odd to me that she would expect you to leave your children in the middle of your family holiday just to go and listen to her problems.'

'Oh for goodness sake,' she huffed, finally realising she needed to say something. She continued to avoid his eye though by going to search for some ankle boots in the walk-in closet. 'I've told you thousands of times now. She's got a lot of stuff going on in her personal life and she's asked me to come and see her so we can talk it through and spend a bit of time with one another. That's it. She wants me to go there and I don't want to insist that she comes here. Why should she?'

'Because it's a damn sight nicer here than it is in shitty Wandsworth,' he said, gesturing outside to the stunning panoramic view that lay before them.

'Look,' said Jennifer, feeling unbelievably claustrophobic despite the never-ending vista. 'I'm not saying it again. *Me* leaving the children is easy. They're happy here and have endless people to look after them. You're not even going to be around for the next week so it's not like we'd be spending any time together, whereas Karen simply hasn't got the funds to uproot herself and Suzy in order to fly over here just because I've told her to. So I'm going to her and that's final.'

'But I could pay for…'

'I know you could pay,' said Jennifer, starting to get angry now. God, if she had really been just going to see her friend he wasn't half being awkward about it. Pretty hypocritical given that he'd been known on occasion in the past to casually announce in the morning that he was off to another continent for a few days, having failed to remember to tell his PA to tell her. 'But I don't *want* you to pay for her and Karen doesn't want you to either. So that's that. Come on, Tim. How often do I ever go away and do anything for myself? Once a year with the girls and that's it. Other than that I'm at your beck and call or with the kids but I really want to do this. I want to be there for my friend when she needs me and it might help build a few bridges at the same time.'

'So what exactly is going on with her anyway?' said Tim, who *still* didn't look totally convinced. He was irritatingly sharp.

'Maritals,' said Jennifer a tad too quickly.

Tim pondered this for a while before saying eventually,

'Well that doesn't surprise me, I suppose. If I were Pete I'd have left her years ago.'

'Ha bloody ha,' retorted Jennifer unenthusiastically. 'Now, does that mean you're going to stop nagging me and let me go with your blessing because apart from anything else the helicopter's here?'

'Fine,' said Tim.

Internally Jennifer breathed a sigh of relief. Only, the feeling that she'd got away with it may have been hasty because just as she was about to head for the en-suite bathroom to sort out her toiletries, Tim came up behind her and grabbed her arm. As she spun round to face him his expression made her gulp. It was flinty and cold, his smile had faded away and his eyes had a warning in them as he said, 'But if I ever find out you've lied to me I'll kill you.'

Jennifer felt petrified so regarded him for a while as she tried to work out the best way to respond. Eventually she decided to go on the offensive. How dare he threaten her like that? She hated him. The sooner she got away the better.

'And if you ever speak to me like that again I'll divorce you,' she replied icily at which point Tim looked thoroughly thrown.

'I was only joking,' he said lamely.

'Well, don't. Because it's not funny and what you've just said is a pretty disgusting thing to say to your wife,' she said, blinking away angry tears. She shoved Tim away.

He was blocking her path and she didn't want to be near him a second longer.

'Well, I apologise then,' he said flatly, unsmiling 'And I'll leave you to pack now. My chopper's here so I might as well say goodbye.'

'I'll see you in eight days,' said Jennifer grimly.

'You will. Oh, and Jennifer?'

'Yes.'

'Make sure you don't forget to pack these. They're vital for a trip to see Karen I'm sure.'

With her heart in her mouth Jennifer turned around slowly only to see Tim clutching a very sexy, very flimsy pair of knickers. She felt sick.

'Oh,' she said lightly, snatching them away from him and stuffing them back into a drawer. 'I won't be needing those, that's for sure.'

'Right,' he said, his face impossible to read. 'I'll be off then, I'll just go and say goodbye to the children.'

'Bye, have a great week in Monaco.'

'Thanks,' he said, and without so much as a peck on the cheek he left.

TUNNEL NUMBER TWO

What Could Have Been—Tim

Joe had been dozing on and off for an hour now, his face a picture of pure contentment, his huge body heavy with sleep. All Jennifer had done during this time was stare at him, for his was a face she could quite happily gaze at for hours on end. In fact, she reckoned she could probably do at least a month without getting bored.

She'd felt the same way when each of her newborns had first arrived in the world. She'd spent hours examining their faces, drinking them in, marvelling at their very presence and at how miraculous it felt to have them in her life. But she'd never felt anything remotely similar for an adult before. For someone who had facial hair and size twelve feet. And yet the comparisons between her feelings for Joe and the unconditional love she felt as a parent didn't end there. It was only the other day that during one of her long, angst-filled telephone discussions with Karen (which she'd come to rely on increasingly as she tried to work out how to untangle the extraordinary mess her life was in), she'd told her friend that Joe was the only person alive, other than her kids, whom she could say with any certainty she'd take a bullet for. Not needlessly of course. She wouldn't do it just to prove a point or anything. That would be ridiculous. Yet, if it was a case of saving either herself or him, she'd sacrifice herself every time, just as she would with each of her offspring. However, if the choice were between saving herself or Tim, she'd scarper out of the line of fire quicker than you could say 'Sorry love, needs must'.

Karen had laughed heartily at this (perhaps with slightly too much relish), before adding, 'If you think about it, it would probably be worth shoving Tim in front of a bullet. You'd get the life insurance for starters. Plus that way everyone would feel sorry for you for being widowed, so when you "suddenly" took up with Joe they'd all be happy for you. Perfect.'

At that point Jennifer had checked herself. Reaching the point where you started fantasising about the untimely death of your husband probably wasn't healthy, even if her best friend had clearly been doing it for years.

Joe's eyes slowly opened. When he realised she was watching him, a slow leisurely grin sprawled across his face. 'Hello you, have I been asleep?'

'Yeah,' said Jennifer, laughing.

'What you laughing at?' he said, still half asleep.

'You've had an hour.'

'An hour? Have I heck?' he said, yawning and stretching out his huge arms before pulling her in for a hug. Jennifer had noticed that his Yorkshire accent had become more pronounced as soon as he'd arrived back in his home county.

'And what have you been up to while I've been resting my eyeballs?'

'Staring at you,' she admitted, totally unashamed. They were both far too smitten with one another to bother trying to be cool. There was no point.

'Stalker,' said Joe.

'Creepy,' agreed Jennifer, nuzzling herself right into him.

'Aah this is such heaven,' he said, his eyes still squinting while he slowly continued to wake up properly. 'You realise we've done nothing for forty-eight hours now,' he added, one hand squeezing her bum appreciatively. 'God I love this bottom you know.'

'I wouldn't say we've done nothing,' said Jennifer, thoroughly enjoying the sensation of having her bum stroked and stretching out one smooth, brown leg from beneath the sheets in order to wrap it round one of his large, hairy ones.

'We've hardly left this one room since we got here,' laughed Joe.

'Yes we have. You even made a roast yesterday. And we went to the pub.'

'For about half an hour,' he said, turning round in the

bed but pulling her arms round with him so that she was hugging him from behind. Jennifer loved the way Joe was in bed. Not just when they were having sex (they'd both agreed that the phrase 'making love' was repellent. Just one of the hundreds of silly yet important things they were in total agreement on) but when they weren't too. He was unbelievably affectionate and often she'd wake up briefly in the middle of the night to find that they were completely entwined with one another.

She nestled into his broad back, inhaling his smell and feeling more secure and happy than she had for ages. For them, the prospect of being able to spend one entire night together was stupidly exciting, so the fact that they were spending seven whole nights in a row together was almost too much to comprehend. It was ridiculous but two days in and they'd already discussed how depressed they were about their little slice of heaven coming to an end.

'Are you complaining? Do you wish we were sightseeing?'

'No,' he said. 'Just being with you is bloody bliss. I don't need anything else. Not even a telly.'

'Wow, now that is love. A proper declaration if ever I heard one.'

'It is. Now could you give my back a scratch please, my little angel? I've got an itch.'

Happy to oblige, Jennifer removed one hand from his and scratched his back.

'Ooh that's better. Thank you.'

'Pleasure, now how about anywhere else? Have you got an itch round the front?' she teased, sliding her hand around him, reaching for his cock which when she found it was already at half-mast.

'Ooh, that's a surprise.'

'You can't blame me, I'm lying next to you,' he said, turning round again so their faces were only centimetres apart.

'I love you,' she said for the five hundredth time that day.

'I love you too,' he replied sincerely, his eyes searching her face. 'So so much. Never leave me will you?'

She shook her head, her eyes filling with tears.

He stroked her cheek 'Hey, little squidger. Don't cry. It'll all be OK.'

She nodded but the tears kept on coming. She was so stressed all the time. No matter how hard she tried to keep it at bay, her anxiety about their situation was never far from the surface.

'You only get one life you know,' he said and his eyes were so sad and so full of concern that she'd probably never loved him more than she had at that precise second.

'Do you want to go for a walk?' she sniffed, wiping her face with the back of her hand. She didn't want these precious few days together to be marred by her constant angst. She wanted to relish every second they had together and to try and just enjoy the present. 'The sun's come out.'

He shook his head and grinned. 'I want to kiss you.'

*

A lazy, passion-filled, self-indulgent hour or so later, Joe emerged from the bathroom, still wet from the shower. 'Come on you,' he said, drying himself vigorously. Despite the fact Jennifer was completely sated she experienced a fresh lurch of potent desire just from looking at him.

'Let's get amongst it, let's get some fresh air so at least we can say we've done something today. Time to leave our pit of passion.'

*

Jennifer loved every minute of their walk through the Yorkshire dales. The countryside was gorgeous. Rugged and hilly and strewn with purple heathers and patchworked with green velvety fields. It was a lovely warm day but not boiling hot like it had been in France. There was a strong wind and the clouds scudded across the sky as if in a race.

'It's so beautiful here,' she exclaimed as they came to the crest of a hill which they'd been climbing for a while. She was completely breathless as was Joe who flung himself down onto the grass.

'Come here you, come and share this view with me.'

She reached out and let him pull her towards him until she was sitting between his legs, his arms wrapped tightly around her. Joe was a large man. Six foot five with the stature to match. She loved this about him. It made her feel small, feminine, protected.

'It's so amazing here,' she said, drinking in the scenery.

'I'm so happy to be here with you,' said Joe, nuzzling her neck with his nose. 'I've dreamed of this and here we are.'

They both stared at the majestic countryside that was spread out before them. It was seven-thirty, the sun was starting to sink in the sky and the light was incredible. Suddenly Jennifer wondered why anyone in their right mind would want to inhabit a city. 'Do you hate living in town sometimes?' she asked, half terrified of what his reply would be.

'Erm…I'm definitely a country boy at heart,' he said eventually, 'always will be, but there are things about living in London I really appreciate. It's a very beautiful city I think and full of so many different cultures. I've learned a lot. Having said all that, I do prefer the pace out here and I do crave this feeling of space at times. I'd be more than happy to move back out again, even if it meant just working in a nice pub that served really excellent food. Nice hearty stuff that was done properly.'

Jennifer digested this. Could she picture herself living out of town? She couldn't see Tim letting her take the children out of the schools they were in.

'But listen, what have we always said the meaning of life is?'

Jennifer smiled, her fears dissipating already.

'Sofa,' she whispered.

'Sofa,' he repeated. 'Home is where your heart is and with the person you want to be sat next to on the sofa and for me, Jen, that is you. So, if that means I have to live out my days in the most overpriced part of London, surrounded by snobby arseholes where I can't afford to buy a beer, let alone a flat, then that is what I'll do so that your kids can keep going to those disgusting schools where they're forced to wear boaters and speak Latin for no sane reason.'

His tone was far less harsh than the words he was saying. Jennifer loved it when he told her how it was.

'Sofa,' she repeated laughing, her heart contracting with its usual mix of love, fear and dread of what she was facing.

'Now, let's take a picture on my phone of you and me with our view behind us.'

They both wriggled round and Jennifer snuggled in as Joe extended his arm around them both so that the lens of his phone was pointing towards them. She smiled into the camera, desperate to milk every second of the time she had with him. Would there ever be a time when they could just be together without constantly pondering life without each other and the situation they were in?

'Look at that little face,' said Joe, his deep Yorkshire

voice laden with affection as he regarded the snap he'd just taken. 'You are a beauty Jennifer you know. Look at those eyes.'

'Don't be silly,' she said. She thought she looked a state in the photo if she were being honest, what with hardly any make-up on and her hair a mess.

'You've got no idea have you? Hey, what's up with you now? Why are you looking sad all of a sudden? Do we need to have a chat?'

Jennifer blinked, loving him for being so intuitive but hating herself for being so miserable.

'Well, if you could bear it,' she said finally.

'Come on then, misery features,' said Joe amiably. 'Let's be having it, squidger, what's on that mind of yours now?'

'It's just…I just…'

'What?'

Jennifer struggled to find the words to convey what had been gnawing away at her for a while now. 'I know it's difficult because we've not had the chance to experience being with each other under normal circumstances but…and again, I know it's a bit wet…but, what I'm trying to say is, if I leave him then we *have* to work out, Joe. I need us to make it. I don't think I could bear to have two failed relationships behind me and, being really honest, I don't want to go through all the pain and upheaval and nastiness of a divorce only to find that when I'm out the other side you've…changed your mind.'

She looked tentatively at Joe to gauge his reaction and was dismayed to see that she'd done exactly what she'd worried she might do by displaying a lack of faith. She'd pissed him off.

'Don't be cross. I'm only being honest. You know all I want is to be with you but...well, the whole thing is just so...it's so bloody big, I'd be lying if I said it didn't scare me and I suppose I just need to be reassured that you really feel the same way as me and that this isn't just about the chase of someone who's not available.'

Now Joe looked deeply offended.

'Not that I think you'd ever do that consciously,' she rattled on, knowing that whatever she said now was probably only going to make matters worse. 'Only Karen did ask me once if perhaps the depth of feeling we have for one another might be heightened by the situation we're in, and perhaps it is?'

Joe lay back on the earthy ground and stared at the sky.

'Talk to me,' urged Jennifer.

'I don't know what you want me to say,' he mumbled, unable it seemed even to look at her. Her stomach flipped as she realised quite how fed up he was.

'Well, just say what's in your head.'

Joe's whole face had darkened and when he still didn't say anything her heart sank. She could also feel herself getting annoyed. Shutting down like this was a waste of time. She knew she was being needy and no doubt annoying but she couldn't help what she felt so what was the point of punishing her? She was on the brink of leaving her husband. It didn't get much bigger than that and she didn't mind admitting she was beyond terrified. Why couldn't he just humour her and give her the reassurance she obviously so needed?

'Please Joe, just talk to me.'

'I've got nothing to say.'

At a loss to know what to do next she lay next to him for a while in silence, wishing she'd kept quiet and ignored her own pathetic insecurity.

She prayed this wasn't going to ruin an entire night or more. What a waste that would be.

However, to her surprise, in the next minute, as they lay side by side she felt a hand reach for hers at which point her stomach flipped back to normal for she knew this was Joe's way of telling her it was all right.

'I'm sorry,' she said, tears racing down her face. She briefly acknowledged that she really did have to address how much she was crying all the time.

He pulled her towards him so she was lying on his chest.

'You're such an idiot,' he said quietly, his voice full of nothing but despair and love.

'I know,' she blubbed.

Joe turned to face her and for a while they just stared at one another, saying nothing. Then he held her face in his strong warm hands and said, 'After some of the things you've just said, I don't think there's anyone else on the

planet I would do this for, but as it's you I'm going to say
it. Again. And then I'll say it again after that if I have to.
I love you, Jennifer. I love you more than any other human
being in this world. I want to be with you. And that's that.
And I'm not him so please don't act as if I'd ever be as
complacent or thoughtless as him because it makes me
feel like a pile of shit.'

'I'm sorry,' she said truthfully.

'And accusing me of only being interested in "the
chase" is just about one of the most insulting things
you've ever said to me. I hate the fact you're married.
I hate the fact that in order to be with me you've got
to break up your family unit. In fact the only thing that
enables me to cope with it is that I can see how unhappy he
makes you. You once said to me that the two issues were
almost separate and that you'd probably have left him
anyway. So why now make me feel dreadful by making
out you wouldn't?'

Jennifer felt wretched. How could she explain that in all
truthfulness if it wasn't for Joe there was probably no way
she'd leave, despite the awful state of the marriage. She
simply wouldn't have the guts. Staying put would just be
easier.

'I'm sorry,' she muttered.

Joe shook his head despairingly. 'Look, I know you'll
be sacrificing a huge amount if you leave Tim but are they
really the things that matter? I can't offer you five-star
luxury and a designer wardrobe, but fuck me Jen, you

wouldn't be the woman I loved if that was all you were interested in. I will always look after you though and I am here to support you as much as I can in every way. I will take on those kiddies as my own and am prepared to sacrifice having ones of my own if it means being with you. But I am not going to sit here and beg you to leave. That has to be your decision. And if ultimately it comes to it and you tell me you don't want to, or that you can't, then I will understand. And I won't hate you. I will still love you but I will let you get on with it. I'll move back here and spend the rest of my days trying and failing to forget about you. But I will say this, and it's not a threat Jen, it's not, but I can't do this forever.'

'Do what forever?' she asked, her heart pounding with fear. What was he saying?

'Be in this state of limbo,' he replied simply. 'Because it's not easy not knowing if you're going to lose your world from one day to the next. I know it's hard for you and I don't want to rush you but at the same time I'm not sure how much more I can take.'

Jennifer gulped and nodded to show she'd understood what he was saying. She had to make a decision soon. For all their sakes.

*

A couple of hours later they were back at the cottage. Joe had opened a bottle of red wine which they were getting through nicely and he'd also cooked a delicious risotto with mushrooms and chicken and tons of parmesan cheese. Ensconced together, away from the rest of the world, they couldn't have been any happier than they were then, just being.

They ate in front of the telly, so that they could keep half an eye on an episode of *Don't Tell the Bride*. It was a particularly funny one because the groom was managing to get everything slightly wrong. By the time they'd got to the bit where the bride was about to discover what dress had been chosen for her, which they both suspected she'd hate, Jennifer and Joe had tears of mirth rolling down their faces. The two of them had been making a stream of sarcastic running commentary throughout the show and now, snorting with laughter, Jennifer managed to say, 'OK, let's play "you look like a princess bingo". Bet you any money someone's about to say it.'

Literally the second the words were out of her mouth, the mother of the bride started welling up on screen at the sight of her daughter in a cloud of satin (which the bride did indeed detest, having wanted something slim-fitting) and uttered the inevitable words, 'Ooh you don't half look like a princess' at which point Joe laughed so violently he practically choked.

'Noooo,' Jennifer wailed, doubled up almost in pain. 'You've got to switch over,' she panted, 'I almost can't handle this any more. Look at her face. She wants to kill her.'

Joe thumped his leg, trying to recover so he could

swallow the mouthful of risotto he was otherwise in danger of choking on. Once he had he said, 'Bloody hell that was funny, Jen. You don't half make me laugh.'

Jennifer swelled with pleasure at the compliment. 'Hey, if we were on this show, what kind of dress would you pick for me?'

Joe gave her a very strange sidelong glance, gathering the last bits of risotto onto his fork. 'What do you mean?'

'What kind of dress would you go for?'

'I'm not marrying you,' he said, not unkindly but firmly, certainly as though he'd given the matter some thought. It wasn't the light-hearted response she'd been expecting.

Jennifer felt quite thrown. She'd only been joking. She wasn't proposing or anything. She was married for crissakes so getting married again was hardly something she was thinking about at this stage.

'OK,' she said, trying not to look offended. She was surprised by how disappointed she felt that he didn't want to marry her.

Joe regarded her for a while, clearly weighing up whether or not to say anything else to go along with his very bald statement.

'It's just you've done it all before,' he explained. 'With him, so I don't see the point.'

Jennifer could be pretty astute when she wanted to be. Sat on the sofa, feet curled under her, she nodded but purposefully dropped the subject. Instead she turned her attentions back to the TV. Then, a little later, once what he'd said had melted away into the atmosphere a bit, she got up and went to give him a cuddle which he was more than happy to receive. Inevitably the cuddle turned into kissing, which turned into groping and eventually resulted in full-blown passionate sex on the floor.

All the while they were having sex, touching each other with a real urgency, kissing, rubbing, licking and sucking one another into an emotion-fuelled frenzy, it was as if Jennifer had had an epiphany. For when Joe had told her he wouldn't marry her, strangely it had perhaps been the most revealing sign of how much he truly loved her. She would never forget how sad his face had looked and although on paper his words didn't seem romantic, knowing him as she did, she had found it to be the most meaningful and heart-breakingly beautiful gesture ever. For what it actually demonstrated was that he had thought about having her as his wife, despite the fact she was still married to someone else. He'd thought about it at length and it clearly pained him that she'd done it before with someone that wasn't him. Of course, what he didn't know was that first time round it had been more of a stressful experience than anything else. The wedding had been so huge it had totally swamped the reasons behind doing it. She'd not really enjoyed it, had felt hugely pressured throughout and had had tiny doubts even as she'd walked down the aisle which she'd valiantly dismissed as jitters.

But he didn't know that and who could tell what ran

through that head of his when he thought about stuff like that. It must be incredibly difficult and she didn't give him enough credit.

Joe loved her.

He really, truly loved her and it was that moment that marked a change for Jennifer, because whereas *he* might not be sure about whether he wanted to marry her, she was. She should be anti-marriage altogether. She'd broken her vows. She'd failed at the whole thing miserably, but then again, was it any surprise? Ultimately, she'd married the wrong person and yet here was the right person, inside her now, loving her to within an inch of her life and there was no way she was going to lose him. So that was that. It dawned on her then that her decision had finally been made.

'What?' he panted now, breathless after an enormous orgasm. He rolled off her and lay flat on his back. 'Why are you grinning?'

'No reason,' she said. 'I just love you and also, I've made my decision. I know what I've got to do.'

TUNNEL NUMBER TWO

What Could Have Been—Tim

The day Jennifer chose as the one she would finally tell her husband she was leaving him began pleasantly enough.

Tim had originally been due back from Monaco the day before but had rung to say he'd been delayed. On the one hand Jennifer was delighted to have another day's grace from seeing him. On the other she could hardly bear the suspense. Still, she'd decided to make the most of her rare time alone with the kids. Aware of how hard they'd been working lately, what with her having been away, she'd instructed the nannies to have the day off. It was so rare that she was in sole charge of her own children it was practically a novelty and at lunchtime she'd thoroughly enjoyed the simple tasks of cutting up the younger one's food, pouring their drinks, fetching the food out of the fridge and laying the table. Thanks to one of her many discussions with Joe she insisted that the children help her with all of this. Joe had pointed out in Yorkshire that if they didn't start helping out with normal domestic tasks they'd leave home pampered to the point where they wouldn't be equipped to look after themselves on any level. Jennifer totally agreed.

Unused to seeing their mother whirling around the kitchen, enthused and for once not looking distracted and worried, the children were responding eagerly and enthusiastically. For the umpteenth time Jennifer resolved to be a better parent and to ensure that from now on she took more control of their upbringing. It wasn't too late for them to benefit from more of her influence and less of Tim's. It wasn't too late for her to be the woman she knew she could be.

At one point Tilly started singing a One Direction song so despite the fact they were still eating, Jennifer went to get her Mac so they could all listen to it and have a bit of a dance, something their father would never approve of and that therefore would never happen when the nannies were on duty. As a result Jennifer and the children were all so busy singing at the top of their lungs, none of them heard the distant sound of the helicopter landing in the grounds.

So they had no idea that Tim had arrived back at the house, meaning that when he entered the kitchen he found them all dancing around screaming '*You don't know you're beautiful*', while using various kitchen implements as microphones.

It was only when Hattie yelled 'Daddy' that Jennifer

realised he was there, at which point she immediately switched off the music.

'What on earth are you all doing?' Tim said, and his look chilled her to the very bone. The happy atmosphere in the kitchen vanished instantly.

Tim looked disproportionately pissed off and Jennifer's heart lurched with dread. Did he know? He looked so angry.

'Oh come on, we were only having a harmless muck about,' said Jennifer, motioning to the children to sit down at the table which they did with no fuss. They never challenged Tim, although recently she got the distinct feeling that Edward, their eldest, wanted to and probably would in the not too distant future. Right now, still out of breath, he was watching his father from beneath his fringe. His expression broke Jennifer's heart.

'Hmm, well I suggest you sit down when you eat in future or you'll get indigestion. Where are Annie and Deck?'

'Gone into town. They needed some time off.' Jennifer's tone was defiant.

Tim didn't say anything for so long that eventually Jennifer felt like she needed to fill the gap.

'How was your trip?'

'Enlightening,' was all he would say and again her heart somersaulted with what could only be described as terror. The vibe she was getting from him was not good at all.

However, then he suddenly turned everything on its head once again, making Jennifer wonder if perhaps she was just paranoid.

'I got you a present,' he said, reaching into his pocket and pulling out a small jewellery box.

'You shouldn't have done that,' his wife replied. She noticed that Jasper was looking a bit anxious, obviously having picked up on the tension in the room. She went to ruffle his head reassuringly.

Meanwhile Tilly was staring down at her bread and cheese and almost seemed to have turned to stone. A stark contrast to the happy little girl who had been bounding about only minutes before, acting her age in the most care-free way. Only Hattie seemed completely oblivious to the strained atmosphere. But then that was Hattie. She was the most robust out of all of them. Jennifer's heart ached with love and guilt on behalf of her children. Living like this wasn't good for any of them.

'I probably shouldn't have,' said Tim, a crooked smile on his face. 'But I have, so open it.'

Jennifer was left with no choice other than to cross the kitchen and take the box from his hand.

'Open it,' he insisted again when she hesitated.

Finally she opened the box only to find an exquisite pair of emerald and diamond earrings nestled on navy silk. They probably cost thousands. They also would have required precisely no thought on Tim's part. She didn't want them.

'Thank you,' she said robotically. 'They're beautiful.'

'Good. Right, I'm off to have a shower. Feel free to pick up where you all left off if you really want. I don't want to be a spoilsport. Besides, if you will insist on leaping around like chimps it's probably best you do it when we don't have any houseguests.'

'Can we put it on again please, Mummy?' begged Hattie instantly.

'Um, I don't think so,' muttered Jennifer and all four children instantly knew that the window during which their mother had been liberated enough to have some fun had shut. They didn't bother protesting and just picked at their lunch until they were allowed to get back to the pool.

For the rest of the day Jennifer felt like she was treading on eggshells and avoided Tim as much as possible. For much of it she sat on a lounger, under an umbrella, her youngest boy Jasper cuddled into her, wrapped in a towel because he'd suddenly developed an earache so needed some serious tlc. As she stroked his hair and watched the others splashing about in the pool, she'd suddenly felt overwhelmed with conviction that bringing Joe into their lives would be a positive thing for her children too. Of course it would. He would be an amazing step-dad. After all, she'd seen him interact with them on countless occasions and while it would obviously take some time for them to adapt to the fact their parents had separated and that their old chef was now her partner, they'd get there eventually.

She was so desperate to speak to Joe but it was ages before she got an opportunity to ring him. Finally, later, once the kids had come in from swimming and had showered and been fed, and the nannies were back on duty, she managed to sneak away. Checking first that Tim was safely ensconced in his study she went upstairs, figuring that the safest place to phone from was her walk-in wardrobe. When his phone went straight to answer machine it was a terrible anti-climax and she tried a further three times before eventually admitting defeat and leaving a brief but urgent message for him to call her.

She put the phone back in her pocket willing it to vibrate and sighed. She hadn't spoken to Joe since first thing this morning. It felt like an age. Probably due to a certain amount of nerves on both parts their conversation this morning had ended up rather tense, which only made the fact she couldn't get hold of him now all the more frustrating. At the same time she knew it was unfair to expect him to hold her hand throughout this. To say it wasn't the easiest of times for either of them was an understatement.

*

In Yorkshire, when she'd informed Joe of her decision to leave Tim, she'd expected him to be jubilant and ecstatic that she'd finally made her mind up.

However, whilst clearly pleased, he'd also been dishearteningly cautious. 'You can still change your mind you know,' he'd even said at one point.

'But I don't want to,' she'd retorted indignantly. 'I'm telling you I've decided and I know it's taken me a while to get here but I know myself and now I've got here, that's it. I thought you'd be pleased. I thought it was what you wanted.'

'Oh it is,' said Joe sincerely. 'It's everything I've ever wanted but I'm just worried for you. I know what this means and the shit you're going to have to go through now. It might be what I want but it doesn't feel like cause for celebration. I'll reserve that for when everything's sorted out and for when we can be happy and start the rest of our lives together.'

*

A few hours later, once all the children were fast asleep, Jennifer regarded herself in the floor to ceiling mirrors which covered an entire wall of her dressing room. She looked fine. In fact she looked good. She was tanned and had gained a few pounds during her time in Yorkshire with Joe, which probably wasn't a bad thing at all. She'd lost a lot of weight lately due to all the stress and had been starting to look gaunt. Now she just looked enviably, as opposed to worryingly slim again. She smoothed down her Marc Jacobs sundress and applied a quick slick of lipgloss before promptly wiping it off again. What was she doing? What precisely did she need to look good for anyway? She supposed it was her version of putting on armour.

Right.

She was ready, or at least as ready as she was ever going to be. She was also ridiculously scared and nervous and there were a million things she'd prefer to be doing at that precise moment. Like eating cat food, prising off her fingernails with a rusty screw, or running a marathon in nothing but a pair of clown shoes, in the rain. Only none of these things were on the agenda. Telling her husband she was leaving him was.

Since that pivotal moment in Yorkshire she'd known what she had to do. Her feelings for Joe had become an unstoppable force. She simply had to be with him and no matter how sad it made everybody short term, long term she fully believed and hoped they would all be better off.

Jennifer took a deep breath, left the sanctuary that was her dressing room and went downstairs to find Tim who was outside, on the terrace, looking at some papers.

It was past eleven. Jennifer had wanted to make totally sure all the children were fast asleep when she told him.

'You OK?' said Jennifer, taking a seat opposite Tim. The moonlight was bouncing off the pool. Everything looked so beautiful. Would she miss it?

'What do you want?' said Tim, looking up briefly.

The look in his eyes made her recoil.

'Um, I just wondered if we could have a chat?'

Tim picked up the crystal tumbler next to him and took a slow, deliberate sip of his gin and tonic. 'Go for it.'

'Right, well I don't think I need to tell you that we haven't been getting on well lately.'

'No, you're right. You don't. You're not even wearing the earrings I bought you which is pretty ungrateful.'

Jennifer immediately felt on the back foot. She'd always known Tim was her superior intellectually. He could spar verbally with the best of them and would always have an answer, a riposte, or a quick-witted put-down. Only today she wasn't looking for a discussion. She was telling him something and that was what she had to keep reminding herself of.

'Look, Tim, I know you don't want to hear this but I have to say it anyway.'

He continued to read his papers which seemed so rude. In a way it helped.

Jennifer cleared her throat and ran her palms down her dress again. She was sweating. 'I think it might be time we went our separate ways, Tim. I've not been happy for a long time now and I doubt you are either. So, while we're still both young enough to rebuild our lives I think we should call it a day and try to do so as amicably as possible for the sake of the children.'

Tim swirled the ice round in his glass which made a chinking sound. For a second Jennifer wondered if he'd heard what she'd just said. She felt a sudden wave of nausea and experienced an intense flash of frustration that

Joe hadn't been on the other end of the phone earlier. She needed him so much. Where was he?

She opened her mouth to reiterate what she'd just said but Tim cut her off.

'So, you have the audacity to sit there and calmly tell me that you've decided we should "call it a day". As if ending our marriage is as important an issue as changing your mind about what dress to wear or what colour paint you're going to decorate a room with.'

'No, of course not,' began Jennifer. 'It's not like that at all. In fact, for what it's worth, it's taken months of turmoil for me to arrive at this conclusion. There is absolutely nothing about this decision that has been light or easy and I am so bloody sorry, Tim.'

'So, how many months exactly have you been thinking about this then?'

Jennifer gulped, steeling herself for the onslaught she knew was around the corner, mind whirring as she tried to second guess why he was asking that. 'Look, you can't pretend you haven't noticed,' she said, trying to avoid answering. 'We've barely been speaking for months. We've been in separate bedrooms the vast majority of the time for years now and I can't remember when we last had sex. This isn't a marriage, Tim, and I know I'm the one saying it out loud but come on, you've never got anything good to say about me, you're always putting me down and acting as if I irritate you, so to be honest I'm surprised you're not pleased.'

'Pleased,' repeated Tim. 'Mm, interesting choice of vocabulary there. You're surprised I'm not pleased that you've taken it upon yourself to be such a selfish bitch that you would actually consider breaking up this family, destroying the children's lives and everything I've been working hard to build up for the last god knows how many years, with zero consultation or regard for my reputation.'

Jennifer blinked. Was that all he cared about? Suddenly she was amazed she'd lasted as long as she had in this sham of a relationship.

'But that's just it,' she said, 'your reputation has nothing to do with our marriage. A marriage is a relationship between two people. Everything else just surrounds it. But our connection has died a death, Tim. You don't love me, you don't even like me.'

'Ah, finally you're speaking some sense because you're right there,' he said coolly, putting down his papers and drink and leaning in to fix her with a stare that turned her stomach. 'I loathe you and do you know why?'

She shook her head, sure he was going to fill her in anyway.

'I loathe you because without me you'd be absolutely nothing. I have carried you since university and you know it. You're a spineless, directionless, useless individual but for some reason I took pity on you and have let you ride on my coat tails for all these years.'

'I've given you four beautiful children,' Jennifer said

quietly, her eyes pricked with tears. What he was saying was so hurtful. So cruel. So disgusting.

'Yes, you've *had* four children. Well done you for being fertile. You haven't given me anything. You're not even a good mother.'

'That's not fair,' she said. He may as well just have slapped her. It would have hurt less.

'Maybe not but it's true. You do the bare minimum.'

'Only because you've always controlled me so much that that's all I've been allowed to do. My only crime is that I've been weak. I've let you steal all my confidence to the point where I've lost control of my own kids.' Even as Jennifer said it, the truth in what she was saying finally completely caught up with her and she vowed then and there that she would change, starting by playing a proper part in how her children were going to turn out. She wasn't going to be dictated to any longer.

Tim stood up and paced the terrace for a while.

Suddenly Jennifer felt incredibly vulnerable. Perhaps this had been a mistake? Perhaps she should have waited till they were back in London.

'You're a lying whore,' said Tim icily, almost from nowhere.

'I beg your pardon?' said Jennifer who was shaking.

'When were you going to tell me about your revolting little secret eh? Or were you not going to bother? Because we both know what this is really about don't we?'

He knows, thought Jennifer. Of course he does. How

could she ever have thought she could have kept anything secret from the omnipotent Tim?

She analysed how she felt. Numb really, but underneath there was also a definite sense of relief. She didn't want to lie any more. She was sick of living like this. To hell with it.

'I love him,' she said calmly.

Tim threw his head back and only then did Jennifer see for the first time a glimpse of how he wasn't just angry but also hurt. She'd damaged him with what she'd done. Of course she had and what could she ever have expected his reaction to be?

No matter how unpleasant he'd been to her he still had the moral high ground. She was the one who had been unfaithful.

'You stupid, stupid bitch,' he said, the cool tone having disappeared altogether. 'And how long's it been going on then? Because naively I had hoped you'd only decided to be a disgusting whore a short time ago, only now you've told me you've been debating whether to leave me for months I start to wonder. You see, I'm not stupid Jennifer, so it doesn't take a great deal to figure out that this is all about your selfishness and desire to fuck someone.'

Jennifer swallowed, aware that without knowing exactly what he knew she should be treading extremely carefully.

'It's not. They're two separate issues. That never would have happened if I wasn't deeply unhappy. I'm not justifying anything but you have to know that wanting to split up with you is because I honestly can't see a way to make our marriage work.'

'I had you followed when you went to "Karen's",' he said, using his fingers to make inverted commas round her friend's name. 'A love nest in Yorkshire with my now ex-chef. I've never known anything so pathetic in all my life. But I tell you what; if that's what you think you want then you're very welcome. Only I'll tell you this for nothing, my dear…'

His use of the words 'my dear' made her feel faintly sick.

'You've chosen the wrong person to pick a fight with because I am going to make sure you end up with nothing. And when I say nothing I mean no money, nowhere to live, no friends and no children.'

'You can't take my children away. You're being ridiculous,' said Jennifer, and though her tone was designed to sound throwaway she couldn't disguise the very real sense of panic that was rising up inside her. He was insane.

'I'm their mother. The law would never allow you to take them from me,' she added, more confidently than she felt.

'We'll see about that,' threatened Tim, taking a step towards her, eyes blazing with fury and contempt.

She swallowed. 'Well there's probably not much point in talking further tonight so why don't we sleep on it and try and have another chat in the morning?'

'There's nothing to discuss,' said Tim, stepping back again and picking up the sheaf of papers he'd been looking at. He sat down and returned his attention to them.

She'd been dismissed.

Happy to get away from him she turned to enter the house, desperate to get hold of Joe and tell him what had happened. Surely he'd be answering his phone by now?

'No doubt you're off to phone lover-boy to fill him in on the latest.'

'Don't be ridiculous,' she shot back immediately, unnerved by his accuracy. She'd literally stopped in her tracks. Shit, maybe she should wait until tomorrow to contact him? Knowing Tim, he might come and listen at the door and there could be the most horrific scene.

'Still, if you really want to speak to him maybe try him. After all, it's been hours since you spoke to one another, hasn't it?'

How could he possibly know that? Jennifer's eyes widened. Suddenly she was scared. Was Tim toying with her or did he really know something?

She turned. 'What are you doing?' she said, no longer bothering to try and sound nonchalant. She didn't care if he knew she was frightened. She needed to know what was going on.

'Me? Oh I'm not doing anything. It's our ex-chef who's been very busy. And on that note, I want to make it very clear that he is not to come within an inch of any of my properties ever again. He also won't ever be working anywhere in London again either, which is a shame for you.'

'What are you talking about?' said Jennifer, her entire body trembling as she tried to digest what was happening. She'd lost control of the situation completely. How could she ever have imagined she could take Tim on?

'Well, think about it,' he said, tapping his temple. 'If he can't work in London then he can hardly stay in the city where your children will be remaining which means you'll have some decisions to make. And in case you still don't get it,' he said patronisingly, 'it means you'll have to choose between your children or an out of work, out of shape chef. So, how are you going to negotiate that one eh, wifey?'

'Where's Joe?' she said flatly, heart pounding.

'Oh don't you worry about him,' smirked Tim.

'Tell me what you've done,' screamed Jennifer who had now officially lost it. She hated him with every bit of her being. He was a cruel bastard. 'If you've done anything to hurt him I will call the police.'

'Oh will you now,' said Tim mildly. 'Interesting that even after all these years you still insist on thinking I'm stupid. Ironic really. Jennifer, do you really think I'd get my hands dirty over this?'

By now Jennifer was in floods of tears. He clearly knew where Joe was and she didn't and the sense of helplessness was so intense she could hardly remain standing up.

'Please tell me where he is?' she wept.

Tim regarded his sobbing wife with contempt.

'Why should I?'

'Because no matter what I've done to you, you can't do this. It's not right and you will damage your reputation if you do something stupid.'

'But I've already explained, *I'm* not doing anything. Look at you, you're a snivelling wreck, it's pathetic.'

Hearing this, Jennifer forced herself to stop crying. Her tears were only aggravating him further and for Joe's sake she had to play this right. The situation was too serious for her to fuck it up by letting her emotions get the better of her.

'OK listen,' she said changing gear completely. 'I promise that if you just tell me what you know, because I can tell there's something, then we can work things out and make sure that no one ever knows about any of it. So come on Tim, tell me what's going on.'

Her tone was calm and measured and a bit like she was talking to somebody who was standing on the edge of a cliff about to throw themselves off. But it seemed to work. The madness which Jennifer had recognised in Tim's eyes seemed to be abating slightly.

'Joe's not far from here.'

'What do you mean?' said Jennifer, who was now wondering if he had actually lost it.

'He's in France.'

'Here? In France?'

'That's what I said.'

Jennifer paused. She was confused. What the hell would Joe be doing in France? Could he really be only kilometres away from here?

'Why? Who's he with?'

Tim regarded her coolly before replying. 'One of my men.'

'What do you mean one of your men, Tim?' Jennifer demanded to know. Once again fear had got the better of her and had turned her tone shrill and hysterical.

'I'm not going to talk to you while you're in this state,' said Tim, marching brusquely past her.

But there was no way Jennifer was standing for that. Not if he really did know anything about where Joe was. Without considering what she was doing, fuelled by rage and frustration she launched at him like a woman possessed. 'No you don't,' she screeched, grabbing at the back of his pale pink shirt.

It was an attack Tim hadn't been expecting and his loafers slipped on the terrace tiles, causing him to stagger sideways before falling to the ground at which point his wife leapt on him and stared pounding his chest with her fist.

'Tell me what you know or I'm calling the police,' she screamed.

'Get off, you're mad,' yelled Tim, trying to protect his face from the punches which were raining down on him.

'Where's Joe?' she repeated, as Tim finally found the

wherewithal to fight back. Grabbing her wrists he heaved her away from him.

'You're insane,' he yelled, flinging her to one side with considerable force. 'Get off me, you fucking lunatic.'

Finally Jennifer's adrenaline started to subside. Panting she reached over to pick up one of her sandals which had come off and slid it back onto her foot. She also smoothed her hair back down and got up from where she was sprawled on the ground.

'Just tell me,' she repeated. Her legs felt like jelly.

Tim regarded her for what felt like an age, clearly trying to decide what to tell her. For the first time Jennifer sensed that he was floundering a bit.

'There's nothing to tell,' he admitted finally, his tone weary.

'What?'

'I just wanted to spook you, make you feel as dire as I do. I have been having him watched though and I wasn't lying about one thing, he caught a plane this afternoon.'

'Why?'

'Why what?'

'Are you having him followed?'

'Why do you think?' Tim spat. 'Because the minute he started sleeping with my wife, what he was "up to" very much became my business. And besides, at some stage I might pay the arsehole a visit and explain that shagging your boss's wife doesn't exactly bode well when it comes to getting a reference.'

'And you haven't done anything else?'

'What do you take me for?'

'OK then,' said Jennifer, whose breathing was just about returning to normal. 'OK,' she repeated, walking away.

'Where are you going?'

Jennifer turned round and was hit by a fresh, over-whelming sense of guilt and betrayal. Now she knew Joe was safe her focus returned to the fact that she'd just imparted the hugest of body blows to her husband. 'To find Joe. I'm so sorry,' she said.

'You will be,' he replied, his face sour with regret and contempt, but this time Jennifer could tell his heart wasn't in it. It was over.

*

The second she was out of earshot she pulled her phone out of her pocket and dialled Joe's number. To her immense relief this time it was ringing and sure enough the ringtone was foreign. She was desperate to find out what on earth he was doing in France. She hoped he was OK.

'Hello, babe, is that you?'

'Joe,' she exclaimed, flooded with relief. 'Where are you?'

'France. I've come to be near you. I've literally just got through passport control and was about to ring you but you beat me to it.'

'And you're OK?'

'Fine yeah course, are you? I was worried you might be mad with me for flying over but I couldn't sit around at home wondering what was going on. I've been a wreck. I know there's not a lot I can do but at least I'll be nearby if you need me.'

'Oh my god I love you so much,' gulped Jennifer. 'Listen, I've got loads to tell you. I'll come and meet you. Give me forty minutes or so and I'll be there. You're at Nice airport right?'

'Yeah, but listen if it's tricky to get away…?'

'It's not, I'm on my way. Just stay put till I get there. Promise?'

'Promise,' he said.

And with that Jennifer grabbed a set of car keys, the ones for the jeep and, without looking back, slammed the front door behind her and raced across the gravel driveway to where the vehicle was parked. Once in the car she turned on the ignition and sped towards the electric gates, the only barrier now that lay between her and freedom. Winding down the window she punched in the code. The wait for them to open was agonising but finally they did and once there was enough space to squeeze the jeep through she took off at such a pace that the tyres screeched underneath her.

She'd been coming to France for years now so she knew the mountain roads like the back of her hand. Joe. She and Joe were going to be together. She couldn't believe it and though it had been horrific having to tell Tim, it was done. She put her foot down a little harder. Now she just needed to get to him.

Heart racing and adrenaline pumping through her system, Jennifer didn't take a moment to gather herself. If only she'd stopped for a second and taken a long deep breath. If only she'd realised that once she reached Joe, they'd have the rest of their lives together and that getting to him minutes earlier wouldn't make any difference. The physical desire to be with him was so immense though that common sense simply took a back seat. The relief of telling Tim after the most painful year of her life was so enormous it propelled her down the twisty mountain roads in a reckless fashion that normally she wouldn't contemplate. She flew round the corners and bends perfectly, driving with accurate precision; but what she couldn't have known was that around the next bend a moped was approaching. A young man was coming back from the bars of Nice. Earlier on that day he'd found out he'd got a promotion so had stopped after work for a beer or two. Now he was veering unwisely into the middle of the road. As Jennifer turned the corner she saw him far too late, and was by now travelling at such a speed that she didn't have enough time to react. The shock of seeing his headlight in her line of vision was so great that she lost control of the wheel altogether and the jeep hurtled towards the edge of the cliff. Meanwhile, the brakes which she'd slammed on so hard simply didn't have time to bring the vehicle to a stop. The man on the moped, who had managed to steer himself to safety, watched in horror as Jennifer's jeep smashed through the low metal barrier at the side of the cliff top and although her death would be instant once she made contact with the rocks at the bottom of the mountain, the drop down towards them wasn't. That fall took five long seconds and the thoughts that flashed through Jennifer's mind and the feelings she experienced in those last few terrifying moments were even darker than the ones Joe would have to live with for the rest of his life.

PRESENT DAY

Max had hit a wall. His own health had taken a battering due to stress and lack of sleep and he was starting to feel quite unhinged. Only yesterday he'd been swamped by a worrying desire to grab Jennifer's inert body and start shaking it in the hope it might wake her up, jolt her out of her coma. It was at this point he finally admitted defeat and rang Karen. Up until now he'd refused to let her take over, worried that the one night he didn't keep vigil would be the night something happened. As Karen arrived, she could tell Max was on the brink of collapse. He couldn't even be bothered to put up any resistance as he had been doing for weeks. Instead he just waved goodbye sadly and ambled away.

Once he'd gone, Karen went to sit next to the woman who'd been her best friend since school, who she'd shared a quarter of a century of friendship with. A friendship she simply couldn't comprehend not having as part of her life going forward. Karen chose not to think like that though. As far as she was concerned Jennifer was going to get better and that was that.

'Hello you,' said Karen. Unlike Max she didn't feel at all self-conscious talking to someone who was in a coma. If anything it was a similar experience to talking to Pete when he was watching West Ham play. 'Do me a favour and get yourself sorted out will you? I miss you, you big lummox.

*

Max had been right of course. The one night he wasn't at the hospital something was bound to happen. It's simply the law of the sod.

It happened at around two-thirty am. Karen was asleep on the visitor bed which was next to Jennifer's. She didn't know how Max had suffered it for all these weeks and now fully understood why he'd been complaining of a sore back. The bed was profoundly uncomfortable, the springs having given up the ghost years ago, and it had taken Karen ages to drop off. However, she was finally sound asleep when the machines around Jennifer suddenly started to beep urgently.

At first Karen wondered if an alarm had gone off. Was it time to get up for work? It was only when a nurse suddenly burst into the room that she remembered where she was, at which point she sprang up, eyes wide with fear.

'Oh my god, what's happening?' she asked frantically.

'Just a second please,' said the nurse as two other nurses also joined her in the room.

The sound of the machines was distressing but not

as distressing as what Karen saw next: which was that Jennifer's face was contorted into the most frighteningly strange expression while her body was jerking in a disturbingly unnatural way.

'Is she in pain?' screamed Karen, wondering what the hell she should do. 'Why does she look like that? Is she waking up?'

But no one would answer her. The room was filling up with more and more medical staff all of whom were far too busy tending to the patient to give any clue as to what might be happening to her friend. They were all shouting at one another, mainly medical jargon which Karen had no chance of ever understanding. They administered something into Jennifer's arm by injection, they checked her pulse, changed her drip, there was more frantic shouting and then finally, finally the machines seemed to calm down, meaning whatever was happening to Jennifer was hopefully subsiding.

Karen was completely traumatised by what had just happened. She'd honestly thought her friend might be dying.

'What happened?' she begged to know, tears rolling down her frightened face.

'Don't worry, she's stabilised now,' said one of the remaining nurses. 'She was having some sort of seizure. She seemed very distressed but she's fine now. You should try and get some sleep and we'll get the specialist to come and talk to you more tomorrow.'

'OK,' said Karen, and her voice came out as a whisper.

Once everyone had left the room, Karen went to sit next to Jennifer. She took her limp hand. 'Hey you. You gave us a bit of a shock there lovely…'

Karen stopped in her tracks.

Then she blinked and went to switch on the bedside lamp to make sure she was definitely seeing what she thought she was seeing.

When the light from the lamp illuminated Jennifer's face she could see that she wasn't hallucinating. There was indeed one very real tear rolling down her now still friend's face. It was quite possibly the saddest thing Karen had ever witnessed. What was going on in that brain of hers? And how could she have missed quite how unhappy she was? If she pulled through this (and after what had just happened, finally Karen was admitting to herself that it was if as opposed to when), she vowed to do everything in her power to make her friend happy again.

The next morning a vaguely refreshed Max arrived back at the hospital only to be told that his wife had suffered some kind of inexplicable seizure during the night.

As Karen filled him in on what had happened, any benefit he'd been feeling from his short break from the hospital was erased totally.

'Max look, I don't know whether I should be telling you this because it's a bit upsetting but at the same time the doctors thought it was a very encouraging sign.'

'Tell me now,' said Max.

'OK,' said Karen, who knew she had to fill him in but was wondering how on earth to broach the second half of her news. 'Well the first thing is, she cried. Or at least I saw one tear roll down her face.'

'Really?' said Max, the mix of emotions he was experiencing at that moment unsteadying him.

'Yes, which is pretty amazing. It shows more or less that there's no way she's brain dead. I mean, she can't be.'

'What's the other thing?'

'She said a word, Max.'

'What? When?' He couldn't believe he'd missed it. His wife had done nothing but lie there for weeks and the one night he chose to be away it seemed she'd practically put on a show.

'What? What word did she say? And when?' he demanded to know.

'At about three in the morning, just after I noticed the tear rolling down her face.'

'And what was it?' Max practically yelled.

Karen gulped and then she made a decision, for sometimes she decided, there was such a thing in life as a good lie. A bloody necessary lie.

'The word she said was…Max.'

'Was it?' said Max, his whole face lighting up and tears springing into his eyes. 'I can't believe it. Oh Jen,' he said, rushing over to the bed and taking his wife's limp hand and rubbing it with his. 'Oh Jen, I love you. Thank you so much. I needed a sign, I really did, and now you've given me one.'

Karen watched nervously, a weak smile on her face. What on earth was going on between Jennifer and Max? Not for the first time she berated herself for not having paid more attention to her friend when she'd tried to tell her that she wasn't happy. It had been easier to assume that her friends were just having a patch. Looking at Max now though she could tell their problems had scratched far deeper than the surface. When had the rot set in?

In the meantime she didn't have the heart to tell Max what her friend had really said and more than ever she prayed that Jennifer would wake up soon. Apart from anything else she needed to ask her 'Who on earth is Joe?'

THE PAST — MAX

Thirty-three thought Jennifer, studying her grey complexion in the harsh light of the bathroom and slapping on yet more pink blusher. She felt more like eighty-three. Eadie was two and a half and Polly was six months and teething badly, so sleep was a thing of the past and Jennifer had never been so desperately in need of a break from the crying, the nappies, the demands. A romantic dinner out would be just the recharge she required.

Of course, in some ways it was tempting not to bother and just to become at one with the sofa like they did most nights, but she'd always said that birthdays were to be celebrated and she was determined that this one would be no exception. So Max had booked a table at a local restaurant, fancy enough that it warranted her wearing something which wasn't leisure wear, but not so smart that the fact she hadn't been to the hairdressers for months was a problem.

It would be such a treat to spend some proper time with Max and sheer luxury to be able to abandon her babies for a few hours of precious, uninterrupted adult time.

She sighed now as she opened the bathroom door and the sound of Polly screaming from her cot hit her in a wave. 'Coming baba, coming.'

Half an hour later, having plonked Eadie downstairs in front of CBeebies and strapped a still grizzly Polly into her bouncy chair, she called Max's mobile. It went straight to voicemail. This was a good sign. He was probably already on the tube heading home.

She left a message: 'Hi, only me, birthday girl. I'm so excited! Eadie's bathed and fed and Polly's bathed, but not fed, because her gums are pretty much on fire. She's basically been screaming all day, but anyway,' she said in a sing-song voice, trying not to lose the plot, 'I can't wait to hand over to Mum and more importantly I can't wait to see you. Can't believe I'm actually going to be getting out of the house and eating with someone who doesn't need their food cutting up or blended. So please hurry. Wahoo. Better go and grab Pol. See you soon, call me.'

One hour later and there was still no sign of Max. Jennifer's mum had arrived and had taken over looking after the girls leaving Jennifer wondering what to do. She felt trapped. By now she was literally desperate to escape the confines of the house but didn't particularly fancy sitting in a restaurant on her own. Where was he? Of all the days to be late back.

She phoned his mobile for the fourth time. Finally he picked up, but as quickly as her heart leapt with joy, it sunk again like a stone when she realised the background noise was of a bar or a pub.

'Where are you?' she said, instantly really cross. Had he not even started the journey home yet? She'd kill him. At that moment she was swamped by a really bad feeling about how the night was going to pan out.

'I'm just having a quick pint with a few people from the office. I won't be long.'

'But we're going out. It's my birthday and I'm ready. You said you were going to take me for a drink before-hand.'

'Well sorry, but I couldn't really say no, they all wanted me to come for one. You know what it's like. You have a nice bath or something and I'll leave as soon as I've finished this one.'

'But I'm ready and I can't believe you haven't left. Why do you need to have a drink with them? Why couldn't you just say that it was your wife's birthday? You see them every bloody day and meanwhile I'm sit-ting here dressed up to go out, with make-up on, for the first time in what feels like far too long, waiting for you!'

'All right,' said Max, 'calm down, bloody hell, all I've done is come for one pint. It's only seven. I'll be home for eight.'

'Only if you leave right now,' said Jennifer, hot tears pricking her eyes. She was unbelievably upset. 'I told you Mum was coming early, and how often do I get the opportunity to go out before the girls are asleep? Never. Whereas you get to go out all the time.'

'All right,' said Max moodily.

Jennifer could tell he was slightly pissed. The situation was getting worse by the minute.

'I'll come now then,' he huffed.

Jennifer felt like bursting into tears. 'Well that's very good of you given that it's my birthday. Or perhaps you'd forgotten?'

'Hardly, as if you'd bloody let me, going on and on about it, like a ten-year-old. Every frigging year.'

Jennifer was stunned. She gulped, waiting for him to realise how cruel he'd been and to say sorry.

'I'll see you soon,' was the only thing he said though before putting down the phone.

Jennifer felt like he'd taken a chisel to her heart and chipped a tiny little piece of it out.

FRIDAY MORNING — THE DAY OF THE ACCIDENT

'You haven't been for a while. It's good to see you.'

'Good to see you too,' said Jennifer, though she wasn't entirely sure it was. She'd taken a break from therapy in order to reflect on whether it was actually working for her or not. On balance she'd decided that it was. She just wasn't a very patient person. Never had been, and yet what had become clear was that achieving anything from the process would take time. There were no overnight answers. Instead, she tended to go away after a session, ponder what had been discussed and perhaps understand more about *why* she felt the way she did but not necessarily what to do about it.

She was also very wary of the constant need to analyse her childhood. It just felt a bit pointless. Her parents had done their best. They were good people. So what if she'd 'married her mother'? The past was done. What she was after was some help with the present. Still, she had decided to persevere.

'So, what brings you back today, Jennifer?' asked

Susan, a petite woman in her sixties with a short cropped hairstyle and disarmingly deep voice, which wasn't the only clue to her voracious smoking habit. Susan's face was considerably lined for her age and there were deep grooves running down towards her top lip. She always insisted Jennifer took her shoes off when entering her house which was where she held her sessions in the smallest of her three bedrooms.

'It's been a bit of a mad week I suppose,' admitted Jennifer. 'Yesterday, Eadie, my eldest, broke her arm. It was horrific.'

'Oh my goodness. How terrible! Is she OK?'

'Yes, she's fine.'

'And you?'

Jennifer paused. Why was it the minute she got in this room she always wanted to blub like a baby?

'Um…' She blinked rapidly. Thankfully Susan realised she needed helping out.

'Tell me about you and Max. Last time I saw you, you had some concerns about your relationship. How are things now?'

'Not great,' said Jennifer dolefully. 'I don't know really. Yesterday, at the hospital, I was so desperate to see him but when he finally arrived all he did was lay into me about what had happened. Like it was my fault. It was so strange. I'd been expecting a hug and for him to ask me if I was all right. How he reacted just highlighted that there's a big gulf between us at the moment.'

'Why do you think that is?'

'I think it's a couple of things really. We've always had a bit of an issue about whether I should work or not and lately I've been feeling quite resentful about sacrificing my career to stay at home. If I'm honest I think I partly only did it to please him. He's a modern man in so many ways but I know he loves having dinner on the table when he gets in. Sometimes he makes me feel like he wants me chained to the sink.'

'What's the other thing?'

Jennifer exhaled noisily, already despairing at what she was about to say, 'He keeps banging on about how wonderful this woman at work called Judith is and it really upsets me because of course the irony is she's a career woman who barely knows what her children's names are.'

'And how does that make you feel?'

'Inadequate, lacking by comparison and also annoyed at myself for not having focused more on what I want to do.'

Susan nodded.

'I get a bit jealous too. There was a time when Max thought I was the best thing since sliced bread. Now I just seem to annoy him. Though perhaps I'm just being ultra-sensitive.'

'Going back to what you said earlier. Did Max specifically tell you to give up work?'

'Not directly. He always said it was up to me but then

would infer that for lots of reasons it would be more sensible if I stayed at home.'

'And what did you think?'

'I think that's the problem. I didn't really know so I just went with the flow and tried to do the easiest thing for everyone. And in many ways I'm glad I did. I've been able to be there for the girls and it's been incredibly rewarding in many ways. Only now they're getting bigger, I suppose I worry about being so financially dependent. Especially with our marriage on shaky ground.'

Susan's gaze never left Jennifer's face.

Jennifer was filled with the familiar urge she often got when she came here to punch her square in the jaw.

'Have you told Max any of this? Have you discussed your fears?'

'I've tried to, but weird as it may sound we never seem to get any proper time together and half the time he doesn't listen anyway.'

She sighed heavily and it occurred to her then how odd it was that she was sitting in someone's box room, on a sun-lounger which had been covered in a throw in order to disguise it, pouring her heart out to a stranger. A stranger who she occasionally spotted doing her shopping in Sainsbury's, no doubt spending the money she'd earned listening to people like her moaning about their lives.

Silence filled the room but Susan's expression didn't change which made Jennifer want to say something purely for shock value, just to see if her expression would change.

After what felt like an endless pause Susan finally spoke. 'Do you think there's any chance at all that you're having a mid-life crisis?'

Jennifer couldn't help it. She rolled her eyes.

'What?'

'I'm sorry, it's just you're not the first person to suggest that that's what all this is about.'

'And, are you?'

'No.'

'No you aren't having one?'

'No, I mean yes I am. I mean…what I mean is, there's not a chance I'm having one. I'm definitely having one.'

For once Susan looked mildly taken aback. This was pleasing to Jennifer.

'OK, so do you want to tell me about that?'

'Well, I think that what I'm trying to say is that I know I am definitely, without a shadow of a doubt, having the hugest mid-life crisis ever.'

'OK.'

'Only I don't think that should be taken lightly.'

'Right.'

'Look, I really hope you don't think I'm being rude, it's just that even when you asked me that question it was almost as if you were dismissing having a mid-life crisis as something I should be able to face up to and get over.'

Jennifer paused in order to give Susan a chance to

defend herself but her total silence appeared to indicate that she'd prefer Jennifer to continue instead. So she did.

'Admittedly, I used to hear the phrase myself and think it was a tired old cliché which applied purely to people who were desperate to regain their youth or just wanted an excuse to wear leather trousers. Only now I'm having one myself I realise it's a far more complex stage. There's a reason it's been given the label "crisis" and I just think people should focus more on that word. You know, Susan…'

Jennifer paused for a moment, trying to find the right words.

'Go on…tell me what you're thinking.'

'Well…I don't think what I'm feeling is as straightforward as simply not wanting to be middle-aged. I think what I'm going through is something I really need help with and I suspect it's the same for everyone who goes through this stage. I know for some people it may manifest itself in dressing like an idiot, or having sex with someone just to validate the fact they're still vaguely desirable but those are just symptoms which stem from suddenly wondering what the hell has happened to you. To me, a mid-life crisis is more about waking up one morning and wondering how on earth you've ended up doing what you're doing. It's the sudden awful realisation that so much of your life is behind you and yet you haven't achieved what you wanted to, in which case it's likely you never will. It's about assessing where you're at and mourning your hopes and dreams and that sort of fizzy sense of confidence you have in your youth when it feels like anything's still possible. Then, once all that's caught up with you, you start to examine other areas in your life at which point if you realise anything is lacking, the crisis just gets worse.'

Jennifer tucked her hair behind her ears. 'Look, if I'm being totally honest Susan, which I know is the whole point of coming here, I suppose at the moment I'm slightly wondering if I can stand to be with my husband for the rest of my life because I'm not sure he really loves me any more. Meanwhile it's also dawned on me that my earning prospects are dismal and that I'll probably never fall in love again which somehow feels like a monumental disaster. Is it wrong of me to want to experience feeling giddy with love again before I die? Is it weird that not knowing how I'm going to fill my time for the rest of my days terrifies me? Because despite not being young any more, I'm also a long way from dead, and with a bit of luck I've still got a lot of life to live. Only now I'm finally wise enough to understand how quickly it's all going to fly by.'

Susan nodded.

Jennifer swallowed hard. 'Sometimes I lie awake at night, listening to Max snore, and I start to feel panic rising, start wondering if I should be grabbing my life with two hands and giving it an almighty shake because I can't think of anything worse than looking in the mirror in another ten years' time and thinking, well, you've had it now. You've lost the opportunity to make yourself truly happy and I don't want to die wondering what could have been.'

Jennifer blinked, determined not to cry.

Susan looked terribly sympathetic. 'And what else?'

'I think it's a stage that shouldn't be mocked because it's actually terribly hard and I can't bear what I'm turning into. I've spent most of this week daydreaming about my past, wondering what life might have been like if I'd made different decisions, or perhaps stayed with other men I've loved. And it's scary because I *should* be happy but I'm not so then that makes me feel selfish and guilty which is even more depressing. I can't even eat at the moment. I've lost a stone in a year but I just want to be happy, Susan. I want to get out of this mire. I want to know that I've led my life in a positive way and that I haven't missed out and most of all, when I ask the question "Is this it?" I want to feel like if it is then that's OK.'

Speech over, the room fell completely silent, apart from the ticking of Susan's clock on the wall. The clock was in the shape of a cow which had always struck Jennifer as slightly absurd. What did cows have to do with time? It's not like they needed to be anywhere.

Now she'd finished, Jennifer wasn't entirely sure where her outburst had come from but actually she felt better for it, if a little embarrassed. She watched the dust motes swirling in the shaft of light that was pouring through the window.

Thirty more seconds of silence passed and Jennifer could feel her face going red. She sat on her hands as she waited for Susan's response and hoped that when it came that it wouldn't be one which would belittle everything she'd just expressed. She hoped Susan had been listening properly. If she had been, then she'd know she wouldn't want to be patronised with something along the lines of 'well how does that all make you feel?'

It took an age but finally Susan's response did come and when it did it couldn't have been more unpredictable.

'Well at least you're thin.'

Jennifer turned in amazement, wondering if her therapist was taking the piss. However, when she caught Susan's eye she was rewarded with a reassuring, wholly understanding wink.

'There is that,' she replied, acknowledging Susan's joke with a watery smile. 'Being a size ten again is pretty good.

'On a serious note though, I want you to know that I for one respect everything you're feeling. This is a really tough chapter in your life. I also want you to have a think this week about what you think the root cause of your unhappiness might be. I can tell that your soul is yearning for some change at the moment, but have you ever considered that by changing what you've already got that you might simply be swapping one set of problems for another?'

Jennifer cocked her head to one side as she thought

about this. This was more like it. This was what she came to therapy and paid forty pounds a time for. What Susan had just said was actually very interesting.

'And, do you not think that whilst you and Max certainly have some work to do on aspects of your relationship, rather than this being all about him, this is actually about you. It's about you working out what you want, about figuring out who Jennifer is and what makes you happy. Because until you can be happy in yourself I don't think anybody else can fill that gap for you.'

'Susan?'

'Yes?'

'Do you ever think that perhaps life should be full of change?'

'What do you mean exactly?'

'Well, why does convention dictate that we should expect to find a relationship which will last forever? Maybe every relationship has a different life span? Perhaps we're supposed to be with different people for certain periods of our lives and as we change and our needs develop, the person we should be with should change too? I think people who find one person who makes them happy their entire life, more than anything, just got lucky.'

Susan pondered this for a while. 'Are you trying to tell me there's someone specific you're considering a change with?'

'No,' said Jennifer hurriedly, 'I'm not. There isn't anyone in my life except Max. In fact, lately I've spent more time harking back to the past as opposed to thinking about anyone in the present.'

'Give me an example.'

'Well, I've been thinking a lot recently about the boyfriend I went out with before Max. He was called Steve. I actually met Max at a party we were at together, and was convinced Max and I were far more suited. Yet I'm pretty sure that Max has never loved me as much as Steve did. Perhaps if I'd stayed with him I wouldn't be feeling like this right now? Perhaps if I *hadn't* given Max my number at that party I would still be with Steve and living very happily?'

'Or perhaps you'd be with Steve and wondering if you should have gone off with Max while you had the chance? It's impossible to say,' mused Susan, 'and it's also very difficult to reflect on the past and remember how we truly felt at the time when our perception is so coloured by the present.'

'Mm,' agreed Jennifer, who was pretty sure this would be one of those comments she'd need to go away and think about before making up her mind.

'Perhaps for next week you should concentrate on trying to reconnect with Max again. Try telling him how you're feeling. I think you could be surprised by the results.'

'Really?'

'Really,' said Susan kindly and it occurred to Jennifer that she hadn't wanted to punch her in the face for a whole twenty minutes. Progress. This was a pretty good session.

'I tried to seduce him last week but it failed miserably,' admitted Jennifer for no other reason than the memory had just popped into her head.

'How do you mean failed? Could he not perform?'

Jennifer wrinkled up her nose, embarrassed. 'No, nothing like that. I just got all dressed up in a bid to make an effort but he didn't even come upstairs to see me when he got home from work so I gave up.'

'OK,' said Susan. 'So Max wasn't actually aware that you were trying to seduce him?'

'No.'

'So what you were really upset about wasn't being rejected, but the fact that when he got home from work he didn't seek you out?'

'I suppose so,' sighed Jennifer.

'Well, perhaps you need to tell him what your needs are. He may be totally unaware of how you're feeling and he at least deserves the chance to put things right. No?'

Jennifer shrugged. She almost preferred it when Susan remained impartial.

'How are the anti-depressants going?'

'I've stopped taking them,' admitted Jennifer.

'Why?'

Another shrug.

'OK, well it's not for me to tell you what you do but I strongly recommend you go back to your doctor and discuss that with him. If you are suffering from depression you need to give them a chance to work.'

'I don't think I need them,' said Jennifer.

'What do you think you need?' Susan asked softly.

'I think, after having talked to you today that I need to talk to Max properly and to try and set aside some time for us to perhaps go away and attempt to sort things out.'

'That sounds like a very positive idea.'

*

A while later Jennifer left Susan's house feeling considerably better than she had when she'd first arrived. There was clearly not going to be an overnight solution to how she was feeling. She still had a lot of thinking to do and it would take time, but one thing she could take control of was trying to save her marriage. It felt like a step in the right direction.

PRESENT DAY

Jennifer's brain was beginning to slowly recover from the accident. Most of the time she was still existing in her otherworldly state. However, these periods were now interspersed with short spells during which her consciousness allowed her to connect properly with the here and now.

After tunnel number two had shut behind her for the last time Jennifer had been beside herself with distress. She'd experienced love on a level she hadn't previously known was possible and then she'd died. It was all so incredibly painful.

She'd been so distraught and grief-stricken that when that depth of emotion had coincided with reality it had been too much to cope with, causing her to suffer a seizure. The machines bleeping had signified the second when her brain had truly engaged with the enormity of what would have happened in France had she chosen that path in life.

Ever since, she'd felt like a wounded animal. Her body was getting stronger though and refused to give up its battle for recovery. This, coupled with willpower and emotional resilience she never previously would have given herself credit for, meant that eventually Jennifer was ready to consider her next move. It was that or give up, but her instinct to survive was stronger. So she'd decided that she had to hold onto the fact that the painful outcome in France hadn't been her true fate, or the one she'd really chosen. It was utterly tragic but thank god none of it had come to pass. Those children didn't lose a mother because they didn't really exist. Joe didn't lose the love of his life. Only then it occurred to her that he might actually exist in the real world...but the idea was too mind boggling to even contemplate.

She turned her attentions and focus to the fact that there was still another tunnel to explore. Tunnel number three was beckoning to her. Its light entranced her, beguiled her and promised something completely different to the experience she'd just had. This would be her life with Steve. With sweet, good looking, gentle Steve. Surely this life would have been more straightforward? The first two tunnels were completely sealed off. The third was waiting and shining brighter than ever.

TUNNEL NUMBER THREE

What Could Have Been—Steve

Steve whistled appreciatively. 'You look stunning, babe. Absolutely stunning. Let me take a picture.'

Jennifer struck a pose. Hands on hips she stared suggestively down the lens of his digital camera.

'Flipping heck,' said Steve, looking at the result. 'Check you out.'

Jennifer came over to have a look and had to admit it was a good one. She looked quite the vamp.

'Doesn't she look like a model, Mum?'

'Ooh she does,' agreed June, frantically dusting and arranging her commemorative plates in one of her glass-fronted cabinets. She'd bought the entire set on QVC a fortnight ago and had been beside herself with excitement when they'd arrived earlier. There were eight plates in total and each one depicted a different member of the Royal family at various events. The one which featured Princess Beatrice grinning inanely had become a secret favourite in an '*it's so bad it's good*' sort of way.

'Lovely colour. I like you in brights.'

'Thanks,' said Jennifer, who was pleased with her new dress. She felt sexy in it. It was bright pink, quite fitted and showed off her figure. Being with Steve these last couple of years had given her a newfound confidence in her body. He complimented her every day and always seemed to mean it sincerely. He always noticed when she'd had her hair done, or when she was wearing something new and had an opinion on what he liked her in which she found very sexy. Yes it was important to dress for yourself, but it was an added bonus if how you looked made your boyfriend want to take your clothes off. He hadn't asked her yet but one day Jennifer suspected that if ever they got that far, it might make shopping for a wedding dress far easier too because he was even able to verbalise his idea of a beautiful looking bride (hair up, dress which wasn't too big). Though having said that, whenever he alluded to their future together, a few doubts had started to creep in recently. For a long time now Steve had just assumed they'd stay together forever but seemed to have forgotten along the way to ask her what she felt about this.

'Right, Mum, I'll see you soon. I'll be staying at Jen's for the next few nights or so,' said Steve, grabbing his jacket.

'Oh really? All right then love,' said June, looking downcast.

'What?'

'No, no it's nothing,' said June, rearranging Prince

Andrew into a more prominent position and relegating Princess Anne firmly to the back. She had a most definite pecking order.

Jennifer tried to ignore the nugget of irritation which was building in her stomach. She hated it when people said 'nothing' when clearly there was 'something'. With June there was always 'something'.

'Come on,' cajoled Steve, his voice laden with patience like he was talking to a small child. 'Let's be having it. There's obviously something on your mind and we're not leaving for this party till you've spat it out.'

Jennifer didn't necessarily agree with this last statement. If June took too long she for one would definitely be off.

'Honestly, it's nothing.'

'Mum…'

'No, it's silly really,' said June, 'it's just I assumed you were coming back here so I went and got everything in for a roast tomorrow.

Steve looked stricken. 'Oh no, did you?'

Eager to leave, Jennifer quickly assessed the situation. 'I tell you what,' she chimed in, 'why don't we just crash at mine tonight as planned? That way we don't have to spend a fortune on a taxi or leave the party early, but then we could always come back here tomorrow for lunch couldn't we?'

'But what about you getting to work on Monday, babe?'

Damn. To be fair Jennifer hadn't totally thought that one through but she could hardly backtrack now. 'Hmm, well…I guess I'll either have to go back home tomorrow night or I could just leave here very, very early on Monday morning.'

She was rewarded for her peacekeeping efforts with a ridiculously grateful smile from Steve who she knew hated upsetting his mum. The two of them were extremely close and it was just another aspect of Steve's comparative warmth she'd always appreciated and had been surprised by when they'd first got together. Tim had barely given his mum the time of day. He'd never been able to get her off the phone quick enough, always answering her questions with bullet points and hardly ever bothering to enquire after her. But Steve checked in with June daily and told her everything. They had an amazing relationship really, although lately Jennifer had found herself wishing he'd stick up for himself a bit more when she was being bossy. Sometimes it seemed like she had her son wrapped around her acrylic nailed little finger.

'Really?' said June. 'You'd come back tomorrow? It's just since Derek and I split up Sundays can be so lonely. But only come if it's not a pain.'

It would be a pain. A massive pain. Jennifer had been desperately excited about spending a rare day in bed doing nothing. Now they'd be trekking across town with hangovers, but to hell with it, at least she wouldn't have to cope with Steve feeling guilty and fretting about his mum all day. Plus they'd get fed.

'Course it isn't a pain,' said Steve. 'How could it be a pain when it involves having one of your roasts?'

Jennifer cringed.

'What roast is it anyway?'

'Your favourite,' said June. 'Beef.'

Steve pulled a face similar to the one he made during orgasm, sort of cross-eyed with bliss. He rubbed his hands together. 'Nice one, Mum. Can't wait. Right my gorgeous, shall we go?'

*

On the tube, Steve thanked Jennifer profusely. 'I'm so sorry babe, I know you were really looking forward to lying in all day. It's so kind what you did and so typical of you to be so unselfish.'

'That's all right,' said Jennifer. 'As long as you promise me that next time you'll make it totally clear, days in advance, that we're definitely not coming back. So she doesn't get all that bloody food in.'

'Hmm,' said Steve, looking torn, clearly debating whether or not he should be divulging what he was about to tell her next. 'Actually, I kind of did to be honest, but I think she just loves having us around so much she chose to forget.'

Jennifer wished Steve hadn't told her this. If June had in fact manipulated them into coming back to Leytonstone tomorrow it was actually very irritating, especially since she was now facing a horrible trek to work on Monday. Suddenly she felt far less inclined to be doing June the favour. Dammit.

Steve picked up her hand and gave it a little squeeze. 'I'll make it up to you, babe.'

Jennifer took a deep breath, and tried not to let anything ruin the night. She'd been looking forward to this party for ages. It was Esther's boyfriend Toby's best mate's party and promised to be a really good night. According to Esther there was going to be an amazing DJ, loads of booze, plus all her best friends would be there. Toby was a good laugh too so his mates were bound to be up for it.

'You know what my mum's like,' persevered Steve. He could tell Jennifer was fed up. 'Like I said she just loves our company and you know how lonely she gets.'

'I know,' said Jennifer, only she couldn't quite leave it at that. Usually she never dared criticise the mother-ship but today it felt warranted. 'Only perhaps, just occasionally, you could try putting me first? After all, we do spend a lot of time bending over backwards to make sure she's happy and if I'd known she was being sneaky I would never have offered to go back tomorrow. You always go on about how she wants to see both of us, but it's kind of annoying because she doesn't really. She wants to see you. Not me.'

'That's not true, babe,' said Steve looking genuinely

aghast. 'She loves you. Only the other day she was asking when she's going to be a grandma.'

'And what did you say?' asked Jennifer slightly frostily.

'I said as soon as I could persuade you to have my babies.'

'Well, you're going to have to wait a bit longer I'm afraid.'

'I know,' said Steve, 'one more year.'

As the tube rattled through the tunnels, Jennifer despaired. Steve insisted on hanging on to that 'one more year' for dear life. She'd only said it to shut him up. She definitely wanted to start a family at some point but they weren't even engaged yet and she hated the pressure. She loved Steve very much but his constant nagging to have a baby was starting to get on her nonlactating tits.

'And again, her becoming a grandma has got nothing to do with me. It's the baby she's after,' she added through gritted teeth, her mood worsening by the second.

'All right,' warned Steve. He was a softie all right but not when it came to his mother and Jennifer knew she was treading a fine line before he got annoyed, although given the mood she was in she wasn't sure she cared.

'Look, I'm sorry OK, and I know it's going to be a bit of a ball-ache tomorrow but we can laze around until at least ten thirty and it's not *that* much of a big deal going back. At least we'll be getting Mum's roasties.'

Jennifer battled with the urge to tell him she'd always

found his mum's 'roasties' a bit oily and that what she really fancied tomorrow was a nice dirty Chinese take-away.

'Oh shit, I forgot to tell you, babe,' said Steve, wisely changing the subject. 'You know Mum entered me in for that competition?'

'Ye-es.'

'They've only gone and been in touch. They want to get me in for a meeting or something. Or maybe even a, hang on, what did they call it? Oh yeah, a screen test.'

Steve had chosen his timing well. This was an instant distraction.

'I can't believe you didn't tell me. That's hilarious!'

'I know, although I reckon they probably only looked at her entry because no doubt she keeps the entire company afloat with her spending habits.'

Jennifer laughed. This was golden gossip. She couldn't believe Steve was only just telling her now and it certainly helped improve her mood.

'So are you going to go? When is it?'

'Nah,' said Steve dismissively. 'Can you imagine me fumbling my way through a "screen test"? I get embarrassed enough as it is just having my photo taken, let alone talking on camera.'

'Still,' said Jennifer, 'can you imagine what a house-wives' favourite you'd be?

Steve frowned, assuming she was taking the piss.

'I'm not joking. You've seen the usual cheese-balls that work on those channels. I saw one the other day who was so brown he looked mahogany, his suit was shiny and his eyes were slightly too close together. You'd be the fittest thing they'd ever clapped eyes on.'

Steve rolled his eyes and shook his head.

'Seriously babe, I reckon they'd love you. Plus there's nothing you don't know about DIY so it's not like you wouldn't be in your comfort zone.' Jennifer laughed, mainly at herself. 'I can't believe I'm encouraging you but you never know. You might find you're good and I bet they'd pay well too.'

'Well, you're very sweet baby but somehow being *Price Smash*'s DIY expert isn't exactly a dream I'm up for pursuing. No matter how much Mum insists.'

Jennifer felt a definite sense of satisfaction that for once it looked like he was going to defy mummy dearest. Steve was right, if he were to work on one of her beloved shopping channels she'd be the happiest woman ever. Still, in this instance she was kind of on June's side. She couldn't see what he had to lose. He was a great plumber but in terms of broadening his horizons, prospects and earning power this could be his big opportunity.

Jennifer tried another tactic. 'She'll be devastated if you don't go. She'd never forgive you. I heard her telling Sue about it only the other day. She was so pleased with what she'd sent in and to be fair I was very cynical about it. I reckoned so many people would enter that you wouldn't stand a chance, so she's done well. I bet hundreds entered.'

'Hm,' said Steve, still not looking wholly convinced. '*Price Smash* is hardly QVC though is it?'

'Oh I don't know, I'd say it's definitely up there.' At that point Jennifer started chuckling. 'Oh my god, listen to me. What have I become? I'd never so much as glimpsed a shopping channel before I met you. Now I'm a bloody connoisseur.'

'I know,' laughed Steve. 'It sort of seeps in though doesn't it? Even I nearly got sucked in the other day. I sat down to have a beer, fully meaning to switch over and watch something proper. Next thing I knew I'd watched ten minutes of someone talking about an air fryer and was on the verge of buying one.'

Jennifer cackled whole-heartedly before eventually spluttering, 'How much do you reckon she spent last month alone on crap from those channels?'

'Dread to think,' said Steve drily. 'I caught her buying a steam mop the other day and that disgusting necklace she gave Sue for her birthday, I know for a fact was bought from one or other of them. It might even have been *Price Smash* actually.'

Their shared despair of both June's viewing and buying habits succeeded in defusing what otherwise could have become a row and for much of the remainder of the journey they sat together in comfortable silence. As the train finally pulled into Hammersmith however, Steve leaned in and whispered, 'One day you're going to be the best mum in the world you know, babe. Even better than mine.'

Jennifer laughed.

'What?' said Steve, looking a bit miffed that his stab at being romantic was being giggled at.

'Bloody hell, Steve,' she exclaimed, 'until the day I give birth you really are not going to let it lie are you? You've got to change the record! You make me feel like a walking womb sometimes.'

Steve shot her back a rueful grin. Then he shrugged and made a renewed vow not to bug her too much about getting pregnant. He didn't want to put her off.

'Honestly,' said Jennifer shaking her head and feeling really irritated, 'you're a nightmare and I need you to give it a rest a bit. I've told you, I don't know how many times, that at the moment I need to concentrate on getting this promotion at work. After that we'll see, in a year or so.'

'Good,' said Steve, grinning to the point of stupidity.

TUNNEL NUMBER THREE

What Could Have Been—Steve

The party was in full swing by the time they arrived. There were loads of familiar faces and as soon as they'd set foot in the hallway, they were engulfed by friends. Drawn towards the music, and being pulled enthusiastically along by the hand by Lucy, Jennifer had headed straight to the makeshift dance floor in the lounge, her free arm in the air, moving in time to the strains of the funk which was being played. Meanwhile, Steve had bumped into Pete and had gone off to replace the warm beers he'd brought with him for cold ones which were sitting in an empty bin surrounded by bags of ice. Pete had seemed genuinely pleased to see Steve so Jennifer knew he'd be all right. All Jennifer's friends really liked him but then he was easy to get along with so becoming part of their group had been an easy transition.

'There she is,' said Lucy, shoving Jennifer in Karen's direction. 'She's been pining for you.'

'Yeah,' screamed Karen, upon realising her friend had

finally arrived and barrelling over to Jennifer. If the sweat patches under her arms were anything to go by she'd clearly been dancing energetically for a while.

'It's too loud for me here,' yelled Lucy at the top of her lungs, 'I'm going outside for a fag.'

She left them to it, right by the speakers where the mixer was set up. She was right. The music was loud enough to make your ears bleed.

'You all right?' yelled Karen.

Jennifer took a deep breath in preparation to scream back her answer.

'Yeah good,' she shouted, 'just glad to be here. It took ages.'

'Oh well, you've done your stint at June towers for the week. Now you can chill, babe.'

Jennifer was about to fill her in and explain that actually she couldn't and that she'd be trekking back there tomorrow but decided it would only inflame her annoyance which she was doing well to keep a lid on at the moment. Plus it would be too much effort to make herself understood over this racket.

'I haven't seen Esther,' she yelled directly into Karen's inner ear instead, which was the only hope either of them had of hearing each other. The volume was ridiculous. The police would be round soon no doubt.

'Upstairs I think,' said Karen, pulling a face. 'Her and Toby were having a massive barney about something when Pete and I arrived.'

'What about?'

'What?'

'I said what about?'

'I think he was eyeing up Rochelle. You know Rochelle? Silly cow with the massive tits. The one Esther hates.'

Jennifer couldn't make out what she'd said so she just nodded and smiled enthusiastically.

'How's Steve?'

'Good.'

'No ring yet?' teased Karen.

'What?'

Karen tapped her ring finger.

'No thank god,' laughed Jennifer, only half joking. 'He'd rather get me up the duff first anyway I reckon.' It had become a standing joke within the group that out of the two of them it was Steve who was eager to settle down and have babies while Jennifer was doing her best to cling onto her last vestiges of freedom.

Just then the music changed and someone saw sense to reduce the volume to a less painful threshold. The funk came off and suddenly one of Jennifer's favourite house tracks came pouring out of the speakers, causing her to squeal with delight.

'Wooooh,' yelled Karen, hands aloft.

Jennifer turned round to show her appreciation to the DJ only to find that he'd gone and that someone else had taken his place. Someone who perhaps wasn't deaf?

The guy behind the CD mixer had dark hair, an attractive lop-sided grin and was only wearing a scruffy T-shirt and black jeans yet managed to look really good. Just then he caught Jennifer's eye. She didn't need any more encouragement than that to go and tell him how much she appreciated his choice of track. 'Oh my god this is such a tune,' she squealed, scuttling over.

He nodded his head, smiling at her girlish enthusiasm. 'Better get dancing then,' he said, shooting her a grin.

Jennifer did as she was told and for the next couple of minutes danced with gusto to the tune that sent shivers down her spine whenever the chorus kicked in. At one point she and Karen clutched onto one another and just jumped around together. By now a far larger group had been attracted to the dance floor.

'Who's the DJ?' panted Jennifer, after the fifth brilliant track in a row.

'Max Wright,' said Karen. 'He's cute isn't he? He's a mate of Drifter's.'

Jennifer looked blank.

'You know Drifter don't you? Toby's cousin's ex.'

Jennifer shook her head.

'Why?'

'No reason, I just love the music he's playing. It's brilliant.'

'Do you want a drink?' asked Karen. 'I'm going to see if I can hunt down some vodka. If I can't I'll probably go to the offy. Do you want to come?'

'Do you mind if I stay here for now? I want to dance a bit more.'

Karen nodded and disappeared off into the crowd. The party seemed to be filling up by the second.

Jennifer turned to see if anyone else she knew was about. As she did her eyes met with the DJ's again. She'd sensed him watching her a few times when she'd been dancing and now he was looking directly at her. He gave a small nod of his head. Jennifer smiled back and acknowledged to herself that if she wasn't attached she'd probably be making a beeline for him right this second.

Right. Definitely time to find Steve.

It took her a while to find him. By this point the party had crossed the line from being pleasantly heaving to unpleasantly packed. The stairs were three people deep and not one inch of carpet could be seen now. After a pretty unpleasant ten minutes of barging her way through small groups of people who were so engrossed in what they were doing they were reluctant to move, she finally found her boyfriend in one of the bedrooms. Even then it took her a while to detect him because the room was so full of smoke she could hardly see into it. There were about eight lads in there doing shots of limoncello. Pete was one of them. In fact, it was obvious he was the main instigator and that when it came to the acrid yet sweet smelling smoke which hung thick in the air he was also the culprit. He had an enormous joint hanging from his lips and Jennifer watched amazed as he offered it over to Steve and he accepted. Steve wasn't a big drinker and certainly never normally smoked pot or went anywhere near drugs, which was probably why he was looking a bit green now.

'Hey gorgeous,' he said, looking up, finally realising she was standing over him. It had only taken two whole minutes for him to have noticed her. Oh god. He was wasted.

'Hey, you all right?' she enquired gently, aware that he wouldn't want her to make him look like a loser in front of the other guys by exposing how out of it he was.

'Yeah good,' said Steve, beckoning to her to come and sit next to him on the bed. His hand was all floppy and limp. She perched on the end of the bed, very conscious of the fact that she was the only female in what felt like a male dorm. Steve tried to sit up more so he could give her a kiss. He missed her mouth a bit and ended up smooching her cheek. She had to resist the urge to wipe her face with her hand. She felt like she'd been kissed by a Labrador.

He reached over and rubbed her leg which was fine. But then he sat up and started kissing her neck and stroking her hair which was a bit weird given that there were seven other people in the room. She tried to pull away without drawing too much attention to them but clearly failed.

'Oi oi,' said one lairy-looking bloke.

'Get a room you two,' said Pete, and Jennifer felt her face redden.

'If I want to kiss my beautiful girlfriend then why shouldn't I?' proclaimed Steve. Pete pretended to stick his fingers down his throat and replied, 'Because you show us all up mate, and I'll have Karen moaning at me later saying "you don't show me as much affection as Steve shows Jen" blah blah blah.'

'Er, I am in the room you know,' said Jennifer, firmly pulling away from Steve's hands now which were still trying to stroke her. He was getting on her nerves. How had he got so out of it so quickly?

While Pete turned round to concentrate on the serious business of doling out another round of shots to everybody, she took the opportunity to turn to face Steve properly. He looked stoned. His eyes were bloodshot and his expression was positively dopey.

'Babe, I hate to say it but it's still pretty early, so don't get any more out of it because we've got to get all the way back to Leytonstone tomorrow, remember?'

Steve's face instantly clouded over. 'Urgh, you're not still going on about that are you? I wish you'd give it a rest. Honestly, you're making such a big deal out of it,' he slurred.

Jennifer was outraged. 'Oh my god,' she fumed, in a seething whisper she hoped no one else could hear.

'As if! I was hardly having a go. The opposite in fact. I was trying to look out for you and was only saying that if you get too wrecked you'll pay for it tomorrow. But if you want to be like that, then do what you want.'

Steve sighed heavily and she could see him trying to come up with a good defence but it was never going to happen. He was looking really peaky now. Pale and a bit sweaty. She gave up. She didn't care what he had to say anyway. She was incensed. He was being an idiot.

'I'm going back downstairs,' she said, shaking off his right hand which was trying to paw at her again. As she left the room, she heard Steve calling out, 'Oh babe come on, come back a minute, I didn't mean it.'

She cringed. Great. Well done Steve. Now they'd all know they were arguing.

Back downstairs, the party was starting to lose its appeal. There were simply too many people and many of them obviously hadn't been invited. No one dared go up to the group of unsavourys who were loitering in the hall, to ask what they were doing there but their presence leant an uneasy atmosphere. Jennifer searched for Karen for ages but failed to find her anywhere so assumed she must have gone to the off licence. She did bump into Esther and Lucy though. 'Hey,' she said delighted to see them until she realised Esther's face was tear-stained and that Lucy was leading her by the elbow like an old lady. Her mascara had clumped and she had rings of black eyeliner halfway down her face.

'Oh my god what's happened?'

'It's OK,' said Lucy, on Esther's behalf. 'She's just split up with Toby. He's been a total prick.'

'Oh no, why?' asked Jennifer, but Lucy shook her head and pulled a warning face, telling her not to enquire further. 'OK, so what are you both doing now then?'

'I'm going to take Esther outside and make sure she gets in a cab. I'll either come back or I might just get in with her,' replied Lucy.

'OK,' said Jennifer, feeling really sorry for Esther who was clearly so drunk and upset that she couldn't even talk. Jennifer watched as she shuffled off, Lucy keeping a firm grip on her.

'You OK?' said a voice.

Jennifer turned round and was pleasantly surprised to see the man she already knew was called Max standing there. 'Oh hello. It's the DJ who isn't deaf.'

Max grinned. 'It was a bit painful before wasn't it? No doubt it will be again. Drifter's on for his next set. Do you fancy a drink?'

'What you got?'

'Rum,' said Max, pulling a bottle out of the back pocket of his jeans.

'Don't mind if I do.'

Max gestured to a small two-seater sofa which had been dragged up against the wall and which had miraculously just become free. 'Quick,' he instructed.

*

'Ah, bloody brilliant. I've been dying to sit down for ages,' said Max once they'd successfully nabbed the seats. Jennifer had to admit it felt very good to sit. Her heels were starting to kill her.

'So, how come I've not met you before then?' asked Max.

'Don't know,' shrugged Jennifer, taking the bottle which he was handing to her now and taking an enormous swig. Man alive that was strong.

'Because I've met Karen and Pete a few times now but you've never been around.'

'International woman of mystery me,' replied Jennifer.

'It's Jennifer isn't it?'

'Yes, and you're Max?'

He nodded. 'So Jennifer, international woman of mystery, have you got a boyfriend?'

'Yes,' she said, turning to look him straight in the eye. Her tone almost defiant.

'And who is he?'

'Steve.'

'Steve eh? And what's Steve like?'

'He's lovely. Obviously. Or I wouldn't go out with him.'

'Fair enough,' said Max, grinning and taking the rum back off her.

'What about you? Are you single?'

'Yup.'

Jennifer looked around the room. A couple were snogging up against the opposite wall. They were both so drunk it was pretty off-putting and rather grim to watch. You could see their tongues rotating.

'Nice eh?' said Max.

Jennifer pulled a face. 'I hate public displays of affection like that.'

'I'm not sure if that counts as affection,' Max laughed. 'More like desperation.'

They sat in silence for a while, Jennifer wondering if perhaps she shouldn't be going to find Steve. Only she knew he was fine and actually they had found a pretty good spot here and she was reluctant to give it up and return to stalking round the house looking for something to do or someone to talk to.

'Great set earlier by the way.'

'Oh good. Glad you liked it. To be honest I haven't DJ'd since my university days but Drifter was desperate for me to help him out so he didn't have to do it all night.'

'Ah, well that answers the next question I was going to ask which was do you do it for a living? Only, there's a girl at my work who's looking for someone good for her thirtieth.'

Max regarded her in a way that she liked. He was very sexy. She suspected if she wasn't attached he'd be flirting with her. She turned away. She didn't want to encourage him or give him the wrong impression.

'Well, you never know, if it was for a friend of yours perhaps I could come out of retirement,' said Max, which only confirmed what she'd just thought.

'OK great, are you expensive?'

'If it's her birthday I'm sure I can come up with a reasonable rate.'

'Ah, I like that,' smiled Jennifer.

'What, that I'm cheap?'

'No, that you would be generous because it's her birthday.'

'Well they only happen once a year. Obviously.'

'Which is exactly why I've never understood people who can't be bothered to celebrate. I always celebrate mine by doing something. In fact my whole family make a big deal out of everyone's birthday. Always have done.'

'Even as they get older?'

'*Especially* as they get older. I mean, a birthday isn't just about the day itself, it's about celebrating another whole year of living isn't it?'

'Heaven forbid your boyfriend ever forgets yours. I can tell you feel quite strongly about this.'

'He wouldn't forget,' grinned Jennifer. 'Not if he knew what was good for him.'

Her gaze drifted back to the couple across the room who

were now really going at it. His hands were everywhere, up her skirt, down her top. It was horrible.

'So where's Steve now then?' enquired Max.

'Upstairs. He's a bit wrecked to be honest.'

'Ooh, upchucking is he? Last of the great romantics.'

'Oi you,' said Jennifer, giving him a bit of a nudge. 'I'll have you know Steve is ridiculously romantic.'

'Is he now? In what way? What's the most romantic thing he's done for you then?'

She toyed with telling him to mind his own bloody business but in the end decided he was only having a bit of fun so went with it. 'OK, well he's always telling me I'm beautiful.'

Max nodded. 'Well, he's got a point there. He's a lucky guy your Steve and I hope you know I'm only being like this because I'm disgustingly jealous of him and totally unable to get a lovely girlfriend like you myself.'

Jennifer laughed. 'You're terrible.'

'Why? It's true. Now come on, I'm intrigued. What else does he do? You've got to tell me because maybe I can learn from this. Does he compile playlists of music which remind him of you?'

'No,' admitted Jennifer, thinking that actually that would be quite nice. Steve had never massively been into music, certainly not as much as she was.

'Really?' said Max. 'I'm surprised, I would have thought that would have been a dead cert. But the two of you have a song obviously?'

Jennifer wrinkled her nose up. 'Um, not really you know.'

'Oh OK, maybe I'm thinking too inside the box,' admitted Max. 'It's just when I saw you dancing earlier I assumed you loved music and that you'd be the sort of person who would always have a song for everything. You're a good dancer by the way.'

'Thanks,' said Jennifer blushing.

'So, out of interest what is your favourite tune?'

'Impossible to answer,' she shot back. 'Totally absurd question if you don't mind me saying because it depends on the mood doesn't it?'

'All right Miss Pedantic, then how about if you could only ever hear one song for the rest of your life and you *had* to choose one or have your tits burnt off with a soldering iron. What would it be?'

'"Bittersweet Symphony" by The Verve then.'

'Interesting,' mused Max. 'Rum?'

She took the bottle and swigged from it greedily. 'We're like pirates,' she said, gasping as the strong liquor trickled down her oesophagus.

'Not really,' said Max in a way that really made her giggle. 'I've got all my teeth for starters, I haven't got scurvy and I'm not wearing an earring. You look a bit like an addled old sea dog admittedly, but only a bit. Anyway, back to your romantic boyfriend, I want more details.'

'Why are you so interested?'

Max shrugged. 'Well, my options are to sit here and

chat to you about life and the universe or get forced to DJ for another hour and a half which I really can't be bothered to do. Besides, I've played all my best tunes already, trying and failing to impress you.'

By now Jennifer was thoroughly enjoying herself.

'Right. Well let's just sit and talk rubbish then because the last thing this party needs is the scrapings of your DJ barrel.'

'Pirate barrel,' added Max. 'Right, let's continue the interrogation then. What else does Steve do for you that's romantic?'

'OK then,' she began. 'He cooks for me a lot.'

'Nice. And of course he does. I can tell we're dealing with a proper twenty-first century perfect specimen of manhood here. What kind of thing does he cook?'

'All sorts,' lied Jennifer. The fact was Steve did cook for her regularly but only ever a variation on one thing. Breakfast, which always comprised of four of the following—sausage, bacon, beans, egg, grilled tomatoes, mushrooms and toast. She'd probably had every possible combination and she loved his breakfasts, though did sometimes wonder if he'd ever experiment with anything else. When questioned he always said there was no point learning to cook when his mum was so good.

'I've heard this before you know,' said Max. 'That being a dab hand in the kitchen makes girls go weak at the knees. I'll have to brush up. I can pretty much only do roasts and curries.'

'Well that sounds pretty impressive,' said Jennifer truthfully. 'Chuck in a mean spaghetti bolognese and I reckon any girl would be very happy with that.'

'So what else?' persisted Max. 'He cooks, he tells you you're beautiful but what else? Has he ever whisked you away to Paris in the spring, bought you flowers for no reason, showered you with thoughtful gifts, written you poetry, or are these sorts of gestures all too trite and cliché for perfect Steve?'

'Aha,' said Jennifer triumphantly, glad to have finally come up with something. She'd been starting to panic. 'I tell you what he did do that was very romantic. He bought me a piece of the moon for my birthday.'

The expression on Max's face was not what she'd anticipated at all though. Rather than impressed he looked thoroughly offended.

'What?' said Jennifer, feeling herself get embarrassed and faintly wishing she'd never mentioned it.

'You are kidding me?' said Max. 'You're not telling me you're the kind of girl that thinks that sort of thing is actually cool? You've suddenly gone right down in my estimation.'

'Why?' she squealed, blushing furiously.

'So you're telling me that your boyfriend handed over good money for some bullshit piece of paper that says you own however many square feet of the moon?'

Jennifer didn't say anything, but gave him a look designed to warn him not to take the piss too much.

Not that he took any notice.

Max laughed, holding his sides as the concept really took hold. 'Let me guess, did it come with a revolting teddy bear to go with it?'

'No it did not,' lied Jennifer, hating Max for being so spot on but hating herself more for having given Steve's lunar purchase as an example of something romantic when at the time she herself had thought it a truly senseless gift.

'But who did he think he was buying it off?' gasped Max, really enjoying himself now. 'No one owns the bloody moon so no one has the right to sell it. I tell you what, if I go and make a nice certificate on the computer that says you own some of the sun will you buy it off me for fifty quid?'

'Shut up you,' said Jennifer, though she couldn't help but smile a bit. It was pretty ridiculous when you thought about it.

'Is that really romantic or just gullible?'

'Well, if anyone was to colonise the moon then at least I could claim my piece of it,' she said lamely, remembering what Steve had tried to tell her as she'd looked blankly at her pointless 'certificate' wishing it was a top from Whistles.

'Yeah, cos that's bloody likely isn't it?' wheezed Max. 'That's really likely to happen in our lifetime. Mm, let's inhabit a freezing cold oxygen-less satellite we can't breathe on.'

'You're very sarcastic aren't you,' said Jennifer, turning away so he couldn't see how much she was starting to laugh.

'And of course if anyone did decide to inhabit the moon and managed to find a way to do that without dying, then traditionally wouldn't it be the people who colonised it who'd be the ones staking their claim? Not numb-nuts like you, all the way down here, waving your meaningless certificate around and berating them with your teddy bear.'

Jennifer narrowed her eyes but Max was laughing so hard now it was becoming increasingly infectious and eventually she was laughing as much as he was. The truth was she completely agreed. At the time she'd told her friends how sweet and meaningful she'd found Steve's present but deep down had wondered how anybody over the age of nineteen could have fallen for such a load of garbage.

Still, he could tone it down a bit.

'Screw you,' she said to Max, elbowing him in the stomach while he was bent double laughing.

*

A few hours later and it was most definitely time to leave. The police had been round to warn them to turn the music down, people were starting to look like they needed to be horizontal and Jennifer was concerned that Steve was going to vomit everywhere if she didn't get him back to hers soon.

'Come on,' she urged, trying to heave him up from where he was slumped on the bottom stair, his head leaning against the wall for support.

'Coming,' he slurred, just about managing to stagger to his feet.

'Where's your jumper?' barked Jennifer who'd really had enough by now.

'Shit. My jumper. It's upstairs, let me go and get it.'

'For god's sake,' she tutted.

'Why are they so annoying?' said Karen, who was also in the hall, shivering with tiredness, waiting for Pete to stop male bonding with someone so they could leave.

'I'm starting to feel like a bloody sheepdog,' despaired Jennifer.

'Exactly. I'm gagging to get this bra off too. It's really digging in now.'

Rather than wait in the hall any longer, Jennifer decided to pop back into the lounge to say goodbye to Max where he was back on the decks. They'd been keeping each other entertained most of the night and she'd found him great company. Steve had been unable to leave the bedroom for the duration and although she'd sat with him for a while, stroking his brow and reassuring him he'd feel better tomorrow, after a while his 'whitey' had started to bore her. As a result she'd ended up hanging out with Max for the majority of the party. He was really bright and funny and challenged her more than Steve ever did. It was quite refreshing.

'Hey you,' she said, giving the back of his arm a little tap.

'All right? You off then?'

'Yeah, so I just thought I'd come and say bye.'

'Bye,' he said.

It was sharp and to the point. Jennifer felt a sharp little stab of disappointment at his lacklustre farewell. However, just as she was about to walk back into the hall the unmistakeable sound of the sweeping strings from the beginning of 'Bittersweet Symphony' filled the room.

Her automatic response was to turn and walk back in. She was so happy to hear it. Back in the room she pointed at Max to acknowledge his gesture and, touched that he'd remembered her favourite song, blew him a kiss.

In return Max did something tiny but intimate that felt even more romantic than all the compliments she'd ever received from Steve, and definitely beat all the extravagant gifts she used to get from Tim. He raised his right hand up, made a little fist and patted his chest right where his heart was and gave her a look that told her all she needed to know.

Her stomach whooped with real delight and with that fluttery feeling of butterflies. Oh god what was happening here?

Having managed to stay in control all evening, convincing herself they were just getting on well as friends, suddenly she didn't know what to do. She should go.

Sensing her quandary Max left his post and came over. 'Can I give you my number?' he asked over the sound of the tune's beautiful violin chorus. 'Actually, scrap that because you'll never ring and I'll spend the rest of my life staring at my phone, or getting all excited when it does ring only to discover it's my mum, so can I have yours?'

Jennifer honestly did not know what to do.

She had a boyfriend. A boyfriend who wanted to have her babies.

A boyfriend who was sweet and lovely to her. A boyfriend who was currently upstairs, staggering around no doubt, trying to find his jumper.

But she was attracted to Max on so many levels and he wasn't the only one who had picked up on how well they got on. They'd really connected in a way that seemed quite rare.

'I don't think I can,' she said eventually. 'I'm sorry.'

She turned to go but giving it one last shot Max said, 'Well, at least let me take it so I can talk to you about DJing at your friend's birthday. In other words let me take it in a professional capacity.'

Jennifer smiled, her mind racing, knowing that what he'd just done was to provide her with an excuse. 'Bittersweet Symphony' was still playing. She was feeling quite tipsy and was annoyed enough with Steve to reason that just giving out her number hardly equated to being unfaithful. It would almost be rude not to if all he wanted to do was talk about playing at Jackie's birthday party.

*

And then, everything in the tunnel froze for a second, like a film which had been paused. In that moment the past collided with the present and Jennifer found herself circling her twenty-five-year-old self. And it was the strangest thing because of course she knew precisely what was supposed to happen next. She knew that she simply hadn't been able to resist the pull of Max and that she'd had a feeling deep within her gut that she would be insane to let him slip through her fingers. Furthermore, she knew that any second now she would get her lipstick out of her pocket and write her number down Max's arm, thus ruining her favourite lippy in the process.

*

'But, as everything started moving again, none of the above was what she saw and Jennifer now understood that this was the point where 'what could have been' was about to become apparent for the first time since she'd entered this world. So far what she'd experienced was what did happen. What she'd remembered and reflected on so many times over the years was there to be relived, perfectly vivid and in full Technicolor. It was so bizarre to recall how she'd felt that day. She could practically feel her younger self's indecision, could see her conflicted mind swirling and knew it was the exact point when things could have very easily gone the other way.

And in this version she said, 'I can't. I just can't give you my number. I'm really sorry.' Then she tore out of the room and into the hall where she hauled Steve to his feet and left before anything else could happen.

*

As for Max he went home alone and lay in bed thinking about the girl in the pink dress and how he hadn't met anybody remotely as pretty and funny in years and what a lucky, lucky bloke that Steve was. His last thought before he fell into a deep, dreamless sleep was that he hoped that one day Steve would give her a song that could be theirs. That seemed to be the least she deserved as opposed to what he suspected might be a life sentence of cuddly toys.

PRESENT DAY

As far as the doctors were concerned, Jennifer was doing really well. She was making progress and her condition had now been stable for a week. What they had no way of knowing of course, was that inside she felt desperately sad.

Meeting Max again had been the most surreal of her experiences so far. She had been flooded with memories as she recalled how good they'd been together back in the early days of their relationship. The nostalgia had been overwhelming and she couldn't believe either of them had ever forgotten what had pulled them together in the first place. He was her Max. Her funny, sweet, good looking, bright, laid back, clever Max. How had they managed, over the years, to forget what they had together? How had they let becoming parents change them into different people? How could he ever have even contemplated risking everything they had for a cheap fling? Suddenly she wanted to get back. She needed to get back, for lots of reasons, one of them being to tell him how angry she was.

But she could sense that her body hadn't yet caught up with her mind and so was powerless to do anything but wait. Her physical self still needed longer to heal. What should she do?

In the end it appeared she didn't have much choice. Apparently she had to see this through and so she found herself floating down tunnel number three again, where she would find out once and for all what life with Steve would have brought with it.

TUNNEL NUMBER THREE

What Could Have Been—Steve

Jennifer and Steve sat in the car, both gazing fixedly ahead at the windscreen. The weather matched their mood. It was a grey, bleak, miserable day.

She was the one to break the protracted silence first by suddenly sniffing loudly before rummaging in her handbag for a tissue.

'We'd better get going hadn't we?' she suggested, voice tight. 'You don't want to be late.'

Steve sighed heavily and by way of reply simply turned the key in the ignition.

While he was putting his seatbelt on Jennifer asked, 'Is there really no way you can get out of going in? Surely if you said you'd been violently sick they'd have to cope without you somehow, wouldn't they?'

Steve shook his head, his face despairing. 'I'm not lying. No point letting them down.'

'OK.'

'What about you? Where do you want dropping?'

'Um…' Jennifer's brain felt utterly blank. She decided then that there was no way she personally could put herself through going into work when feeling like this. 'If you've got time to, just drop me home. I'll phone and say I'm going to work from there for the rest of the day.'

'Fine.'

*

Twenty minutes later Jennifer waved goodbye to Steve and shut the door behind her. She had thought she'd prefer to be with him but as it turned out it was a relief to be alone. Besides, Steve was a big boy and if he thought going into work was the best thing to do she wasn't going to stop him. Perhaps he needed the distraction? There was so much to say to one another. Only not yet. They needed time to absorb. Time to digest.

Unsure what to do with herself, she pottered aimlessly about the kitchen for a while. It was already pretty tidy but she still wiped all the surfaces and unloaded the dishwasher, drawing comfort from the mundane tasks. Once there was nothing left to clean she made herself a huge doorstep sandwich stuffed with cheese, ham and mayonnaise, which she chewed morosely at the table.

Once she'd finished, despite feeling totally full, she decided to have a piece of cake as well. It would be total comfort eating but frankly it was comfort she was after. She was dealing with so many different emotions at the moment; relief, horror, grief, pity and above all a huge sense of injustice. Her stomach churned at the mere thought of how they were going to cope.

'Cooeee,' came the familiar voice of her mother-in-law. She heard the front door slam. Her solitude was destroyed. She felt like screaming.

'You home, Jen?'

'In here,' she called back, glancing at the clock. Damn. Just for once, she'd thought she'd have the house to herself for a change. She could have sworn June had said she wouldn't be back till gone six.

'What are you doing back so early?' she said, trying but failing not to sound accusatory. Not that June noticed.

'Sue had to leave. We were at the Marks and Spencer's cafe having a nice éclair and a cup of tea when she got a text. There was some emergency,' she said, bustling in, arms laden with shopping bags. 'So her daughter-in-law needed her to pick up the little one from nursery. Janice was obviously only too happy to help. That little girl is the love of her life.'

Jennifer smiled a rueful smile, used to these kinds of veiled digs.

'Anyway, have you set the Sky plus? Stevie boy's on in a minute isn't he?'

'He is indeed,' said Jennifer. 'I was going to watch him with a piece of cake and a cup of tea.'

'Good idea, get the kettle on then, love. Though I'm

not sure you want to be having any cake. You'll lose your figure before you've even got preggy,' the older woman cackled.

Jennifer's jaw literally dropped. What a bitch. She hated living with her mother-in-law sometimes. She could still hardly believe she'd allowed it to happen. Yet it made perfect financial sense of course. She and Steve were saving a fortune between the two of them each month and had already built up a pretty impressive nest egg. Their wedding had been stupidly expensive and if they wanted a chance of buying a place of their own this was the way. Still, at moments like this she'd sooner rent for the rest of her life.

*

As Jennifer and June sunk into the settee, Jennifer felt a dull ache in her lower abdomen.

'I'm just going to the loo,' she said dully to her mother-in-law.

'Well hurry up,' June flapped. 'He'll be on in a minute.'

Jennifer thought she would probably get over it if she missed a few minutes but didn't say anything. In the privacy of the bathroom however, once she'd seen the inevitable tell-tale sign that once again there would be no baby that month, she wept. She may have been far cooler about getting pregnant when she hadn't wanted to be, but the minute she'd decided it was time to go for it, it had become her be all and end all. She and Steve had been mutually upset every month when their attempts kept failing. In fact, more recently, it had probably been her who'd been most despondent as every period had arrived with sickening punctuality.

Right, she needed to be strong. Firstly because she was not ready to discuss anything with June yet, and secondly for Steve. She fumbled under the sink for a Tampax, splashed her face with cold water, washed her hands and went to join June in the lounge just as the title music for the *Price Smash* DIY bonanza was about to begin.

'Good afternoon and welcome,' said the heavily made-up blonde who Jennifer had met a few times and actually quite liked. Her off-screen persona wasn't nearly as brassy as her on-screen one. 'You're watching *Price Smash* with myself Debbie Pierman, and Steve Barrett, our resident DIY expert. Hiya Steve.'

'Hiya Debbie.'

'Now, over the next two hours, we're going to be bringing you some incredible deals on big name brands from the world of home improvement aren't we, Steve?'

'Yeah that's right, Debbie. Not only have I got a leaf shredder coming up for you but also a power drill from Black and Decker and a pressure washer from Kärcher which we're selling at the lowest price it's ever been.'

'He's so slick,' said June.

Jennifer nodded and was relieved to see that on screen at least Steve appeared to be OK.

*

Later that night, Jennifer lay in bed half watching a film, passing the time as she waited for Steve to come in.

It was gone midnight when the door finally opened, and Steve tentatively peered round it, trying to detect whether or not his wife was asleep.

'Hey you,' said Jennifer.

'Hey,' said Steve, coming in properly now he knew she was awake and going to hang his suit jacket up.

'Are you OK? How was work?'

Steve took off his tie then sunk heavily down onto the end of the bed, narrowly missing Jennifer's foot under the duvet. He hung his head and massaged his temples with his thumb and finger for a while but didn't say anything.

Jennifer crawled across the bed to where he was and stroked his back at which point her husband turned around. Her heart ached as she realised he was crying. Clearly the ordeal of having to go to work and then not only having to appear normal but having to talk about power tools for two hours straight, while looking as if he actually gave a shit, had caught up with him. As sobs wracked through his tired, stressed body his shoulders began to shudder. It was so sad. Jennifer's heart actually contracted with pain.

'Oh Steve,' she soothed, her own tears finally catching up with her properly.

A while later, having let it all out, they lay in bed, facing one another. Eventually Jennifer decided to ask the question which had been on her mind all day.

'So, what are we going to do? Do we adopt?'

Steve sniffed and raised a hand to stroke her hair. 'I don't know. I don't think I want to. I just don't think it would be the same.'

'But you're not ruling it out?' whispered Jennifer, who also had no idea at this stage how she really felt about anything.

'No, I'm not ruling it out,' said Steve.

Jennifer leaned in to kiss him on the mouth but Steve pulled away. 'I'm sorry. I can't. Not tonight.'

'I'm not trying to have sex,' she said. 'Just a kiss.'

He pulled her in close and kissed her on the top of her head. It would do. It was closeness Jennifer was after.

'Everyone's going to laugh,' he mumbled into her hair.

'What?' asked Jennifer, bemused and by this point utterly exhausted too.

'When it's this way round. Blokes get the piss ripped out of them.'

Jennifer was moved to half sit up. 'I'm sorry,' she said softly, resting on one elbow, 'but if anybody thought this was an appropriate thing to take the piss out of someone for, then frankly they're not worth knowing.'

Steve shrugged and gave her a strange look which took her a while to decipher.

'Oh my god. You want to say it's me don't you?'

Unable to say it Steve shut his eyes and turned over.

Jennifer started to cry. It was all so shit and so bloody unfair. Why them? Eighteen months they'd been trying for a baby. Eighteen months of shagging on cue, not drinking, peeing on sticks and taking supplements they'd endured, interspersed with bitter disappointment every four weeks or so. All of that time, money, energy and effort had been used up, only for Jennifer to find out that her fit, seemingly virile husband who had desperately wanted to be a dad ever since she could remember was firing blanks and had as much hope of conceiving as he did of becoming president of the United States.

Steve turned round, his face full of despair. 'I'm so sorry Jen, and I will completely understand if you want to leave me.'

'Oh you silly sod,' she sniffed. 'No, I'm just a bit flabbergasted that you care so much about what other people are going to think. Personally I think we don't tell them anything. It's none of their business, and I for one will just say that we've had trouble and that it's not going to happen. End of story. I don't think either of us need to go around filling people in on the details.'

'OK,' said Steve, looking sheepish. 'But also…if you do want to leave me and find someone who can give you children I'd understand.'

'Are you kidding me?'

'Kidding me,' said Steve, his eyes full of bitter disappointment and despair. 'Good choice of word.'

Jennifer laughed through her tears. 'Oh come here you.'

She held him tight and slowly could feel some of the tension starting to seep out of his body. They clung on to one another in this manner for hours, united in their grief for the family they would never have.

'I love you so much,' said Steve at one point. 'I can't believe you're not going to leave me.'

'If you even so much as suggest that again I'll be livid,' said Jennifer firmly.

It was three am by this point. The digital clock by their bed displayed it in green. Sleep for either of them seemed unlikely now.

'But…'

'But what?' said Steve, his expression one of pure panic.

'Please don't totally rule out adoption. There are lots of children out there with nobody to love them.'

'I know,' said Steve. 'I know. I love you, Jen.'

'I love you too. And Steve?

'What?'

'I'm so so sorry.'

PRESENT DAY

Jennifer was getting used to finding out things she never could have predicted. Poor Steve. Of all the people to be infertile. Sometimes life didn't half play cruel tricks on people.

For a while Jennifer pondered over the lives she could have had and the children she'd borne in each of them. If she'd been with Aidan she'd have had endearing, sweet Nathan who she knew she would have loved fiercely with every inch of her being. Then there were the four children she'd shared with Tim, each one lovely but very much a product of their upbringing and ultimately all to be damaged by losing their mother at such tender ages. Then she thought of Polly and Eadie and with a stab of potent, maternal love, her insides lurched with a sense of urgency, another sign that slowly reality was taking hold. She needed to return to them. She needed to feel their small bodies in her arms. Her little girls. Her real, living, breathing, little girls who thrilled and drained her every day in equal measure.

Suddenly, Jennifer could sense that her experience was

beginning to draw to a close. Something was either going to change or end soon. But first she had one more journey to make. She hoped, really hoped, that everything was going to be OK. Not perfect. She would probably never expect that ever again because she no longer believed it even existed, but OK would be just fine. OK would be nice.

TUNNEL NUMBER THREE

What Could Have Been—Steve

Jennifer got out of the shower and wrapped herself in a towel before removing her shower cap. She'd been to the hairdressers earlier and hadn't wanted to ruin her hair before the party. She was very pleased when it tumbled out and didn't look frizzy.

'You all right, gorgeous?' called Steve from the bedroom where he was also getting ready. 'You excited?'

'Very,' replied Jennifer, applying a nice generous portion of Lancôme moisturiser to her face. As the steam started to clear from the mirror she regarded her reflection. Her hairdresser had done a great job. All the grey was covered and recently she'd started having a few low lights which helped soften everything up a bit. She was confident that once she had her make-up on and was wearing her nice new Phase Eight dress, she'd look really nice, elegant, 'good for her age'. Although when your age was sixty you were never going to be exuding a youthful bloom or the kind of sex appeal you once had in your thirties and to an extent forties. Still, one of the few advantages of getting older was that you tended to care less about things that weren't really important in the grand scheme of things. Walking past a building site and not being whistled at wasn't the end of the world. These days Jennifer was happy to blend into the background and be a spectator rather than the main event. As time marched on she had an increasing amount of life to look back on and less future to worry about which enabled her to enjoy the present more.

Her patience levels had definitely improved too. Take the arrangements for today for instance. The person she'd been in her twenties would have spent the last few weeks panicking that it wouldn't be perfect, that people would be bored/not come/hate the food. As it was she'd taken all the planning in her stride, knowing that of course her guests would have a lovely time and that if the caterers she'd hired to do a barbecue weren't very good, it wouldn't be the end of the world. Perhaps people should put off getting married till they were in their sixties, she mused idly? For if she had her time again, she certainly wouldn't waste all that energy fretting over tiny details no one cared about.

'Who's dressing your mother?' she asked, poking her head out of the en-suite as the thought suddenly occurred to her.

'I'll do her,' replied Steve, bending down from where he was sat on the edge of the bed, levering his shoes on with a shoe horn. When it had come to what suit he was going to wear he'd been spoilt for choice. As one of *Price Smash*'s highest sellers he was provided with a new suit every quarter. Over the years he'd accrued so many that he regularly sold them on eBay.

'Thanks love,' said Jennifer, glad he was happy to do it. She wanted to quickly paint her nails and getting June dressed would have meant she couldn't.

*

Three hours later, glass of champagne in hand, Steve stood under the gazebo which they'd had erected on the patio the day before. He tinged his glass.

'Hi everyone, can I have your attention please? And don't worry, I'm not going to try and sell you anything.'

The forty or so assembled guests laughed with varying degrees of gusto determined largely by how much they'd had to drink. Jennifer experienced a huge pang of thankfulness as she surveyed the scene. So far the day had been blissful. The garden and house looked fantastic, the weather had held, the food was delicious, and everyone seemed to be enjoying themselves. To be surrounded by all their friends and family was a wonderful thing and so rare too. She loved the mix of generations present and it was great watching her parents, who were both still in rude health, catching up with some of her friends. She could tell they were having a wonderful time, as was June who, despite driving Jennifer mad on a daily basis, had earned her respect over the years. She may have been in a wheelchair for the last five of them but today she was sat upright in it surveying proceedings almost regally. Of course she loved the fact that so many of *Price Smash*'s presenters were currently standing in her back garden.

*

'Come on you rowdy lot, listen up now,' bellowed Steve, a huge grin on his face.

Jennifer felt a swell of pride. Steve had aged very well and was still incredibly good looking. He hadn't let himself develop a paunch unlike so many of her friends' husbands. She glanced now at Pete who was still tucking into the remains of the buffet. That must be at least his third plate and the way his shirt was straining to contain his belly suggested that one small portion would have been plenty. Some people mocked Steve for being groomed and taking care of his personal appearance, which he did because of his job, but she had no complaints and knew his fitness levels contributed to his still healthy libido.

As Steve waited for quiet, some people persisted in carrying on chattering, forcing others in the crowd to eventually do some very loud ssshhing until those who weren't listening finally shut up.

'Thank you. Right,' began Steve. 'So, as you know we're all here because, as hard as it is to believe, Jennifer, my beautiful wife, has turned sixty years old today.'

A few people cheered and someone at the back did a wolf whistle which made everyone laugh.

'Jen, I don't want you to go anywhere near that man,' joked Steve, pointing at the culprit. 'He simply can't be trusted. Take it from me I know,' he added, winking at his work colleague to show he was joking. 'Jen, actually where are you, babe?' he said scouting the crowd, one hand up to shield his eyes from the sun. 'I want you up here next to me where we can all see you.'

'I'm here,' she waved, from where she'd been attempting to keep a low profile by the buffet table.

Lucy who was stood next to her gave her an encouraging shove.

'Well get up here,' Steve insisted.

There was another loud cheer at which point Jennifer realised she definitely should have served the food earlier. They were all three sheets to the wind. Grinning madly she went up to join her husband.

'Come here beautiful,' said Steve, loving the whole thing and waiting for the cheers to subside. 'Now, I just want to say in front of all our friends and family that I honestly feel like I owe you my life, for you, Jennifer, are the kindest, most unselfish, gorgeous woman ever to have walked this earth.'

Jennifer could feel herself welling up. Steve had never been anything but lovely to her. Sometimes he drove her mad, like when he insisted on watching his *Price Smash* shows back as soon as he got in, or when he refused to go to the theatre or watch anything that wasn't certified a 'blockbuster', but over the years he'd almost drowned her in love, partly due to the guilt he felt over not being able to give her a child. Still, she'd always tried to reassure him that she was happy with her lot. Having their own family simply hadn't meant to be. It had taken a while for true acceptance to arrive but she'd got there in the end. Strangely she'd been experiencing fresh pangs of grief recently as she'd contemplated not just never being a mother but never being a grandmother. Though she refused to dwell on it for too long, knowing that in so many other ways her life was very blessed. There had been some massive advantages to not having children, ones which they reminded one another of regularly. Over the years she'd witnessed how the very tiring years when children first arrived had damaged some of her friends' relationships, had turned marriages stale and left people with no energy for anything until they resembled empty, tired husks. Without anyone else to focus their time, energy and indeed money on, she and Steve had been able to concentrate on themselves and what they wanted to do. There had been periods when unlimited time for one another had felt like a luxury they didn't want, but she simply had to look at the upside or die bitter and full of sadness which would never do. Determined never to lead a life which felt even remotely empty she and Steve had made every effort to achieve the opposite. As a result they were one of the most well-travelled couples she knew, having toured round the continents of India, Africa and America. They'd climbed the Himalayas, raised £110,000 for their charity and, thanks to Steve's ever increasing salary at *Price Smash* and not having to shell out on dependents, had never had to worry about money to fund all these ventures. They entertained constantly, played golf, did yoga and took classes. Their lives were full to the brim. Different to the one they would have had given the choice but a perfect example of making the most of your lot and probably far more diverse.

'Not only does she look after me,' continued Steve now, 'but she's always helped take care of my old mum, the duchess, June. All right Mum! In fact, we should all raise a glass to my mum because without her, shopping channels would probably go bankrupt. In fact, if you don't believe me, take a look at how many figurines are crammed into our cabinets. And in case you were wondering, four combination ovens for a three person household is three too many but there's no telling her is there, Jen?'

Laughing, Jennifer shook her head in agreement and gave June a little wink who in turn cackled away, adoring being the centre of attention.

'So here's to June,' instructed Steve and there was a long pause as everyone drank from their glass and then raised them. 'To June.'

'And watch out Kevin Jameson. She's got her eye on you,' he quipped which again got a raucous laugh from the *Price Smash* crowd. 'Right, lastly I'd like to thank Jen's parents as well, Lesley and Nigel, you've been a constant support to us both over the years. Nigel, we still can't believe you ran a half marathon only twenty years ago for our charity. I'm not sure we'd want to see you attempt it now but what an achievement that was, mate. I'll never forget it. And also, Jennifer's gang of friends, where are you girls? That's Esther, Karen and Lucy who between them have given the two of us five godchildren in total. We may not have been blessed enough to have our own but they've made sure that we've had lots of wonderful little people to spoil at Christmas. Of course they're all grown up now and it's so lovely that three out of the five could be here today. We really do love you as our own, don't we Jen?'

She nodded, a huge lump in her throat constantly threatening to ruin her eye make-up.

'You've honestly all enriched our lives, well, apart from the time Suzy stayed over and wet the bed... Sorry Suzy! You were only four, it's all right, we know you wouldn't do it now. Although the way I'm drinking today...I might.'

Another huge laugh.

'Anyway, on a serious note you've really all meant the world to us.'

By now Jennifer had properly gone. She frantically tried to stem her happy tears with a hanky.

Steve leant in and gave his wife a kiss on the forehead. 'My darling Jen, you're one in a million and if we could please now all raise our glasses to my wonderful wife. To Jennifer. Happy birthday, babe.'

'To Jennifer. Happy Birthday,' said everyone pretty much in unison.

*

Much later Jennifer was slumped on the sofa with her best friend. The rest of the guests had left, either having been seen into cabs or, in a couple of cases, had arguments about who'd drunk less and swerved off into the night. Jennifer hadn't wanted Karen to leave though so she and Pete and their daughter Suzy had decided to stay over. Suzy, Pete and June had all hit the sack leaving Jennifer and Karen to have a good gossip and to laugh from time to time at Steve who was snoring loudly, passed out in the armchair.

'Bless him, he's wiped out. Ah, you're a lucky girl you know,' said Karen, patting her friend's wrist.

'I do know,' said Jennifer and it was the greatest feeling in the world to actually mean it.

'Not many people can say their husband adores them like he adores you.'

'Pete adores you,' said Jennifer.

Karen gave her an arch look and raised one eyebrow. 'I'd say adores is a bit strong,' she countered. 'Tolerates more like.'

'No. Don't be silly.'

'Oh we're all right,' said Karen. 'We're fine and I'm very fond of him even though I do wish he'd take a leaf out of Steve's book and do a bit of bloody exercise.

These days it's like going to bed with a big hairy buffalo.'

Jennifer snorted.

'It is! When he rolls on top for a quickie I feel like I'm getting crushed,' she complained.

'Yeah well, I think you two are great and you've got lovely Suzy,' said Jennifer, the drink making her sound more wistful than she would ordinarily allow herself to be.

'I know, love,' said Karen, 'although you know she sees you as her second mum. You are her second mum.'

Jennifer squeezed her hand. 'Right you, come on. Time for bed. Now we're old crones and eligible for our bus passes we need all the sleep we can get.'

'We do,' said Karen, heaving herself reluctantly from the sofa. 'Love you, Jen.'

'Love you too,' said Jennifer, going over to attempt to wake up Steve so she could get him up to bed where they would both sleep very soundly.

FRIDAY — THE DAY OF THE ACCIDENT

Jennifer was ready which had taken a huge effort. Max had somehow managed to mess up the entire house during his day off. When Jennifer had returned home from her therapy session she'd walked in only to find the girls' bedrooms in a complete state. Every toy had been pulled out in the lounge and nothing had been cleared up from lunch. Still, she'd managed not to say anything. The kids were having a lovely time playing with their dad and despite her broken arm and how uncomfortable her cast was, Eadie was in good spirits. So that was the main thing.

Later though, the minute Max left the house to go to the gym, it meant Jennifer only had a small window of time to get everything ready for her night of seduction. In order to have the children fed, bathed and in bed, the house tidy, the dinner on, herself looking attractive and wearing sexy underwear underneath her clothes, she'd had to run around like a woman possessed.

She was finally ready now but slightly concerned she'd be too exhausted for the sex she was making all this effort for.

Nevertheless, as she crept out of her bedroom, she felt a flush of excitement as her satin G-string rode up her bum. How anyone could wear these for non-sexual pursuits she had no idea but she was happy to suffer it for tonight. She went to check on the girls. By some miracle it seemed they were both actually asleep. Yes!

Then, just at that second, Eadie, who on the contrary was still very much awake, rather ruined the moment by calling from her bed, 'Muuuumy.'

Damn. Jennifer cursed inwardly. She should have known it was too good to be true.

She tiptoed into her bedroom. 'What is it?' she asked, slightly impatiently. She and Max so desperately needed to have a good night together she'd worked herself up into a bit of a state. 'Come on now,' she said to her daughter. 'It's time to go to sleep.'

'I'm not tired though.'

'Yes you are,' insisted Jennifer, halfway out the door again. She wanted to make a nice mushroom sauce to pour over the steak.

'What time is it?' said Eadie, refusing to play ball though and sitting up and looking around as perky as a meerkat, waving her plaster-cast about.

'Ten o'clock,' lied Jennifer.

'Ten o'clock?'

'Yes, it's very, very late.'

Eadie didn't look convinced. She wasn't stupid. Apart

from anything else it didn't feel like ten o'clock, probably because it was only quarter to eight.

Just then they both heard Max's key in the door.

'Daddy!'

'OK, that is Dad and I'm sure he'll come up quickly to say night night, but then we're going to have some grown up time, so I want you to go to bed like a good girl. If you go to sleep nice and quickly I'll buy you some sweets tomorrow.'

'Can I have a magazine too?' said Eadie, spotting an opportunity.

'Eadie,' hissed Jennifer, her patience starting to wear thin. 'Don't you blackmail me. I'm getting cross now. Just *go to bed.*'

Jennifer left the room and went downstairs to see Max.

'Hello,' she said, 'how are you?'

'Good, that was full-on today. Legs are going to kill tomorrow. I need a shower. Are the girls already in bed?'

'Yes, well Polly is. Eadie's still awake. In fact, can you quickly say goodnight to her, then with a bit of luck we can have our dinner in peace.'

'Mm smells lovely, what are we having?'

'Steak, salad, jacket potatoes with sour cream, and corn on the cob.'

'Oh wow,' said Max. 'Fantastic, I could eat a horse.'

'Well you'll need to leave some room for me,' said

Jennifer, in an attempt to get the whole sex thing rolling. Her comment was rather lost however because Max was looking straight past her.

'Hello Eadie Beadie,' he said, managing to ignore what Jennifer had said quite magnificently and gazing up at his daughter who had just appeared at the top of the stairs, arm aloft. She looked like a mini angel of the North.

'What are you doing?' spluttered Jennifer. 'You promised Mummy you'd stay in bed.'

'All right,' said Max, 'calm down, she's not doing anything. It's not even eight yet anyway.'

'See,' said Eadie triumphantly.

Jennifer gave up. Leaving them to it she took a deep breath and headed to the kitchen to make her sauce.

By the time Max finally appeared, showered and wearing a T-shirt and checked pyjama bottoms, dinner was on the table.

'Ooh this looks amazing,' said Max appreciatively. 'A bit of red meat's just what I fancy.'

'Me too,' joked Jennifer, injecting tons of innuendo into her voice and wondering if she should flash Max a bit of stocking so that he'd get the hint. 'Is Eadie asleep by the way?'

'What do you think?'

Jennifer groaned. 'Do you think she wants us never to have sex again for the rest of our lives or something? It's like she knows.'

'It doesn't matter,' said Max tucking in. 'She'll be

asleep soon enough so let's just enjoy our dinner, take our time, savour it, and by the time we're done and maybe have had another glass of wine she'll be out like a light and we can go upstairs and have sex.'

'OK,' said Jennifer, feeling calmer. Honestly, once they'd got tonight out of the way she was going to ensure they got back into a routine of having sex far more regularly. Leaving it this long meant she was actually nervous. Not in an exciting, butterflies in the stomach type of way either. Instead it had reached the point where having sex with her husband felt like some sort of barrier she had to cross. She knew this was a slippery slope and was terrified of starting to view Max as her best friend or housemate. She needed him to want to be physically intimate with her and vice versa. Simply put, occasionally having your husband's penis inserted into you was what marked your relationship out as special and different to the one you had with everyone else wasn't it? She picked up her wine glass and pretty much drained it.

'So anyway, how was therapy?' enquired Max, slathering his steak with mustard. 'Helpful?'

Jennifer appreciated him making the effort to ask. She was well aware that really he thought it was a load of old hokum.

'It was fine,' she said. 'In fact, it was good.'

'Good,' said Max, as if that was all sorted then.

'I mean there's a long way to go but…you know…I felt like I really got something out of it today.'

'Eadie, what are you doing down here, sweetheart?' asked Max as their daughter suddenly appeared at the door.

Jennifer glared at her daughter.

'I can't sleep, my arm's itchy.'

Jennifer stopped glaring, felt guilty and rearranged her face into one of concern instead. 'Hang on, I'll go and find the Calpol.'

One hour later and Eadie was finally asleep, Jennifer and Max were both stuffed with food and had polished off a bottle and a half of red between them. Jennifer's face was hot and she could feel her tongue furring up from the tannin already.

None of this was particularly conducive to sex but she didn't care.

'Right, shall we go upstairs then?' she suggested, almost briskly. If she could have done, at this point she'd have just herded him up the stairs if that was what it took. Anything to just get the deed bloody well done.

'Yes,' said Max, 'let me just check in with Judith first though. Make sure everything was OK today, what with me being out of the office.'

'Why don't you do that after?' asked Jennifer, trying not to sound intensely irritated.

'Because I'd rather get it out of the way,' said Max, 'and also because I don't want to disturb her too late.'

Jennifer was definitely quite drunk because she felt like sticking her tongue out and giving the whole notion of him ringing Judith the finger. Still, she found some restraint from somewhere.

'OK, well be quick won't you?' she said, walking as sexily as she could out of the room. 'I'll be waiting upstairs for you…although, actually hang on, I need to take some water up. That wine's made my mouth so dry.'

When did life get so unspontaneous she thought, scuttling back to the tap?

*

Twenty minutes later Jennifer was starting to get deeply pissed off. She'd been lying wantonly on the bed in her temptress underwear waiting for Max for ages now. As soon as she'd got upstairs the first thing she'd done was to check that the girls were definitely asleep. Upon finding out they were, she'd stripped off, only leaving on her new bra, stockings, suspenders and G-string (cheesewire). She'd put on her highest pair of stilettos, glugged down half a pint of water, brushed her teeth and then arranged herself on the bed and waited, all the while contemplating how she was pretty sure that there had once been a time when she and Max had barely been able to make it up the stairs so eager were they to have sex with one another. Making her wait like this was very depressing and didn't exactly make her feel very attractive. It was almost like he'd be doing her a favour or something. As if having intercourse would be his final chore of the day. I mean, why of all times did he have to pick now to phone bloody

Judith? He'd had all day to do it. If he'd been truly looking forward to a night of passion like she had, wouldn't he
have called her earlier and got it out of the way?

From downstairs the sound of Max's phone conversation floated upwards to the landing. It was like pouring petrol on the flames of her suspicion. He sounded so
jovial, so alive, and like he was making every effort to be
charming and engaging. This wasn't helping her mood at
all, and if he laughed that nauseating laugh again she'd be
tempted to take off one of her shoes and stab him in the
eye with the heel.

Another ten minutes later and Jennifer was prickling
with embarrassment. She felt so stupid. She felt unloved,
unbelievably jealous, rejected and because she was trying so hard not to cry, all these emotions were steadily
transforming into crystallised fury. How could he do this
to her? By now Jennifer had given up sprawling on
the bed and had decamped out onto the landing, where
she was squatting on the floor, head stuck between the
bannisters. That way she could hear exactly what was
being said. Their conversation was all fairly innocuous
but also seemed largely unrelated to work. Instead they
were gossiping and sharing private jokes, which only confirmed that this was a chat that they definitely didn't need
to be having now. The rawness of what she was feeling,
combined with how much wine she'd drunk, meant that
by the time he did finally terminate the call, the only thing
she was ready for, was a fight.

'How could you?' she said to a surprised Max as he finally rounded the top of the stairs only to find her crouching on the landing dressed like a prostitute.

'What are you doing? What are you wearing?'

'I'm wearing what I thought you might possibly find sexy enough to want to fuck me in. Only clearly I was wrong. Why did you have to talk to that stupid cow for so long? You knew I was waiting for you up here. It's so rude,' she cried, hot jealousy welling up inside her, like a volcano about to erupt.

'Calm down,' said Max, only fuelling the fire further. 'I told you I had to phone her because I took the day off today to help *you*. I'm sorry it went on for a bit but you know what Judith's like once she gets going.'

'Oh, and I suppose you were physically unable to say something like *"I need to keep this quick because I'm in the middle of something"*. Or, *"I'm sorry Judith I've got to go because I haven't had sex with my wife for so long she doesn't know if I even love her any more"*. Or *"I must dash, my wife's dressed like a slut, only I've got to the point in life where I don't even care because I'd rather be talking to you"*.' Jennifer was so upset that by now she knew she was looking deranged but was unable to stop herself. She just needed to hear him say sorry.

'You're being ridiculous,' Max thundered.

Jennifer recoiled because of course she *felt* ridiculous. There wasn't any part of her that wanted this to be happening. This was supposed to be their evening for a bit of love and romance. Instead, she was dressed in this 'get up' which she'd hoped he'd find really sexy but which was now making her feel like a cheap hooker, and she felt totally embarrassed. Worse still, Judith had impinged on their lives once again. She couldn't stand it.

'You're so out of order,' she cried.

'Oh for fuck's sake, you're being so dramatic. Just because you've had a couple of glasses of wine you act like an idiot.'

'Fuck you,' screamed Jennifer.

'Ssh, keep your voice down, you'll wake the girls.'

Jennifer was trembling with rage and hurt. She took a sharp inhalation of breath in an attempt to calm herself. Max had never taken kindly to histrionics. Plus she really didn't want to wake the children.

'Look, I'm sorry I've got myself into this state,' she said, happy to acknowledge that she was acting like a crazy woman but determined to make him understand why. 'I just want you to try and get how I feel. I've made loads of effort for tonight and I had hoped you might like what I was wearing. I wanted you to fancy me and for us to feel like we used to when we had sex. I wanted us to be close.'

'You look great,' said Max unconvincingly.

'But instead,' Jennifer said, smearing mascara across her face, 'it's just another time which has been domi- nated by Judith, who you know I feel insecure about as it is.'

Max traipsed wearily from the landing into their room where he sunk onto their bed, shook his head and rubbed his face with his hands. 'I'm too tired for this, Jen. I just want to go to bed now.'

*

Following him in, she felt sick. His lack of effort to make things better made her stomach turn. She felt terrified, yet intuition was telling her to keep digging. Why should she let him get away with this shitty treatment? Why was she constantly apologising all the time? It wasn't fair. It wasn't *all* her fault and she was fed up with being made to feel like it was, like she was mad.

'I think you have feelings for her. Do you?'

Suddenly Jennifer knew that this was the crux of the matter. Probably had been for weeks.

'Oh Christ,' said Max, sounding angry now.

'I mean it, Max. I want to know. Do you have feelings for Judith? Because I think you might. I think that's why you hardly look at me these days. I know you think I'm a mad, crazy cow but you're the one who keeps making me feel like that. You used to make me feel beautiful and loved and happy and now I'm just miserable all the time and feel like I'm constantly waiting for you to announce something.'

Max looked pained and refused to even glance in her direction, staring into the middle distance instead.

'I don't have feelings for her,' he said quietly.

'Swear on the girl's lives,' said Jennifer so menacingly that Max actually gulped.

And then he did something that practically cracked her heart in two. He finally found it in himself to look at her briefly but then couldn't hold her gaze or say what she so desperately needed him to say. So he looked away again and sighed. A heavy, sad, terrible sigh that felt like such a huge sign of betrayal that Jennifer thought she might actually be about to have a panic attack. Her whole body went cold and clammy. She wondered if she was going to be sick or faint.

'You'd better tell me everything,' she said, 'and I mean everything.'

Even as she was saying this, she was wondering if this was the end of her marriage. It was so surreal. Could this be the end of life as she knew it? She willed Max with every cell in her body to make it all go away. To look at her in such a way that she would know he was playing with her, trying to be funny. Only that could make this all OK. But he didn't.

Instead he said, looking truly wretched, 'Jen, I swear there's not really anything to tell. Nothing has actually happened and that's the god's honest truth…'

'But…'

'But nothing,' he repeated, getting up and coming over to her.

'Don't lie to me,' she warned him and as he reached over to touch her arm her entire body flinched, a totally reflex action. It was as if subconsciously she was scared he would harm her. This was harming her. The pain she was experiencing was on a physical level. Again she wished fervently she wasn't dressed as she was and yet it hardly mattered.

'Tell me.'

'There's nothing to tell.'

'But you'd like there to be.'

Max gazed at her, his expression bleak, his eyes searching hers as if he hoped to find an answer through her. And then he shrugged, almost imperceptibly, and that was all she needed to know.

'Have you had sex with her?'

'No…'

'But?'

'I haven't…actually slept with her.'

Jennifer froze and for a fraction of a second time seemed to stand still. The house fell silent, and then she ran. Stopping only to discard her heels, she hurtled out of the room and practically threw herself down the stairs in a bid to flee. Downstairs in the hall she desperately searched for something to put on her feet that didn't come with a six-inch heel. These would do. An old pair of disgusting gardening shoes her mother had left the last time she'd been round. They were far too big but Jennifer didn't care, she just needed to be away. To escape from what was happening. She couldn't breathe. She'd go to Karen's. That's what she'd do. She wouldn't stop to think until she'd got there. Wouldn't stop to contemplate what this all meant until she was safe with her friend. Karen was only ten minutes away. That's where she'd go.

When Max came thundering down the stairs after her she only increased her efforts to get away but he tried to block her exit by standing in front of the door.

'What are you doing? You can't go out of the house dressed like that,' he said, his face frantic. 'Jen, just stay so we can talk. You've got it all wrong anyway.'

'Oh I don't think so,' she cried. 'In fact, the only thing I've got wrong is putting up with your bullshit for this long. Now get out of my way.'

'Look, calm down,' tried Max again, using the same tone he often used on the kids. 'You can't go out dressed like that.'

'Fuck off,' she spat, grabbing a coat from the hooks in the hall and shoving it on. She grabbed her phone from the hall stand so she could ring Karen and then, with every bit of strength in her body, shoved Max out of the way so that she could wrench open the door. Once free she sprinted down the road as fast as her oversized shoes would allow.

*

Max didn't know what to do. He suspected she'd be going to Karen's, or to start a new job as a pole dancer. Either or. Part of him thought it was probably for the best that she took some time out to calm down. Another part of him wanted to run after her, to grab her, hold her and tell her it was all going to be OK. Suddenly he was hit by a monumental urge to simply say sorry. How had they got here? How had he let things get to this point? She was right of course. Over the last few months she'd picked up on his absence. Not a physical absence but his mind had been elsewhere and rather than admit it he'd let her think she was the one to blame. It was ridiculous and in that second Max was only grateful he hadn't gone the whole way with Judith. Thank god. Though what he didn't want to examine too much was that this was more down to circumstances than his own restraint. Tonight he'd seen the hurt and grief an affair would have caused and it had been the sharp reminder he'd needed that he didn't want to lose his wife. He loved his wife. He wanted to throttle her sometimes and Judith's attentions had been desperately flattering but from this moment forward he needed to sort his life out. It had all spun out of control.

He felt totally drained. Making sure the door was on the latch he walked out and stood at the gate where he called down the road. 'Jen, what the hell do you think you're doing? Come back. For goodness sake, you've made your point.'

She didn't so much as look back though and eventually she was a pinprick at the bottom of the road. The boring bloke from number forty-two who'd witnessed everything and been rubbernecking quite spectacularly, gave him a judgemental look as he passed the house. Max returned it with a glowering frown.

Right, there was nothing he could do. He'd leave it for a bit, let her cool off and then send her a text telling her he loved her and that he was the biggest idiot on the planet. With that last thought, Max was just about to head back indoors, when he heard the ungodly sound of screeching tyres, a sickening crunch and a scream. From what he could make out the sound had come from the end of the street. His heart skipped a beat and the fear Max experienced in that second was white and petrifying. And then he did something he hadn't done since school. He prayed.

PRESENT DAY

One of Jennifer's eyes, her left one, slowly opened. She couldn't focus on anything specific. As light flooded in it took a while for her retinas to adjust. They had become so accustomed to a vista of black. Everything was very hazy, very blurry and before her vision had had a chance to fine-tune itself, the eye snapped shut again.

Half an hour later the same eye opened once more and then the second one fluttered open as well. Only this time Max was in the room having just returned from the canteen where he'd bought himself a packet of Highland shortbread and a cup of tea.

'Jen,' he cried. The sound of his voice penetrated through to Jennifer who knew he was talking to her. She knew Max was there. Where was *there* though? That bit was all a bit foggy and she was pretty sure that although she'd like to ask him, she wouldn't be able to. Articulating anything would be impossible at the moment. She wouldn't know how to.

An hour or two later and Jennifer's brain and body were making huge leaps back into the real world. The doctors had swarmed around her as soon as Max had raised the alarm. Blood had been taken to check for levels of serum glucose, calcium, sodium, potassium, magnesium, phosphate, urea, and creatinine. Then, as Max had known they would, they'd wheeled his wife off to perform yet another MRI brain scan on her.

A while later and the results were in. As far as they could tell at this stage her brain was showing no signs of permanent damage, although it would be a long time before they could completely confirm it. After five long weeks Jennifer was officially coming out of her coma.

Max couldn't believe it. What he had prayed for each day was happening. It felt as close to a miracle as anything he'd ever experienced.

For the next couple of days Jennifer would wake up for short bursts, and sometimes be profoundly confused and at other times relatively lucid.

The moment when she recognised her husband and was finally able to speak was the best of all.

'Hey you,' he said, stroking her hand gently with one finger. She was looking right at him and not as though he was a stranger as she had been previously.

'Hey,' she said. 'What's happened?'

'You were in an accident, Jen. You got hit by a car. You've been asleep for weeks. We didn't know...' Max stopped, took a gulp and composed himself.

'Eadie and Polly?'

At this Max was almost overwhelmed by relief and

happiness and it took every bit of his willpower not to break down. 'They're fine, Jen. They're absolutely fine. I don't think either of them ever doubted they'd be seeing you again. I think they reckon you're Sleeping Beauty.'

That was more than enough for her first proper conversation though and as the doctor urged Max to let his wife rest again, Jennifer fell into a deep sleep.

'Is she OK?' asked Max as he tended to every time she did this. 'She hasn't gone into a coma again has she?'

'No,' said the doctor, who happened to have been making his rounds. 'Don't worry; your wife is doing phenomenally well. Recovery usually occurs very gradually though and Jennifer will take a while to acquire the ability to respond for any decent length of time. However, I really think her outlook is extremely positive. But, just be prepared for your wife to still appear confused at times and try not to worry if she does. It's totally normal after somebody has been in such a deep coma.'

It was a good thing the doctor had warned him about this because later on that night in the early hours Jennifer started muttering in her sleep. Max, who had been sleeping fitfully on the camp bed (which by this point in time he officially hated and viewed as an actual instrument of torture), sat bolt upright. 'Jen?' he whispered, but when it became clear that she was only sleep talking he got up and went over to see what she was saying.

The next day, Karen brought the girls into hospital in the afternoon during visiting hours. They'd all decided that with so much less machinery around her it was time for them to finally see their mummy again.

It couldn't have gone better. The timing was great. Jennifer was awake and clearly aware of their presence. She was so happy to see them. Just the fact she recognised them was another incredibly encouraging sign that she was on the road to a full recovery. Eadie and Polly had been lectured at length about not wearing their mother out and were rising to the occasion beautifully, being quiet and good as gold.

Until at one point they asked if they could sing a song to her. 'What song?' asked Karen.

'"Gangnam Style"?' suggested Eadie.

'No, that's probably not the best idea,' her godmother vetoed. 'Why don't you sing Mummy a lovely lullaby instead? "Rock a Bye Baby" or something?'

The girls obeyed and as they started to sing Karen took the opportunity to take Max to one side and ask, 'How are you bearing up?'

'Good,' said Max, an emotional wreck. 'I just can't believe this is all going to end OK.'

'I know. Thank god.'

'Karen?'

'Yes?'

'I'm so sorry you know. I never ever wanted this to happen and I can tell you now that I will spend the rest of my life making sure she's happy.'

'I know you will,' said Karen sadly. 'And it's fine. You

really don't need to apologise to me. Besides, now you can apologise to Jen herself.'

Max looked sheepish. It was obvious Jennifer had confided in her friend pre-accident that things weren't great. Not that she'd know the worst of course. He had no idea how much Jennifer herself would remember either. The suspense was nothing short of horrendous.

'Listen,' reassured Karen, 'I understand and I don't judge anyone else's relationships. After all, you get to our stage and learn that life isn't black and white like you think it is when you're young. It's bloody grey.'

'Fifty shades?'

'Ha ha,' said Karen. 'And no, more like one thousand shades of grey, but it's all going to be fine. It'll all work itself out now that Jen's on the mend. I know it will.'

'Thanks,' said Max. 'For everything. For all your help with the girls, everything.'

'You're very welcome,' said Karen.

'Oh, and by the way,' said Max, 'I was thinking of making a donation to the hospital.'

'Oh, nice idea.'

'Mm, I'm buying them a single bed with a really comfortable mattress so that the next poor bastard who ends up kipping in here might have a chance of actually getting some sleep.'

'Good one. Now, Max, do you think we should stop Eadie and Polly singing now? Otherwise I'm just worried Jennifer might actually wish she was back in a coma again.'

'Oh god yes yes,' agreed Max, jolting back to the here and now and realising how right she was. The caterwauling was pretty terrible and Jennifer was looking glassy-eyed, dazed and a bit exhausted. 'And excellent sick joke by the way. Jen would approve.'

'Thanks,' said Karen.

EPILOGUE

Six Months Later

Karen, Pete and Suzy, and Jennifer's parents, were on their way over for Sunday lunch. It was early December and the kind of day you wouldn't go out in unless you absolutely had to, or unless someone else was cooking you a lovely leg of lamb and an apple crumble. The house was full of the smell of cooking, the girls were playing peacefully in the front room with their Play-Doh and Max was working out what sort of wine they should have with lunch and generally pottering about the kitchen pretending to be helpful. From the outside looking in, the scene was one of total domestic bliss. Which is precisely why no one should ever make assumptions about what's going on in anyone's household other than their own.

Jennifer may have looked content, but as she peeled and chopped carrots, what she was actually wondering was whether or not anybody would be able to hear her if she were to turn the volume on her iPod right up, go into the utility room and scream at the top of her lungs.

As she plunged the carrots into boiling water, Max slid up behind her and kissed her neck. 'Hello, beautiful.'

She resisted a strong urge to elbow him away. Physical contact between them still made her feel tense.

'OK?'

'Yeah, you?'

'I'm good,' Max said sincerely. 'I'm just happy that you're so much better.'

'Good.'

'...and I think you and me are heading in the right direction aren't we?' he added hesitantly. 'In fact I think you should try sleeping in our bed tonight.'

'Maybe,' said Jennifer, nudging him away. The constant effort he was making almost repelled her. She bent down to open the oven to check on the meat. 'This needs to rest,' she said, swatting away clouds of steam with a tea towel.

'You're not going to leave me are you?'

Jennifer's stomach churned. 'Don't be silly,' she said just as the doorbell rang.

Max looked so worried and full of despair that for a brief second Jennifer wanted to give him a hug and to tell him it would be OK. But she didn't. Instead the two of them manfully rearranged their expressions so no one would have a clue what was really transpiring.

Lunch was a raucous, slightly chaotic affair. Jennifer had to eat her meal one-handed with a fork because Eadie insisted on sitting on her lap throughout. Ever since the accident she'd demanded constant affection. Not that Jennifer minded in the least. She couldn't get enough of her children either. Their physical presence was a comfort, especially as she was unable to shake off the feeling she'd had for months now. That she was standing on the edge of a cliff trying to decide whether or not to jump.

After the meal, people slunk away from the table to go and sit in the lounge until finally Karen and Jennifer were the only ones left. As they half-heartedly cleared away, and whole-heartedly picked at cheese and drank wine, Karen decided to tackle something she'd been meaning to bring up for ages.

'How much has Max told you about when you were in the coma?'

'Not a lot,' said Jennifer, grabbing a clean tea towel from the drawer. 'He's mainly filled me in on how uncomfortable his bed was. Why?'

'OK,' said Karen, idly wiping a drip of custard from the side of a jug with her finger before sucking it off. 'It's just there was one night, you had a seizure. I was there.'

'Oh god, you poor thing. I don't think I did know that. That must have been horrific.'

'Wasn't the best night of my life,' admitted Karen drily. 'But anyway, the point is, you said a word out loud.'

'Did I? Was it "make-up bag"?'

'That's three,' snorted Karen, laughing.

'Vodka?'

'No you arse. You said Joe.'

Jennifer immediately stopped grinning. 'Are you serious?'

'Yes. Jen, have you met someone called Joe? Because things between you and Max seem very strained.'

'No,' said Jennifer, arms suddenly slack in the sink which was full of washing up and soapy suds. 'That's so weird. Max also told me I said that name one night.'

Karen looked worried.

'...and this is going to sound odd, but it's like...somewhere along the line I have known someone called Joe because every time I hear the name, I honestly want to burst into tears. It's so frustrating. I feel like my brain knows but can't tell me. But then I've had it a bit since the accident with other things.'

'Had what?'

Jennifer struggled to put it into words. 'I'm not sure really. Just this feeling that I'm really lucky to have you in my life for instance and...like...I don't know...like I've lost things. Like when I hear that name, or sometimes when I look at the kids I get this huge pang of emotion. I don't know. I'm probably going mad.'

She looked so unsettled that Karen got up to give her a hug. 'Come here you.'

Jennifer abandoned the washing up, dried her hands on a tea towel and took her up on her offer at which point she started to sob quietly into her friend's shoulder.

Karen held her at arm's length and looked stricken. 'Jen, what the hell is going on? Tell me.'

'I just don't think I can forgive him,' said Jennifer, eyes full of tears and panic as she finally confessed what she hadn't had the courage to tell anyone else. 'I wish I could because I look at the girls and this house… Then I think about the life we have, the friends and how this is my family. But I'm just not sure I can do it any more. Part of me hates him and I don't know if I'm meant to be with him any more. I nearly died, Karen.'

'I know, but you didn't. You're here.'

'Exactly, so I'm determined to make the absolute most of whatever I have left. I don't want to be doing anything because I think I should, or because it's perceived as the right thing to do if it doesn't *feel* right. One day the girls will be grown up and have lives of their own and I know it would be awful and really hard in many ways but if I was on my own I would cope. I would bloody well find a way to make it work.'

Karen spoke firmly. 'Jen, this is crazy talk. I thought you'd come to terms with everything. Max is so bloody sorry and he'll never ever, ever look at another woman as long as he lives. Isn't he entitled to one mistake? He didn't even sleep with her.'

'So he says,' she sighed, her expression anguished. 'But that's hardly the point. For months I was torturing myself while he was busy fantasising about having it off with that awful disgusting woman. I'm so angry with him Karen, and it's not going away. I want it to. I can't tell you how much I want it to because I don't want to lose my lovely life because of his stupidity. I was happy for a long time. But if I can't love him any more…' she trailed off. 'Do you think I should just settle for the children's sakes?'

'I'd hardly describe what you've got as settling. You've got a lovely family and a great life. Plus, no matter how determined you are, I don't know if you *would* cope if you left. It's bloody hard out there these days,' whispered Karen urgently, conscious that the kids had suddenly thundered down the stairs and were now in the hall. 'You'd have to sell this house, you'd be a single mum, the girls would suffer and, I hate to say it, but between the two of you there wouldn't be enough money to run two households. It would be a nightmare.'

Jennifer sighed, tortured by confusion. Everything Karen had just said was true. She wasn't stupid and had already considered all of this. Yet, for whatever reason, all she'd been able to see for the last few months was her life stretched out before her and that there were two directions she could go in. Two tunnels almost, only one was a far easier route to take. She could continue as she was, in what felt like a damaged relationship, full of resentment. And who could tell? Perhaps with a lot of hard work and effort they would get back on track.

But there was another way. Only when she tried to look in that direction, she had no idea what its future held. All she could be sure of was that it was full of uncertainty and difficulty but also of hope, excitement and change. It was one where she would start again, on her own, as Jennifer

Drew. This route thrilled her as much as it terrified her. The familiar versus the unknown. Safety versus risk. Head versus heart.

'But listen,' added Karen, 'at the end of the day I can't tell you what to do because only you know how you feel so whatever you decide to do, know that I am here for you. One hundred percent. Always.'

It was exactly what Jennifer needed to hear.

Later that night, after everyone had gone, Max put the girls to bed. As soon as they were settled he came to join Jennifer on the sofa where she was vaguely watching the news.

After a few minutes he took the remote control from her and turned the TV off.

'What are you doing?'

'I need to know, Jen. I'm sorry but I can't carry on like this any more. I need to know. I can't go around pretending that everything's OK any more because we both know it isn't and it seems the harder I try the more detached you become. So are you in or out? Because if you're in, you have to forgive me. You have to find a way to forget and to let me in or we don't stand a chance. But if you think you can't do that, then I need to know, for once and for all, because the not knowing is killing me.'

Jennifer stared at her husband knowing that their fate lay entirely in her hands. Which tunnel would she choose? She thought back to all the times she'd had to make a decision in the past and knew that none of them had ever been as far-reaching as this one or would ever have as much impact on all of their lives. She was in control now. She needed to make a decision. Perhaps she already had.

* * * * *

ACKNOWLEDGEMENTS

Writing a book is a solitary activity. Getting it on the shelves, however, is a hugely collaborative effort, so I have a lot of people to thank. Enormous thanks must go to my publishers, MIRA. I am so happy to be with you and your enthusiasm and passion is refreshing and wonderful. In particular, many thanks must go to my brilliant editor, Sally Williamson, and fantastic agent, Madeleine Milburn. Like David Seaman, you are both a pair of 'safe hands'. Unlike David Seaman, you're pretty and don't have big moustaches. Thanks must also go to Claudia Webb.

Writing this book has coincided with a pretty turbulent period in my life. Thanks to my family for seeing me through it. There are times when that 'blood is thicker than water' business really rings true and times when frankly your family are the only people who will put up with you. Of course, they don't have much choice. You're related, you're not going any-where and there's no getting out of seeing you over Christmas. So thank you for steering me through to the other side and not drowning me along the way. I don't know what I would have done without you all and will never forget your kindness, patience and support. Dad, Sally, Mum, Mauro, Jessica, Isabel, Paddy, Jim, Harry and Imogen, you are the best bunch of freaks known to man and I love you all to bits. As ever, thank you also to those of you who read an early draft, gave me notes and encouraged me to carry on.

Ooh, after that rather earnest bit I find myself suddenly over-come by a strong desire to dilute it by writing 'big shout-out', like I'm on the radio—I might go with it… Big shout-out to Lily and Freddie, the two best kids in the world. You're both spectacular little monkeys and I look forward to embarrassing you for many more years to come. I know only too well how lucky I am to have children who people actually like inviting round for tea. Thank you for being so gorgeous and for being kind. Kind is good.

My friends. What a bunch! You're all fabulous. I'd like to mention the usual suspects of course, my life-long friends Becky Rolfe, Alessia Small and Stroma Inglis. And very special thanks must also go to Fiona Wright, Nigel Mitchell, Charlotte Woodward, Laura Slader and Carmel Allen for various reasons, which mainly involve them being incredible, caring and/or helpful friends in one way or another.

As for Sarah Jane Wright, I don't even know where to start, so we're just going to have to go out for cocktails and take it from there. I love you loads and don't know how I'll ever thank you.

Now, last, but definitely not least, to Ross. Not a day goes by when I don't think, 'God, you're tall.' Then, after that, I ponder on how lucky I am to have you in my life and to have your friendship. You're amazing, a one-off, and I can't tell you how much I appreciate your input on this book (you were right about the ending, of course you were) and everything else you do for me, including making me laugh, a lot. I could go on, but know how much you hate compliments and how unbelievably bad you are at taking them, so instead I'll just say, 'Sofa' and hope that that says it all.

Author Q&A

Do you have a favourite character in *If You're Not the One*? Why, and what inspired you to write them?

Jennifer is my favourite character in the book. She's by no means perfect (who is?), but I really like her and can relate to her enormously. The idea for her story came to me during a period when, like Jennifer, I was trying to figure a few things out. On paper she *should* be happy. But she's not and is hurtling towards a mid-life crisis, unsure of what she wants. We meet her at a time when she's wondering if there should be more to life and is asking herself, 'Is this it?' I would imagine she's not alone. We live in confusing times, encouraged to reach for the stars, to have the best career, the best relationship and not to settle. Of course, there's a lot to be said for safe and steady and secure, but only as long as it doesn't trickle into dull, unfulfilling and suffocating. Previous generations were programmed just to get on with things and people's reluctance to 'put up and shut up' these days is often labelled as selfishness. Is it, though? I'm not sure. This is why I like her character so much and why she was such a joy to write. Jennifer doesn't have all the answers and I truly believe that, like her, most of us aren't completely happy all of the time or completely miserable. Instead, most of us have good days and bad. Life can be beautiful and also sad. As a result, she feels very real to me and I loved exploring how all the different relationships she experiences make her feel and, to a degree, act in a different way. She's also funny. All the best people are.

Which man do you think Jennifer would be happiest with and why?

I think the man who was her real soul-mate and with whom she had the most passionate connection was Joe. Of course, their feelings were dramatically heightened by the situation they were in, but I like to think that, given the chance, they would have made each other very happy.

With the book as a whole, I wanted to demonstrate that most of the time, when we break up with someone, it's for a very good reason. More often than not our instincts are correct. Therefore it was important to show that had she stayed with Aidan or Tim she would have been fairly miserable. However, I was also determined to show that had she stayed with Steve she could have been quite content, thus destroying the romantic notion that there's only one person out there for each of us. After all, if your parents emigrated to another country when you were a child, it's unlikely to imagine you would never meet anyone you were compatible with and that you had in fact been destined solely for the boy up the road.

Would you like to be able to see what 'could have been', like Jennifer does?

I'm not sure! I think it's something we all wonder about and not just in terms of relationships. I often ponder what might have been had I chosen a slightly more standard career path, for example. I think perhaps it's better we can't and that we just live in the moment and try not to have too many regrets and have faith in our own decisions.

If there's one thing you'd like readers to take away from *If You're Not the One*, what would it be?

That our lives are all made up of a series of small and large decisions which determine everything. Who you choose to share your life with is the most far reaching, for it affects not just your emotional needs but also where you live, your financial status, your friends, extended family, etc. I wanted readers to form their own opinion about Max and Jennifer to a degree. They've got a lot going for them, but the effort has gone. I don't think the book necessarily provides any concrete answers, but I do believe it throws up lots of questions and I hope this makes it an interesting and thought-provoking read. I also set out to try and demonstrate that from the outside looking in it can be easy to imagine you know how people feel or what it's like to b them, and yet no one really does unless you're in those four walls or in that person's brain. Most of all, however, I simply hope that it's an enjoyable read with some sad bits and some funny bits that passes the time enjoyably and makes people want to tell their friends about it. (Not much then?!)

Where do you write—are you a paper-and-pen girl or a coffee-shop with a laptop sort?

Laptop all the way. It's terrible to confess, but my seven-year-old son and nine-year-old daughter have far better hand-writing than me these days. When I write a card or something, it's like I've forgotten how to write with a pen. Forgotten how to *hold* a pen even. To be honest, I don't know how anyone could bear to write anything in longhand. What happens if you want to edit a chunk or move things around? I'd have to totally change my approach if I had to write in longhand as I tend to sort of pour my thoughts out on to the screen and then go back and make sense of the jumble after. This would not be at all practical if using a pen. My next deadline would probably need to be about 2038. And half of that would have been taken up just looking for a pen, as in my house they disappear as soon as they're bought. Full respect to pen wielders. I don't know how you do it.

What do you love most about being a writer?

The satisfaction of creating an entire world and the people who inhabit it. It's the best job in the world and the only really hard aspect of it is coming up with what your next idea is going to be. Once you've cracked that, though, there's nothing better than a day when it's all flowing and at times you've made yourself chuckle or (and this has been known to happen) to cry at what you're writing. Those are the moments when you know you're on to something good. The fact that this all happens in your own head in solitude does at times conspire to make you feel like a bit of a nut-job admittedly, but it's also a lot of fun. The absolute best thing about being a writer, though, is that your only commute is to the kitchen to get caffeine-based drinks, you can wear your most comfy (revolting) 'leisure wear'

…nd no one knows if your hair's greasy and you look like a total minger.

What piece of advice would you give to aspiring writers?

Have a good osteopath on speed dial. When you start to hate your manuscript (about fifty thousand words in), take a break for a few weeks in order to get some objectivity back. Don't write with your audience in mind, otherwise you'll start fretting about whether your mum will approve and end up restricting what you want to say. Know where you're trying to get to. It's obvious, but every story needs a beginning, a middle and an end and it helps enormously if that has been thought out before you begin. Don't forget to read other people's books! Reading keeps you inspired and keeps you tuned in to what will make your writing interesting and good. Also, think about what the point of the book is. To my mind there isn't any point if there isn't a point. And lastly, don't give up. Rejection is par for the course, but if you love writing, you should continue anyway. Do it for the love of it and with a bit of luck one day your perseverance will pay off.

Champagne or a cup of tea?

I drink more tea than champagne. I hope to reverse that in the future and aspire to be more like Joan Collins in many ways. I love the idea of wafting around casually brandishing a flute of the fizzy stuff because it's simply all I'll drink. In truth though, I tend to find champagne a bit acidic and on occasion to cause reflux and dry mouth which tends to lessen the glamour factor. Tea, however, rocks. As does vodka, white wine and gin. OK, now I'm just listing types of alcohol…

City or country?

I don't think I could live in the country full-time. Or at least not while I'm still working. I'm an urban chick at heart. I was born and raised in London and love the hurly burly of the capital. Having said that, an escape to the coast or the country is like medicine for the soul when the traffic, noise and grime

have all got too much. I'm so 'city' that a walk in totally fr̶e̶
air literally makes me feel like I've been drugged afterwards. I̶r̶
a good way. I guess the ideal is a bit of both.

Topshop or Gucci?

Hmm—I'm not sure that during these strange economic times
I could ever justify spending hundreds of pounds on a skirt
or belt, but that doesn't mean to say I wouldn't love a Gucci
handbag. It's pathetic, but like most females I am simply
designed to be excited by a new handbag or shoes. No point
fighting it. It's just basic biology. So, I'd say Gucci for a treat, but
good old Topshop every day of the week if I needed some new
clothes I could actually afford and that didn't make me vomit
in my mouth, due to sickness brought on by anxiety and guilt
after paying at the till.

Tell us a bit about your next book…

My next book is one I'm very excited about. There are some
big themes going on. Life, death, family, love and the nature/
nurture debate all feature. It's a bit different from
anything I've ever written before inasmuch as I've had to do a
fair bit of research for this one. It involves some scenes which
need to be totally spot-on in order to do it justice. I love lots of
the characters and the protagonists' mum is probably my favourite. I don't want to give too much away, but I hope that it will
make people laugh and then make them cry in equal measure.

WHAT DID YOU MISS OUT ON BECAUSE YOU FELL IN LOVE?

Kate Winters might just be 'that' girl. You know the one. The girl who, for no particular reason, doesn't get the guy, doesn't have children, doesn't get the romantic happy-ever-after. So she needs a plan.

What didn't she get to do because she fell in love?

What would she be happy spending the rest of her life doing if love never showed up again?

This is one girl's journey to take back what love stole.

Last year Jane Lockhart was a bestseller. This year she's blocked.

Unfortunately, Jane Lockhart has ground to a halt on the novel that's going to save the neck of her struggling, indie publisher and ex-boyfriend, Tom Duvall.

As Tom sees it, the trouble is that Jane's success has made her too damned happy—and she can't be smiling if she's going to finish her latest misery-lit hit, right? So, to break her block, he sets about ruining everything in her life that's making her happy…

Now a major motion picture

Three superstars. Three secrets.
Who will fall first?

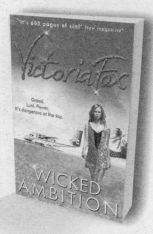

Some will do anything for fame.
Others will do anything to bring
the famous down.

For Robin, Turquoise and Kristin, the spotlight
shines brightly. They've reached the glittering
heights of stardom, but in the shadows lies the
truth... An exposé could be their end.

'It's 600 pages of sin'
Now magazine

It is every mother's nightmare...only worse

Janine wants her child to live a normal life, so she lets her precious daughter go on her first overnight camping trip. But when Janine arrives to pick up Sophie after the trip, her daughter is not with the others.

Janine will not rest until she finds her little girl, because Sophie isn't like every other girl... she suffers from a rare disease.

Who could have taken her child and what will happen if they don't get her back?